FOOTBALL'S FIRST LOVE AFFAIR

150 YEARS AGO AT THE BIRTH OF COLLEGE FOOTBALL

Ω

Rutgers versus Princeton
1869

J. D. Tylus, Ph.D.

FOOTBALL'S FIRST LOVE AFFAIR

150 YEARS AGO AT THE BIRTH OF COLLEGE FOOTBALL

Ω

Rutgers versus Princeton
1869

Copyright© 2019 by J. D. Tylus
All rights reserved

J. D. Tylus, Ph.D.

AUTHOR'S NOTE

It was just over 150 years ago on November 6, 1869, when the American love affair with college football started. It all began on a cold, blustery afternoon in New Brunswick, New Jersey. On that day in 1869, a team from the college located in Princeton traveled to play a team from Rutgers College. They met on a field that was situated along the current College Avenue and at a site that is no longer visible in its original form. But the history that was made there that day has not been lost and the roots for the future of what we have come to know today as college football were permanently planted.

To anyone who follows college football, they know using the word "love" of the game is not overstated as the emotions generated when following one's team for many is nothing less. The passion felt for their school by each fan takes them from the highs of victory and the joys of a shared bond to the jealousy with rivals and the depths of despair when one's love has lost.

With each new season comes a new life awakening. Families are forged amidst smoke and beverages at tailgate barbecues like the pleasantries shared at a wedding reception. Memories are forever implanted in minds through the eyes of those bottom to bottom in rows of stadium seating that will become a common lore. Lyrics of songs and frantic cheering, with actions like car keys dangling to signal a critical third down play, need no explanation to the properly initiated within the fold. Bands swaying to music and aisle dancing to a shared beat creates a euphoric and unique trance-like state within the fan that one normally can only find in the comfort and safety of one's own home.

So a love story set within the real historical events seems totally appropriate as one spins a tale around the birth of college football. It is a love story that is essentially impossible to separate and it will always remain intertwined.

As you read ahead know in advance that this is a work of historical fiction. Characters and dialogue within this novel were created to help entice the reader's interest where often non-fiction databases too often fail. But know that while the dialogue is purely fictional, there are many real events and even names that have not been conjured from the author's imagination of a time gone by. Many of the names have been respectfully included so the portraits that hang on walls or that are within worn pages of old text can breathe life again to share a story about which they were once a part.

And it is a glorious story. It is a history of which the actual names used were the architects of what would become one of the United States greatest traditions. A love of college football.

Rutgers and Princeton (then known as the College of New Jersey) played in the first college football game in history on November 6, 1869. And after that day, the world was never the same again.

Introduction: Part I

"A lingering debate: The First College Football Game!"
Rutgers Campus Earlier Today

   The relaxed dorm life of that afternoon on the Rutgers campus was shattered quickly by one single shouted word from his roommate.
   "Seriously!!!!"

   Instinctively, he jumped from his chair toward the sound and reached out in an attempt to take the laptop from his roommate's hand. He had seen this reaction once before and he remembered all too well the disastrous results of his roommate destroying the previous valuable piece of technology by throwing it against the wall.
   However, before he could get to grab the laptop away, his roommate had yelled again and stepped back too quickly. Now his roommate held it aloft in his left hand and started to pace about their small living quarters, his eyes literally red with bloodshot anger welling up within.
   He took another approach. "Calm down," he said gently to his roommate, slowly edging back away and trying not startle him further.

   "No, seriously, you think they can just do that?" his roommate stammered out at him, like a man possessed.
   "No one is doing anything to you," he answered slowly in an attempt to get him to relax.
   "Damn right they aren't going to do anything to me. I won't let them; that is why! But I am so sick and tired of them trying and me just getting dumped on."
   "You?" It was hard not to sound incredulous even though he valued the laptop and did not want to explain to his parents again why it had been smashed. "Really? You can't think that trivia question posted on the internet is about you?"
   "Yes, me, that's right! It is about me. And it is about you too although you are too blind to see it! This is about both of us and millions of others who call New Jersey our home. Good Americans! That is who we are and we don't deserve to keep getting treated like this with this kind of crap being posted!"

"Again, calm down. They are talking about college football here for Christ's sake, not about taking away your right to vote. Don't you even think maybe you are over-reacting just a little bit? "

"No!"

Suddenly, as if it just dawned on him that he had been shouting at his friend, the roommate paused for just a second as he took a deep breath. He lowered the laptop from above his head to his side. But as he started to speak again he still waved it about like a toy flag. His voice was filled with an angry passion as he laid out all the historic wrongs that were constantly being inflicted upon his home state.

"Just look at what they have already taken from us. Go back in time and watch as New York steals the Statue of Liberty and claims it as their landmark even when everyone knows it resides on an island in Jersey's waters. The wild-west Texans think they invented the gun when their first Colt revolvers were being produced right here in Patterson, New Jersey. Some movie producers in some unknown southern wetlands think they discovered the first wild woods creature and get a television show about it when the Jersey Devil lived in our swamps before they were even a state."

His roommate's face grew redder with his temper and voice volume rising again as he continued on with the list of transgressions that others had wrought on his state.

"Toss in the eroded fields across our Jersey roadways to get people between Philly and NYC so the two of them can even have a city and they treat us like dirt! Or pretend that Hoboken's Sinatra is a New Yorker or Las Vegas star forgetting he was born here instead of there. And then the basic facts we live with every day like the Giants play in the New Jersey Meadowlands and that team still calls themselves the New York Giants. Even an idiot can see a list with no end in sight."

"Please calm down. It is not like there is some conspiracy theory at work out there against our state."

"Oh no!"

"Well, I think you are over-reacting about this football thing. Look at what has you so wound up today. It was one question in some silly online trivia contest!"

"No such chance at talking me out of this amigo. I do no care if it is a one question trivia post. We cannot let anyone twist the facts anywhere. The sport was invented here. It started here. It was first played here. It stays here. End of discussion and damn those who try to cheat us out of our past!"

"Really, does all of this even matter in the end?"

"Yes, you fool, it matters."

"I mean, is it really that big a deal?"

His roommate looked like he might swing at him for making light of the issue. Instead though, he spoke to him like he was an idiot alien ignorant about what he felt should be obvious to anyone.

"Look, football was first played in New Jersey between two New Jersey colleges and the first ever national college football champion team was from New Jersey."

"And?"

"And!?!" his roommate amped up again instantly and half yelled out as the back of his hand smacked on the computer screen. "Now we read this trash that Yale was the first true football champion in this online posting? They played in the first real college football game? They didn't even have a team when the first game was played."

"It is only internet social media babble and I seriously hope you did not just crack my screen."

He had barely gotten the words out when his roommate moved on, totally ignoring any remark or concerns about possible damage to his personal property. Again, his roommate moved about the room with the computer clenched in his hand spewing out a review of the online historical inaccuracy in a trivia question he had just read about which had ignited the outburst in the first place.

"Sure Walter Camp helped modify the game at Yale. But modifications do not make something first. Further, did you know that Yale, Princeton, and Rutgers attended and put the updated rules together at that time in that meeting? And did you know that famous meeting was actually requested by Yale to organize what would be the first intercollegiate football association just to try and agree upon common rules for the game? In other words, my friend, a game and sport they acknowledge already existed and were simply looking for a way to improve upon the structural components."

"I did not know that," he deadpanned back with his eyes still following the waving computer.

"And Rutgers was at that later day meeting too. One of our reps there was Howard Fuller who wrote our college song we so love and still hear at every football game, *On the Banks of the Old Raritan*."

"Again, I did not know that piece of trivia either."

"Any football historian who cares about the facts knows that meeting was in 1873. That was four years after that first game was played here in New Jersey at Rutgers against Princeton in 1869!"

"No, I can honestly say I did not know any of what you just shared."

Then, as if someone had turned a switch to slow him down, his roommate sat on the frayed edges of the couch in their dorm room and spoke in a quieter manner.

"And do you know why we should care?" his roommate calmly asked rhetorically before answering his own question.

"Because, in the beginning, it was only about the game. They played for the glory of a win for their college. They played for school pride and the honor of being called the best. It wasn't a business or a pathway to a future occupation, like so many may attempt to personally use it today."

"Just a game. So we agree. Now that we agree can I have my computer back?" he snuck in a reminder about the valued item still casually being swung about in his roommate's hand.

"Yes, wise-ass, it was a game," his roommate stated, totally ignoring the computer request. "But it was also more than just a game. Teamwork. Teammates. One together for a common cause and the honor of their school."

"But it is just a game, and can I have my computer back?" he repeated the phrase again.

"Damn right!" His roommate, suddenly rejuvenated, jumped back to his feet. "The best damn game ever created too. And, no, it was not born at Harvard or Yale or at Notre Dame or USC or any other place. Rather it was born right here at Rutgers University in good old New Jersey. This is the only place that can all itself the birthplace of college football!"

"Seriously people know the game was first played here. It was just one stupid trivia question on the internet. You've heard them say it and show our logo on the Big Ten Network every weekend with the line about Rutgers University being the birthplace of college football. They send that message out to millions at a time with any football game to be shown across the country."

"And never let them forget it!" his roommate smiled at him.

He could not help but smile back. "You know, honestly, I hope there will always be someone out there just like you who will be sure they never do forget it."

"Why thank you my kind sir."

The sarcastic reply finally sounded like his roommate normally sounded.

"But while I appreciate your passion, please leave the crazy-day antics and shouting for someone else."

"Sorry. But we do need to remain vigilant that no one steals more of our Jersey state heritage. No one on our watch gets to re-designate a new location for the start of college football! There are too many out there always trying to put us down here in New Jersey. Too much fake news about us." His roommate then added as he looked him in the eye, "And I am glad you and I are finally seeing things the same way."

"Right. Now give me back my laptop!"

Introduction: Part 2

"Setting the Table to This Story"
Guest Room at Her Daughter's Home
1938

    The room on the back of the house was small. The first thing anyone would notice was that it was crammed full of framed pictures. Portraits. Family group shots. They were all over the walls. They also sat on top of everything.
    Pictures adorned all five large pieces of furniture which had been squeezed into the room in a manner that left them almost touching each other. These main furnishings consisted of a bed, a radio console, a dresser, a trunk, and the chair she was seated in. Next to the chair was the one small furniture item. A small fold out tray table – which also had two framed pictures on it.

    He hated that he had agreed with his boss at the radio station to come out here and visit her. It was just another fan-based letter. He argued they should have ignored it altogether. Maybe, at the most, he could have recognized the author with a simple hello while they were on the air one day on his show.
    But no, his boss wanted him to take up the offer and go out and talk to this old lady.
    His boss was insistent. Hear what she has to say. It might make for good chatter or even add some color commentary one day on your talk show.
    Sure. Sports talk show star and reporter taking advice from an old lady. Here he is gathering notes from an old woman bundled in some scarlet and black sweater. The matching colored crocheted blanket had her wrapped so tightly in her overstuffed chair he doubted she could even stand.

    When he first came in the room, she had motioned for him to sit on the bed and she had watched him without making a sound as he tried to push pictures aside to even find an open space.
    Even worse than negotiating the tangled mess of picture frames, he noticed his eyes had begun to water as soon as he entered the room. He was sure it was from the lingering toxic mixture of stale perfume, the lilies

in a red vase and what had to be Bengay ointment that permeated the air. The choking smell, he thought to himself, so typical of an old lady's lair.

He hated this assignment.

"Heard your story broadcasted last week about no one previously able to prove when football was invented," she finally spoke without any formal introductions. "Heard you then unveil that you personally have now officially decided when that was."

"Yes ma'am," he replied choking back the desire to gag from the stuffy air. "All opinions before me. But facts are what matter, you see, when talking about history."

"Is that so?"

"It is," he said not attempting to mask the boastful sound in his voice that so many accused him of. "A lot of speculation has been out there on this subject. But I've studied it thoroughly and there should be no debate about what I decided any longer," the final words coming out like a formal announcement.

"And I think I heard you decide in your talk show that the first game was at Harvard and that Yale is the first champion?" she asked.

"That is what I have come to conclude. Harvard was where the first real game was played and not just some imitation of it. Yale should be considered the first real college football champion. My research endorses this conclusion," he boasted.

"And you call yourself a college football expert?" she looked at him through the top of her bifocals.

"I like to think that I am a student of the game who continues to study it," he answered, responding back with a more defensive tone at the sudden bluntness of her statement. "But I also see myself as a man who fully understands the historic implications of how it came to be what it is today."

"So then you know your Walter Camp and Alonozo Stagg references. You know your Knute Rockne stories and the legends like the Galloping Ghosts and the Gipper? Maybe you can even repeat the tale of who threw the first forward pass?"

"Simple summaries with details about the sport," he smiled back. "Especially when it comes to the foundation makers and especially the firsts in college football. I know all about them as they are all a part of my job!"

"I also figure then you would be able to identify William Gummere and William Leggett from your research. Which one do you credit as the key man?"

"I am not sure I know what..."

"And who do you credit, from all of your studying and reading that you supposedly have done, with the first points? Do you credit Stephen Gano or George Dixon?"

"Who?"

"And how about the original M.V.P. award that should have been given out? Did you think that should have gone to Jacob Michael due to his personal impact on the contest even though he was not on the winning team?"

"Look, I am not sure I know exactly what you are referring to."

"How about the simple things then? First tailgate party? First appearance of the famous flying wedge that would dominate the sport for years? The first college cheer? The first use of school colors to identify a team? The first college football rivalry? The first pep talk and game strategy?"

He did not even attempt to answer this time.

"Son, do you even know what the score was and who won the first game that took place in New Brunswick?"

"First game?"

"Yes, that first Rutgers versus Princeton football game back in 1869."

"Oh, that version of the game. I am pretty sure that contest went to Rutgers. Of course, that is, if you go by one side of the story. But I would not call that the first football game," he clarified.

"So you said, incorrectly I will add, on your radio show last week," she quipped.

"With all due respect ma'am, the real first game based on any style of actual United States of America football play was between Harvard and Tufts. As for first college football champions, Walter Camp's roadmap indicates that should go to Yale. I know about the Jersey game you are referring to. But until they created several required rules to be implemented, the game of football had only resembled a mixed version of soccer and rugby," he added with an air of academic confidence back in his voice.

It was her turn to smile now. The expression on her face, though, was not of joy. Rather, her smile had the look of someone who is showing pity for the simple ignorance of another human being.

"Ah, the joys of the revisionist historians," she said without emotion. "And idiots. But before we talk football, I will note, the role of revisionist in life is not all bad. Truth be told, in many cases, if it were not for the revisionist historians there may be no push to go back and try to remember the past at all."

"Ma'am?"

"Actually, I even prefer those authors honest enough to enlighten their readers at the start of what they are espousing that everything is typically a form of historical fiction since no full record can ever be found of any historic event. Cliché about winners writing history, you know. It is like you seem to feel you should be doing, good poor uninformed sir, always reopening the past for interpretation."

"I am not sure I am following you."

She smiled again. This time it was in a more warm-hearted manner like one would see in an exchange between a young scholar and an elderly woman who was no longer concerned about personal accolades but was more impassioned with helping a future generation appreciate the lessons learned in life.

"Well, young man," she leaned forward. "If you have a moment, maybe I can help set the record straight for you about any error you have made or any doubt you have in your mind related to the origins of college football. Give me a chance to show you how wrong you are about the Harvard thing and hopefully even you will put the title back with Rutgers and Princeton where it belongs."

"I am all ears," he answered with a chuckle at the audacity of this old woman thinking she would be in a position to teach him about the game.

"You see, while some may wish to take and make their moment in history more important than the prior souls who participated in it, the reality is that some facts can never be changed," she pointed out to him as he watched her still all tucked into her chair with her scarlet and black sweater and blankets.

"I am not altering history ma'am. Facts are facts. But go ahead and build your case. Try and make me a believer about the Rutgers and Princeton game being unequivocally the first college football game. I would love to hear what you have to offer. Try to change my mind. But know I believe I have already resolved from my research that great debate which had persisted over previous decades."

He then clarified for the older woman what he expected to hear from her that could make him change his mind, figuring this might save some time and avoid her disappointment when he left.
"Even before you start, I feel we must have several ground rules."
"Of course," she acknowledged.
"The true historian shows documents and records that can be triangulated and leave no room for argument about the event. This can be very difficult for you," he warned her.
"I believe you have documents that show records of the November 6th game played in 1869 as a first. That is ahead of any other contest. Earlier you even reported knowledge of that football game," she reminded him. "I know of no one that challenges that record itself."
"No," he admitted. "That is true. But again, I contest it was not the original college football game. It was just an odd soccer-like competition in my book."
"The football historian most would rate as the finest of his time, Parke H. Davis, researched all early contests extensively. If you read the history he reported in the *1933 Spalding Football Guide*, he came to the conclusion that Rutgers and Princeton were first on all accounts. You can read, can you not?"
"Parke Davis is dead and the conclusions in his opinionated work in the eyes of this researcher should be buried with him," the man responded without any acknowledgement of the 'his ability to read' comment.

"Okay," she sighed as she saw how stubborn he was going to be and began to dig in.
"So let me weave the documented facts into a story with people representative of a time period. Let's use that revisionist historian license you have used to spin a little tale of what I will admit up front is part historical fiction. I will use the recollections from those who played as well as the college records left behind by those who attended at both Rutgers and Princeton. Did you know they called Princeton the College of New Jersey in 1869?"
"And the purpose of creating this imagined tale for me to prove an actual historical point?" This time he ignored her tidbit about the name altogether.

"I believe that it is the charm of the human engagement with the sport that made us all fall in love with it from day one. This did not start later. I believe that it was the emphasis of rivalry and the joy of victory that melded together all future games that would eventually arrive on the scene. Forward pass or not, that day at Rutgers was the day college football was born."

"Again ma'am. Remember I see the first real football game at Harvard and first champ as Yale."

"Sir, I will yield right at the start that the ongoing Harvard and Yale or even the Lafayette and Lehigh rivalries might have taken place later without this inaugural event in New Brunswick. I would also hope they more closely resemble the current game rules as they have taken place more recently."

"Unfortunately for Harvard and Yale and your theory though, a previous football game predated all their contests," she stated with an emphasis on the word *predated* before continuing.

"But for this debate sir, let's remember the point I am proving is that what you see in games, like even more modern competitions at Notre Dame, Texas, Alabama, or California, is just a continuation of what first took place in New Brunswick in 1869 and the spirit of a sport we have all grown to love."

"Okay. So sell me on the connection," he stated, smug as he had been when they first started talking. It was obvious he was now appearing anxious to move the discussion along as he glanced at his watch.

She smiled sweetly again at him before responding, even as his unbridled arrogance and general rudeness seemed to seep out from every pore of his body.

"You see, dear, it has always been a game about passion and the desire to win. That was not created at Harvard. The need to vanquish the enemy in a way that allows the victor, if only for a short period of time, the chance to bring honor to their college and the ability to claim that they are the champions of a college sport. That championship feel was not first felt at Yale."

"So real football is defined by championships?"

"Yes and no. We all play to win in life young man."

"Power, money and accumulation of showy material wealth through greed then? That seems like it is always the metric in determining the ultimate human victory," he interjected.

"Yes, sadly I can see how you would jump to that. You probably even believe that. And, yes, they are all tools to demonstrate personal influence," she noted before explaining the difference.

"But the playing of this sport has a more unified purpose to demonstrate excellence. It has the ability to galvanize the population of an entire campus and college community to see within a contest the credibility it can bring their school and their home. Thankfully, it does not carry the same inhumane carnage as a military campaign. But it does evoke the same visceral feelings that overwhelm those on the winning side of a battle. It also overcomes those on the losing side of that same event and leaves them gloomy probably longer than the victor's joy of winning lasts. In many ways, it is the ultimate human desire to say that our collective group is better than our opponent. College football provides that venue which is more palatable in this manner than any other social contest invented."

"Interesting. Go on." He had settled back in the chair, genuinely seeming to be absorbing what she had to say but also clearly calculating his final points he wished to make.

"And college football at its inception, you see, was built with that intent. It was at the very core of the Rutgers and Princeton game. It is still serving that purpose in the same way today. New first down chain crews and balls shaped to facilitate an easier forward pass do not change the base elements."

"The same?"

"Even down to the inspiration for our college youth and the elderly alumni singing off-key college fight songs and being willing to stand out at a grill in the cold and rain in a pre-game ritual of community-building hours before the contest is set to begin."

He chuckled before extending his challenge again.

"So tell me your story. As I can see I will not be able to leave until you have provided it to me. Go ahead and see if you can make a believer out of me. Victory for you is Rutgers and Princeton etched forever in history without further debate as the first ever college football game played. I will even consider one or both of them the first champion. But let me warn you. A loss for you is I do not see the connection today and I walk away from here an unchanged scholar. In addition, you agree to preach what I have decreed to any remaining elderly friends you may have who may ever broach this topic."

on your radio show?" she asked.

". broadcast the results there and repeat it in public every chance I get in the future."

She leaned forward in her chair and looked him straight in the eye. "Game on!" she declared.

The sweet elder advisor sound was suddenly gone from her voice. It was replaced now with the tone of a wise lioness who was about to spring her trap as she made one last remark before she settled in to tell her story.

"I suggest, sonny, that while I talk you start preparing your speech for when you lose."

1
"The History Begins"
Early in September 1869
Trenton, New Jersey

The elder Gummere gave his son's shoulder a stiff pat as the two of them prepared to part ways.   This was as close a physical gesture of endearment he ever allowed himself with his son. There were never any further signs of emotion between the two of them.

"So this is the last go at it, young man."

The older man's gravelly voice was firm and cold. The sound perfectly matched the dark suit jacket, high-buttoned collar and formal simple black cravat tie he always wore.

While hard for a casual observer to understand, this was not an indication that the father lacked a deep level of compassion for his son. He did love his son, just as he loved his other children. He truly saw his children as an extension of himself and wanted them to succeed. He knew they were his legacy to this world.

His wife watched this from behind the darkened screen of the front door.

She was out of their direct line of sight. Although she did not like this parenting arrangement, she understood all of the social norms too. She had previously explained this privately to their son and other children many times over the years. She just hoped that what she had shared was believed by their beloved boy, William.

"Yes, sir," the young Gummere dutifully responded with an equal air of cold detachment while standing obediently in front of his father. Hat in hand, he always played his part as he had come to know it.
"As your father and the family patriarch, I am bound to provide some final conveyance of my and your mother's expectations for you as you head off this last time."

The senior Gummere took a moment to clear his throat for effect.
"This time you have spent at your college is not one where we saw any gain for our family fortune. While I sincerely hope you feel your studies there have given you what you needed, it is now time that you decide how you will take what has been given and turn that cost to us into something more meaningful for our family. It is time for you to make your mark on that place this year so our investment there was worthwhile."
"We all know you reached the age of 17 this past June. Some may have considered you young when you first started your college studies. But I remind you that you were older than your brother, Samuel, when he first started. For many boys at your age, they have already begun to advance past their boyhood schoolwork and into their adult careers as men. They were providing for their families while you have had the luxury of simply living for your own personal gain. That we are sending you on for another year of college this year is no longer just an opportunity for you to just sit, listen and absorb. No, it is time that you step up to start being seen as a leader in that community."

Reaching a hand out and placing it on his son's shoulder as if remembering there was a second person in this conversation, he asked forcibly, "Do you understand what I am saying? That this is the only way your schooling will advance your future financial gains?"
"Yes, sir," his son replied not allowing himself to show the least bit of fear from his father's direct gaze.
"Good. Good."

The older man let go of his son's shoulder. His eyes looked off toward the clouds as if they held in them the words of the speech he was to about to make while crossing the blue sky.

"It has been decided that when you complete this year you will return to study law in my office here in Trenton. You will be at my side in an apprentice role along with Samuel. Remember, I will not need a boy for that; I will require a man."

"Hopefully your studies have prepared you to pass an oral exam with the judge to be admitted to the bar," the father went on. "Hopefully your academic setting has also trained you to be professional and ethical in your interactions with clients. Hopefully your place in that academic community will earn you the respect needed to gain the following of others who will become the basis for your clientele. Failure in any of these avenues will disappoint me to no end. You do understand that, do you not?"

"Yes, sir."

"So for several more months we will continue to measure your success by knowing you are reading the great books of the world and by scoring well on all the professors' assignments. The basic expectations of a schoolboy. However, young man, you must make a commitment to yourself, to me and to our family that you will take steps in establishing yourself as a leader among your classmates that will bring attention to you above all others. Realize as you leave, William, the time is now. Make this year the one where we can finally be proud of what you are to become. I expect when we speak again I will have learned how you have made a difference and helped establish our family future!"

"I will do my best sir."

The boy's comment was met with the hard steely gaze of his father which bore into him. His father stared at him without comment for several seconds. When he spoke he emphasized each word without shifting his eyes from his son for emphasis.

"Not just your best, William. To be of future value, you must do better than the rest."

"Yes, sir."

"Now off you go to both your studies and to the step you will take to finally show some worth!"

There was no further verbal exchange between father and son. There was no handshake or simple hug. The speech was completed. The elder Gummere now held his chin high and shifted each of his thumbs under the lapels of his jacket, as if posing for a sculptor to make a marble statesman's statue.

The younger Gummere nodded to his father and walked off.

He glanced back at his father only once and wondered if the older man was even looking at him.

William tapped the shoulder of his younger brother who had been waiting fifty feet away at the fence line. Bags in hand, the two boys moved up the dirt street toward the center of town to catch their ride.

˜ His mother, still unseen by either the father or son, said nothing as she watched her two sons walk away.

Small tears fell from her cheeks.

Unlike her husband, she cried just as she always did when her sons left for school.

Still standing behind that door, she now looked over at her husband's stoic figure. While her sons did not know it, she knew that her husband held that pose to keep from showing any similar type of outward emotion. Though he would never say it to his sons, he also hated to see his sons leave them.

The truth was that it always left an empty void in their home and caused pain in both their hearts.

Yes, they did both love their sons.

The two brothers, William Gummere and Samuel Gummere, walked to the depot, paid for two tickets, and got on the small, duel horse carriage that would take them east.

As it pulled away from Trenton, the hack jostled William as it shifted off the stone street to the rutted dirt pathway of the turnpike that connected Trenton to Princeton.

The movement caused William to accidently bump into the arm of the passenger next to him.

William nodded to this large bearded man hoping the simple gesture would excuse his physical intrusion and possibly even break the ice with this stranger to open up a conversation that would help kill the time on the trip.

The man did nothing to acknowledge him.

William looked at his brother on his other side. He could tell his brother was already drifting off with the rocking of the cab.

Silently William shifted his gaze back out the window to the trees and farmlands slowly passing by.

Make his mark.

His father's message now reverberated inside William's head.

A child is of no value until he has provided something of worth for the family.

Stern words from his father, William thought, as he weighed what had been said against his outlined future plans. Stern words, he told himself again, but words he must find a way to make come true.

Make his mark.

But how do you stand out above all the rest and become remembered after one's time has ended at college when everyone there is trained to act the same?

For today, he thought to himself, he had no answer.

As the rhythm of the vehicle now lolled him off to sleep too, his mind escaped from the challenges his father had presented him with and returned to the last item he had enjoyed reading about before leaving his father's Trenton household.

The newspaper had highlighted the excitement coming out of the British Isle about the advances with the London Football Association. The article focused on the efforts of a man named Ebenezer Cobb Morley who had been the captain of one of the football clubs at that time. He was recognized for spearheading the attempt at formalizing the rules between the football clubs at the Freemason's Tavern in the heart of London and drawn up rules for the sport. The article praised Morley for his work. It noted that while a fight still existed among local clubs with how they wanted the game to be played many, even in America, were starting to talk about the Federation or "the Morley way."

William enjoyed reading about the author's praise for Morley.

He loved the part that stated Morley had taken the first step in creating this new game. He loved that it was a sport where men could prove to each other who was the best man. And when they defined what was best they defined it not only as a personal skilled athlete, like the fastest runner. No, best was seen as the leader of a team of men against men. The author had concluded that, without question, Morley would go down in the annals of British history as having changed forever the face of British sports.

That was making a mark! As this crossed William's mind, he involuntarily smiled.

However, what captured William's fancy, even beyond Morley's fame with writing a rulebook, was how being a victor on the athletic field changed into sheer hero adulation among others.

Morley was being praised and hailed as a hero beyond the book readers.

His worshiping crowd now included those watching the contests being played. And among the fans, William was sure, there were young men who cheered his every move. Surely, there were also women who learned about these exploits and seemed to want to throw themselves to be in a position to be with the victor.

As William dreamed along with the rocking of the carriage, he pictured his life as if he were Morley.

A star being carried off the field of play on the shoulders of his mates.

They would all sing his praise in unison and, along with those who had watched the game be played, would cheer his name out loud.

Hail our hero! Hail Gummere!

Like a gladiator in the Coliseum, in his vision, he was surrounded by a multitude of followers. Each one who cheered him after the other was more in awe of his accomplishments. Instant fame.

Teammates. Writers. Old men. All talking about him. Young children wishing they could be him. Strangers stopping him in a restaurant to shake his hand. And the young ladies? They were all over him. He could see it now. As he spoke to these female fans with their parasols twirling. All of them nearly fainting as they dropped their parasols to their sides each time he passed them on a promenade.

That was making a mark!

He awoke suddenly.

Wiping his eyes, his daydreaming faded away and the image of Nassau Hall came into focus as the hack slowed its pace.

He shook his head to clear the cobwebs that lingered. His father's voice rolled back.

Was it only about becoming a community lawyer? Was that the life his father envisioned for him in his predetermined personal destiny? Or should there be more to it? Was his dreaming to be something more heroic, like being Morley an international hero, just another one of those childhood fantasies his father had told him to forget as he implored him to enter the regular adult world?

Could these gates into this college in Princeton really hold behind them the passage to his future?

Gummere sighed as he stepped from the carriage with his brother at his side.

The old passenger who had been sitting next to him pushed past them both, completely ignoring him again.

As he watched that man walk off he thought to himself that only time could tell if people will one day pause because they recognize it is me.

He looked at his brother and nodded toward the Princeton gate. "Let's get going!"

2
"A Second Departure"
September 1869
Readington, New Jersey

Any daylight that had appeared earlier was already fading fast as the train lurched forward to pull away from the Whitehouse Station train depot in Readington, New Jersey.

A soft rain had started to fall just a half hour earlier. Now one could barely make out the outline of Abraham Van Horne's old 18th Century tavern from any window of that train as it moved ahead out of Hunterdon County and crossed into Somerset County.

The *Central New Jersey* line was a quality railroad that linked the western portion of the state with a passageway from Pennsylvania to New York City. It hauled both people and raw materials and the rail line was a critical part of the equation that brought monetary stability to the population around Whitehouse Station.

It was also the vehicle which helped provide the financial footing for the family that supported George H. Large who was now in route on its rails to New Brunswick.

George's father was originally a dealer in lumber and coal, establishing his business throughout the local region. With the advent of routes for trains throughout key cities, his main economic gains had been through the shipping of iron ores. In time the family prospered.

But George's father was quick to lecture his son on the hard work needed to extract the natural resources to make the business run and the

What happened several days later to him, as it related to the song, also continued to haunt his thoughts.

He had been in the center of their small village and, as he walked past one of the few shops in the town proper, he had overheard a gentleman discussing that night and the same song.

"Brings me to '61 every time I hear it, it does."

The old looking man who had spoken was seated next to a second man as George had walked up on them accidently invading their space and private conversation.

George noticed the other man was much younger and had a rustic looking crutch. It had a badly worn top with a dirty cloth wrapped around a wood cross piece underneath it. The crutch stood out as it was strategically propped up against a wooden beam within easy reach of the man next to his chair.

On closer inspection, George could see that this man did not have a right leg below his thigh. His pants leg was folded and pinned where his knee would have been.

"Morning," George had awkwardly interrupted their chat.

The two men nodded back without speaking. It was the kind of physical action intended to acknowledge someone without inviting them to talk while expecting the stranger to keep walking by.

But George had skipped the social cue and kept talking that day.

"I heard you talking about that song the band played this past weekend at the bandstand. I thought it was amazing and I know it stirred all of our patriotic hearts!"

Both men stared back at him with annoyed expressions on their faces. The older man appeared to be looking George over as he sized the intruder up.

"You 18?" he guessed George's age after several seconds of an awkward silence.

"Yes," George had admitted. "Actually almost 19."

The man huffed.

"Sir?" George had asked.

Slowly the older man explained his reaction.

"Son, I appreciate your interest in the music and the respect I know you are intending to show now. But I also sense that your enthusiasm is misplaced when you hear a song like that and translate it to your boyish ear. It is a song that was meant for a group that you would have probably belonged to had the war been several years later or if you had been born several years sooner."

"I am not sure I understand."

Patiently the old man had gone on as if it were critical to him that this uninitiated young man did understand his point.

"To fathom the true meaning of that song and that moment at the bandstand you would have had to of served. You would have had to have been in the fight. You would have had to of witnessed the blood and the carnage. You would have had to have been there, like Charlie and me, to have suffered through the loss of life and loss of limbs. You would had to have been a part of it!"

The man with one leg kept his eyes to the ground while the older man continued.

"So, you see, that song called us off to battle. It was our song. It is not meant to be a fancy dancing or clapping tune for others now to hear. The meaning of that song changed on the field of battle forever from a call to arms to a day of memorialized remembrance. It evolved with us until it became a part of us and a reminder of all that was lost. The song is not meant to be the highlight for others of a happy evening at a park."

Before George was able to apologize for sounding like he had tried to glorify war and their suffering by his enjoyment of the song; the man with one leg looked up at last and spoke.

"It is also a reminder though, as President Lincoln said, that our comrades did not die in vain. It calls to us that through their sacrifice all other lives are better today for it."

A moment of silence passed before the older man spoke again. This time he looked not at George but rather at his friend seated next to him.

"It is a powerful song. It speaks to us that we did the right thing when called upon. We did not shirk our duty. It is a song that reminds us that regardless of how the rest of our lives play out, at that moment in time we served a true life's purpose. It reminds us, we were a part of it while others were not."

Those words stuck with George Large.

Within the spirit of that song, the old man knew his life had a purpose.

George wondered if he would someday hear a song call him in that same way?

A purpose, Large thought again, as the train slowed while it crossed the Raritan River Bridge on its way into New Brunswick.

When will I hear that call and define my life's purpose?

Rutgers College sat a short distance away from him now.

He thought about the often tedious days of study and the routine he was expected to follow. He also thought to the special bond he felt with those at Rutgers who were engaged in the same self-building exercise with him.

They were classmates now but all would soon be joining the world. He knew his role in school. Study and learn. But was there supposed to be something more to it? Was there more than the memorizing of what others had learned before him? How was his time supposed to be different and provide meaning and a future purpose for him?

Large looked around as the others moved to exit the train. They all seemed to know where they were heading as if they each knew their place and purpose.

But what is mine?

This year, Large vowed to himself, I shall work hard to find my purpose. This year I shall find a way to give greater meaning and glory to those with whom I have been associated.

He now walked to the lodging place near the campus where he would lay his head each night, anxious to get settled in before embarking on his next year of learning.

He passed a small marker that designated the site as the prior tavern location named the Red Lion. From his first day at Rutgers it had been shared how the original students had met here for classes. Now gone, the building's past still held the imagination of those who entered Rutgers each year seeking to advance themselves. It had served a purpose of providing the foundation from which all future Rutgers students would move forward.

A purpose. George Large repeated the words again.

He then said a small prayer out loud to remind himself of the higher calling his faith instilled in him after he heard the chapel bell ringing across the campus and the streets of New Brunswick.

May I be so blessed to be a part of something so grand that will make a positive difference in the lives of so many who will come after me. May that be a part of my purpose found here at Rutgers this year.

With that he pulled his bag to the door of the residence that would serve as his home while at Rutgers College for the remaining semesters.

3
"College as a Business"
September 1869
Rutgers Campus

    The strands of Brahms' *Lullaby* lingered in his head as the professor crossed the grass field that made up the commons grounds. Mud rimmed the sides of his boots as well as his pants legs as he moved along.
    Up ahead, at the end of this field, was a quiet cross street where on the opposite side was a small hill. At the top the beauty of the Old Queens building was now clearly in his view.
    This sighting on the Rutgers campus always made him feel better as he went about his daily routines.

    He hummed louder to the musical notes clicking in his mind. Unlike the average music lover, he did not simply embrace the lyrics or sound of a song. No, instead his math-focused mind actually counted the beats and explored the symmetry of each stanza.
    How people would see him as odd if they only knew of his fascination with reconstructing music this way he thought. Still, he loved how the link between math and music always provided a respite from the more intricate calculations his brain wanted to process throughout a day.
    Not that his was any unique discovery about a math and music connection. But he loved to relate these types of tidbits to his students to see if it could spark their imagination with learning.
    And the September breeze that blew across the campus brought with it new students with minds he hoped would be eager to immerse themselves in thinking beyond the constraints of a traditional curriculum.
    Oh how he loved his position at Rutgers College with the new Scientific Studies section that had recently been instituted.

    He chuckled now as he thought about his colleagues and their conversation earlier that day.
    It felt good to laugh now. But it had taken him a while to get to this point as he had been quite agitated during the actual discussion itself.
    He knew Rutgers had come so far to where its work was now heading.
    It was a new direction away from the basic traditional framework it had once practiced. True, it had taken a virtual purging of faculty staff by the Board of Trustees ten years earlier and a formal separation from church

control to get them on the road there; but the real world did deserve a place in academia regardless of the traditionalists who had feared any type of change. Murray was thrilled Rutgers was moving, if slowly, in this progressive-minded direction.

He thought about Professor Cook, an outspoken voice of reason from those days who had been one of the only members of the faculty to be retained. It had been Cook who had recruited Murray from his position in Albany, New York to this very campus. How fitting it was that his work with this man had helped secure the financial footing so critical to the continued mission of Rutgers a year later.

Upon arriving at Rutgers, Cook had scared Murray by telling tales of the old days filled with painful meetings and a threatening lack of collegial respect that had radiated between members of the faculty. The curriculum was meant to be adhered to and any deviation in lesson or expectation was seen as a form of heresy on the highest level punishable by faculty isolation. Cook had told him of instances where members of the faculty would unexpectedly appear in the lecture halls of others just to see if they could catch a colleague preaching about anything beyond the agreed upon central points.

Cook told Murray it had been a nightmare. Murray had agreed with his colleague when he arrived at Rutgers that he would help lead any fight that attempted to draw the mission of the college backward to those dark days. Together they would always push Rutgers toward the future.

Perhaps that was what had made Murray wince as he thought back to earlier that day.

True, he would expect objections from those with strong ties to the fundamental teaching of a Church mission on the campus. They had a "divine purpose" with their point of view, Murray liked to say.

But even members of the rest of the college, like those in the newly emerging Scientific Section, were prone to falling into the trap of wanting to only teach how they had been taught themselves and not see their goal as always updating instructional practices as new information was created from beyond. College was about discovery and not memorization in Murray's book.

There was no question those around him were some of the most learned men in their fields in the United States at that time. Yet they still struggled to separate even the most basic scientific things from the religious texts they adored as the core to all learning.

He had always expected a good challenge, just on the principle of things, from the Reverend Theodore Doolittle. He was a professor of rhetoric, logic and mental philosophy.

But brand new adjunct mathematics professor Edward Bowser and the young math tutors themselves wanting to hold on to all the old ways of teaching and learning? At times they appeared even more conservative in their approaches, or at least their line of reasoning, whenever the topic of curriculum and studies came about at their staffing meetings.

That was the catalyst of today's argument that bothered him the most.

Bowser had started it all with one critical complaint.

"How are we supposed to move them forward with their math backgrounds being so bare? These students may have a basic understanding of arithmetic when it has logical visual representations. But this is not enough to meet the higher level rigors of college level algebra."

"Ciphering skills," Isaac Hasbrouck the formal math tutor moaned. "That is all that many of the newest students are entering with. Even then I find they are challenged with reciting anything beyond the basic multiplication tables."

"They are just not interested. That is the basic problem with each of these students today," Bowser stated. "Math takes discipline and they appear to lack natural skills or a willingness to work hard."

"Maybe part of the equation that is missing is you," Murray had interjected with the hope of redirecting them. "If you would just make the problems practical and show students how it has meaning they are more likely to be interested. Beyond that, they are also more likely to learn and retain what you wanted taught."

"With all due respect, sir. The problem is hardly the instructors. Staff has shown they have an expertise to be reckoned with," Reverend DeWiit Ten Broeck Reiley, who was the Professor of Latin, chimed in.

"I agree. Deflecting the problem to staff when it is clearly the lack of study on the part of the students is foolish," Reverend Dr. Jacob Cooper, who was the Professor of Greek Literature, added.

"Dr. Murray I feel that we were so far ahead of these students today compared with when we undertook our first college classes," Bowser explained. "It is just that these students lack so much and then seem to want to provide so little effort in mastering what is expected of them."

"I've heard some of the same students making fun of the value of the classics as if they know it all," Reiley cut back in. "Then, when they are tested on the material they fail to relay any substance in their essays or even show they have any understanding in simple quiz assignments."

"I believe the solution is to go back to a more rigid design for their program and regain that fundamental framework from which they should be learning." Reverend Cooper now stood as if making a political speech. "We cannot abandon the older established basis of college studies on the Rutgers campus. While I understand your desire, Dr. Murray, is to expand critical thinking on a different level, we must be cognizant of what the elite colleges like Harvard and the College of William & Mary are both committed to with their traditional studies."

"Gentlemen I respect your opinions on the need for a basic level of knowledge on various subjects. But I reject the notion that we must live in the past when we are supposed to be training minds for the future."

As the words left Murray's lips, it was his turn to stand to lecture the group.

"However, while you may be engrossed in developing language skills and memorizing historical orations; I am more interested in the actions of my own staff recognizing that our field is not only one from the past, but also one that will develop creative minds for tomorrow."

Doolittle's face had a tinge of red as he spoke.

"I object to your inference that mathematics has more value to it compared with a course of studies in any other area. Are you to tell me that wrestling with the great debate over the moral mysteries of both our faith and the logic by which we live our lives is not of the greatest value for every man?"

"Of course not," Murray shot back. "We do need a moral code built on fundamental religious beliefs and societal rules founded within a context of the betterment of the whole. But what I am advocating for is that we need to have students not just memorizing facts and regurgitating the information we expect to hear from them. We must find a way to light a spark that will cause their minds to want to explore new ways to improve our lives and the world around them. Anything less, honestly, is criminal."

It was Reverend Campbell who put a quick end to this momentary deviation from the set agenda.

"Dr. Murray, I will assume that there was no intended ill will toward the church in what you are thinking."

"Of course not, sir," Murray had replied.

"Fine. Then let us move on."

They were the last words allowed on that subject – for that day.

As that meeting had later teetered on with talk of finances and where any new revenue would be focused, Murray had caught himself thinking about how he really should not have challenged his math team in front of this larger assembled group.

All three of the math staff sat in the meeting with hurt looks on their faces now. This made Murray feel badly that he had ever said anything.

Murray loathed the thought that he now had a group to supervise and that he too was turning into an administrator. Sure he understood the needed responsibility. Without fail he attended each administrative function and performed his duty as both mentor and disciplinarian in supervising those in his charge. But he did long, each day, for the simpler life of being only a research professor and teacher independent of the demands of babysitting other adults in his life.

This was clearly one of those times.

Well, he would fix it with his team later he had promised himself. Now he was forced to listen to the money chats and watch the others on staff who tried to realign the college mission to the past.

As usual, they sat that day and reviewed everything on the typical business agenda. It ran the gamut from lack of funding to the need for building space.

It never ceased to amaze Murray that Reverend William Henry Campbell, who served as the President of Rutgers at the time, would not clearly embrace the complete benefit of shifting away from the courses of the past to a more focused union with occupational realities and the sciences.

To bring in much needed financial support for the college, it was essential to market the future possibilities to the entrepreneurs. They were the ones who were amassing wealth at great rates through the current power of industry and ingenuity and held the key to financial support.

Of course Reverend Campbell had been among those who cheered Cook and Murray as they helped shepherd dollars through the application of the land-grant process. He was beaming with pride as Rutgers "won" in its battle with the College of New Jersey in Princeton in the fight over which New Jersey school would be the beneficiary of the Morrill Act's windfall.

Yet, as the funding stream opened, even the Reverend Campbell had a hard time acknowledging the funds were to establish something totally new and were not intended to simply prop up the established way of college operational practices. Murray had to remind himself, time and again, how difficult change could be for some even in Reverend Campbell's position.

While he wanted to race and embrace the possibilities of a new frontier in education he did not have to wait for Reverend Campbell to remind him, as he would each week in Chapel, that the Rutgers College mission was initially based upon raising young men to fill the ranks of churches with an educated populace to minister the Word of God to the masses. The seminary was still a crucial anchor of many schools and the supporting congregation was essential.

In the case of Rutgers this was the original underpinning of the college from the Dutch Reformed Church. With the College of New Jersey in Princeton, it had been the Presbyterian mission.

Reverend Campbell himself was the Professor of Biblical Literature along with the student's required coursework in Moral Philosophy and Evidence of Christianity. Campbell was also, as the President, in a unique position where all things divine could not be lost upon those things financial.

Like it or not the college was still a business. Campbell used to negotiate the terms of any philosophical change with the synod that had overseen the operations. He also never shied away from approaching the leaders in industry and business who were so essential with their potential financial gifts.

As the President, he knew, he may want to talk instruction. But in the end, it was all about money.

Even this morning's discussion on the status review of the centennial celebration planned for the upcoming year had really been about promoting the college to entice additional funding.

The irony to Murray in this whole discussion was that this Rutgers Centennial was being planned for the wrong year. The planners refused to acknowledge it so they could have this fundraiser.

Like the whole college community, Murray was familiar with the debate that never seemed to end about the official date of the founding of the college. The two sides dug their heels in on whether the charter for Rutgers had been drafted in 1766 or, as claimed by others, in 1770.

The 1770 group wanted this date to be accurate so that they could have a 100 year celebration in the Spring. They wanted a joyous event filled with lecture and pageantry to rightfully recognize the history of Rutgers College. And, of course, this was needed to bring moneyed pockets to the college to donate.

Murray, along with those who he felt valued fact over fiction, ascribed to the 1766 school of thought. Due to their research on the topic, and the reality that the college had long announced 1766 as the year of origin for decades, it was a falsehood that in the long term would not benefit the history of the school.

This group held that it was unfortunate that the leaders of the college forgot to hold a formal celebration in 1866. But the event should not now be based upon a second document that talked about a 1770 date just to cash in by having a celebration.

The reality was that Governor Franklin granted a charter in 1766, four years earlier, and their research provided support for this.

The problem for Murray's group was, at this time, the 1766 document itself could not be located.

Earlier that day, when the first comment about 1766 had been made, the remark opened up a heated debate again about proof from the 1770 group.

As a man of science, Murray could not help teasing his colleagues on the 1770 side who demanded proof while holding occupations in religious-based courses. He liked to point out that "proof" was not supposed to be as fundamentally important as "faith" to them. Why change their blind faith mantra for physical evidence logic just for the desire to hold a 100 year celebration?

They had just growled back at him.

To himself, Murray would admit Rutgers actually needed an event like a centennial celebration to bring folks out and to pay for their fun. The college was short on revenue.

He was in tune with the reality that all colleges needed money. Rutgers had never met its intended numbers with enrollees, even from its earliest days. Fears about fiscal tightening with an up and down economy struck each faculty member regardless of the course they taught.

Still, do you sell out for a later charter date just to raise cash?

He should have just let it go. But he had argued with the staff.

What a day so far! He had insulted his new charges first and ended the session by angering the zealots anxious to have the centennial celebration. And without a funding source, it all might come crumbling down.

Murray now walked across the campus thinking about the future financial foundation of Rutgers College. How do we get our Board of Trustees to actively recruit investors beyond a one-time centennial spectacle.

They needed their Board and others to be proactive and seek industrialists and businessmen who could make the connection between the value of expanding college research to foster new ideas with the potential financial gains to be found by creating and communicating best practices for emerging occupational fields.

For this, the study of both science and engineering were clearly the keys to the future.

Like Professor Cook stated, there would always be a need to feed America and the mission of any future college should hinge on the science of agriculture and how to end the fear of starving in a modern era.

Grow a better America through advanced education. That was a slogan that could attract resources.

The question that haunted Murray time and again was how to build a loyal backing from men in fields when they tended to disassociate from a college because of their perceptions that it was simply a brewing pot of future clerics and philosophers?

Such was the dilemma for any college structure that prided itself first and foremost on a Classic Liberal Arts foundation.

But who could help promote the message that a college could be about focusing on solving the issues of science and engineering through research?

"Dr. Murray!"

He heard his name called out and it broke straight into his thoughts.

Running across the street was a face he instantly recognized from a recent meeting with the Board of Trustees and a session where several graduates had come back to speak on their recent ventures.

"Mr. Voorhees," Murray responded back.

With a smile and a handshake, the two men exchanged pleasantries as they strolled forth together.

"So what takes you away from your law practice and brings you back to the campus today?" Murray asked.

"I am actually running a personal favor for a young lady I am very fond of," Voorhees replied.

"Ah, the charms of young love," Murray joked.

"Well, one might say that. But when you are married you suddenly realize at the same time that it is not so charming to be sent on an errand. This is especially true when you have to stop what you had planned to do so you can track down her brother who is still a college student because she is having a fit unless you run him some extra food."

Murray smiled. "And what happens to be the name of the young academic here?"

"George Large."

"Oh yes, I have heard the name. Supposedly a bright young man and true to his namesake of being one of the larger young men here on campus although this class appears to have several a little shorter than average in stature."

"I suppose they all seem smaller when compared with those of us who have now fully grown up in life after leaving Rutgers," Voorhees stated in a boastful tone.

"Class of '56 – correct?"

"Always good with numbers, there, Dr. Murray. Yes, Rutgers Class of '56. Before the War and when men were still groomed to be men."

Murray laughed. "Well John, I hope that we are still producing the same high quality graduate that will make a difference on the world he encounters after leaving our hallowed halls."

"Oh, I did not mean to infer you are not doing your job here, Dr. Murray. No, quite to the contrary. At the same time I think they are entering a world so different from the one that nurtured us. It is a land stained in bloodshed and one which cannot afford to see that same crisis of rebellion tear us apart again. It is a world that needs to break its foundation of separation due to the root troubles of ages past and instead realize that a joint mission moving forward together is the only true direction."

"Nobly stated," Murray said without any hint of sarcasm.

"It is true," Voorhees continued. "The investment we should be making in these students today is more about building team membership skills. By learning the benefits of cooperation they can combine on joint ventures that can alter where we are heading as a nation. I tell you, as we hear constantly in our law offices, there are new inventions needing patents every day. There is so much evolving with industry that to step backward and just re-study the past, as I hate to say I felt I was often doing while I was here in college, seems criminal with the pace of change taking place across our society today."

"You should have brought your excitement to my discussion this morning," Murray noted.

"I am sorry, I forget myself," Voorhees calmed down. "I know of your work with bringing the sciences in to Rutgers and of the efforts you and Professor Cook made in procuring the Morrill Act funding. That is not lost on those of us who have walked these footsteps in New Brunswick before."

"It is that information which you shared before that is so critical to helping direct our college on its next phase," Murray stated. "We should not be isolated within these walls of our campus without a voice from the economic realities of what our nation and our young graduates will need."

"Funny, as you say that about the future I am still drawn back to my classical studies. What you said rings of what we memorized."

"And that would be?" Murray asked.

"No man is an island, entire of itself. Every man is a piece of the continent, a part of the main," Voorhees quoted.

"John Donne," Murray noted.

"1624, *Devotions upon Emergent Occasions*," Voorhees added.

"Impressive," Murray smiled again.

"You know that piece of prose from a poet has stayed with me throughout my years after leaving my college studies. Funny how often it comes back to remind me that we are all a part of something bigger. A part of something that we need to re-connect with while there is time."

"Alumni!" Murray stated out loud.

"Pardon?"

"Oh, nothing," Murray replied. "Just a random thought passing through my head that somehow found a way to pop out."

"Good ol' Class of '56." Voorhees looked up at the edifice of the Old Queen's building in front of them on that slight rise of a hill which was the defining feature of the Rutgers College campus. The copula of the main academic structure on campus, its features had been built with the intention of drawing in both man's mind to the power of learning and his eyes always upward toward the pathway to God.

"So will we see you on the campus again soon or is this to be a one-time casual happenstance?"

"You know, I might see if I can make it back to see the commencement ceremonies and enjoy the festivities of the centennial," Voorhees said with a sound that he would commit himself to at least one more visit.

"And what would it take to make you a regular visitor. Maybe a regular who finds a way to support the future mission of our students like you so eloquently just extolled the necessity of to me?"

"Are you suggesting I re-enroll Dr. Murray?" Voorhees laughed. "I do not need to remind you that even if I were to come back I doubt you would see much of me beyond the classrooms with classical studies versus the science hall I suppose you envision."

"No, our former Rutgers graduate," Murray patted him on the back as he smiled. "My hope is that you come back with money clip opened in hand to help fund our whole college mission. A mission that you may realize, with your input in how we shape our future course offerings to match what you have just spoken about, is one worth investing in for the betterment of all."

"And to good Old Queens I suppose," Voorhees added.

"Yes, to the birthplace of Rutgers and her storied past along with the stories here yet to be told."

"Did you ever think about going into marketing or sales, Dr. Murray?"

"I market science every day for the sale of its knowledge to our young people," Murray smiled back.

"So true. Well, find me an entertaining reason to come back to the campus and you never know what I or others who are alumni might bring," Voorhees said. "I am sure there are others among our prior ranks more willing and more capable of offering the support you need. At the same time, they need a reason to be here to be inspired and not through artificial avenues of speeches and pamphlets extolling the virtues of an educated mind. Rather they need to find the inspiration and the passion to want to re-enjoin and be a part of something bigger and grander."

Murray nodded in agreement as Voorhees continued.

"As my classical studies although littered with dead men and ancient tales of woe so clearly explained, there is nothing that inspires giving and love of an institution like the joy felt in the post celebratory moments of a victory hard won. Create us that forum Dr. Murray and I believe the alumni with their gifts of dollars and donations of time, just to belong once again to that type of environment, are sure to appear in mass. Give us something to cheer and I am sure that gifts will follow."

"John, it has been a pleasure," Murray said as he extended his hand and bid the visitor goodbye. "My best to the Voorhees family and all from prior Rutgers classes when you chance to meet them. I will be sure to see what opportunities arise to 'create that forum' from which alumni can feel invested again."

"You do that, Dr. Murray. And be blest as you mold the young minds."

Voorhees headed off to track down that current student, George Large, the brother of his wife.

Murray paused for a moment before entering the building to start another day's lecture.

He thought back upon the question he had been wrestling with at the time of his chance encounter with John Voorhees, alumnus and member of a large legal and political New Jersey family.

How to build a loyal backing from men in fields that would disassociate from a college because of their perceptions that it was simply a brewing pot of future clerics and philosophers?

Murray smiled as he opened the door. Of course, start with those who already should have a loyalty to the institution itself and a vested interest in seeing its name increase in prestige and honor. Start with the alumni. But how to bring them back and re-engage?

Create a forum where they wish to return and be inspired by what they see when they arrive.

Voorhees had the general concept, now this faculty member needed to develop what that forum could be. Where can that gladiator spirit and crowd excitement of the Roman Colosseum be found?

4
"A Hot Early September 1869 Day"
Princeton, New Jersey

Several of the College of New Jersey's finest young men walked along Nassau Street in Princeton proper as they moved from their morning exercises to their Cliosophic Society student club meeting.

The group joked and talked playfully in the warmth of the midday sun. They were enjoying themselves as they pushed each other and laughed at the crude stories they manufactured.

It was a rare permitted break from the routine of the dorm and classroom life imposed upon them. In many ways they felt like convicts who had escaped from their prison routine for fresh air whenever they exited the campus proper.

The college had expanded from its initial single building, Nassau Hall, which once housed everything from classes and library to sleeping quarters. The East and West College buildings and the Whig and Clio Debating Society buildings provided students with more space in which to conduct their daily lives.

There was also no question that campus housing on this Princeton campus created for the students gave them a more unified feeling of comradeship when compared with their New Brunswick student neighbors who lacked the same campus housing option at Rutgers College.

One of the biggest advantages of having housing to live in on campus was the security it provided. It also afforded a setting for the opportunity to continue debates and discussions about what had been shared in lectures earlier in the day.

The disadvantage of having housing to live in on campus was that with the security came closer monitoring of the students. This left them with little personal freedom at times to do anything beyond being allowed to continue their studies after the day's lectures had ended.

Within days of arriving each year back on campus, the routine and structure of this arrangement caused the students in the College of New Jersey to grow anxious and claustrophobic and look for any distraction from their "learning chores."

Their foray for this small group of students this day, or so they had explained to those who supervised them, was being done in the name of "wellness." Really it was an excuse to escape the claustrophobic feel of the whole college setting around them.

This group of students had requested the time to attempt an activity which would both strengthen body and mind. They proposed, and it was approved, that they be allowed to debate while in physical motion. It was approved to support the importance of exercise on building personal moral character. Off they went, walking and debating, at least for the first ten minutes of their stroll.

Unsupervised by any direct authority, their conversations meandered through a variety of topics that rarely joined back to the stated purpose of the assigned theme. Instead they talked about everything from their favorite foods ever eaten to the overly fat lady they saw cooking them.

As they walked and talked, feeling jovial with their new found freedom, they were met with a horrible shock at the sight of what suddenly lay ahead.

Standing in their pathway in full formal attire looked like the entire faculty of the College of New Jersey. Side by side these men stood out in stove pipe hats and sporting canes in hand to add to their distinguished airs.

They were directly in front of Professor Arnold H. Guyot's house. Ex-President Reverend John Maclean was positioned neatly in the center of the group next to the new President of the College, Reverend James McCosh. In all the boys counted quickly nine faculty members assembled together as if for some form of meeting. From first glance it looked like they were conducting themselves as if they were on a float in a parade.

The students froze for a full minute, unable to move at the sight.

As several of the faculty seemed to turn in their direction, they each were certain that their personal ramblings had been overheard and would now come back to haunt them with a punishment. The students nearly choked on their words as they re-grouped and attempted to put together phrases in their conversation to redirect it back to what they were supposed to be discussing.

Stunned at seeing this august group assembled as it were, the younger men then stumbled over themselves to try and prepare some formal greeting.

"Good day, good sirs," one of the student group was able to finally call out.

The distinguished looking gathering barely blinked in their direction, engrossed instead at the photographer organizing them into some alignment for a photo shoot.

At that moment, out of nowhere, a young boy of about ten years of age emerged from the corner of the house. He was chasing a round, inflated ball that was bouncing precariously ahead of him.

"Andrew James," a thick Scottish accent bellowed out. "Get that confounded thing out of here and back with your playmates!"

The students stopped in awe at the admonishment of his son by the new President of their College.

The young boy caught up with the ball and, without touching it with his hands, stopped it mid-bounce on the ground by his feet. Without any hesitation, he gave the ball a fierce kick re-directing it back toward where it had just come. It lifted quickly out of the sight of the students across the street. Young Andrew James then disappeared after it with a chorus of young voices yelling from the back of the house in the area where he had directed the ball to fly.

"What's the matter lads, never seen a star kicker boot a ball before?"

Again, the students stood open mouthed and in awe of the Scottish voice that played out across the street.

"Where's the respect?" one of the other faculty members called out as if he were just now noticing the small group of college students there in his presence.

Immediately, the students took off and tipped their caps in mandatory fashion in the direction of the assembled faculty members.

"Who let you go free at an hour such as this?" another yelled out. "Chapel and study only today!"

"Now, now," President McCosh chided the faculty members. "There is nothing better than a chance to walk about while studying. I gave them permission to do so and I cannot imagine there is anyone here who would object to such an action."

The faculty members appeared to take a step back at the rebuke by the President in front of their young charges.

Gummere thought he could detect a slight grin on the face of President McCosh as he moved across the street toward the students who were still frozen in their tracks.

"Out debating, what was it now? Oh yes, about the importance of fasting I believe I was told," McCosh spoke loudly for the larger adult group to hear him as he stepped closer.

None of the students even blinked as he closed the distance toward them.

McCosh moved in among the students who ringed him in a small circle. His voice, noticeably lowered in volume from his earlier call, addressed the students in a manner that suggested the conversation was for their ears only and not for the assembled faculty across the street.

"So, what did you think about my son's ability to kick?" he asked to no one in particular.

He was met with total silence.

"Makes me wonder, with all of you so anxious to get in your exercises today, if any among you have the same skill or ability with the likes of a ball?"

One student, Dutch Boughner, cleared his throat and offered, "Well sir, several of us have on occasion kicked a ball around before."

"Several of us were actually pretty good at the game they called ball-own and they used to play here on campus regularly a few years back," a second student commented.

"Ball-own?" McCosh questioned. "Never heard of it."

"It was a pretty violent kicking game that brought together two large teams. We actually still play a version of it now and then but the original version of the game was eventually frowned upon," another in the group chimed in. "So many of the younger lads always getting injured."

"True," said another student. "But we do still take every chance to play something like it and some of us actually find ourselves kicking the ball about on a regular basis when we are not caught up completely in our studies, sir."

"So you do kick the ball around?" McCosh responded. "And your skill level lads? Is it as good as what you just saw from my son A.J. there today?"

"Well sir, I am not exactly sure," came back a meek response.

"We are supposed to be building men here," McCosh answered. "I thought I had heard even when I was across the pond that the athletic prowess of the lads in Princeton was something to be amazed with. Guess it would be as good a time as any to see how we are progressing on that front."

"Sir?'

"This way," McCosh stated as he turned and moved back across the street, leaving no doubt about his intentions for the students to follow him.

As directed, they moved cautiously behind him without saying a word.

"What now..," one of the faculty members called out to the procession but was cut off by McCosh's arm raised with his hand in a stop signal.

The faculty members watched as the students passed them and shifted toward the rear of the house and to the lawn adjacent to the property. Assembled there were several boys of various ages chasing the same round ball that young A.J. McCosh had earlier kicked back to them.

"I'd drop the hats and coats lads," President McCosh stated now out of the direct line of sight from any member of his college staff. "Time to see how you measure up!"

McCosh called over his son and the other boys who had been kicking the ball about. The college students took off their hats and caps and coats and ambled out on to the grass field where McCosh had gathered the younger boys.

"Okay lads," McCosh gestured with his hand. "Count off and seven of you head over that away. The rest of you stay here and get ready to go in as substitutes if the time comes."

The younger boys ran over to the opposite side of the field. McCosh tossed the ball to his son and called out, "Okay Andrew James, show them how it's done."

With that, the young boy maneuvered the ball forward, dribbling it with his feet toward the opponent's goal which was made from two tree branches planted points down into the ground.

The college students were slow to react and watched as the young boy deftly moved the length of the field and booted the ball in between the two uprights.

"What's the matter with you?" McCosh yelled out at the college students. "You just let a ten year old make a fool of you all!"

The younger McCosh dropped the ball at the feet of the college student closest to him and jogged back to the other side of the field.

The college student shrugged his shoulders and started to dribble the ball forward as he had seen the young McCosh do toward them. As he approached the younger boys, in mass they swarmed toward the player with the ball. Although smaller in stature, they caught him totally by surprise when they ran straight into him and knocked him to the ground.

Instantly two of the boys kicked the ball forward. One of the college students suddenly came to life and ran toward the ball but before he could get there the boy kicked it forward and the ball took several high hops toward another teammate. As it looked as though the ball would bounce over his head, the player batted the ball with his fist toward a teammate in front of him who hit it with his hip toward a third teammate. Again the ball bounced higher and this teammate batted the ball with his fist toward the young McCosh who, without hesitation booted the ball again with a mighty kick straight through the two uprights.

"They did it to you again!" the elder McCosh yelled out. "Getting whipped by a bunch of 9 and 10 year olds! You are embarrassing the College of New Jersey with your gamesmanship!"

"He cheated," one of the college students called out.

"In what way?" McCosh demanded defensively. "Watch what you say as one of those lads is my son!"

"He used his hands. They can't do that!"

"And they ran right into our teammate and drove him to the ground. That's not allowed either!"

The Reverend McCosh let out a laugh that rolled across the make-shift field.

"Okay, Andrew James. You and your friends go back and work out yourselves. Seems I have some pretty lassies who are afraid to mix it up the way the contest is intended to be played now," McCosh instructed his son and his friends.

"Sir, I was just saying," the college student who had first objected spoke out. However, he was cut off before he could complete his sentence.

"Hold it, Andrew James," McCosh told his son. "What is it that you are saying lad?"

The college student took a deep breath and, in a composed voice answered, "I think we get it now and are ready to take them on. We thought they were playing soccer when we first saw them. I think this is that new federation rules football we have been hearing about."

"So you have heard of the game," McCosh stated.

"Read about it," Gummere stated, looking around at the other students by his side. "We've been playing a little of something similar to this on our free hours last year, but we had no formal teams. I had actually hoped that we might create a club around this sport here in Princeton."

"Good. I am encouraged to hear that." McCosh signaled for his son to kick the ball back over to the college students. He called out as they were about to receive it, "Let us see how you do with knowing what you are supposed to be playing this time!"

As they prepared to move forward, they called out to each other to do exactly what they had seen McCosh's son's team do.

This time, in a more aggressive manner, they started forward dribbling the ball. They kicked it from player to player but, as soon as they neared the young McCosh, he sped past the college player who was dribbling the ball and batted it away with his fist.

Like a herd of gazelles on the run, they all raced after the batted bouncing ball. One of the college players caught up with it first and, before kicking it, lifted his forearm into the face of the charging ten year old who was closing in on him. As the ten year old sprawled backward from the blow, the college player booted the ball as far as he could. Unfortunately for him it was intercepted by the young McCosh who appeared to be everywhere.

The young McCosh headed forward. This time two of the college players, acting either as they thought they were supposed to or acting simply out of frustration, both pounced on the younger and smaller player bringing him to the ground as the ball squirted forward. It bounced toward a college player who batted it with his fist toward a teammate who, as soon as the ball arrived to him, turned and kicked it toward the goal. The ball itself swerved wide and rolled out, once again, toward the street.

"Okay. Okay," the elder McCosh called out. "Enough for now."
One of the other ten year olds chased the ball while the younger McCosh pushed himself up from the ground and wiped the dirt off his face.
"Sorry," one of the college students said to the ten year old as he looked at his smaller size and the scrapes that appeared on the younger boy's face and arms.
"Sorry?" the young McCosh responded. "I thought you were a bunch of daisies when we first started and then you come on like that. Great improvement. That was bloody amazing!"
"Language!" the elder McCosh scolded his young son.
Instantly the young boy's eyes widened at his father's stern stare. Obediently, he shrugged his shoulders and nodded. But, as he looked back up he turned toward the college student and gave him a wink while whispering, "Next time you go down."
"Okay, enough of that too," the elder McCosh said to his son. "Go get yourself cleaned off and time for your friends to start heading off to their houses on their own."
"Yes sir," the younger McCosh said.

President McCosh turned his attention back toward the college students and moved toward the side of the property as they watched. "Come on over here," he called out to the group.
Slowly they moved forward and grouped around him as they waited for him to speak.
"You were correct, Mr. Gummere. That is a version of the new football they are playing overseas," Dr. McCosh started. "Claims it makes men out of boys and prepares them for the rigors of life. It is quickly becoming all the rage. It is similar but different from soccer as you seem to be aware. Not that I have anything against soccer or rugby for that matter, but I love to think that our young men will always be at the forefront of any new

challenge that presents itself in this world. So if we are solid at playing a sport that has existed for many years like cricket; that is grand. But knowing we can quickly adapt and instantly be the best at the next test in life – that is even better!"

McCosh looked over the group before speaking again.

"So, you wanted to get your exercise today? My plan is that you will get more of it in the immediate future. A healthy mind can only be attained with a healthy body. Personally, I love the idea of gymnastics for young men. It is a powerful sport to build personal endurance and strength. However, it may take a while to get that going since it requires a gymnasium and equipment."

"In the interim," McCosh continued. "I believe this football game will help build the mental toughness and teamwork that is equally important in turning you into men. As Mr. Gummere noted before, it is the newest form of sport coming to us from the British Isles. I would like you each to start mastering it right away so you can stay ahead of those who are younger then you, like my ten year old son, and already embracing it. And since you expressed an interest Mr. Gummere, starting at the end of this week, do you think you can have a training club formed to practice with my son's group? What do you all think?"

"Yes sir," came back as the collective response along with Gummere leading the call.

"Good. Good." McCosh noted. As he turned and started to move away, he turned back to the college students who had yet to move.

"One more thing. Next time I expect to see more personal toughness when called out. When you speak we do demand respect. But we also desire a sense of fortitude exhibited in all manner of body and speech that demonstrates confidence and poise. Confidence with respect. You can provide both in all interactions with me as well as with the staff. It is also what I expect when you meet with anyone else. The men we are building here at the College of New Jersey should always cause those who meet them to walk away knowing they have just met a new world power. Mind you we do not want to come across as pompous, entitled, self-centered princes. No, we expect men of dignity and of the highest moral manner whose skill and scholarship earn the instant respect of all they meet!"

The students just stared. Their mouths were open but no sound emanated, as if they were in shock.

McCosh cleared his throat before he finished off. "Now get back to your walk and debate about, what was it going to be again, the benefits of fasting? Oh, and the two of you who hit my son, I will be sure to address that at a later date."

McCosh then started to walk away from the group and moved back around out of sight at the front of the house. But as he walked, he spoke loud enough for the boys behind him to still hear. "The thought of it, willing to hit the College President's young son. And right in front of him!"

"What was that all about?" Jerry Sharp, one of the college students, finally blurted out when McCosh was gone from sight.

"Getting ready," Gummere answered.

"For what?"

"Whatever we face with the next challenge in life," Gummere's steely voice replied.

"He is a strange man, William," Charlie Darst, another student there, remarked. "You have to admit, that was odd."

"Polite and inviting. Challenge us and then insult us. Command us and then reprimand us. And all within a matter of minutes. That doesn't seem crazy to you?" Sharp asked.

"I liked his style," Gummere stated without hesitation. "I think there is something about him that is right on the mark." Then, looking at the surprised faces around him he added, "Even if that was unexpected and definitely strange."

"Like him or not, I wonder what he plans to do to us for hitting his son?" one of the college students asked. "Do you think he will remember?"

"As off the wall as his temperament was; all I know is I hope he remembers it was you who hit him and does not think it was me!"

"Very funny!"

By this point, President McCosh had now continued past the faculty members without even commenting to the group assembled there. The ex-President, Maclean, had joined him as the two of them walked away and back toward the main part of the campus.

"Well John, think I made an impression today?" McCosh asked his retired predecessor.

"A permanent one," Maclean responded without delay. "Both on the students and the faculty."

"You think the staff learned a new perspective?"

"All I can say is that it put them a little on edge, James. They did not know what to make of you. Not that you should ever feel you need to be like me but they definitely appeared shocked by the actions and interactive way you engaged the students. If nothing else, I guarantee they are coming away from that encounter with thoughts about what is happening here and are asking each other what is this new fellow planning to change in the way we have been doing things."

"As intended," McCosh came back. "As intended."

"Caution, is all I would say," Maclean answered. "This institution has earned its reputation by maintaining the highest of standards. It has avoided the folly of experimenting with mixed methodology instructional practices or watered-down curriculum. Excellence demands a rigid path for her subjects."

"I understand," McCosh answered.

"The faculty will rebel on you if you try to tear away the foundation that all this historic greatness has been built upon. Lose the faculty and you lose the College."

"Again, I appreciate your thoughts on the subject and respect the work you have done and all that the College of New Jersey has accomplished during your tenure." McCosh glanced back toward the disappearing image of the faculty behind him. "I just hope the faculty appreciates and respects the work we now have ahead of us."

The faculty members, still assembled at the front of the house, watched as the current President and ex-President ambled away from them up Nassau Street.

"What was that all about?" one of the faculty asked aloud, echoing the same question offered by the college student earlier.

"I have no idea," one of his colleagues responded.

"Disgraceful and undignified," a third faculty member offered. "Not the way I feel a President of the College of New Jersey should carry himself when meeting with students!"

The faculty group grew completely quiet and leered out with stern faces as the college students appeared from the field behind the house where they had just recently engaged in their short physical game of football with the younger boys.

The college students, again immediately drawing on prior required practice, tipped their hats or caps at the members of the faculty but said nothing to them as they passed by.

As they moved out of earshot one of the faculty asked, "What message do you think was sent to our students today? That it is fine to act like a group of hooligans in a public display like this whenever they want? What type of young men does he think we are trying to produce here? Men of class and formality or street urchins to mingle with the common throng?"

No one answered. Instead, each faculty member pondered their new relationship with the incoming President and wondered what their future roles may be.

The day had started so positive for them. The new President calling the faculty together in this informal setting. A social gathering of mutual respect. Then that discussion, albeit short, before the students had arrived and as they waited for an impromptu group photograph to be taken. It had run a different course from what most felt a new college president would say to his experienced faculty.

McCosh had been polite and professional with them, no question there. But his statements about moving into a new era where academics placed a higher level of importance on the practical world versus the classics that were the very foundation of where young men needed to be fashioned from? What was the meaning behind those words?

Would this new President not understand his purpose of protecting the faculty from outside invasion of political rhetoric and influence from businessmen intent on re-writing the curriculum to create a training ground simply for their narrow niched occupational pathway?

And then this sport and activity emphasis with his son and the college students? Not only highly unexpected but clearly inappropriate. Did he not realize the necessary boundaries that needed to be maintained between the students and the staff? Did he not appreciate the dignity that his office was intended to bear on the operational practices of the school itself?

So quirky. So strange. Now, feeling so out of balance.

As the group split up and headed back to their personal activities for the day, no man left without wondering what the next day would bring and an uneasy feeling about what would be expected of them.

For President McCosh, that was exactly how he had hoped the staff he was about to lead would start to feel. A little cognitive dissonance was good for the soul. To ready men in your charge to meet the next great battle you needed to keep your own sword sharp. Eliminate the classics – of course not. But find a way to prepare them for the future and not the past – that was where these faculty members needed to be thinking each and every day themselves.

Gummere saw the young McCosh jogging up toward the grounds as he crossed back over the pathway.
"You were pretty talented out there," he called out to the young boy.
"And I hope you all get better," the child shot back.
Gummere smiled without saying anything else. This kid had a strong personality. This kid had a sense of self confidence. This kid felt he could take on and beat anyone else in the world. Gummere chuckled and stated to himself out loud, "This kid reminds me of me."

5
"The Annual Rivalry Taunt and College Prank"
New Brunswick: Inside A Local Public House Tavern
September 21, 1869

It was an old cannon.

On first glance there was nothing special about it. Small by the standards for this type of weaponry, one would pass by it on an average day on the street in Princeton without looking back.

But the story of this cannon went all the way back to the American Revolution. The debate over who actually owned the cannon was almost as old. The right to place the cannon within their city proper pitted the people of New Brunswick and Princeton against each other as they saw the cannon as one of those unique historic relics worthy of being their own memorial.

They both claimed ownership. For now, Princeton held onto it and the people of New Brunswick demanded it back.

On closer inspection though, this was really a fight about community pride.

And fight they did.

The tale revolved around the story of the birth of America. With a patriotic passion every resident extolled the essential role that all of New Jersey had played during that first "true" winter of the war when Washington's troops were struggling to survive. The elders of Princeton and New Brunswick spoke with pride about how imperative the actions in New Jersey had been in determining the outcome of the war and in helping the United States Army on a major step toward securing eventual victory and, with it, the independence and nationhood for the country.

The commonality in the story always ended at this point.

Depending on where in New Jersey the story teller resided, they typically moved on to explain why the cannon played a more critical role in that local community's contribution on the road to American independence. In reality they were bragging that their overall community contribution to the American war effort was greater than their other neighbors in New Jersey. They deserved the trophy for their ancestors' efforts. And the trophy, to each of them, was that cannon.

In Princeton they talked about the Battle of Princeton. They repeated with great detail the events a week after the victory against the Hessians at Trenton. In Princeton was when Washington surprised the British again at the start of that cold January and swung the momentum in the American's favor. And when they defeated the British in Princeton, many claimed, it was done with the cannon they held on to as their rightful memorial now.

In New Brunswick, the emphasis was about the critical cover locals and soldiers provided to the retreating Continental troops and the skirmishes around New Brunswick. The story tellers here would note that the army may have been victorious in a small battle near Princeton. But when the troops were weary and in danger of capture in December 1776 it was the fight in New Brunswick that saved the day. They loved to highlight, with a dash of bravado, the colorful exploits of Alexander Hamilton's horse artillery delaying the British advance in New Brunswick that allowed the American army to escape. Of course, they would point out, this was done with the cannon that now resided incorrectly in Princeton.

In New Brunswick they would also boast about a second engagement later in the War that saw Colonel Daniel Morgan and General Mad Anthony Wayne chase Howe's troops across the Raritan and out of New Jersey. Of course this was supported by the courage of those in New Brunswick and done with the missing cannon they claimed that would have been on hand.

Who cared if there were two altercations in New Brunswick, the Princetonians would counter. With pride they would then remind listeners that Princeton was once the capital of the entire fledging country at one stage in the grand American Story. In this retelling, the nation's capital was always protected by their cannon.

The argument knew no end. The constant debate to claim the cannon as their rightful property and a visual symbol of victory was always inflamed with jealousy and anger.

This anger resonated in New Brunswick. When the cannon they once had disappeared after the War, many there believed their missing cannon was taken by people in Princeton.

In Princeton they swore that the cannon currently on their town grounds had always been their property. They acknowledged that it may have been loaned out at one time after the War, but that did not change their right of ownership. Any attempt to try and take it would never be allowed.

And so it went back and forth over the years as both groups of residents demanded that they be allowed to display the cannon as a symbol of local pride.

To two groups of college students, this was the perfect challenge that could not be passed over within their existing school rivalry. Get or keep the cannon for our side.

Whether it started with an attempted theft by the Rutgers students or the original theft by the College of New Jersey in Princeton, it became an annual activity to see who would get to keep it at day's end. For the last few years, the townspeople of Princeton were the proud victors with the cannon remaining on their land. But this feud knew no end.

So when September started each year, as soon as new students arrived on each campus, the locals would incite them with the story of the stolen cannon.

It was only the second formal day of classes that day in 1869, on the Rutgers campus, and the talk had already started again.

It never helped that the students in Princeton and the people of Princeton took every opportunity to taunt the New Brunswick youth and general populace with the question of, "Have you found your missing cannon yet?"

This was the very question that was posed to a first year Rutgers undergrad late in August, before his classes had even started, when he was teased while visiting Princeton.

Sharing the tale of his visit to Princeton got the tempers boiling back in New Brunswick that evening again among several young Rutgers students seated in a crowded local tavern.

It began as typical public meal time boasting. Just like so many average young college students tended to do, they bragged about how they planned to re-shape the world. This time they pledged to avenge this insulting behavior enacted by the people of Princeton.

Within earshot, the townspeople in that New Brunswick tavern were also frustrated. But their anger was generated with how exhausted they were from the annual bragging by Rutgers students about acts of honor and redemption that never seemed to materialize. These men already harbored a dislike for all "spoiled college boys." On this hot night it was now painful to hear how these Rutgers students sounded so full of their personal predictions of grand deeds. Rough to absorb when you knew that the average working man actually did the daily things that made life happen around them.

A growling, gravelly voice caught the Rutgers students' attention.

"So what are you going to do about it youngins?" The question was thrown out by an older patron in the tavern house that evening.

The students, who were seated socializing over their meal at a central table near the New Brunswick regulars, grew quiet on the topic of rude Princeton students.

"I think it is disgraceful that we have these high-browed intellectual sophisticates in our midst every year doing all this book learning and yet they never have been able to figure out about how we are getting our poor community property back," another loud-voiced older patron chimed in.

"I suppose they teach 'em how to lace their knickers and learn 'em how to do that fancy talk all day but never take the time to make men out of 'em." A third townsman spoke out even louder, intending his comments to be heard by everyone in the tavern.

"Bunch a dandies they tend to be. Sad but true," the first man reported back. "Every year the same thing. Same old talk about making tomorrow different or better by reading about the past. But they never step in to fix a major slight to the good people here who tolerate their very presence in our town every year."

"And what is it that you all feel we should be doing?" one of the young college students finally asked back toward the older group of men.

"Go and get it!" one of the townsmen shot back. "Do we really need to give you directions on how to get off your arse?"

"You lads sit there talking all high and mighty and throw in a quote from some ol' dead guy in Greece or Rome and think that makes a bit of difference in the real world?" The oldest townsman of the group now stood and continued to speak as he moved toward their table.

"Every year we hear about how great the college boys are supposed to be here at Rutgers. Then we get word out of Princeton about how much better their young men are who attend their college. They remind us that they have the real College of New Jersey."

Now the other three townsmen walked over to join the old man who had moved to where the students were seated. They also stood at the side of the table and looked down at the college lads.

"Insult you personally little boy about the cannon and now you just take that too?" the first old man continued, nodding his head in disgust.

"Youngsters, you will soon learn in life that you are no one until you have acted with a purpose. You are no one until you actually accomplish something of worth as valued by others. You are no one regardless of your fancy clothes. Those vocabulary words spit out in perfect diction don't mean a thing when all you have to back it up is the story of your father's lineage or someone else's worldly triumphs."

"What should you do?" laughed another in the townsmen group. "I think you boys here should embrace the chance to do something others actually care about. Don't let those Nassau boys piss in your beer all your life with tales of how they got the better of you. Hell! Go get the damn cannon back and teach them a lesson for a change!"

The townsmen kept the comments coming.

"So some College of New Jersey boy teases you about not finding the cannon and all you do is sit and whine here? You all riled up here this evening? Seriously, you have to ask us what to do?"

"Either fluff your skirts and petticoats and do nothing but chatter about it like some gal-boys as you appear to be doing tonight or go make 'em pay for insulting you in public like that."

"Ask me what to do? You obviously didn't punch him in the mouth like I would have already done for saying such a thing!"

"Me too! Versus crying like you all are about their, what was the word you were using? Audacity?" The old man just shook his head from side to side.

"Live boys, before all you can do is piss and moan telling stories about what you wished you had done."

"Teach 'em pompous asses down in Princeton what's for!"

"Put up in action or shut up and go back to your studying about what great things other people do!"

"And if you don't, please don't frequent any establishment with real men in it while you sit and cry!"

With a disgusted look on his face, the oldest man flipped his hand in the air and turned and walked away without any further comment.

Stunned, the Rutgers students watched as the group of older townsmen exited the establishment through the door with him.

Finally, breaking the silence, one in the Rutgers group spoke out.

"Great! Now we're getting told off by old men?"

"Not told off," another student corrected him. "Getting set straight."

Then for the next two hours the students no longer discussed the merits of conjugating verbs in Latin or the upcoming assignment with

Algebraic analysis. The young Rutgers students instead ramped up the energy within them convinced it was time to take action. They came to a conclusion, collectively, that this was a sign to act and swift action would make a point to the locals as well as those arrogant Princetonians once and for all that the men at Rutgers would be a force to reckon with and not be humbled by anyone's windy bluster.

Emotional desire shifted to strategic planning. Planning shifted to real steps to take and instructions for each student to follow. Time and place set, plan in motion, they crossed hands on top of each other and swore allegiance to getting this done. They swore protection if discovered to each other in the group. They swore their action was not just an act of revenge but rather a noble cause that would bring glory to the name of Rutgers College and restore the prestige to the good people of New Brunswick.

Three more hours later that Tuesday night, seven students left the grounds of the Rutgers campus and headed in the dark toward Princeton. They understood they were risking the consequences of the curfew requirement and knew that they even risked the chance of expulsion. They had sworn their loyalty to each other not to share a thing with anyone else regardless of the outcome. No personal gain here if they succeeded. No broken loyalty by ratting anyone out within the ranks if caught.

They were joined together for a higher calling as they stole away. They acted tonight for something they all deemed more important than the daily ritual obedience to the rules. They acted to restore the reputation of a community. They acted to restore the faith from the community in the men of Rutgers College. They acted for the pride of the collective whole versus one man's glory.

So inspired, they felt emboldened as they set forth.

The strategy they had outlined appeared simple.

There was a night train that ran from New Brunswick to the station in Princeton near the campus. They wagered this would likely be near the site of the cannon.

Once in Princeton, they planned to move on foot in the dark of the night after the train ride and into the town where the cannon was said to be standing.

Together they felt seven strong young men would be able to wheel the cannon from its position in the town to one of the nearby farms. There they would un-hitch the cannon itself from the gun carriage wheels and drop it into a fallow field.

They would then cover the cannon over with mud, sticks and leaves in this temporary hiding place. They would place some type of marker by it so they could find where they had buried it at a later date when they wanted to retrieve it to bring it home to New Brunswick.

Then the plan was to take the now lighter, cannon-less gun carriage and wheel it back to town and deposit it back where they had originally found it. The goal was to do this in five hours in order to get to the train station and leave Princeton on the early morning train back to New Brunswick. If all went as planned they would make it back in time to New Brunswick to go to classes.

It might be a full night without sleep and a great deal of physical labor. However, even if they would have to force themselves to stay awake in their classes the next day, it would be worth it. If they did it right, nobody at Rutgers would even notice they had been missing.

They laughed as they had finished their preparations. Each one of them in the group wished they could actually be able to see what took place in Princeton the next day. Somebody there would wake up and likely go right past the spot without even noticing it was missing. Then somebody else would inevitably realize the cannon was gone. All they would find would be that set of wheels and no cannon.

Then it would be their turn to tease the people of Princeton about having "lost" their cannon!

In high spirits, they raced that night to the New Brunswick train station and hopped on the train.

The ride to Princeton had taken some planning but turned out to be the easiest part of the foray.

As soon as the train pulled into the station in Princeton, the hand drawn map that one of the Rutgers students carried soon proved less than accurate. Instantly they got lost wandering around in the dark looking for an item none of them had actually laid eyes upon before.

"How hard can it be to find a cannon?" one of the group had asked.

An hour later, they all agreed it could be very hard to find.

After walking around for over an hour they began to get irritable from both their inability to locate the cannon and a lack of sleep.

Then, near the corner of Dickinson Street and Canal Street, one of the students spied a stack of pails that had been left from a day of whitewashing fencing near someone's personal property. On closer inspection, the pails appeared to each to have some paint still in them.

Seizing on this discovery and getting exhausted from traipsing about late at night in their futile search for the cannon, one of the young men suggested an alternate plan.

"Look, I don't know about you but I am not sure we are going to find this cannon and I also do not want to leave without paying the people of Princeton back in some way. What do you think about taking the paint in these pails and writing words all over the face of the College building?"

Whether it was a great idea or they were just so tired of looking for the cannon, they each agreed with the new plan and secured the pails and brushes that had been left there for the next day's use by the painter and jogged in the direction of Nassau Hall.

While Princeton was not a bustling metropolis or even a large town by any standard, there was still some level of human activity out and about even at that late hour. As the young men with the pails moved across the street, a set of eyes saw them and thought their behavior was odd. Assuming that it was students from Nassau Hall, he gave the actions of the young men some leeway. But, as fate would have it, this one man who saw them ran into two professors from the college who had been out studying stars. He passed on the word to them that he had seen what appeared to be several students running toward the campus building with buckets in their hands.

As soon as the Rutgers students had arrived at the steps to Nassau Hall they had immediately begun to write on the stone entrance. In sloppy writing from half-spilled paint, they etched out the words, "May all thieves rot in hell with any stolen cannon."

As one student started to fashion the letters to "Rutgers" alongside the initial statement, the Rutgers students heard the voices of two older men calling out.

"Hey there!" a call rang out from the dark. "What are you doing there!?!"

Already prepared to run if anyone approached, they hurled the pails away and darted at a full sprint for the open grounds perpendicular from the two approaching men.

"Stop!" cried one of the two men coming up on them in an authoritative tone.

The students ran even faster.

They weaved through two streets and along a fence line to a field without looking back.

Within a few minutes they did not see any sign of these men pursuing them any longer. Winded, they retraced their steps and slowly approached the train station near the campus.

Suddenly a new panic climbed over them. They realized they would be caught red-handed by the men chasing them from Nassau Hall if they waited here at the train depot.

"We need to find another way back."

"We can't walk back to New Brunswick!"

"Maybe we can find a carriage."

"Seven of us!"

"I'd rather walk then wait here!"

"Why not at least hoof it to the previous station we saw up the rails that was before this one."

"Princeton Junction?"

"Yeah- I say let's get out of here. I am starting to feel like a caged animal just waiting for someone to come. I would rather keep moving before we are caught like sitting ducks."

"Alright, let's get going."

There was now suddenly more noise across Nassau Street coming from the direction of Nassau Hall. It was apparent that others had now joined the first two men who had interrupted the Rutgers boys from their painting spree and yells could be heard in the night about catching the vandals.

Not needing anymore coaxing, all seven Rutgers students simultaneously bolted away from the station benches and raced alongside the tracks following the path of the train toward the next station.

"You know a train will not be at this station either for almost three hours," one of the students noted after several minutes of running and as they each had pulled up to an opening by the tree line to catch their breath.

"So, what do you suggest now? We run all the way back to New Brunswick?"

"No, but I would rather continue past this closer station to put some more distance between ourselves and anyone who might be following behind us. What is the next train stop up the line?"

"The next train station?"

"This is crazy!" one them muttered out while still gasping for breath.

"The Plainsboro Depot in South Brunswick," one of the others called out.

"I say we keep on moving and not wait here. This is just too close to the campus for me."

"I agree. What harm can it be to keep on moving toward the next station?"

"I'm not sure. Do you consider a heart attack harm?"

"Look we do not have to sprint there. We can jog or even walk fast if we have to so we can keep together if some of you are too winded to run any further."

"What if we miss the train at the next stop because we don't get there in time?"

"It is probably only two or three miles away from here. We should be fine if we keep moving."

"You don't think if they want to hunt us down they wouldn't think to keep coming up the line after us?"

"Maybe. But I would still rather be further away."

"Enough talking. I say we start jogging in that direction."

While several of them groaned at the thought of walking at all they did start at a slightly slower pace from their previous run, but still one that had them heading quickly toward their next destination.

Two hours later, on schedule, a steam train pulled into the depot in South Brunswick. The Rutgers students had made it there with time to spare.

At the station they had decided to break into three separate groups of two pairs and one threesome while they had waited there. They milled about the station in this manner and each concocted a story they thought they would use as an alibi for why they were getting on a train at this time of day and at this location if anyone from Princeton approached them.

No one ever asked.

The morning train eventually arrived in New Brunswick before the sun started to rise, the darkness playing heavy on their exhaustion and the desire to sleep with each of the Rutgers seven. As soon as the train pulled to a stop, the young men stepped off and scurried back toward their respective domiciles with the intent of freshening up and hustling directly to chapel for morning prayers.

The last instruction to the group had been that no one was to say a thing about this to anyone and no one was to skip morning chapel to sleep in. Miss the third day of classes and each of them knew that people will notice.

Each student nodded at the other as they left the group and found their way indoors at each of their individual residences.

Inside, some were greeted with a "where have you been?" Others were able to sneak in to their boarding location going undetected. Regardless of the internal welcome, each student hurriedly got himself ready for class. Each student then raced back to the campus anxious not to stand out by being seen entering anywhere late this day.

6
"Consequences?"
September 22, 1869
Princeton

President McCosh watched as the students moved about the markings that had been painted on the ground and also upon the building owned by their college.

The white lettering was badly smeared.

Various liquids were being poured over the paint. The remnants of the white lettering were vigorously being scrubbed away with rough straw and horsehair brushes and were slowly vanishing with the watery wash.

Each of the young men who came out of Nassau Hall made statements about this being the work of the students from Rutgers. There were no formal markings to verify this besides a painted letter "R." The single letter must have been the final thing being painted when Professors Comas and Morley had come upon the vandals after being tipped by the townsmen on their way off the campus the night before. While it was just an "R," most believed the letters "utgers" were intended to follow it.

Even without the name of the other college, the consistent remark going around was, "Who else would care about a cannon?"

The common laughter from the lads at Nassau Hall was over a spelling error.

Clear to all who saw it was the misspelling of the word "cannon." The painted word had included an "e" instead of an "o" as the second vowel.

As they laughed, the Princeton students all swore that this was a solid clue and proved that this work was done by a Rutgers student as they couldn't spell and were such poor academic scholars.

The general mood was surprisingly upbeat around the campus considering that the school had been victimized by outsiders in this manner. Even the fact that the students in Nassau Hall had been called upon to clean up a mess they had not created did not seem to diminish the positive sounds being heard among the students.

The activity from the night before also brought the arrival of several Princeton townspeople as general observers. They were equally curious to see for themselves what evidence there was of the raid that took place. Each visitor brought along some thoughts about Rutgers in general after hearing the Princeton students talk and added their views on the losing traditions in New Brunswick as evidenced by the issue of ownership of the cannon itself.

"Just draws attention in all the wrong ways to those poor fools up there," one of the townspeople commented.

"They already live in an inferior community that is getting heavy with smoke from factories and sewage from too many people congested in a small area. Now they act like ruffians in the night harming the good place others live. Seems like someone should do something about that to keep them in their place. A lesson to those Rutgers schoolboys is definitely called for here."

The advice was relatively consistent throughout the day.

President McCosh heard numerous times that the young men of Rutgers College should be brought to justice and held accountable for their actions with some type of consequence.

President McCosh listened without casting judgment about anyone to each of those who came by. He only acknowledged that, if the tables were turned, he would investigate among his own students as he was sure that President Campbell would be doing at this time at Rutgers College.

New Brunswick

Back in New Brunswick, the story of the events in Princeton started to spread across the school and into the town well before the day was out.

Talk ranged from minor vandalism done to buildings in Princeton to massive destruction of personal property. Several shared that it was once again a failed attempt at taking back the cannon which was always followed with a painful moan on the part of any listener. This was also made worse when word leaked about the poor spelling that the Princeton folks saw as indicative of the fools at the New Brunswick grammar school.

Still, the prevailing tale was that the Princeton elders were angry at this wanton display of disrespect to their community and would demand that New Brunswick come up with the funding to pay for any physical damages.

President Campbell, in charge of both the academic structure and the student affairs at Rutgers, met with the various leaders of the town and listened to their thoughts on what they had picked up from the gossip and the rumors being thrown about.

Some of these town leaders highlighted how this had created an embarrassment for the community and ruined the positive opinion people had about the proud city of New Brunswick. Others noted that the reputation of Rutgers College was less than what one would hope already and this harmed it further. Each of them emphasized numerous times that they would not pay one cent if Princeton sent a bill to them to cover any of the damages regardless of what those damages eventually turned out to be.

Campbell was patient as each person demanded he take action with this. He promised he would investigate within the student body. Then after speaking with members of his faculty he would gather what additional information he could to render a decision on next steps if he discovered that a student or students had been the guilty party.

Some in the group that first met with Campbell thought that maybe a town committee should be called in to review the manner in which the vandals from the college had possibly tarnished the reputation of New Brunswick. They expressed how this might help the students understand the seriousness versus just getting a scolding from their college administrator before being expelled.

Campbell listened, respectfully, and then reminded those present that he had followed that suggested pathway of using a town leader to head an investigation not that long ago with a local vandalism incident. He also pointed out that alternate process had not turned out any better than an internal review would have.

When they started to challenge that statement Campbell walked the town leaders through how the staff at Rutgers had actually reached out to get the help of one of the local boarding-house owners who also served as a local Justice, James S. Nevius, to assist them. He explained how Justice Nevius was brought in to conduct the investigation and the interrogation of the Rutgers students to determine which one of them had been involved with the destruction of the campus latrine.

Campbell then highlighted to the townspeople how even in their own backyard, and with the blown up remnants of the latrine still providing a distinct odor in their midst, Justice Nevius had not been able to resolve the mystery of who had been responsible for that act.

They grumbled at the thought they would not be involved in the process but left without further requests after Campbell reminded them what the charge had been for the failed service Nevius had provided and that the cost of the actual replacement latrine was less than what Nevius had cost them.

That evening, after classes had ended for the day, new rumors continued to show up and be shared quickly among the students speculating on what had taken place and who had been involved.

One school of thought was that it had been the members of the newer fraternity, Zeta Psi. Once suggested, word spread that this was the type of prank that they would have done and that vandalism of another college was easily something that members of Zeta Psi would have engaged in as a ritual for membership.

Instantly several members of the fraternity and others who knew those connected to Zeta Psi insisted that this had not been the case.

By nightfall, while some students had made their predictions and shared their own rumors about who may have been involved, the reality was that no specific student had acknowledged their role in the events of the evening before.

Still, often due to the listening ears of those adults around the students as they tossed out possibilities, several names were "leaking" forward through the staff and on to those in charge.

Before President Campbell addressed the student body as a whole the next day he had already heard the latest story being bandied about that the students who "may" have participated had taken a pledge of loyalty to the school and community of New Brunswick before embarking on their journey to try and restore the stolen property from Princeton.

This cannon raid loyalty story kept coming forward as the hours progressed.

Later, Campbell was told, these same students who had sworn their allegiance to each other not to report out on the events with the cannon had done this to support the other students who were there. Students shared with this story that, to date, not one student had broken that pledge of honor.

To the students at Rutgers College this level of loyalty sounded heroic.

To the Princeton official who had appeared in New Brunswick to investigate on the part of their community this was unacceptable nonsense.

Seated in Dr. Campbell's office, Campbell knew if this man's anger was indicative of all the patrons down in Princeton, this event would not go away quietly just due to the passing of time.

"We demand restitution as well as punishment for those involved," the Princetonian stated as he banged his fist on President Campbell's desk.

"Nothing less will suffice. You must take immediate and swift action to discourage future shenanigans among your students here at Rutgers. This action must be done in public and not in some private manner so all can see justice has been served!"

"We are investigating and will take appropriate action once we have gathered all the facts," Dr. Campbell calmly replied in a professional tone.

Then, with an air of arrogance intended to project his own personally perceived level of importance in the world over not just this college president but all of the people of New Brunswick, the man smugly sat back in his chair and closed out with one final statement.

"What you should be more embarrassed about though, Dr. Campbell, even beyond the disgraceful action of vandalism, is the lack of intellect and character on the part of your students. Have you heard that even with the schooling you have provided them they still misspelled the word cannon?"

Campbell, once again, did not take the bait.

"Thank you for sharing your thoughts in such an objective and unbiased manner," Campbell responded, still seated at his desk while the man stood red-faced in front of him. "Please know that I will take your input into account as we conclude our investigation."

President Campbell had listened politely to the complaint and the demands being made.

He made no excuses on the status of things but did acknowledge that using someone else's paint without paying for it and vandalizing someone's property were not actions he would ever support or want to encourage.

Still, President Campbell thought to himself as that man chuckled out loud at his comments about the "ignorance" of the Rutgers students, there is an even higher level of ignorance and not just the obvious arrogance among the Princeton people if this man is representative of how they all think one should act in matters of this nature.

President Campbell stood to signal the end of the conversation. He reached out his hand to the gentleman and excused himself from their meeting stating that he needed to continue with his investigation. The gentleman from Princeton huffed and nodded, still obviously agitated. Without turning back the man from Princeton exited the room.

At this point three Rutgers students were ushered into the office of President Campbell.

They stood before him while three staff members moved to President's Campbell's side. Campbell had retaken his seat behind his desk.

The three young men were dressed in identical outfits common for students at that time. Jackets, ribbon ties, dress slacks and low cut boots, not one standing out from the other. They carried their caps in their hands in a respectful manner and stood at attention in front of the College President waiting for him to speak to them.

President Campbell looked into the eyes of each of the three students before him and then shifted his eyes to glance down at a stack of papers he had arranged on his desk. He flipped through the papers in silence. After studying these papers for what seemed like an eternity, he cleared his throat and spoke.

"I suppose each of you know why you have been brought here today?" Campbell asked the students without looking up from the papers that he continued to flip between his two hands from left to right on his desktop. His voice was rhetorical in nature and it was clear he did not expect a response.

The boys understood the magnitude of the situation and said nothing.

"When actions take place that can injure the reputation of our College it is my responsibility to control the damage and take steps in correcting such injury."

"Do each of you understand this?" This time as he asked this he looked back up at their faces.

"Yes sir," they answered collectively.

"I suppose each of you have heard about what took place on the college grounds in Princeton with the theft of local paint and the acts of vandalism?"

"Yes sir," the three responded in unison again.

"At the same time, I do not suppose any of the three of you present today came in here with the intent to state that he is the party responsible for the damage inflicted in Princeton on the grounds of Nassau Hall at the College of New Jersey now almost two nights ago?"

"No sir," the three answered without hesitation.

"Or with the intent of telling us who among the Rutgers students may have been involved?"

"No sir," they answered again without delay.

"I did not think so," Campbell responded.

He stood as he continued to slowly speak. His hands behind his back, he walked to the side of his desk while looking at where the boys were standing.

"So this being the case, I am led to believe that you are waiting for someone else to turn himself in and I should move on to ask the others where they stand on the same questions."

Silence.

Campbell tapped his fingers on the edge of his desk. He looked at the staff now instead of the three students but his comment was clearly intended for the students.

"So I suppose you wish for me to blame someone else so that the reputation of the college can be preserved and the most important core values of integrity and character can be preserved as a part of our mission?"

There was silence again, but only for a moment.

Then, one of the students took a step forward and spoke.

"Sir, with all due respect, while I give you not a name of one who was involved in the events that have been rumored to have taken place in Princeton in retaliation for the stolen cannon; I would gladly allow you to select me to be punished in the manner you see fit for the good of Rutgers. I would gladly sacrifice myself for the good of my school and my classmates."

Campbell moved slowly toward the student who had just spoken. "So, you claim your innocence but you wish to be the one given the consequence?"

"If that is what is needed for the good of all others I would willingly sacrifice my standing for all of my fellow Rutgers classmates versus you randomly selecting or requiring another student be used as an example to appease the Princeton community."

"The same for me," the second student suddenly blurted out as he stepped forward.

"The same for me too," the third student followed suit boldly in the same manner.

"And if I told you that all three of you have alibi's that appear solid and that I do not suspect any of the three of you? You would rather that I not proceed with my questioning and simply carry out a consequence with the three of you knowing that it is wrong?"

"Sir, if you feel that justice would be best served in this manner," the first student stated.

"If it restores what is needed for the good of all the Rutgers students here and those who came before and those who will come after," said the second.

"And I would be willing to be the lone student held accountable if you wish to allow these other two students to be excused," said the third.

Campbell moved slowly back behind his desk.

The three boys stared straight ahead without making eye contact with him.

Once again Campbell took his seat behind his desk and tapped his fingers slowly on the top of his desk. This was now the only sound that could be heard in the small office.

After a full minute, Campbell turned to the staff member standing at his side and directed, "Please escort these three students back to be seated with the rest of the student body. I will join you shortly."

The staff and students exited the office without a word being said.

Inside the chapel, the wooden pews framed the students into an organized body. The uniformity of position and dress made them look like toy soldiers seated as if awaiting an address. The cavernous structure was dimly lit by candles and this cast an imposing shadow across their faces. That the majority of light came from the front of the facility lent to the feel that the speaker about to address them had the power of the Almighty supporting his mission here on earth.

The assembled group of students sat perfectly quiet in their rows as they awaited President Campbell's appearance and, more importantly, his words. They clearly understood the enormity of what might take place that evening.

The students and staff present there seemed to hold their collective breath as Campbell entered and made his way directly to the lectern. He had no papers or notes in his hands.

Campbell paused when he reached the podium and took a deep breath and closed his eyes for a moment as if in reflective prayer. When he opened his eyes he placed his hands on either side of the top of the finely crafted wooden stand and not another sound could be heard in the entire place besides his voice as he started to speak.

"When the news reached me of what had taken place in Princeton, I was immediately saddened. That such an act would be taken by anyone was not good. Such an action spoke of lower moral values. It showed a lack of caring and compassion for others. It was without question, wrong."

"However, even worse, word came almost immediately to me that the accused were likely members of the Rutgers College student body. This was even more difficult to digest."

"While vandalism and the destruction of private property can be repaired, the insinuation that one of our young men would act in such a devious manner was an indication to me that others do not believe that we are developing young men with high moral character at our institution. Our mission is not to simply memorize the historical problems of the world better than any other scholar before us. No, our mission is to help grow minds and develop individuals who as citizens will take actions to help make this community and this country a better place for all to live in."

Campbell, scanned around the room at all the faces looking back at him.

What the students saw reflected on his face was a stern judge about to pass his sentence on them all.

"A sadness, I tell you again, a sadness," he stated while shaking his head.

"So what to do about this?" Campbell asked. "Where do we go with the information that was shared?"

Now he glanced toward the guest from Princeton who was seated toward the rear.

"Yes, I have conducted an investigation. Yes, I could convert the line of questioning to one with a more aggressive manner. I am sure there are some who would prefer a modern day Inquisition for any issue that arises that involves someone else."

"But my purpose, no the College's purpose, is to improve and not shift backward in its thinking when handling the learning process with its students. So while the political binds that often tie me within my capacity as a school administrator often dictate next steps; here I propose the following summary and restitution."

"First, until the constabulary are able to produce factual evidence of who actually perpetrated the actions at Princeton that night, I will not pull any student from his course of studies on mere supposition. Nor do I plan to lose an additional minute of valuable faculty time on an investigation when they should be engaged in the teaching process of our students."

"Secondly, we will send forth some form of an act of contrition to the good people of Princeton. The goal would be to signify that we do not condone what happened and to support them in their appropriate level of grieving for such an act. What that action will be, I am not yet sure. But it will represent a sign of our condolences even if this is seen as an apology on the part of the Rutgers College community for what has befallen those in Princeton and no student has been found guilty."

Campbell could see the man from Princeton squirming in his seat and not looking pleased.

"And, for those who appreciate scapegoating on any level, I ask you, the students of Rutgers College assembled here today the following questions."

"Who among you, if one student is to be sacrificed for the good of the whole, is willing for the sake of your classmates to be that student who is extended the consequence?"

"For the clarity of those in our midst I ask now of you, our students, who is willing to be the one who falls so that the others may stand and a great College continue to rise above the triviality of the rest of this world?"

A student immediately stood and called out.
"I, sir. I will take the consequence for my classmates."
A second student rose quickly behind him. "I sir."
This was followed by a third. "Sir, I will be that volunteer."
The answer was instantly followed by the same reply across the student body. Within sixty seconds every student was standing and cheering out – "I volunteer!"
The chorus of "I" continued. Hand clapping and feet stomping matched the cadence. Somewhere within this spontaneous reaction, a chant began.
"If one did it, we all did it!"

Campbell watched for several seconds longer before he raised his hands to quiet the group. He directed the students to be seated again.

Once they settled and quieted down he continued.

"Let this stand for any observer to carry to their home within or away from New Brunswick that the character of our students here at this college is strong. Let it be known that the young men being developed at Rutgers College understand the risks and have a willingness to sacrifice for the greater good. While so unlike Peter in the New Testament, their public acknowledgment of support today demonstrated the entire student population at Rutgers College showed its true spirit and with this they have shared their true personal and united values."

"United, you students have pledged an oath to honor the birth and growth of our college. Upon entry, you vowed to respect and care for your fellow classmates and the greater community. You are asked to be selfless in danger and in times of concern. While I deplore the destruction of property, that greater willingness to sacrifice for others is on full display at this time and a thread from that fabric shall not be pulled apart to separate the greater good. Without question the story from this incident is to tell those beyond our campus that this is an institution where young men who aspire to greatness are born. Today, you should be proud to call yourselves loyal sons of Rutgers!"

"I call this investigation over. Good day, men of Rutgers College."

With that, President Campbell suddenly turned and left his place behind the lectern. Without looking back he walked directly to the doorway and exited the room.

Cheers erupted from students across the room.

Chants rang out about *Old Rutgers*. Cheers went up hailing *Glory to Old Queens*.

Soon there was a singular chanting sound. It almost had a musical rhythmic feel to it. The sound of feet stomping on the ground joined back in.

Row by row the young men exited in a march and chanted as they went.

"Rutgers rah!" was a guttural sound accented by those stomping feet and fists pumped in cadence with the beat.

The enthusiasm of the young men in marching fashion as they exited the church and headed out into the streets of New Brunswick was now on display for the onlookers from the town. They clapped along as if cheering a parade as the line of students processed out into the dimly lit evening.

"What was that?" Dr. Murray asked Professor Cook who was standing next to him as they watched the students walk away from the meeting they had just attended.

"The students or President Campbell?" Cook asked back.

"Both!"

"For them it was a much needed unifying moment," Cook responded after thinking about the question for a moment and now pointing out toward the disappearing student lines.

"And with Campbell?"

"For him - the great moral conflict of being swayed by an inspiring action before the reality that you need to develop a consequence in some way for an injustice that was done elsewhere."

"What do you think Campbell plans to do next?" Murray asked.

"We will see, my good sir. But I hope that whatever he figures out that we must do to square things in Princeton will not eliminate that spirit we just saw from our young Rutgers charges. That spirit is so badly needed for the good of the future of our college, Dr. Murray. I truly believe it is a spirit that will decide one day if there will even be a future for our college."

7
"Institutional Symbolic Actions"
September 27, 1869
Rutgers College

"Yes, they will attend."

President Campbell was emphatic on this point as he explained what would take place to his faculty who were gathered in his office.

Everyone in the group looked back at him without a single comment.

The room was dark with two flickering lamps lighting the interior. These lamps barely provided enough light to expose the images of the men scattered around the room. Smoke from their pipes and cigars filled the space and added to the heavy feel of the air.

President Campbell's explanation of how a group of Rutgers students would be chaperoned to attend this upcoming event in Princeton had been presented in full detail.

He noted the general stated purpose.

The activity had been proposed by the people of Princeton to have a setting where the Rutgers College students' desire to let the prior incident be in the past could be witnessed as proof of their sincerity. It was supposedly offered as an olive branch with a goal of reconciliation between the two schools and their young charges.

However, to all the Rutgers staff gathered there, this participation sounded like going with the intent to beg for forgiveness. It looked like an acknowledgment of guilt. Worst of all it posed, to those who tried to visualize how this event could play out, an opportunity for possible public humiliation of the Rutgers students in front of a Princeton audience.

They had been in the meeting for slightly over an hour.

The regularly scheduled agenda was thrown away due to the circumstances now at hand. The normal procedures and protocol of allowing faculty interaction and input was put on hold. President Campbell had been the main speaker and he made it clear that the decision had been reached. He had given a broad overview of why he had elected to take the path he had now chosen before finishing up by assigning the tasks to put the plan in motion.

"Professor Murray, I ask that you help select the students who will be a part of this delegation."

"Yes sir," Murray answered back without inflection in his voice or challenge.

"As for the adult faculty chaperones for this event, I have already determined that our adjunct professor and two tutors will assume this as a part of their assignment here at the College."

Bowser looked over at Dr. Murray who shrugged back at him and silently mouthed to him the single word, "Sorry."

Campbell continued talking about the expectations moving ahead. He clarified again that while some may disagree with this plan proposed by those from Princeton, his hope was that this delegation's appearance at this function would finally put to rest the distractions of the conversations related to the act of vandalism.

The room grew quiet when he finished.

"Before we leave today sir," Professor Doolittle stated in a formal manner, awkwardly breaking the silence. "I did wish to share how impressive your handling of this matter has been to this point."

"Here, here," the group called out and tapped their walking sticks to the ground or patted the arms of their chairs for a sound similar to applause.

Doolittle paused for a moment as he waited for the noise to settle down.

"I am sure there are men in Princeton, and especially down at the College of New Jersey, who are furious more was not done to punish a random student here at Rutgers. Please know that everyone we have spoken with within the community of New Brunswick has expressed their personal regards and positive feelings about someone taking a stand against Princeton and their original theft and insulting behavior aimed at our community."

"Thank you Professor Doolittle and all of you for your support during this incident," Campbell replied.

Campbell now looked out at the distinguished men in front of him. He knew what many were thinking about the difference between his prior strong stand and the plan he was now requesting them to follow. Rather than ignore it, he addressed it head on.

"I do know what the real intent was within this letter pertaining to this request from President McCosh and Judge Olden in Princeton. Please know that has not been lost on me while reviewing the options in front of us. I truly appreciate, as many of you have surely deciphered, that the actual message is meant to impress upon me the need to control our students while seeming to extend an opportunity to move forward."

"You do know sir, with all due respect," Murray inserted. "The staff at the College of New Jersey may appear to be offering the olive branch but this action will be interpreted at the minimum as a taunt toward our school's reputation. More likely it will prove to be a humbling experience on the part of our Rutgers students in a setting that we are about to place them in."

"I appreciate your observation," Campbell said. "Please know though that there are times when, even in the face of where we are in this situation, we do need to see if we can alter a negative pathway both Colleges appear to be heading down. I fear that pathway can lead to no good for Rutgers in the end."

"We need to be the leaders in righting the direction. While it may seem that in accepting this invitation to attend that we are admitting that our students were wrong in the eyes of others even though our investigation found no guilty party, we need to stop the petty fighting and bickering that has evolved between the Colleges. This, I believe, is a step we must take to right the direction. We do not go on bended knee. We go with noble intent regardless of their true motivations."

"And the specific directions for us that evening sir?" Adjunct Professor Bowser asked.

"As chaperones my expectations for you should be clear at this point. No mischief on this night. No lost student who attempts anything foolish. I do not want anyone being accused of anything by anyone that night. This is a chance to remove a tarnish on our campus we need to rid ourselves of. This needs to be a time to start back on equal footing." Campbell was emphatic in his charge. "Regardless of our feelings about this matter, the reality is that there was a theft of personal property that night and vandalism. Proven or not, most out there believe it was our young who perpetuated the crime. As molders of their character we can never appear to tolerate that."

"And the ability to un-tarnish their young reputations? This is accomplished by?" Hasbrouck, the tutor, asked. "Their appearance there makes them come across as the guilty. Boys brought to the gallows after their sentencing versus innocents at a ball."

"Noted, Mr. Hasbrouck. But to prove we lead only young men who embody good character I want you to help them stand tall and behave as they should. Have the young men socialize. Let them build a feeling of community between people of their own generation. Have them show their good manners. Have them engage with all others there in conversations where they can impress the elders in Princeton with their knowledge. Provide them the venue that night where they can demonstrate their intellect and hopefully help us all restore the image of Rutgers as a campus of academics versus a collection of untamed fools who cannot spell," Campbell clarified.

"Anything formal to expect while we are there?" Hasbrouck squeaked out, fearing that President Campbell was tiring of questions from the members of the traditional faculty let alone the support staff as he was currently employed.

"There is no formal apology or unique hand shake or special gift that you will bring if that is what you mean, Mr. Hasbrouck. I am sure that Judge Olden or President McCosh may attempt to gather folks and make a speech. My hope is that it is not too offensive to Rutgers or to our young men there. However, prepare yourself and your young charges not to overreact as it would not surprise me if whatever they say will come across as condescending toward us," Campbell added.

"And if President McCosh is attending sir, you do not wish to be present yourself? You do not think that they will see this as a slight in your non-attendance when they are there?" Murray asked.

Campbell paused for a moment before responding. He looked hard at Dr. Murray. It was as if he was calculating if he wished to say anything or not directly to Murray.

Finally, almost clinically, he turned his eyes and talked instead to the group as a whole.

"Gentlemen. I do not know how to make this any plainer." Without pause he continued in a very formal manner.

"Our three selected staff will represent the school. Dr. Murray, you will handpick the best and the brightest in your estimation from the student body to represent the College. They will go and socialize and demonstrate that our students are not barbarians."

Then looking directly back at Dr. Murray he added, "I am a theologian first. This embeds me with hope for mankind. However, I am also politically astute in the secular world and understand the implications of going to an event in this manner and the perceptions that may take place among those who are present. Tail between legs some may call it here and I am sure there will be those there who see it the same way. The goal, however, that is not to be forgotten is to present a positive front and then see if we can shift the future discussions away from this attempt to pull each other down and instead try to build each other up. This starts by publicizing the positive qualities of our students, not mine."

Professor Atherton looked like he grimaced and Campbell saw it. Instantly he requested an explanation.

"Professor Atherton, something I said that is bothering you?"

"Well sir," Atherton began, paused as he thought about if he should continue, then went forward as he realized he now had no choice. "With my military experiences I just never saw where two parties could come together, especially ones who had a natural desire to want to make the other look bad, and walk away with anything gained. It is not natural. The hatred makes one want to destroy the other not walk away hand in hand rejoicing about the merit of the meeting."

"How about Appomattox, Professor Atherton? Grant and Lee?" Campbell countered. "They left respecting not only each other but also both left with their honor and dignity intact."

"I suppose anything is possible," Atherton replied quickly getting the point that the President had discussed this matter long enough.

"Very well. Select the students who will attend and represent our Rutgers College wisely Dr. Murray," Campbell directed the professor.

Then, turning to the chaperones for the event he added one last set of instructions.

"And Misters Bowser, Hasbrouck and Adkins: please make sure you keep the students you take under control. We await both your return and your positive report."

"Good day gentlemen," Campbell announced.

With that he moved to the door, opened it, and turned back to face the group. Through his actions he indicated that it was time for them to leave.

8
"Opposing Views"
September 30, 1869
Princeton Campus

Several young men were crowded into the hot dorm room in the East College building. Without room to spread out around this small space, they were packed in so closely it was hard to breathe.

Two of them, unable to find a place to sit down, were left standing and leaning up against the wall. Two others were seated with their legs crossed on top of each of the two small beds. Four more actually sat on top of the small table that covered the center of the room. They sat there with their feet on the sides of the arms of the two chairs on either side of them so they would not hit their knees in the faces of three others who were seated below them on the floor.

It was crammed tight.

A candle burned inside the hurricane lamp positioned in between the two students seated on the table and the light flickered against their faces as they spoke.

"So we are supposed to just act as if we are their friends that night?"

Gummere looked back at the student who had just spoken before turning to hear from another voice across the room.

"It is a social event. You know we do not get to partake in activities like this every day. I think we should just lay low and not cause trouble while in public and especially while we are at Judge Olden's house. It is about keeping our reputations intact. For the good of ourselves, I say we ignore them and just remember that every man is able to weather any storm like the sailors say about life at sea."

"Ignore them? Is that even possible?"

"It beats being polite with them."

"So they honestly think we should go there and treat them as our friends?" Mixsell asked.

"They have to know how much we detest them," his roommate added.

"I honestly cannot stand them!"

"Is loathe too strong a word for how I feel about them?"

"It is perfect for how I feel about them."

"No one said we had to be friends. The directive was just that we show up."

"What a pitiful lot that group is up there at Rutgers."

"If I was them, I do not think I would show up," Charlie Parker suggested. "I cannot even imagine walking into a place where you know you have failed and at the same time have to beg forgiveness for your effort in failing. We are so sorry we failed to steal the cannon. We are so sorry we did not know how to spell the word cannon."

The group laughed.

"Seriously, Charlie is right," Jacob Michael, typically called Big Mike by his fellow classmates, stated. "Think about it. They lost the cannon years ago. The whole town fails at getting it back. They end up putting some whitewash, misspelled at that, on our steps after not stealing the cannon back. Now they have been required to show up in front of the whole Princeton community and basically say they are sorry. That is humiliating."

John Weir twisted the end of his mustache and, in his slow southern gentleman accent added, "I actually feel badly for the Rutgers lads."

"Seriously? That group of horses' asses?"

"You didn't let me finish. I would feel bad for them, however, this is for their own good as nothing builds character like a little public embarrassment. Maybe it can even build men out of them one day."

Several in the room chuckled.

"So do you think we will be expected to say anything that night?" Nissley asked.

"What do you mean?"

"You know, like a speech that tells them what they have done wrong or what they should show their gratitude for in being invited here?"

"I could hear that speech now." This student rose as he spoke and took the stance of a Roman Senator.

"To Rutgers College. Wait. I believe you are supposed to be a college but are they teaching you anything academic that you have actually learned yet up there for that designation?"

"Did you know I heard at one time they were going to be a prep school at Rutgers? It was all about them not making gains with enrollment or succeeding as they were chartered to accomplish. When the state legislature voted they left it one vote short of taking it over. If the plan had pushed through, they would have been a prep school to our college. That was also at the same time we were named the College of New Jersey."

"So we became the College of New Jersey and they became?"

"What is the term for a lesser college?"

"A lower school," Big Mike joked.

"A non-college?"

Once again there was laughter across the room.

"To the members of Rutgers Lower School Non-College!"

"Where your graduate's highest aspirations should have been to one day be academically strong enough with enough study time put in to eventually enroll here in Princeton as a first year student."

"I feel bad that they never get anything."

"You know Nissley may be on to something," said Parker. "Maybe we should offer them another chance at something."

"What do you mean?"

"Well, they have lost at the cannon battle. They lost really badly at baseball. They lost at rowing. They lost at being named the state college. They lost their academic standards when they were forced to lower their admissions requirements so they had enough students able to attend."

"We get it. They are losers. But what are you suggesting we offer them?"

"I'm thinking that maybe we offer them a new challenge. We start with something that gets them going a little so they feel compelled to accept our offer. You know, a remark or two about something about how the cannon war is officially over with Princeton the victor. Then we discuss how tough it is to lose-"

"Or so we have heard from other losers like those who happen to attend Rutgers College," another student interjected to more laughter from the group.

"Good. Good. Then we note that we know they lost at baseball and again at crew. But, knowing that it is hard to continually live in the shadow of defeat, we still want to give them another chance at competing at or possibly winning at something."

"Then we ask them what they think they might win at."

"Then we offer to beat them at that too!"

"What can they offer that they can honestly win at?"

"Nothing."

"Definitely!"

"Don't you think they know they can't win at anything too?"

"Then why would they accept?"

"Like I said before because it will be a public challenge. And even when one knows that they will be shot dead by a better marksman in a duel, no public challenge can ever be let to pass."

"So we meet up with their little New Brunswick delegation at Judge Olden's home. We offer them a chance at losing at the challenge of their choice in front of all that are present."

"That is definitely better than talking to them pretending they are our friends!"

"Here's to the other college that happens to also be in New Jersey!"

"What other college?"

"The lower college!"

"The non-college!"

"No. Here is to our opponents known only forever in the future to all as the losing college!"

Eventually the scheming and lingering small talk broke off as the joking wore down.

After a few more rounds of small group chatter about Rutgers and the students there with their feeble prior exploits in athletics, the boys picked up their things and moved out the door and started to shift away to other rooms in the East College building and or on to other places.

The mood had definitely changed from the initial negative thoughts of having to politely socialize with their disliked peers in New Brunswick after laughing through rounds of planning to corner the visitors with another chance of embarrassing them.   As the hour grew long and the day now grew short, most finally settled in to go to sleep with the common belief that they were to prepare to face their foes in some type of competition that they would defeat Rutgers at again adding one more layer of insult to the reputation of the other college in New Jersey.

   Whispering could be heard by the final participants that night as they drifted off to sleep.
   "Who does decide what we compete at?"
   "Who cares? We will win at whatever they decide they want to lose at."
   "Do you ever fear that maybe we are a bit over-confident?"
   "Not at all. To win you have to believe in yourself."
   "Makes sense."
   "And since we never lose and they never win, there really is nothing to fear."
   "So true."
   With that common thought having been shared in so many separate rooms at the same time throughout the campus, the last light in Princeton was finally extinguished for the night.

9
"The Challenge and Elizabeth…"
October 2, 1869
Princeton, New Jersey

It was a beautiful mansion by any standards.

As they approached the entranceway to the property, every eye shifted instantly to the lighted tall columns. Riding in, the students and chaperones each let out a collective, "wow!"

It was breath-taking.

Everyone who inhabited any spot on the land across this region of the Jersey countryside was equally awed by its size and beauty even if they saw it every day. Most people also knew of the marvelous history of the building as well as the story about the site and its owner. To any visitor who was not similarly informed, the locals instantly saw it as their duty to bring them up to speed.

The mansion, named *Drumthwacket*, had been continually expanded while the owner pursued a lifestyle of a gentleman farmer as well as a businessman. The original structure elsewhere on the property had been his childhood home. It was much smaller and was a reminder of the humble beginnings he had begun life with. He left this childhood home to make his fortune in New Orleans or so the local story went. When he returned to New Jersey he not only continued his business enterprises he also shifted to what many felt was his true calling in life in the fields of politics and state government office.

As the owner grew in name and stature, the house also grew in size and began to take on a personality all its own. It was at this time that the owner gave the home its name. Legend had it that *Drumthwacket* was a combination of two Gaelic words that were roughly translated to mean that this was *the* home "on wooded hill."

By the date of this party the owner was 70 years old. As everyone in Princeton knew, State Supreme Court Justice Charles Smith Olden had held many powerful positions. Besides being a current Supreme Court Justice and a member of the legislature, Judge Olden had previously been the Governor of New Jersey during the early years of the War Between the States.

He was truly a man of both wealth and political power and he was often seen as one of the most influential men not only in New Jersey but also across the growing nation.

Due to his term as Governor, many still called him by that title, Governor Olden. However, whether one called him Governor Olden or Justice Olden when addressing him and regardless of their political affiliations; all felt welcome when they were in his presence. He had that naturally engaging personality and when he entered a room he was always seen as the man who was in control.

But as people first arrived this night it was the house that was on display for the Fall Festival.

The home itself seemed to invite the entering guests through its large portico.

This front of the mansion was accented magnificently by six Ionic columns of a brilliant white. People moved into a two and a half story grand center room once they passed them. This center section of the household served as the social gathering spot between two rooms positioned on either side.

Normally this area served as the regular base of "polite" entertainment for the well-known and well-connected of New Jersey. On this night though, the whole population of the greater Princeton area showed for the main social event of the year open to the common public.

At the grand entryway outside and then all along the interior were mums boldly setting off the area in an orange glow. The petals were illuminated by the bright candlelight from numerous candles burning throughout all the rooms. There were limited numbers of other flowers scattered about in vases, reminiscent of summer now gone by. The color in the northern fields had started to fade with the first of the night frosts signaling an early winter set to arrive. Greens were hung across the railings and were draped from corner to corner along the ceiling. Taken together the decorations provided a feel of a healthier outdoors ahead of the impending winter as well as a symbol of this jovial celebration.

A large glass bowl was filled with punch and was set on the far side of the room. It stood as an artistic centerpiece across from the entryway. Numerous glasses were staged around it in symmetrical fashion. Along each of the walls wooden tables covered with white cloths held a variety of refreshments and small appetizers from which the guests could select. Several waiters dressed in black jackets circled the rooms with trays filled with other goodies to eat.

The guests themselves represented a broad array of the Princeton population.

It was clearly an economically more diverse part of the community from what normally attended the regular social events held at *Drumthwacket* throughout the rest of the year. There were the regulars, the local elite, dressed in their fine attire as they would be at any other time they were out in the public eye. Clothing may not make the man, but it clearly designated the occupational class to which the wearer was associated.

Each of the male guests were dressed in the best outfits they could afford. All men had ties affixed to high collared shirts; but that was the only common feature. Even the make of the shirt or the quality of the ties varied greatly. While ministers' jackets mixed with humbler broadcloth coats and tailored suits stood next to home pressed wool, each item represented that man's best finery and their socio-economic status in the society. Top hats were shed at the door as the guests entered the hallway and glancing at the check-in area one could make out an assortment of older formal beaver skin stove pipe hats along with the increasingly popular bowler hats.

Also speckled throughout the crowd, worn by ex-military men, were the occasional blue's once donned by some who had been a member of the United States military force. It served as a reminder to so many of just how recent the calamitous events of the Civil War had been, not yet five years past. These jackets and pants, often faded in color and with strings pulled at the seams where a limb was missing, also served as a sign that not all who served on the winning side of the conflict were able to return to livelihoods that provided any degree of personal wealth.

In similar fashion, the women were decked out in their finest personal attire they owned. Floor length dresses and skirts swept over the tops of their hidden shoes below. The color choice for a gown varied little as they were mostly dark in shades of greens, browns, blacks, and dark blue. Actually, the only real variation of major color the women adorned was often seen within the various headpieces they elected to wear.

Like the men, the outfits also advertised their personal station in life, or at least the wealth that was accumulated in their household. While the social barrier that existed between the have and have nots which separated them in their daily lives was once again on display; the spirited event allowed for one evening of a true mixing of the people of Princeton.

It was a night where simple faces rose above the bustle and fashion could at times become hidden by the sheer size of the crowd.

It was into this festive environment that Elizabeth Warren walked.

Elizabeth's mother was initially at her side, as she typically was every day. Unlike the normal day though, as they entered the main room, her mother left Elizabeth to go visit with others as soon as she saw several acquaintances who waved out to her. She left Elizabeth to herself.

Less personally engaged with those in the Princeton community, Elizabeth moved about the room virtually unnoticed. She nodded pleasantly at those she passed by. Still she remained happily silent and content in feeling that within this crowd, while folks were polite, it did not stand out that she was alone.

Not that being alone was anything Elizabeth had not grown accustomed to.

Princeton in 1869 would definitely have been classified as a village versus a bustling city. And with this size, all the trappings of a small town setting were to be found.

True it could claim a proud national connection with a history filled full of a revolutionary war past and the distinction of having served as a capital of the fledging United States in its infancy. It could boast of a fine college and of a core of families who resided in fine estates around its center with wealth growing in parallel with the nation.

Still, as Elizabeth glanced about the room and seemed to know the name of almost all of those faces, she understood that this corner of New Jersey was still very provincial at its core.

She was also aware, much like she knew who they were and their personal stories, each of those faces in the crowd knew her personal life story as well.

The male conversation that evening, as one would expect, was about the day's news headlines relating the events on Wall Street.

Talk was flying all around about speculation that the nefarious business partners, Jay Gould and Jim Fisk, were being accused of attempting to manipulate the gold market into the panic that had ensued the prior day. It was obvious that several men were licking their financial wounds inflicted by this trading scheme that they had been unable to detect until it was too late to escape. The market's tumble that took place was already being dubbed "Black Friday."

Still, while national and world news would punctuate the air in an attempt at sophistication, Elizabeth's ear could already pick up on the side comments about what certain guests were wearing.

Gossip was rampant about anyone who was not standing presently in the company of the chatting mouths. Little cliques dictated who the comments would be directed toward. These comments ranged from "oh those poor dears, I wonder how they survive" to "if I had that kind of money I think I would make a better choice."

Fall festival, the time honored tradition of celebrating the season of the year when the crops were all harvested, had its roots in the farming history across the land. It was a time when the farmers gave praise for another bountiful gift. In its earliest days the festival been held in September at a local church. Growth in population and the number of non-farmers had made the original purpose blurry and the religious ties were separated when the churches proved too small or formal to host the events.

The image of the farmers, though, were still at the center of the Fall Festival. Elizabeth suspected it was the reason that the dirt farmers were invited to mingle on this night with the rich. Judge Olden probably referred to the farmer part of the guest list as the "authentic" participants and saw them much like he saw the orange mums out front, like part of the decorations.

The original rural setting that defined the Princeton region was still the basis of its very fabric. Yes, to get there the average rider had passed the expensive homes that outlined the approach to the college grounds. Commodore Stockton's massive structure, named Morven, elicited awe from its sheer size while an Italianate Villa often generated the most speculation of what lay inside. Prospect, a model farm and the property of Thomas Potter, had neatly trimmed and ornate flower beds which helped draw everyone's eye toward the grandeur of the castle spire and elaborately fashioned frame.

Yet the majority of folk who were here this evening represented those who toiled on self-supporting farms each day around the town proper versus bankers or lawyers or the newly minted entrepreneurs. Most of the farmers even rarely ventured into the town itself with the exception of the times when they came to trade their surplus goods or shop for necessities or participate in the great communal gatherings each Sunday at the various churches.

But every farmer, on this evening, came happily to join in at the home of the gracious Judge Olden.

"Gracious Judge Olden," Elizabeth repeated the oft-echoed words in the crowd to herself.

As she looked out across the room she wondered, almost out loud, if it was truly the act of a gracious man. Or was this simply another political trick of a shrewd businessman to garnish votes by inviting the poor? In the end, did he hold this Fall Festival party in his home as a unique way to bribe people for their support and their vote?

It was not lost on Elizabeth that an entire part of the community was not present.

Clearly missing were the good people who worshipped at the Witherspoon Street Presbyterian Church. That community within Princeton had educated leaders there who had graduated from Lincoln College in Pennsylvania and who without question were among the most intelligent in their local surroundings. She also smugly wondered why Judge Olden did not invite those individuals as he always announced he had invited all the important people and they represented one of the most important parts of the African-American community in New Jersey.

Guess he is too high and mighty to include "all" people Elizabeth thought as she questioned Judge Olden's guest list omissions. All that rhetoric about meeting the needs of every man woman and child in Princeton. Does he really care about everyone in Princeton? Seriously?

She looked over at the group gossiping on the opposite side of the crowded room.

Probably over there talking about me right now. They are just as bad as Judge Olden. Oh, do I really want to be in here with all of these evil people!

Then she caught herself and Elizabeth chastised herself for thinking this way. My word. It is a party after all she told herself. Judge Olden was definitely a benevolent host. Stop it. Move on with your life. Elizabeth knew she needed to be less cynical of people. Stop over analyzing everything. Just enjoy the party and the fun of the gathering itself.

"Excuse me ma'am."

The voice shook her from her thoughts as she felt a slight bump of a body making contact with her side.

"Sir?" Elizabeth responded in a startled manner, looking at the gentleman standing next to her with a cup in his hand.

"Oh, excuse me ma'am," the man repeated himself. "It is just so crowded. I apologize for bumping into you like that. I hope I did not jostle you in a way that caused injury or insult. It is just that everyone is pushing about for space and I—"

"I assure you I am fine," she cut him off from his stumbling patter.

"I do apologize, as I fear I may have spilled some of the punch on your gown." He nodded awkwardly toward her side where it was apparent that he had doused her with punch when he had bumped up against her.

Elizabeth glanced at the obvious watery stain. The liquid had run its course from her waist along the side of her leg to a small puddle that now formed on the ground near her foot. This dripping action made the young man even more embarrassed at his actions.

"Here, let me." He pulled his handkerchief from his pocket and reached out toward her skirt starting to rub it downward. Just as quickly as he had started, he suddenly stopped as he realized what he was doing now touching this female stranger and his face turned a brilliant shade of red.

"Oh my," he said, with his face now turning two deeper shades of the blushing red hue. "It appears I am destined to just make a fool of myself here with you tonight."

Elizabeth took a small step back.

While she would not normally have given a strange man any leeway, she did take pity on him as he appeared to be genuine in his apology. She was also intrigued at how he was equally flustered in his social awkwardness about a woman. There was a gentle innocence about him.

"May I?" she asked, extending her hand and taking the handkerchief from him. She dabbed at the wet area on her dress to dry it.

The darkened color of the wet area showing no sign of receding, Elizabeth could sense that the man was staring at her in horror at the thought that he had permanently stained some expensive gown. It was evident he did not know that this was a homemade skirt.

"Oh my," the gentleman exclaimed as he continued to look at the damage he had wrought with the spill. "I am so sorry! It appears I have ruined your formal gown!"

How quaint, Elizabeth thought to herself, before replying.

"This old thing," she thought she heard herself coo in a manner so unlike herself. "Do not think twice about it, good sir. I am sure that it will be just fine when it dries."

"You are too kind, ma'am," he replied. "Please, at least, let me get you a fresh cup of punch to drink versus spilling it on you this time."

"That really is not necessary. I can get my own," Elizabeth responded back, now in her usual independent sounding tone.

"No, it is the least I can do," he answered. Without looking back, he squeezed forward through the crowd toward the punch bowl.

Elizabeth watched while he shifted among the bodies and he moved into position to fill two glasses. It was then that an all too common voice chimed in behind her.

"Cute feller," it came in with its mature sound. "I could see from all the way across the room he looked like he was in pain talking to you. What did you do to him to make him fetch you a drink?"

"Mother," Elizabeth half sighed without turning around to acknowledge her. "I am amazed to hear that your prying eyes didn't see all that happened before he headed off on his punch quest."

"Try speaking nicely to this one," her mother coached. "I hear he is one of those young men from New Brunswick. He is here as a staff chaperone on behalf of that Rutgers College to watch their students. Word is they have all the young boys here at Old Nassau in a twitter about his presence."

"You never cease to amaze me in how fast you can gather intelligence on every living male in our vicinity mother. You really could have been a Union spy for Mr. Lincoln."

"I'm off!" Her mother swept past and away as she noticed the young man had turned from the punch table and was now headed toward them.

"Please behave yourself and be polite," were the last words Elizabeth swore she heard her mother loudly whisper. It was more a command versus a suggestion about etiquette.

Elizabeth watched as the young man maneuvered through the crowded room, his eyes focused on balancing the punch inside the cups as guests moved about him without paying him any mind. Her mother's information about his connection to the college in New Brunswick seemed to be confirmed by his less expensive attire and youthful appearance. She suppressed a chuckle as she thought of her defining him as youthful and that he was probably her same age.

"Here you go ma'am," he held out one of the punch glasses to her.

Be polite. Her mother's words reverberated in her head.

"Thank you. This was very kind of you." She took the glass with both of her white gloved hands and nodded gently in his direction.

"Again ma'am, I am so sorry about your gown," he replied with the same hint of the nervousness he had demonstrated earlier.

"Elizabeth," she stated.

"Ma'am?"

"Elizabeth," she enunciated slowly but still trying to sound polite and not condescending as she spoke. "My name is Elizabeth Warren. I really do prefer it to the use of the word ma'am."

"Oh, yes," he smiled. "Please forgive me."

"And you do not have to apologize each time you speak," she added. It was too late to catch the words before they exited her mouth. She knew it sounded a little ruder and abrupt then she had meant it to be.

"Sorry-!"

He cut himself off as soon as the words left his mouth.

"There I go again. I know I have sounded like a fool since I have first, literally, bumped into you. I would apologize again but I now realize how boorish that has to sound."

Elizabeth smiled, grateful to hear his actual personality finally emerging.

"Not at all." She paused before asking, "And what is your name?"

"Oh, I can't believe I forgot to do that," and he reached out his hand.

"Let me introduce myself," he said, starting to sound more relaxed. "My name is Christopher Adkins. Also, I promise you I am much brighter then I have appeared so far this evening to you."

"So I have been told, Mr. Adkins. I understand you are associated with the College in New Brunswick."

His eyes narrowed in quizzical fashion. "And who would have told you that?"

Elizabeth gently turned his shoulder so he now faced toward the small group of older women who were across in the far side of the room. "See that huddle of bonnets in the far corner pretending not to be looking this way?"

He looked out across the room. He saw four women who suddenly appeared to turn away and be interested in investigating something that was down at their feet.

"That is the group who would best have served as town criers in days of old. They all seem to know everything about anything that may be going on. They also feel it their moral duty to inform everyone within earshot what they have discovered."

"Interesting," he noted. "And with this large assembly of people what is their sudden interest in who I am?"

"Do you see the one trying the hardest to not be seen in the back? The one who is clearly sneaking peeks at us now? That is my mother, Mrs. Annilee Bell."

"Ah, I see her now." He gave her a small wave of his hand.

Instantly the older woman pretended not to see him and Elizabeth's mother turned to become engrossed again in a conversation with the other three women at her side.

"Yes, my mother," Elizabeth sighed. "She is very well intentioned, mind you. But she is clearly something of a busy body."

"And she told you about me? How?"

"She raced over here the moment she saw an opening. It was when you left to get punch at the table. She basically ran to let me know that she had already learned you were one of several gentlemen here this evening from Rutgers College."

"That is kind of cute." Adkins smiled.

"Well, is she correct?"

"Yes, she was correct on that account," Adkins laughed. "I am here as part of the formal party dispatched from Rutgers at the beckoning of President McCosh from here at Nassau Hall to our Rutgers College President Campbell. It is supposed to be a sort of symbol of peace between the schools after the botched cannon episode."

"Oh, tell me you were not one of the vandals that night?"

Adkins laughed again.

"No, I am one of the chaperones. I was sent this night with my tail between legs because we know our students were in the wrong and that the good people of Princeton were so kind in not pressing charges against anyone involved."

"As odd as this sounds, and I do have to say they did create a mess, I also heard that they were such poor thieves that if they had been charged no Judge could have found them guilty of a crime."

"Yes, they did botch it up."

"I just do not get what the attraction is with that cannon."

Adkins paused before responding.

He was not exactly sure how to put into words the youthful exuberance of the students who had attempted to steal the cannon. He also was not sure he wanted to mention the passionate disdain those in New

Brunswick felt toward the Princetonians who flaunted the fact that they still had the cannon.

When he spoke, his words were guarded. Still, it was hard to mask his feelings about what he saw as the cause of the situation.

"Well, let me just say that there are some in New Brunswick who are tired of the joking. They are bothered that certain members of the Princeton community seemingly taunt them with having taken the cannon from its proud place in New Brunswick to begin with."

"So you are accusing the people of Princeton of stealing the cannon from New Brunswick?" Elizabeth seemed to instantly flare up. "Seriously you do not believe that? Are you trying to justify what the Rutgers' students did recently as a fair response to any juvenile joking about who has the cannon?"

"Well," Adkins started to explain how he did feel the action was justified but stopped. He thought better of it as he saw the determined look in Elizabeth's face.

"No, Ms. Warren, I was only explaining that our purpose here tonight was to accept the olive branch and help forge a future between the two colleges with a renewed shared purpose with learning."

Elizabeth, realizing that her temper had spiked to argue a point that really meant little to her, calmed herself before talking. "I do believe that gesture would be appreciated by all."

"I am curious," Adkins stated as he glanced back again toward Elizabeth's mother. "Did she add anything else about me?"

"No," Elizabeth smiled happy to be off the cannon topic. "Her intelligence gathering did not provide much detail besides the basic observation that several of the Princeton gentlemen here, especially a group from the College, are not pleased with the Rutgers presence at this event."

"Yes, I could sense that when I first entered the room. I guess the cannon thing must still have some people a little hot and bothered." He chuckled as he thought he saw Elizabeth blush slightly at the reference to her quick rise in temper seconds before. Suddenly, the smile on his face vanished as his look became more serious.

"Mrs. Bell?" He said it slowly as if just putting two puzzle pieces together.

"Your mother's name is Mrs. Bell? And you introduced yourself as Elizabeth Warren. Please tell me I have not made an even bigger fool of myself by intruding in here to speak with the wife of a husband who will be jealously charging in to protect the honor of his wife at any moment?"

"Now that would be a scene to talk about," Elizabeth responded, and looked away out at the crowd.

"I am correct?" He sounded nervous.

"No. Captain Warren, my husband, was one of the casualties of the War. He fell at the Battle of Cold Harbor outside of Richmond while he was serving under General Grant. Ironically it was the last day of the battle there. He was killed assaulting a position the army never took. They left the field right after he was killed that day."

"I am so sorry," Adkins offered.

"There you go apologizing again, Mr. Adkins," Elizabeth looked him in the eyes.

"I know but bringing that up and at a party —"

"Mr. Adkins. There is no way you could have known. It is not like you had anything to do with it. So, again, there is no need to apologize."

"Thank you Mrs. Warren," he said.

"I prefer Elizabeth," she answered him. Her voice was softer and did not have a harsh sound this time. "I assure you, since I have taken off the black veil and joined the rest of society, I have been going about my daily business of living. Elizabeth and not Mrs. Warren is what everyone else calls me."

Adkins smiled.

It was a gentle and warm smile, Elizabeth noticed. It was the type that brought about a sort of calming effect on anyone.

"Well, I still feel I have made a mess of things so far tonight and no, I am not about to apologize again," Adkins joked. "Please know that this awkward appearance tonight that you have witnessed is not who I normally am. I actually do not stumble into people or get lost over my words every day. I do not ruin women's dresses or ask insensitive questions at fun occasions."

"Mr. Adkins, it does sound to me like you are trying to apologize again," Elizabeth cut in. This time her voice was less corrective and more pleasant. And she smiled.

Before Adkins could reply, loud shouting noises rang out from nearby.

Instantly the sound drew everyone's attention. Immediately the bodies in the room were drawn toward the growing commotion in an attempt to see what was happening just outside the mansion.

The words were hard to make out but the angry tone was clear. Instinctively Adkins recognized one of the yelling voices. That was a Rutgers student.

He pushed hard to get ahead of the crowd surge that was pushing forward in the direction of the noise. As he moved, he separated from Elizabeth and left her behind.

Adkins' swift action got him to the portico ahead of most of the crowd.

There on the portico, standing face to face, were two young men who appeared to be about to engage in some form of physical combat. Teeth clenched and fingers tightened into fists, they looked prepared to square off and set to attack.

Beside each man were two or three other young men. Each of these individuals looked similarly heated up with an expression of anger and hatred clearly etched on every face.

"You heard what I said," the one young man shouted in the face of the other loud enough for all to hear. "I said take your Rutgers College moron friends with you. Go back to your studying about pigs and chickens and get out of a college town that appreciates real knowledge and has real standards and expectations with academia!"

"You are just another one of those typical father's dandies here. All laced up like some refined wealthy mother's boy pretending to know what real life is!"

"Oh you think so! Well I have two pistols if you want me to blow a hole in your head at twenty paces. Or maybe you would prefer swords if you wish for me to puncture your heart. As you may soon find out I also have these two fists ready to pulverize your nose! I am all ready to go. Just pick your poison and, just like always, the men from Old Nassau will beat you Rutgers ladies down to the ground!"

Adkins at this point, along with several other older men in the group, forced themselves in between the two who were ready to start as combatants. They pulled the boys backwards to create some space between the two groups.

Adkins literally had the young man from Rutgers who had been nose-to-nose now in a chokehold to restrain him from lunging back toward the other group. His grip tightened around the youth's neck. But it did not cut off the words as they came spewing out of his seething young body.

"Any time. Any place you bunch of pompous school boys!" He shouted. "And to all of you here making fun – we didn't want that damn cannon anyway! We always intended to just leave a mark that we were here. We were just letting you know we can come here anytime we want to get it!"

"Try to take it now you big mouthed daisy!" came back a yell from one in the other group. They were all also being held back by other adults around them now.

Adkins looked to his left. Mr. Edward Bowser, the Rutgers math adjunct professor and a large man himself, had another of the Rutgers students in his hold.

Adkins watched as that young man sneered at the whole Princeton crowd. Then in an evil-sounding tone the student stated, "Oh we could get it right now. But there is too much joy in knowing that you will never be able to sleep any night again. You will hear a noise and jump for fear that we are coming to take our cannon and bring it back to its rightful place in New Brunswick in the future. Best you sleep with one eye open now. For I make you this promise. That cannon will be taken home to New Brunswick on the night when you least expect it!"

"Aww, such bold talk from a school that loses everything," one of the Princeton boys yelled out.

"Played much baseball lately boys?" came another Princeton voice.

Laughter rolled out across the Princeton crowd.

"How is the water at your Raritan boat house? Heard you always have a nice view of the backs of the other skulls as they pull away to the finish line!"

Again, loud laughter followed. This time it included the students and adults from Princeton.

"Come on boys," Adkins heard Adjunct Professor Bowser say to the young man he held. He gestured to the others from Rutgers who were there. "Time to go."

The Rutgers chaperones herded the students with them to the carriages that had been pulled up along the street.

"Have a bumpy ride home you losers!"

"Do not forget to look at our cannons on your way out!"

The jeers continued.

Behind the students from Princeton Adkins could now hear several adult voices requesting that the young men calm themselves.

The Rutgers students, now under close physical supervision of the staff, exited without further comment.

Adkins glanced back as he stepped into the carriage himself.

The crowd on the front steps resembled a mob. The lights about the building looked like angry torches now versus welcoming lights to a party as they had once been intended. Some of the older guests were yelling along with the students for them to go back to New Brunswick. Others appeared to be holding the group back in check so that a fighting posse would not pursue them.

Adkins scanned the faces for any sign of Elizabeth Warren but did not see her.

"Let's go," Adkins turned back and ordered the driver to leave. Instantly the carriage pulled off.

10

"I hate them," the young man at Adkins' side uttered as the clicking of the hooves turned to thumps with a change of the road surface. The carriage had moved from the pounded gravel in the street of Princeton proper and on to the pure mud of the turnpike as they headed back toward New Brunswick.

Adkins said nothing as they rode on and left behind the crowd at Princeton. A million thoughts swirled through his head.

President Campbell was going to be furious with them at how this turned out.

First there had been the failed cannon raid.

Then the embarrassment of what the students had done with the vandalism.

Now this public spectacle and reality that the situation was now worse between the schools.

Their mission had been a failure.

Adkins was not looking forward to what lay in store when they gathered back at Old Queens. After this debacle it was not hard to think about himself first. He began to wonder if his role as a tutor would be terminated early. He saw his dream of becoming a professor being derailed before it had ever really had a chance to start.

One simple task. That was all that he had been given. Make sure the students were able to mind their manners. As they rode away he had obviously failed.

He wondered if President Campbell would call him in by himself to issue some edict that he would be terminated for his failure in keeping the students straight as a chaperone on the trip. Or maybe all of the staff tutors would all be brought in together and then dismiss them as a group. He could see it now, Hasbrouck and Bowser there on either side.

Of course Hasbrouck's innate ability with mathematics as a tutor and Bowser's ability as an author on the topic of mathematics would definitely give them an edge if the College needed to make an example of only one of the three of them. If they only needed one scapegoat it would most likely be him!

Adkins looked over at the three students seated in the carriage making the ride back to Rutgers with him. He was sure their expressions were no different from the students in the other two carriages that were following them and being watched by Bowser and Hasbrouck.

An argument about a cannon.

It may seem so simple and silly. But the basis of any argument never changed. Being made to do what someone else says to do and being forced to feel that you are being humiliated in some way in the process was bound to lead to resentment. Tonight it led to a fight.

Adkins shook his head in frustration.

It had been a stupid assignment they had been sent on anyway. How foolish to make the boys do this public penance for something they really were not sorry they had done. Add insult to injury, making them bow down to the lads at Princeton in all of their finery.

No, the division between the two colleges was greater than anyone wanted to admit.

Who cared if the jealousy came from either the money handed to Rutgers by the state when it was selected as the recipient of the funding from the Morrill Act or the historic argument over who had the higher quality academic experience on campus? These were adult topics of debate.

But somehow these sentiments had clearly spilled over to the students. At each college it burned at the core of everything they were about. Belonging to any group and identifying with it gave you a certain desire to protect it from outsiders. Whether President Campbell at Rutgers or President McCosh at Old Nassau wanted to admit it, the student bodies did not see each other on a common mission to unite together in higher learning.

No, to the contrary, they saw each other as the competition. They saw the graduates of each other's college poised to take the better job offer or societal opportunity. They felt the inherent need to defend the label that was bestowed upon them as a part of the brotherhood of their school. Their tribe.

A silly canon?

It wasn't really about wanting a cannon. It was really about pride. The pride in being better. The pride in beating one's opponent. And that was what the students at Old Nassau were – opponents.

Again, Adkins looked at the three students in his carriage, each lost in their own thoughts as they rode on toward the college. He had to admit to himself, he was much closer to their way of thinking versus some peaceful bond that his President had intended to forge. Listening to what had come off the tongues of the folk at Princeton, he knew they were in the same boat as these three young men. They made it clear about what they felt about seeing the other as a friend. It was evident that both saw each other as an enemy.

Adkins chuckled to himself as he remembered his own temper rising as he had been speaking about the ritual of the cannon just before the disruption had broken out.

At that thought, another image played in his head. That woman! Elizabeth Warren.

Her face now took the focus among all the other things twirling about on his mind. As the horses made their way northeast, it was her picture that calmed him from his troubles. Her face so beautiful. He knew she must have noticed how he had been charmed by her every action and the way that she carried herself throughout their short exchange.

Enchanting! That was the word he was trying to think of to describe every part of her being.

It was with his memory of her pleasant smile and her confident manner that finally drew in his full attention and all the bad thoughts about all that had gone wrong that night started to slip away.

Elizabeth. What a wonderful name. As he tried to recreate every detail of her and what had been said, he felt himself start to drift off to sleep.

11
Princeton, New Jersey

It was late when they arrived back to their house in Princeton that night.

"They are still asleep," Elizabeth said as she returned to the kitchen area. "I thought for sure they would both awake as soon as we came in."

Her mother poured the warm water into the cup and stirred the tea with the silver tea spoon. It was one of the family's prized valuables.

"I suppose they would have woken up earlier with all that screaming from Judge Olden's home at the way that racket was going on. I know it made me panic a bit," her mother said.

"Mrs. Annilee Bell," her daughter stated in a firm but loving tone. "You were one of the first who would have been out on that portico if you weren't so busy being nosy about what I was talking about with that young gentleman from Rutgers at the time!"

"True," her mother smiled. "I was kind of disappointed I had to hear about what started that fuss with the school boys out there instead of witnessing it first-hand myself."

"I am sure that will not stop you from repeating it to every relative and stranger who had not heard the story before."

"Well dear," her mother replied. "I know one way you can keep me from constantly re-telling that story."

"And what would that be?"

Her mother leaned forward with a devilish, good-natured, match-making grin.

"If you want to tell me that the conversation with the Rutgers gentleman was more engaging for you. If maybe it might have a long term impact, like a future date. Oh that is the story I would much rather talk about and add to, for example, when he comes to call on you. If that is to happen then I could be convinced to stress that instead of a silly argument when others ask me about the evening."

"Mother, I told you. There is nothing that took place worth repeating," Elizabeth answered back.

"So you tell me that you were not interested in that professor?"

"Mom, we barely spoke," Elizabeth countered.

"Well I liked him," her mother stated. "He had a nice smile. And I have to tell you I thought I noticed a little spark there with you."

"No. No sparks mom."

"Darling, it has been five years."

"I know mom."

"You know I can relate. When your father passed that same year as your brother Timothy, I never thought I would be able to pick myself back up and get going again. But I owed it to you to make sure that you were able to receive all that life can give."

"And you know I am grateful mom."

"In addition, Elizabeth, I owed it to myself."

"Yourself? Mom, you never ever so much as went to a social gathering with another man after father died. All you did was care for me."

"That is partially true. Your father was the only man in my life, and had been for so long. Plus I was older. When he died I saw no need for another man. But do not fool yourself into believing that my life was only dedicated to you. I got so much joy and happiness from being with you that you gave my life meaning when your father was no longer here." As her mother said this, she leaned forward and touched Elizabeth's check gently with her fingers.

"And mom, I have two wonderful children that I now share my life with. John Warren may not have been the perfect man or even in my life for very long. But he gave me these two children who are at the center of my world now."

Her mother leaned back in her chair, now sporting a more exasperated expression on her face as if she had been down this road before many times.

"And they are wonderful children. But, my dear, your situation is so different from mine. You were so much younger and your time with your husband so brief. There is still so much out there that I know can help bring love into your heart. It fills you with another kind of joy that your children cannot bring you."

"Mother, we have had this talk before."

"And as nothing has changed, I am sure we will have it many times again," her mother smiled back.

"Look, I have a fulfilling life. Beyond my children think about the success I have found with our business. And don't forget that this has been accomplished while still managing our farm and home. There are not many who could brag about such a fine millenary shop in town and, while our farm may be small, it does sustain us in so many ways."

"I am not saying that you are not busy, my dear. Nor am I suggesting that I am not proud of how you have grown up so self-sufficient and able to deal with all that life has dealt you. But there is still so much more."

"Mother, I do love you. But even though everyone in town sees you as the teller of tales instead of being a businesswoman; the businesswoman is who I have tried to fashion myself to be," Elizabeth declared.

"Listen missy. Know that my chatting with the population of Princeton is what brings them back to the shop to visit. Then, hopefully while they are listening to me fill them in on what they should know, they buy something from you." She did not sound defensive as she spoke. Rather she came across as very confident in her role that she played in the workings of the shop.

"And I realize how I could not have even thought to open the shop without you here to help with the twins," was all Elizabeth got out before her mother cut in again.

"And a joy that has been to my heart. But all the more reason to understand that there is more to life than working and raising your children with me."

Elizabeth sighed. There was no way to reason with her. She also had no desire to argue with her mother. Her mother was a strong woman, one who Elizabeth truly admired. Still she felt compelled to push on.

"Again mom, I do love how you have helped me with the children and all that you have given me. But, like you, I did have a husband who I also loved very much and got to experience so much with."

"Oh, Elizabeth darling, I have told you so many times that your life experience with him was so different from mine with your father. Understand that you cannot even compare the two time frames in which we lived. I lived in a less worrisome, if at times more economically challenging, period. You were a war bride, rushed together."

"We were in love," Elizabeth interjected but knew it was pointless once her mother got started on this topic.

"Sweetheart, there was no length of time to know if it was truly love. You were so young, and so was he. And though God bestowed you both with the beautiful twins that you now have; the two of you never lived together long enough to share what couples who are married over time define as love."

"Mom."

"No, Elizabeth, hear me out. There is so much more to life versus that excitement of first meeting someone. True, it brings your inner soul to light in a whole new way. I know that the time you did get to share must have been beautiful. But the reality of that time shared together is something totally different. He left for battle ten days after you were wed. He visited home, once, to see his children after they were born. He left again as a heroic soldier and, I know, as a future wonderful father. But darling, when he was killed, your life died too more than it should have."

"Mom, you know I appreciate you sharing your thoughts but," Elizabeth again was cut off before she could finish.

"You have to keep living Elizabeth. You have to keep being a part of something bigger then what you are now."

"Mom, please know that I do feel very fulfilled. And also know I do not believe that I need a man to complete that type of life goal for me at this time."

"What about this professor tonight? Was he so bad?" her mother prompted her.

"Obviously you failed to gather the dirt on him like you typically do with so many others," Elizabeth chided. "To be clear, he was from Rutgers College. But he is not a professor. He is simply what they call at a college a tutor of students."

"A teacher of some sorts?" her mother asked.

"I guess you could say that."

"So he was a learned man. Close enough," her mother stated triumphantly. "And as such, he could challenge you to think and learn and grow in ways that I or the ladies who visit your millenary shop will not be able to push you to keep learning."

"Mom, a tutor means that he is still learning," Elizabeth backed her off.

"As are we all," her mother reminded her before stopping.

After a moment of quiet thought, her mother suddenly came back with an inquisitive, "And how did you find out that he is a tutor? Did he call himself that?"

"No, I overheard some people speaking about his position after he had exited the festival."

"So you were the one snooping about this time. Let me tell you something darling. You must have been interested if you were asking questions about him afterward," her mother pointed out.

"Mother, first I was not snooping. I simply overheard the comment. Secondly, you know I would never ask a direct question to anyone about a man. A widow with two children inquiring about a man in this or any other town in America would get her branded in such vulgar terms that she could never again show her face in the light of day."

"First," her mother began in the exact same manner her daughter had just spoken to her. "I hope that you understand that listening in on others speaking and snooping are the exact same thing. And secondly, never let anyone ever make you feel that because you are a woman what you say in a legitimate social setting should make you a social pariah."

"Mother I didn't say that. Besides you are well aware of social conventions and if anyone even thought I was asking about that man-"

"Darling by now you know, if you wouldn't ask about him I certainly would. Besides," her mother smiled at her. "According to you I am bound to be spreading gossip and rumors about everyone to everyone and that would include you and that young Rutgers fella even if I have not yet learned his name."

Elizabeth chuckled. She did so much love her mother.

Her father had been a wonderful father too. Flawed like every other person in a variety of ways, but he had always been there to offer her encouragement until that summer when her brother had caught the pox. Her father died of the same ailment less than two weeks after her brother, leaving her and her mom to fend on their own.

Her mother was a hard worker. She always had to be.

Her father had been a rather sickly man and her mother pitched in with everything even while he was alive. Her mother would tell stories, even back then, about the frontier and the women who went west on wagons and how brave they were. She used those stories every time Elizabeth got scared that they may not make it or whenever she felt that the work asked of her as a ten year old on a small farm was too much to handle.

The millenary shop had come about at the right time really by accident.

Elizabeth had been taught by her father how to read and write, one of the greatest gifts someone could ever give another he would say. He always loved books. Every chance he had he brought her new material to read helping increase her vocabulary and understanding of the world around.

One day several years after her father died Elizabeth had been in town with her mother when one of the older women, Mrs. Justice, asked if anyone could read the newspaper for her. Elizabeth stepped forward and read the article that she had been handed by the older woman. In it was a story about the war which had broken out between the states. It told about the first real battle fought at a place called Bull Run. She read out loud every detail to Mrs. Justice. Once she completed that, the old woman asked her if she would come to read to her each day at her millenary shop she would pay her.

Elizabeth came to the shop, late each day after all the chores had been completed at the farm, and learned about hats and fashion and business from the older woman in exchange for reading her the stories in the newspaper. There was much admiration for each other. Elizabeth was amazed that a woman could operate and basically own a business. In turn, Mrs. Justice explained how she was in awe of the intellectual powers possessed by her young reader. A bond grew quickly between her and Mrs. Justice and she became like an adopted daughter to the older woman.

As Mrs. Justice's eyesight continued to fail, her even older husband would escort her to the shop each day. One day he explained that Mrs. Justice was not coming in to the shop to work because she was feeling too poorly. He asked Elizabeth if she could help run the shop on a regular basis in Mrs. Justice's absence. He mentioned that her nephew, Johnathan Warren, had moved to the area. He would be coming in to help around the shop with the financial aspect. Mrs. Justice had full faith in Elizabeth that she could handle the detail work of the shop.

The next day Johnathan Warren entered the shop.

It was that day Elizabeth met her future husband and the father of her children.

While Elizabeth ran the shop all day with two other ladies, the young Mr. Warren would arrive in the late afternoon to review the ledgers and make the daily deposit of any transactions that had taken place. He was recently in New Jersey, visiting with his Great Aunt, when she had taken ill. They saw him as the grandchild they never had. Mr. Justice convinced Jonathan's father that he would apprentice him and pay for his schooling at the Princeton Prep Academy.

Jonathan thrived in this arrangement. He immediately grew attached to Elizabeth and shared her love of reading and talking about the great philosophical questions posed by man throughout time.

A year later, near the end of 1863, seeing his Great Aunt's failing health gave her a short time on this planet Jonathan Warren proposed to Elizabeth knowing it would make his Great Aunt happy. They married just two weeks later.

It was also at this same time Jonathan elected to join the army. That same War that brought Elizabeth into Mrs. Justice's life and which led Jonathan into her life was not done shaping her future. Once again it played a big part when it took Johnathan away while they were reshaping the very structure of the world in which she would now live.

Within a year of getting married, Elizabeth had given birth to a baby girl and baby boy. Mrs. Justice had passed away weeks after the wedding itself. With her passing, Mr. Justice willed the millenary shop to his nephew which, in his wartime absence, was actually being run by

Elizabeth, pregnant and all. This was much to the chagrin of many of the smaller-minded people who resided in Princeton proper.

The elderly Mr. Justice passed away two months after his wife. Childless, but never having saved much in terms of personal wealth, the proceeds from the sale of their home paid off the deed to the millenary business which was now in the name of Mr. Jonathan Warren.

Jonathan visited home on leave for several days in 1864. He saw his twin children during that visit home for the very first time. Elizabeth watched, ten days later, as he rode back off to again join the Union army and now with the rank of Captain and the expectation of leading other men.

It was just a month later that Elizabeth learned Jonathan Warren, her husband and father of their twins, had been killed at the Battle of Cold Harbor just outside of Richmond, Virginia.

At first, Elizabeth was not sure what to do.

She was a mother with two infant children at her side. Her mother toiled with her on a small farm that barely created enough to subsist on when the weather cooperated. Now she heard a rumor in the town that she would have to turn over the deed to the millenary because of her husband's death.

As unfair as it may seem, a local lawyer had explained to her, no woman owned and operated a business. Men were required to sign and own such ventures.

As she thought back on those days, she was sure that Mrs. Elizabeth Cady Stanton who stood this year up in front of Congress as the first woman to express anything to them on any topic would not have agreed.

But that was now and so many miles away in Washington DC from where she was living then in Princeton. To the small-minded folk in this parochial town at that time the advice they gave was what they also truly believed, not that their opinions had actually changed about a woman's role any more recently. The common school of thought was that there was a place for women in society in their view of the world and it did not include anything beyond raising children at home or assisting male ventures only when males called for it.

Elizabeth remembered the day she and her mother, twins in tow, walked in to the church and both felt a hush come over the chatter that had preceded them in the entrance hall. One of the older women came to her side and offered up that her husband might be interested in becoming partners with her at the millenary. She explained how her husband would, as the male, become the owner and she would, as the female, be provided the opportunity to keep working there for as long as she liked.

Elizabeth remembered how her mother calmly spoke with the woman and thanked her for her support during such a time. Elizabeth remembered how hard it was to fight back the tears as she had carried the twins into their home later that day. And Elizabeth remembered how she was ready to give in and seek male support with ownership of the business.

However, what stood out the most that night was how her mother argued with Elizabeth.

It was a War that was keeping all the men away and, rules be damned, no one was better equipped to run that shop her mother had stated. No objection Elizabeth could raise seemed to deter her mother's spirited retorts.

Elizabeth remembered the final piece of advice her mother gave. "Darling," she had said in her usual way of trying to control any discussion with her daughter. "Just see the fuss that will happen the day any person, man or woman, walks into that shop and tries to pry it away from you. It is rightfully yours to keep. It is your husband's and, until the day you die, you hold fast to the statement that he fought for this country to secure his right to have that shop and that you, in his name and yours, will not let anyone take that dream away."

Her mother was right. The War had changed the landscape. No man entered the shop with an officer of the law to seize the property. No judge decreed that they would not allow the business to continue.

So, through lack of any external force attempting to take it away, Elizabeth came to work each day. She opened the store and the business continued as it had before Mrs. Justice had died and when Mr. Justice and then her husband Jonathan had been seen as the living deed holder of the property.

And, through hard work the shop actually not only survived but, after the War's end, it thrived. True, it did not bring in anything in the way of a fortune. However it did provide for Elizabeth, her mother, and her two growing children. Of course, Elizabeth's skill as both a businessperson and as a mother was aided by her own mother who shared time raising the twins and keeping their small family farm alive beyond the millenary doors.

"And so, my dear," her voice cut through Elizabeth's thoughts. "How about we take a day trip to New Brunswick this week?"

"Why would I do that?"

"To look for material for the store?"

"I thought we were fully stocked."

"Elizabeth, first, you know our store is never fully stocked. And second, you never know who we might accidentally run into if we happen to stop by that Rutgers College while we are there."

"Mother, you are hopeless!"

"But you, my dear girl, are not."

12
Rutgers College
October 4, 1869

The soft rain that had pattered against the windows of the Old Queens building at Rutgers College when they had first entered stopped and slowly the sun came out but a chill still permeated the air. A light breeze appeared and instantly started to dry up all evidence of the initial wet weather. However, inside, the men were oblivious to any activity outside their halls that did not pertain directly to them.

Rutgers President William Campbell shook his head slowly side to side as the talking stopped.

The assembled faculty knew this was not a good sign.

A man well respected for not only his work as a teacher and public orator, Campbell was also a skilled executive and those around him were aware that his analysis of the situation would be the one that mattered in the end. Of course, this did not mean that ultimately it was a decision that the trustees and even the remnants of the General Synod with the Dutch Reformed Church would not have to agree with. With so many with interests in the educational and financial workings of the school, he would also have to check in with all the traditional sources of influence as well with the recently expanding interests and power forming among the alumni base on such a critical issue that would draw public attention.

"Gentlemen," Campbell strongly enunciated the word as he began his summary.

"There is no need for further discussion after hearing this review. Plain and simple this is not good for the reputation of the college. Young men, our students, engaged in a near brawl at the home of Judge Olden and interrupting a very public affair at his private residence? This is all at an event, mind you, that is central to the whole Princeton community and was intended as a time when our young men were there to extend an olive branch to put behind the shenanigans related to their cannon escapade."

"Again, sir, it was also the actions of the youth there from Princeton that provided the catalyst. They created that stage for the altercation. The students at the College of New Jersey there were at least equally if not more responsible for that public outburst," Dr. Murray interjected.

Campbell's eyes had that authoritative glare as they looked out toward Murray. The power of this stare kept Murray from saying anything else and not another voice chimed in to defend Murray's point.

Campbell eventually started speaking again.

"Like a tribe of barbarian idiots our boys acted. A bunch of unmannered fools is surely how it has been reported throughout the town of Princeton. For that matter I am sure by now word of this has spread to the far reaches of the state. I do not need to remind anyone that in the eyes of everyone out there, we are responsible here, gentlemen." He paused a moment to survey the faculty but let his eyes remain on Murray before continuing. "We are responsible not for the conduct of students at another college or from another community, Dr. Murray. No. We are responsible for the behavior of the students who are here in our charge. We are responsible for the young men who belong to Rutgers College. Young men, mind you, who we as staff were chaperoning at this event at the time it took place."

His remarks were not debated.

To the side of the room, Adkins felt a lump in his throat as he thought about what he was doing when the altercation had broken out. Talking with that lovely lady and nowhere near those in his charge, he was sure he would be singled out for his failure to fulfill the role he had been assigned.

Campbell rose from his chair and he moved from behind his desk toward the window. All eyes were upon him as he spoke.

"As I look out on our grounds and beyond our campus I see the unrest every day. We are not a world apart living in some isolated learning bubble here at Rutgers protected from the machinations of political interests. Like it or not we are a part of that world. And it is a world that is quick to judge and constantly pulls at the very support and loyalties which are essential for our survival as an institution. The lessons from the recent War between the States are an example to how much the events in the world can cause havoc from afar at our school at any time. But this is beyond the intrusion of worldly events in my eyes. Within our own domain there is a growing discontent between maintaining two colleges in one state and the seeds of discontent are being fueled by so many who have their own agendas."

"When Cook and Murray helped win the grant for our scientific school to start and the state chose us over the College of New Jersey, you all know how we celebrated here that day. You also know how the faculty was instantly feeling at that exact same time in Nassau Hall. It was a great day and a great victory for Rutgers. However, when there is a great victory there is also a great loss. With victory comes but a temporary joy. With a loss there is a permanent and constant internal pain that will not go away until that loss can be erased. Revenge is a powerful driver of men's actions."

"I truly believe this great gift that was bestowed on our college has caused the rift that underscores all that we are facing on every front. Yes, a massive rift. Or what did you call it earlier, Mr. Atherton?"

"A rivalry, sir," Professor Atherton said. "It is the common form of competition that has grown between colleges across the country and not just here though. I witnessed it firsthand as a student at Yale and again when I served in the Union Army-"

"A rivalry," Campbell cut back in without averting his gaze which appeared fixed on some distant object as he continued looking outside through the window. "Thank you Professor Atherton, I do know what the term means."

"Yes sir," Atherton responded in his typical military deference to rank tone.

"As I was saying, this rivalry that now appears to be getting championed among the students at each college has grown from what was an adult funding debate to an all-consuming passion with anyone connected with either college or community. I know well the history of the two towns and I understand there are roots of this fighting that go way beyond the more recent land grant award. However I do not want this rivalry also producing negative images of our scholarly mission. We have come too far with our work to establish this as an elite institution of higher learning. I need not remind you that in the minds of a conservative body who truly embraced the concept of the birth role of this college as being linked to the mission of the seminary; we have already broken away from the historical boundaries that had been the impetus for their financial support of this college in the first place. That purpose, as you well know, in the eyes of the Rutgers founders was to produce Godly men!"

He now turned to face the assembled group.

"I also believe that we are at a critical juncture with defining how others in the secular world see us too. With that, like a jealous relative, I do worry the gentlemen at the College of New Jersey as well as those who favor the growth of Princeton over New Brunswick as the state community of choice and prominence want to find ways to paint us beneath them. Our enemies I fear are determined to make us out to be the deficient place of learning."

"I have heard echoes from various voices already about their classical studies in Princeton being more sophisticated then our program. I have heard musings that the students we now admitted to form the Scientific School here at Rutgers may not have the same formal training and background as those admitted to study down in Princeton. I have heard, even from several of the Rutgers alumni, the Princeton supporters are going to great lengths to seize on any opportunity to ridicule our expectations and our new offerings to make us look like ignorant farmers versus established scholars."

Campbell had now walked back to his desk. Instead of sitting back in his chair he placed both hands firmly on the desk. Standing in this manner, he leaned forward toward the faculty members and his voice elevated with a passion in it that surely betrayed his love of Rutgers College.

"In no way do we want our reputations besmirched. In no way do we want to stand back on any remark made by any person about our mission of graduating young men with skills and a sophisticated understanding of both the practical logical life trainings and a fuller embodiment of what it means to be one of God's children and America's citizens. In no way do we want any discussion of a perceived weakness in our program, our research work, our teaching or our knowledge of defining right over wrong to go unchallenged. No gentlemen, I do not want any of you leaving here today with that thought or belief that I do not support action over inaction when it comes to protecting our college."

Campbell now stood straight up and appeared to look, not into their eyes, but over their heads. As he spoke he seemed to be engaging some higher power.

"We can never let the young men and their families or the people of New Brunswick or our trustees and supporters who have moved across the state and this nation -- we can never let any of them ever feel that we are not building the dream that they share in! Even when there are detractors in Princeton who do this only with the hope that by belittling our good name while they attempt to give prominence to their own; we must find an appropriate way to meet each improper reference head on. Still, while that rebuttal must be swift and clear, it must always be conducted with the utmost dignity and class."

He shifted his eyes on to the faculty in a way that each member of the staff thought he was making his comments directly to each one of them.

"That said, we cannot tolerate acts like the improper social conduct of the young men at the festival at Judge Olden's home in Princeton. We cannot appear to condone unlawful actions like vandalizing the property of members in a surrounding community even if they may have stolen property from our good citizens in New Brunswick. We must make this clear to our students and not allow them to go off the rails. In some way we must let those beyond our walls know that this improper display has been dealt with as we are a school with high expectations for all our young men in every activity."

Looking now to Professor Atherton, President Campbell instructed, "George, as you have served in the Union Army, maybe you are the best to handle this escapade with a little formal discipline and help clarify the correct manner in which a gentleman interacts when confronted with such a dispute as the one which arose at Judge Olden's."

"Sir?"

"My thought is perhaps a more robust schedule of managed and orderly physical activity through drilling might dampen some of the desire and energy for these night time raids while at the same time sending out a message about applied discipline. That is the military way, is it not?"

"Yes sir," Atherton acknowledged the charge.

"As for the rest of you, tutors here who were there as chaperones included, your academic work has been outstanding. Do not let this unfortunate event or any possible foolish chatter lead you to believe otherwise."

Now looking specifically at those who had raised questions during their initial part of the meeting, Campbell continued on.

"Yes Mr. Bowser. I do understand the difficulty of chaperoning young men at any time and especially at such a social event when they were in, shall we define it as, hostile territory."

"Yes, Dr. Murray. I do understand that I myself may have handicapped them with the directive that they were to attend with the intent of some form of apology and failed to outline specifically how this would be accomplished without specific instructions. For the record, my hope was that their mere presence would have confirmed that they were gentlemen of good character and this, in and of itself, would have restored the general public perception about the quality of a Rutgers College student. Please know that, in hindsight, that may have been the wrong approach and I do appreciate you taking the time to point this out earlier."

Mr. Bowser, the new adjunct math professor who had been the lead chaperone that night, almost appeared to blush at the comments. His initial anger over the event and getting called to the President's office had started the discussion. When he had been called upon he had spoken his mind and stated that the venture had been a flawed plan at the outset. Now, hearing President Campbell taking responsibility for the evening, Bowser felt awkward that he had presented his thoughts in the deflective manner in which he had.

Before Bowser could say anything to apologize, Campbell asked the group as a whole, "Is it true what I am being told that our young Rutgers scholars lost in this game called baseball to the young men down in Princeton by that large of a score?"

"Unfortunately it is true. They were slaughtered." Adkins heard himself reply and shifted immediately back in his chair as he realized that his place in the room that day was to remain silent as the lowest ranking member of the faculty. As soon as the words left his lips, he could feel everyone's eyes turn on him most likely admonishing this protocol blunder.

Campbell smiled. "Well Mr. Adkins. We need to make sure that our young men are not seen as a group of dandies and are known instead as healthy able-bodied champions. We do not need anyone making jokes at our expense by finding a weakness with our young charges in mind or body."

Adkins kept his eyes down as he nodded politely in agreement at President Campbell.

"So as we move from here today, I want to make sure that we are clear about our next steps. I will communicate with the trustees and board. While I will not do it yet, I will most likely make a point of making a contact of some sort with President McCosh in near the future. I have to figure out a way to make it clear that, while we do not condone the actions of our students with the cannon vandalism act or their behavior at the social event, we are concerned about what appears to be a deliberate attempt to besmirch our reputation as an institution by members of their community."

Campbell now moved toward the doorway, a sign that he was ending the group meeting.

"Again, I do not want anyone leaving here today without the knowledge of how much I value each and every one of you and your contributions to this college. I do not have to mention Dr. Cook or Dr. Murray's names anywhere without immediately those beyond our campus acknowledging their brilliance. Like them, as I see in so many of you, there is that skill to enhance our reputation as an incredible institution of higher learning. At the same time I believe you have been modeling the very moral fabric to which we want our young men to aspire. I thank you for your passion with what you do and in the manner in which you pursue it. For all the loyal sons of Rutgers, blessings on you and yours."

With that, President Campbell opened the door to the room and the faculty took the cue to exit.

13
"The Chance Meeting?"
October 4, 1869
New Brunswick, New Jersey

They stood at the corner of Somerset Street and College Avenue where the college met the downtown area of New Brunswick.

Dr. Murray shook hands with Adkins and Isaac Hasbrouck, the other tutor, as he parted ways with them and headed toward George Street with Mr. Bowser.

"Please make sure that they have their assignments reviewed and committed to paper before the day ends," he stated to both men as he left.

"We will," Hasbrouck assured him. "Christopher is heading off to catch up with two of the students now. I have an appointment in several minutes I must run to, I but will require the two who are in my charge to burn the candles on both ends so it is completed in a timely fashion."

"Well that was some meeting," Adkins stated to Hasbrouck as the two men watched Murray and Bowser walk away. They looked away after they saw that the two men were now heading off in their own different directions. "I did not predict that being the basis of what I thought President Campbell would be saying to us today."

"Me either," Hasbrouck agreed. "I thought for sure that we were going to get a firm lecture with some kind of formal warning about our performance at a minimum. To tell you the truth I even had thoughts that the events in Princeton, as we were the ones who had been in charge, might have led to our dismissal. Even mentioned it to my wife last night to be prepared in case I was out looking for new employment after today."

"I was thinking the same thing," Adkins noted. "I guess the night did not turn out to be as big a disaster as I had previously feared."

"Disaster? For you?" Hasbrouck joked. "What about that young lady I saw you with. That looked like you were taking steps toward a possible personal conquest of getting her name and maybe even a future date."

Adkins smiled. "Small talk, my good man. Nothing but small talk I am afraid."

"Looked pretty serious to me," Hasbrouck answered back. "As a matter of fact, if President Campbell had requested me to testify why the students were free and able to get into the outburst they ended up getting into I was going to have to let our President him know that it was because you were distracted as you were so busy trying to get the attentions of that Princeton woman."

"Good thing I guess he didn't ask then," Adkins laughed back, in a lighter mood now that he was relieved that the President's meeting hadn't ended with more dire results.

"I actually thought she was kind of cute and even pretty by the standards of most men," Hasbrouck teased. "Clearly not in your league."

"Seriously?" Adkins responded. "My league?"

"Face it Christopher," Hasbrouck replied. "She was pretty and that clearly puts a woman like that out of my league, let alone your league. I put your playing field more around elderly scullery maid or haggard witch with no teeth."

"Oh you are so wrong," Adkins shot back. "There is no lady who would be in your league that I would not also be able to catch."

"Catch? You make it sound like a fishing match," Hasbrouck jested. "So what do you make of this lady you approached then? A white fish, flounder or a grouper?"

"For the record, I only associate with royalty," Adkins stated loudly and boldly. "If I were looking to land a woman who had the label of a fish, that fish-woman would have to be some kind of princess-like creature. Is there such a thing as a queen-fish? That is what the woman from last night would have to be if such a thing exists. A queen fish!"

"Mr. Adkins?" a female voice called out from behind him.

Adkins spun around with a quizzical look on his face at the sudden sound of his name. With eyes wide open, he froze as he stared at the figure now directly across from him barely several steps away. No noise came from his motionless, slightly parted lips.

"Mr. Adkins?" she repeated.

"Mrs. Warren?" Adkins finally sputtered out, still startled at her sudden appearance.

"The lady from Princeton?" Hasbrouck's whisper to him sounded equally shocked.

"I am out of here," he then announced to Adkins, catching his composure first and pretending that their business at hand had been officially over.

Hasbrouck tipped his cap as he brushed past the two women and instantly moved to head off up the street without any further comment. This left Adkins alone where the two men had originally been standing.

"Elizabeth," she reminded Adkins as she came up to him. "I hope we did not disturb something important," she said as she nodded in the direction of Hasbrouck's form which was not looking back and was hurriedly scurrying across the street.

"No, no." Adkins now stuttered as he glanced over his shoulder. As he watched Hasbrouck disappear he panicked as he thought to himself, I hope that these ladies had not heard his earlier comparison of her to a fishing trophy.

Adkins took a deep breath as he attempted to try and regain control of his nerves.

"I mean, why yes. I know it is not Mrs. Warren. It is Elizabeth."

He cleared his throat attempting to sound more in control. Politely he welcomed the woman beside Elizabeth and he added as he tipped his hat, "And Mrs. Bell, if I correctly recall your name."

"Oh, he is even more pleasing to the eye today now that I finally get to see him up close," Mrs. Bell observed, intentionally embarrassing her daughter.

Adkins smiled, grateful at the older woman's attempt at adding some levity to what so far had been an awkward situation.

"I am sure it is only because you had to try and look at me through the dim candlelight last time," Adkins replied. "It is the daylight now and that is known to help everyone's general complexion so they do look healthier. I can assure you, my appearance has not changed."

"And witty," Mrs. Bell noted. "I am sure I would have had a better look had there not been that disturbance between the students back at Judge Olden's place. Such a shame you were forced to run off the way that you did before we even had a chance to formally meet that day."

"I would normally tell you how personally sorry I am at all the fuss that was created that evening by our students and the disruption it caused that party."

Adkins paused and looked toward Elizabeth.

"However?" Mrs. Bell asked.

"Well your daughter made it clear that night that she does not care for a man who apologizes and I am fearful that may be a family trait and I do not wish to insult you too."

"Oh, Elizabeth," Mrs. Bell smiled. "He is charming."

Looking now at both women in front of him, Adkins asked the obvious question.

"So what do I owe the pleasure of this visit today ladies?"

"Chance, Mr. Adkins," Elizabeth answered quickly. "Pure chance."

"Chance?"

"Yes. I hope you understand that we both had to be here today on a business errand searching for needed items for our millenary shop back in Princeton," Elizabeth explained.

"Is that so?" Adkins nodded.

"So our meeting, as you can see, is purely by chance," Elizabeth reiterated. "Please do not try to read anything else into it."

"And I suppose that they have this special material here in New Brunswick that can only be found on this part of the academic campus?"

"No, dear," Mrs. Bell cut in. "It was down in the main part of your town here in New Brunswick and not up here on this little hill for your college."

"So then you did elect to come to see me on the campus?"

"Well no," Elizabeth stammered.

"Oh, Mr. Adkins our story is very simple" Mrs. Bell cut in. "I figure I better explain it before my daughter here starts blubbering on about some foolishness that makes no sense to anyone. For her sake, I suppose, I also do not want you to falsely start thinking about any conspiracy on our part. The fabric we needed was at a store in town. I had requested that we take a walk about as we had a little time to kill before our train goes back today. We did just happen to walk in this direction when I thought I saw you. I asked Elizabeth to introduce me because I had not had that opportunity at the festival."

"I see," Adkin noted.

"Believe me sir. While my daughter did mention your name after the party, she is not one who would commit a social blunder by approaching a man in any suggestive manner!"

"I did not intend any harm in my question, Mrs. Bell. I really was just curious-"

"Chance," Mrs. Bell repeated her daughter's earlier term. "Purely chance."

"Yes ma'am."

"But now that we have met," Mrs. Bell changed the tone of her voice to one more suggestive. "Would you care to take a moment to show my daughter the college here? I know it is not as beautiful as Princeton, but I am sure there is something of value to see."

"Value," Adkins responded defensively. Then catching himself, he calmed down and agreed to a tour. "Certainly I would be glad to show your daughter the college grounds. Do you not wish to come along?"

"Oh no," Mrs. Bell waved him away. "I now would like nothing more than to sit these tired bones on that nice bench right over there and take a short rest before resuming our journey back on the train to Princeton. But you go now with Elizabeth and she can tell me later all about what she saw."

Before Elizabeth could object, Adkins turned to her and offered his service as an escort.

She glared over at her mother and seemed to hesitate for a minute.

"I promise I will only show you the good parts," Adkins smiled at her. With that, off they went.

"Well Mr. Adkins." Elizabeth finally felt confident enough to get the brassy and in charge sound back in her voice. "What wisdom do you have to share about your town and your college that anyone would find worthwhile?"

"Truthfully, Mrs. Warren. I feel I may have a little bias here as this town and college have become what I consider home to me."

"Elizabeth," she corrected him about her name again.

"Yes," he replied, but his attention was already directed to his first true love, Rutgers College.

"The place is pure majesty," he continued, pointing toward the weather vane perched high on the cupola of the main academic building before them. Almost affectionately he added, "It is so symbolic. Truly a thing of beauty and a palace to the high ideals we have in our nation about the importance of educating our young to protect future liberties and the well-being of all who reside here."

"I see it as a large brownstone structure, Mr. Adkins. In so many ways this place is the epitome of being hard and cold. Tell me, what makes this large block building so special to you?"

Adkins' smile grew even broader as his youthful zeal and true passion for this place over took his words.

"Oh, you could not be any more wrong, Elizabeth. This is the embodiment of the future and not a prison-like past. This thing of beauty in front of you is Old Queens itself. While construction did not start on it until more than forty years after the founding of the college; it is the emblem of the college itself. While several others claim a long story and links with the past, Rutgers College holds a critical part of the history of this country within her own story since it was one of the first institutions of higher learning in the United States."

"Really?" Elizabeth pointed out with a sense of arrogance evident in her tone. "It seems you have already forgotten that I come from the community of Princeton whose college predates yours in both the country and clearly within the state of New Jersey. If I recall the College in Princeton was way ahead as the 7th college in the country while Rutgers College came along eventually as maybe the 11th college in America."

"It was founded in 1766 on the eve of the events that led us to the American Revolution." Adkins continued on as if she had never spoken. Her interruption had not broken the trance-like aura from which Adkins talked about his college.

Elizabeth watched as Adkins poured out details about the Rutgers Presidents who had served, the recent graduates and their accomplishments, and the current work and credentials of the faculty.

They walked as he talked.

They stopped only for a moment as he would point out a specific marker or some edifice and then complete the related story. She would make a sarcastic comment about the structure or tale, which he typically ignored, and then they would start walking again as he continued on about the marvels of the world before them on the Rutgers campus grounds.

And so the pattern went on.

"This brand new building is the Schanck Observatory," he gushed as they paused again. "It is fashioned after the Tower of the Winds in Athens itself. Can you imagine that! The Greek revival architecture may draw you back to the ancients but the work within this site is filled with the wonders of modern scientific study. Did you know that for the students who get to study astronomy here they get to climb to the top and the roof actually rotates to provide a better view of the heavens above us?"

"I did not know that," Elizabeth stated the obvious, having never seen the building before.

"And the credit for this work really goes to Professor George Cook. I would love for you to meet him one day as he is an amazing man. He worked with Professor Murray and together they put together the plan that brought the funding from the Morrill Grant to support the Scientific School portion of Rutgers College that now exists."

"My understanding from what I have heard is that those were the funds that were stolen from the Nassau Hall students In Princeton," Elizabeth interjected.

This time her comment stopped Adkins in his tracks.

His eyes narrowed and his brow tightened as he suddenly spoke in a very serious sounding tone which appeared to have him snapping back at Elizabeth.

"First. Dr. Cook is a genius and there is no man of knowledge in New Jersey who would dare say a word against him. Likewise for Dr. Murray. Any talk about thievery and trying to connect that word to either of Cook or Murray would only be done by fools who are lower level thinkers and jealous that they failed to have the intelligence to advance such a plan for the benefit of our state. I cannot tolerate that anyone within my presence would ever attempt to besmirch their reputations!"

His reaction caught her by surprise.
She had been teasing him and realized that maybe she had done this too much. She could see this last remark had clearly struck a nerve. Elizabeth could hear her mother's voice inside her head reminding her to be polite to any gentleman callers. She decided rather than to get in an argument over this topic that mattered little to her, she would simply back off.
"I was only stating something I had once heard, in Princeton of course," she said almost sweetly. "I hope you know there was no insult or harm intended to either of these men with my comment."
Adkins sensed now that he may have over-reacted.
Reality quickly set back in that he was speaking with Elizabeth as he saw her beautiful face looking out at him from beneath her bonnet and not a challenger from Princeton's college. Watch yourself, he told himself. You are here with a woman and not here to argue with some editor about a publication involving these two men.
He took a deep breath and struggled to think of what to say next.
"I believe you were telling me about Professor Cook, Mr. Adkins," Elizabeth broke the awkward silence for him. "You make him sound like a true scholar."
"Ah, yes," Adkins took the cue. "You know, he really is a brilliant man. But beyond that, he is an inspiration to the rest of us connected to the faculty and the students. And, I believe you would appreciate as a woman, he is a wonderful family man too!"
"Yes, as a woman." Elizabeth caught herself from adding a sarcastic retort and let it go. Again she heard her mother's voice. "Be polite!"

Elizabeth looked Adkins over as he spoke.
She could tell he appeared to be very new to this type of small talk with a woman and clearly he was awkward in this social context. Still, there was actually something kind of cute about his innocence around her. She also liked that he came across as so genuine and not phony in any way even as he boasted on about his Rutgers stories.
Adkins pointed out the Riverstede building and explained its recent purchase by Dr. Cook. His enthusiastic presentation style stayed on track as he highlighted the family members and the importance to Cook of having them here and near to his place of work.

Elizabeth sighed to herself as Adkins talked about the specifics of the architecture of the house and about trivial facts like Charles Graham being the designer.

Adkins must have realized how trivial his story was getting when he mentioned Graham's role as he stated, "I do hope I am not boring you with too much detail on all of this. I just find it so fascinating that I fear I do lose myself in describing it. Really, I can stop if you wish."

Elizabeth smiled at how sincere he sounded.

"No, not at all Mr. Adkins. I actually am fascinated by this too."

He smiled back and went on with his story. His chest puffed up with pride when he described how everyone at Rutgers saw Dr. Cook having been named the state geologist as one of the grandest honors a college community could have.

Elizabeth felt a warm sensation within herself.

There was something very endearing about him. He was not bragging about himself or his own exploits. He was truly proud to be among men he admired and was passionate about the work he was engaged in with them. He believed in what they and he were doing. He saw this work and this place having a vital purpose in creating the future.

Elizabeth had to admit, his positive manner in which he spoke about everything was actually refreshing. She had grown so accustomed to the small town gossip and rumor mongering in Princeton. It could often be such a little place. She could not think of a day that had gone by when some woman who had shown up in her shop had not turned anything anyone else had done into a cause for ridicule. The small talk that followed always stressed the flaws of others and the weaknesses in every human action.

Yet here was Mr. Adkins. All was good to him and all plans and people had promise.

She liked how that sounded. She liked how this kind of talk made her feel. His passion gave her a sense of hope and a positive feeling about people. This was something that her current cynical world did not foster in any way. As she watched him talk she began to feel a certain attraction to him personally. And she had to admit, this was not just the exploits of the men at Rutgers impressing her.

Even as they came toward the end of his tour, she recognized the joy in his voice as he showed her the simple things around them. Typical of this was his explanation of things like the ringing of the bell in the cupola above them to signal the end of the day's lessons.

"You know the bell was donated by Henry Rutgers, namesake of the college. Colonel Rutgers was a Revolutionary War hero and he might have made a different donation of sort. But no, he donated this bell and what an amazing gift. There is poetry in that ringing of the bell, ma'am. Can you think of anything more wonderful then having this ringing of the bell in his name, every day, to signal that the learning which took place that day may one day make an impact like he did upon the world?"

Elizabeth watched as the students exited from the Old Queens building and out into the streets. She envisioned that each student, while unaware of the symbolism Adkins saw with the bell and their learning, had brought forth knowledge that might change the world. What a beautiful way Adkins had of capturing the meaning of a humble gift by Colonel Rutgers.

At this point they had done a complete circle around George Street and up to College Avenue. Now they were at the top of the knoll on which Old Queen's stood. It was also next to the bench where they had left Elizabeth's mother.

"Enjoy the sites?" Mrs. Bell called out as they approached.

"It really was impressive," Elizabeth replied.

"And, anything else about your tour guide?" Mrs. Bell asked, her active matchmaking attempt becoming obvious and this action making both Elizabeth and Adkins slightly uncomfortable.

"I am sure we have bothered Mr. Adkins long enough, mother," Elizabeth gritted out the last word through her clenched teeth. "Besides, I am sure that Mr. Adkins has other things to which he must attend to today besides us."

Adkins froze, unsure of what to say.

Had he known what she was thinking, he would have had to admit that Elizabeth had been correct with her observations of him earlier. He was awkward and unfamiliar with the social conventions expected between men and women when they met.

He knew that he enjoyed her company. There was something refreshing and even challenging about her that excited him in a way that most of his prior interactions with women had not generated. He could not explain how a simple bumping into her at a party could lead to his immediate interest, but there was no denying that something had sparked instantly within him. As he looked at her he knew there was something about her that caused him to be drawn in.

He looked her over as she spoke about something to her mother. She was beautiful and maybe Hasbrouck was right when he said she was too pretty to be in his league. Funny, beyond her obvious beauty and charms, there were so few details that he knew about her.

Suddenly a sense of panic overcame him as he repeated that thought. He still barely knew almost nothing about her. How stupid, he thought, as he now realized he had missed a chance to let her speak and inform him about who she was and tell him anything about her life.

Now he felt the fool. He had spoken the entire time. She would be leaving and now he would not have the slightest inkling of any information about her.

And now the appropriate social protocol?

Was he supposed to ask them to dine or to stay? If they said yes and agreed to stay for a meal, where would they even go? How would the details work? He had not had a chance to plan any of this out.

He glanced over at Mrs. Bell and spied a sly smile on her face as she and Elizabeth awaited his reply about something.

He was even more aware of the lingering silence.

Would it be considered too forward to ask them to stay and dine with him tonight?

Elizabeth, now believing that Adkins was never going to respond to her last observation about how busy he probably was, announced that so much time had passed and that she and her mother needed to pay heed to the train schedule.

"Again. Mr. Adkins. It really was a pleasure today."

"Oh yes, the train," her mother dead-panned, looking disappointed at the lack of any other comment on the part of Mr. Adkins to her daughter.

"Oh, I am sorry if I delayed you and that you fear you may now miss your train because of my lengthy tour," Adkins started.

"Mr. Adkins, please do not start apologizing again, good sir," Elizabeth reminded him as she had done so often but this time with a gentle smile. "Both my mother and I are responsible for monitoring our schedules. It is in no way a fault of yours."

"Well, at least let me hail you a hack to get you to the station quicker," Adkins offered.

"How kind," Mrs. Bell thanked him. The she added as she smirked at her daughter, "Another very positive quality in a man."

Almost instantly a horse stopped on the corner where they stood and Adkins helped both ladies into the carriage while the driver looked on.

Realizing with a sense of anxiety that they would possibly be riding off without him knowing when or how he would see her again, Adkins acted in a bolder manner than he was accustomed.

"I do hope I will be seeing you again in New Brunswick in the immediate future?" he stated as he looked directly at Elizabeth.

"We do not typically return for several months," Elizabeth replied.

"Oh," Adkins answered, sounding dejected.

"Unless we have a reason," Mrs. Bell suggested.

Not taking the cue, Adkins simply nodded.

"But even if we do not come back to New Brunswick, I am sure that my daughter would appreciate hearing from you again," Mrs. Bell offered.

"Would you?" he asked, hearing Mrs. Bell but still looking at Elizabeth.

Elizabeth smiled and shook her head twice to signify yes.

Instantly Adkins' demeanor changed.

"Then I shall write you post haste," he began.

"Very good, Mr. Adkins," Elizabeth said politely.

"And I promise, I will write to ask you questions about you versus just rambling on about me again," he stated, recalling his earlier thoughts about not knowing anything about her. "I am sorry that I spent the whole day talking about things related to me!"

"You did not spend the day talking about you. You were speaking about the town and college to which you are so proud," Elizabeth corrected. "And again, do not-"

"Apologize," he beat her to the word.

They both chuckled.

As the carriage lurched forward and started on its short ride to the train depot, Elizabeth nodded and waved a gloved hand gently in his direction.

Adkins was still smiling outwardly as the carriage pulled away but inside he was angry at himself. He had almost blown it.

A chance encounter with this woman who had enchanted him that evening earlier down in Princeton. He had been thinking about her constantly since that night even though he had tried to play it cool with Hasbrouck when he had teased him earlier. He had been trying to figure out how he would ever communicate with her. Then she appears like this today.

And then he forgets to ask her anything about herself or even something simple like how he could plan to connect with her again.

He was such a fool.

He walked back toward Old Queens building with his head still spinning.

Now what would he write to her about? He could not think of any time before that he had actually written a letter to a lady. How long a letter should it be? He did not want to scare her off but he definitely did not want to sound so disinterested that he never learned anything about her.

How crazy it was that he had no trouble with advanced math or science but here he was so incapable of putting together two sentences that made any sense when speaking with this woman.

The two ladies had barely spoken when they exited the carriage, stepped from the platform and took their seats on the train. However, as the train pulled from the station back toward Princeton, Mrs. Bell decided it was time to make a point with her daughter.

"Looks like you may have a future gentleman caller, my dear," Mrs. Bell teased her daughter. "That is great because it truly has been a while!"

Elizabeth shot her a glare that could have cut through stone.

"Oh, I know it may just be a letter coming, but I am counting that act as being the start of something good for you," Mrs. Bell continued.

"Really?" Elizabeth shook her head at her mother.

"Oh yes," her mother replied. "Even that is a step in the right direction, dear," and she gently tapped her daughter's arm. "Welcome back to the world of romance!"

"A letter," was all that Elizabeth said back, emphasizing its minimal impact on her life.

Still, as they got on the train and headed back to Princeton, Elizabeth had to admit to herself that she was charmed by the attentions of this young man.

There was something exciting about how this day had gone. In so many ways it was similar even to their original meeting in Princeton. She noticed those butterflies in her stomach were active again for the first time in a long time.

Maybe there is something between the two of us she thought.

Then Elizabeth's practical side started to decipher the message differently from how her heart was telling her to read it. No, that rumbling in her stomach was more likely from the fact that she and her mother had simply not stopped to eat before getting on the train.

She chuckled to herself and, turning her head, saw her mother staring at her.

"Give it a chance, Elizabeth," her mother said before turning away to look out the window on her other side again.

As the train moved toward Princeton, Elizabeth repeated the words to herself.

"Give it a chance." *Okay, but let's wait and see what he actually writes.*

14
October 7, 1869
New Brunswick

They were gathered tightly in a large room at the boarding house where student John Wyckoff resided. It stood along Bayard Street in New Brunswick proper, just outside of the main Rutgers campus grounds.

"Easy guys," John Wyckoff warned the group. "Keep it down! We make too much noise and my landlady down below will chase you all out of here."

"It was a challenge. I was right there when he said it." The student ignored Wyckoff as he spoke, his voice still loud and angry.

The others also seemed to not hear Wyckoff's request and the animated discussion went on oblivious to the fact that the owner of the home where he rented the room would honestly come up and evict them all.

"I think it was meant as a threat!"

"It was just boasting. If not they would have swung at us. They had the chance!"

"We didn't swing at them either and we were also feeling threatened!"

"Those bastards think they are so damn much better than anyone else!"

"Please control your language," Van Neste chastised the other student. "A little respect to those of us who are heading to the ministry."

"Oh, brother. Here we go again. Holier than thou. Forgive me future Reverend, but in here they are the pagan horde and they are threatening our very existence. How about giving us a break on this one?"

"Easy," Williamson cut back in between them. "It was a challenge down in Princeton to compete. That is what has been communicated. Plain and simple."

"With a thick underscoring added in their wording of -- *they have beaten us at everything else*."

"And that is what was intended by them to spark that debate that night at Judge Olden's place. Clearly an intentional push to embarrass us and get our school all wound up," Hawxhurst stated. "Look, I lived down in that area when I went to Lawrenceville School and I know that had to be a pre-arranged plan they had thought out."

"Obviously their plan worked!"

"Look, the real question, regardless of any other outcome or intent, is what we elect to do about it," George Large stated.

"I still say it's just a bunch of bloody arrogant asses there at Nassau Hall, that's all!"

"Seriously!" Van Neste shot back. "Stay focused on the question instead of the insults!"

"I say we take them up on it," Large said.

"Take them up on what?"

"The challenge they supposedly put out there," Large answered.

"But it wasn't anything clearly outlined what they challenged us with?"

"No, but what was clear is the list that they gave about what they feel they have beaten us at."

"Did they really beat our baseball team that badly?"

"Sadly, yes. It was two years ago."

"So we play them at that again? Are we really any better at that sport now?"

"What about the crew meet comment they made? I do not even remember that."

"They were there as an Athletic Club I guess. But if that is accurate, it was really their team."

"So they claim to have started boxing and gymnastics at their college. Maybe that is what they want to try and beat us at next."

"Beat us? That is a lousy defeatist attitude!"

"I didn't say they would beat us only that they claim they can beat us."

"Didn't they also suggest some type of horse race?"

"Maybe. But I think it needs to be more of a team sport. I hate the idea of a one-on-one setting and they have some ringer and they claim they beat us all and it was just their ringer," Large stated.

"So what team sport is there where we can try to beat on them to get our aggression out?"

"What about that football game that we were talking about last year with those league rules that came out of that federation group in England and that they have us running now between ourselves during our punishment sessions after class hours with Atherton?"

"Punishment sessions? I thought it was just a new workout to make us fit?"

"Right! Like they didn't create it to teach us a lesson after the incident in Princeton. Making us march like soldiers in drill formations and run like idiots until we drop. Believe me, that is a punishment technique straight from the military books."

"I do hate the drilling part!"

"Regardless of why we are doing it, I think you may be on to something with the federation football thing. And while I too hate the drilling, I kind of like the football games that we scrimmage with against each other on those days."

"That is what Professor Doolittle was suggesting we get involved with on a regular basis even when the drilling formations end. I think Atherton agreed to it as an option to just running and marching in formation every day because he liked how physical it was."

"And no rifles with live ammunition to shoot at us with!"

"It could actually be to our advantage for a change if they have never played it before down there in Princeton."

"We could start practicing and possibly get an edge."

"Heck, the game is so new we could create some rules that they would never have heard of to turn the game to our advantage."

Van Neste broke back into the conversation.

"You know, they challenge our very ability as men to compete and we sit here and talk about what we should do and how important it is. And then I listen to you give valid reasons why we should accept a challenge of this nature head on. I agree, we should take on this challenge. We owe it to ourselves."

All in the room now listened intently as Van Neste continued to speak.

"But even more we owe it to us and our school, and the reputation of both that we seem to find suffering at the moment, that instead of shrouding what we will play them at in some kind of mystery, shouldn't we come out and openly tell them our plan? That way, if we win, we do not have to feel we tricked them into something or that we have cheapened a victory by some form of deceit."

"I agree with Van Neste," said Large. "We owe it to others to accept the challenge and we owe it to ourselves to be honest in our design of what we are to play."

"Fine. But how do we even go about doing this and getting it started?"

"Well, maybe we put something formal in writing," Clemens suggested.

The group grew silent for a moment as they thought about what was suggested. A formal challenge in written form.

"That may not be a bad idea," someone finally offered up.

"A way to formalize the rules and outcomes provides structure."

"I say we do it that way only if we can use language like they used when they confronted us at the social and insult them with every turn of each phrase back in their faces!"

Williamson laughed now and spoke for the group making the initial idea a formal motion and a unified vote all within one word. "Agreed! How about we think about this tonight and meet over at my place tomorrow on Union Street after dinner to rough out a draft?"

"Sounds like a plan then."

"Maybe we should meet over at Van Nest Hall instead of another tight space like this one."

"Heh!" Wyckoff called out. "What is wrong with my place here?"

"Besides the fact you can't turn around in here without bumping into someone and then apologizing and it smells like sweat and worse than a horse dung unraked street in summer?"

"Nothing," Williamson stepped in between noticing that Wyckoff was getting tired of the teasing after opening up his room to them to meet. "Nothing is wrong with it and we appreciate you hosting everyone here this evening. But if the group gets larger we should meet in a bigger space."

"Okay, we should meet at Van Nest Hall instead," someone suggested.

"Anything else we need to address before we head out?"

"I think we also need to decide upon who will captain our team and actually act as the voice between our two colleges. Things can get pretty confusing if each of us tries to contact them."

"How about Leggett?"

"He's kind of young, isn't he?"

"I suggested him because he is clearly the best player in those scrimmages we have been having with Professor Atherton. He's a natural at the game and speaks well."

"True."

"I agree. He is quick and agile. Fastest man out there."

"He does well calling the scrum is what I like about him. A take charge kind of guy who seems to see the big picture quickly in the game without wasting energy to stop and think about it."

"Is he even going to want to be a part of this? Even his friends this year seem to have trouble locating him as he seems to be constantly at the household of some girl here in New Brunswick."

"He is a man of high character," Van Neste chimed in. "I believe his values and passion for his savior will surely wipe out any talk about his reputation in spending too much time with a girl."

"I don't think anyone was challenging his good moral upbringing. It was just an observation that he might be – distracted."

"I would vouch for him too," Large stated. "I think he will stand up for his mates when called upon. I have no idea about any of his female friend obligations or not. He is dedicated within Delta Upsilon and a natural leader. I think he would be a great choice."

"Anyone object?"

No one called out a veto.

"Okay, then someone needs to invite him to come to our meeting tomorrow."

"I'll do it," Large said after there was a short pause.

"Do you think we need to also alert President Campbell or at least some of the faculty about what we are planning to do?"

"I say we extend the challenge and then see what they think. If the lads at Nassau Hall do not take us up, there is no reason to have discussed it."

"I think we should be upfront and at least let someone in the faculty know," Large stated. "I would be willing to approach Professor Doolittle with the idea. I think I can explain it to him and at least let him decide what we should do."

"I disagree. If the faculty refuses then it could harm our reputation even the worse!"

"What plan would we even share with them?"

"Wouldn't it be worse if we send a challenge and then were not allowed to play?"

"Well let's try to at least get something down on paper first."

"Then we tell someone on staff before we send it?"

"I suppose they are going to find out sometime anyway."

"We just better be sure we know what we are planning to do before we attempt to alert the faculty. Even if Doolittle might appear supportive because he believes in physical fitness and athletics for all on the surface, it does not mean he will support a challenge like this. They may all be against us engaging in anything with the lads down at Princeton after our recent history together."

"Or who knows if his opinion is even the one that would count."

"I still agree with George. We are going to have to tell them some time. I would rather we do it early instead of later."

Turning to George Large now, the student who first suggested not telling the faculty at all simply stated, "You better do a good job of selling it to everyone. Get us a captain. Then get us faculty permission. If you fail we could end up looking like even bigger fools to the lads down in Princeton."

"Or that we are afraid of them."

"Just get it done!"

In so many ways it sounded like a threat. Large did not take it as such.

"I will," Large promised. "I really feel this contest may have a greater purpose to it then we realize. I also feel others, including the staff here at Rutgers, will come to see it that way too."

As they exited from this impromptu meeting, Joen Alfred Van Neste and Thomas Clemens headed over to the Van Fleet's household where Van Neste often stayed to study in the evening.

Jacob Van Fleet had been born in New Brunswick twenty-two years earlier and he had just enrolled at Rutgers that Fall after having worked on his own in the dry goods business for five years. He felt he had a calling for the church and he came back home to his parent's residence in New Brunswick while taking classes at Rutgers College.

His parents seemed to enjoy having him home again as long as he was serious about this new purpose in life with his studies. They did not object to other students congregating in their home as long as it was for academic study.

Van Neste's similar desire with a vocation in the church created a natural bond with Van Fleet and their immediate actions at the start of that term had been to create study sessions where they could both support and challenge each other with their coursework. He had invited Clemens to come with him after he had mentioned some concerns about the paper he was writing involving an ethical issue which asked about Divine intervention in daily life.

Clemens was a year ahead in his studies and his entry into Rutgers College had been created when, as a youth, he had advocated at a town hall meeting for the building of a new school house. Having been raised initially by an Aunt and Uncle in New York City and going in the summer to work as a farm hand in Roicefield, New Jersey; his vocal skill had convinced the locals that he should be sent to further his studies in a college setting.

When Clemens and Van Neste arrived at the Van Fleets, they moved into a room that already held Van Fleet along with two other Rutgers students.

William McKee was from Salem, New York. He was also interested in pursuing a future with the clergy. Like Van Fleet, he had entered Rutgers for the first time that Fall. He had been accepted on special approval as he had struggled with mathematics while his overall understanding of all things religious appealed to the faculty when admissions had been reviewed. Hence, he was there as a student with special standing.

Madison Ball was one of the older students at Rutgers College that Fall. At age 28, he had already experienced a great deal with life in the world having served three years in the army during the Civil War and having previously attended both Knox Seminary and Rutgers Prep School.

"Do all of you know Thomas?" Van Neste introduced the student at his side.

After small pleasantries, Van Fleet asked the obvious question.

"So where have you been?"

"Thomas and I just left a meeting over at Wyckoff's place on Bayard," Van Neste replied.

"A meeting? What kind of meeting, if I may ask?"

"Well, Thomas, I guess it doesn't hurt to talk about." Van Neste looked at Clemens who nodded his approval.

"It seems that the lads down in Princeton sent a letter this way suggesting some form of contest. They indicated that after what had taken place that evening at Judge Olden's home they would like a chance to prove, once and for all, that they are the better college."

"It was even beyond that," Clemens added. "It was like a call to do battle against them. And there on that battlefield they would drive us into the ground."

"Yes," Van Neste admitted. "It was meant to be insulting."

"You would think that they would just leave the issue alone for a while," Van Fleet remarked. "The whole College of New Jersey population has to be aware that we are skating on thin ice up here within our own community after that cannon debacle."

"I don't know," Ball said. "I can see where they might have their fight up right now. I heard that we did get in the last punch, as they say, by painting all over their walls at Nassau Hall while they slept."

"Still, is there any reason to lock horns with us after our own college leadership indicated that we needed to be on our best behavior in the future?"

"I will tell you, when I first arrived at Wyckoff's I was less than interested in engaging anyone in Princeton with anything. But our fellow classmates made a compelling case on the merits of doing something or our reputation as a college may be forever tarnished," Van Neste stated.

Clemens joined in.

"Everything they said earlier did get your blood boiling. The letter was written in such a way that it reeked of an arrogance. It was that same language that makes one detest royals and all those who see themselves as superior to others."

"Careful as we speak of revenge and prideful actions," Van Fleet warned. "It is the very thing that just led to a war within our country where young men's lives were ruined. The Lord does hold us all accountable when we are pursuing anything beyond His work."

"That is true." Van Neste acknowledged the very core of how he had felt earlier. "But I will tell you, that when a group of people threaten to destroy another, there is also Biblical precedent that man is expected to rise to a just cause."

"And you see a contest on the same level as the defense of God's people?"

"Look," Van Neste came back. "I am among those who detest any conflict and always hope that man can find a way through peaceful means to resolve conflicts. Most of you probably know that my father died on the field of battle as a soldier in the Union Army. That loss does come back to me in so many ways by reinforcing the need to seek peaceful means to an end process. But it does not mean that we are to stand idly by as a group attempts to intimidate another or harass them in such a way that it ruins their lives and the good name of those with whom they are associated."

"I agree with Van Neste here." Ball stepped forward as he spoke. "Look, I was injured in the Battle of Donaldson down in Louisiana. I watched good men die all around me as I took part in the siege and assault on Port Hudson. I am sorry to hear about your father. I am sure he was a good man, Van Neste," Ball said as he lowered his voice to show respect.

"But regardless of prior battles fought and the losses that are incurred, one truism always exists. You stand to defend the honor of the institutions to which you believe in. For this, it is our responsibility to never back down in the face of a threat from someone seeking to do harm to another."

"At the same time, this is to be a contest between two colleges. Let us not confuse a game to demonstrate our abilities versus a real battle where lives are lost," Ball declared.

"The similarities abound. This is why when I hear Jacob's reaction I realize it was the same as mine was earlier," Van Neste noted. "But you are correct. This is a peaceful way of resolving a dispute through a game. Hence, there is a potential to right a wrong in a less violent manner."

"I do not know if the contest is any less violent," Clemens corrected. "Football is pretty physical when played against a real opponent."

"You are comparing football to war?" Ball asked Clemens. "What would you know of any such comparison?"

"For what it is worth," Clemens came back at him. "I may not have carried a rifle or been wounded as you were. But I saw my fill of wartime death and violence!"

"Seriously?" Ball stated incredulously. "And how is that even possible given your age?"

"I followed my brother when he enlisted," Clemens explained. "Yes, I was too young to join but that did not keep me from being added to the fife and drum corps for three years. For close to all of those three years I walked soldiers into the line of fire and believe me when I tell you I experienced the same reality of young men dying all around me every day."

"I'm sorry," Ball pulled back. "I did not know. But still, comparing this football game to a war?"

"I did not mean to overstate it," Clemens clarified himself. "But I do see similarities in the way a competition heats up and the intensity it produces when the two sides come together. In no way was that meant as any type of disrespect to those who put their lives in harm's way as they faced down gunfire and cannon blasts. I know they are not the same."

"So this football contest?" McKee now entered the conversation trying to get some clarification. "This is the game that we have been working on with Major Kellogg, Professors Atherton and Doolittle?"

"Yes," Van Neste responded. "We decided that we would pose a team sport of some kind be played as a way of accepting the College of New Jersey challenge."

"Interesting," Van Fleet remarked.

"Interesting or interested?" Clemens asked. "Because as of yet we do not have enough players organized together to field a full team."

"I am not sure." Van Fleet looked at Ball as he replied. "There are several of us who have little time to spend on extra activity outside of our studies. We have come to Rutgers College with an academic purpose and I believe that, at our age, we may not be in a position to be diverted by the distractions of youth that you all may still experiment with."

"Playing in this game does have a purpose," Clemens retorted. "It is about a grander purpose then one's personal studies. For in the end, if we do not fight back against those who attempt to defame the good name of the college we attend, we all lose. The work you will have accomplished here in a classroom will mean little in our society at large if the college's reputation is equated to worthlessness or failure."

"I was irked at the way our lads were treated down in Princeton," Ball observed.

"Well think about it my friend." Van Neste patted Van Fleet on the shoulder. "I too had to wrestle with the concept before throwing in my approval of this pathway."

"But if you do want to join us," Clemens looked at the three who had been at Van Fleet's first. "We are having a planning meeting tomorrow evening where we will generate a letter declaring that we are accepting this challenge and proposing a football game as the means of settling the score. The letter will be sent in the morning post to Princeton."

"So it is full steam ahead?"

"Without question," Clemens answered. "So with you or without you the contest will go on. I just hope that you will consider joining us."

"It also looks like William Leggett will be named the team leader," Van Neste added in a more neutral negotiator tone clearly not wanting to lose the chance they would join the team.

"Leggett?" Van Fleet thought about the name for a moment. "Young fellow and I am aware of him already. He is passionate about his calling with the Church."

"That is the word that is out there about him," Van Neste agreed.

"And he feels it is a good course of action to take even with our busy schedule of studies focused on the Lord's work?" Van Fleet asked.

"Well," Van Neste paused for a moment. "He has not actually confirmed his position as team captain. But George Large is letting him know he has been selected by the others for this important role and I have been told that he is not the type who would let his classmates down."

"George Large talking William Leggett into playing. I can imagine that will be an interesting conversation."

"That it will," Clemens chimed in. "But he was pretty confident and I sense just as passionate about the need to play and win this game."

"I hope he convinces him then," Van Fleet answered.

"So you do care after all," Clemens slapped Van Fleet on the back. "I didn't think you would let your studies keep you from supporting your classmates as a fellow loyal son of Rutgers!"

Van Fleet looked at Clemens before speaking.

"I promise you only today that I will pray on it."

"And if you hear Leggett decides to join us and lead?"

"I will assume he has answered your prayer, Mr. Clemens," Van Fleet replied without committing himself to anything further.

Van Neste then added, "We will know he has answered our prayers when enough loyal sons take the field and not before that."

Van Fleet smiled and nodded at his classmates as he replied. "Understood."

15
"Captain?"
October 8, 1869
New Brunswick

Class ended and the students left the Old Queens classrooms. They sprawled quickly out in various directions from the hillside and into the various parts of the community of New Brunswick.

George Large made a point of walking in step this afternoon with classmate William Leggett.

"So what makes you seem to be in such a hurry today?" Large asked his fellow college mate.

"Each day seems to be shorter than the one before it," Leggett replied.

"Heading to the household of the lovely Miss Parsell, I suppose," Large posed.

Leggett stopped and looked at Large. "And what is it to you if I were?"

"Oh, I did not mean anything of it William," Large stepped back a step as he spoke. "It was just a guess. You missed our last Philo meeting and somewhere I had heard others talking about the amount of time you seemed to be spending there lately. Seems no one has seen much of you lately."

"And, again, what is this to you?"

Large shrugged his shoulders and huffed before starting.

"Look, several of our Rutgers lads were together again yesterday evening. The topic of the events down in Princeton have really gotten a bad hold of them – well me too."

Leggett nodded. "I'm aware."

"Good. Good," Large commented and continued to talk as he and Leggett started to walk again.

"Seems the fellows here are pretty sore about how they felt they have been getting treated by the boys down at the College of New Jersey and the people in Princeton in general. They have been outright obnoxious about everything from these small competitions to an even bigger issue of who has the better college."

Leggett said nothing but continued to listen.

"I suppose there is nothing wrong with them wanting to tout the virtues of their program at their college and even gloat a little about how they have been successful in winning certain competitions lately against us. What really irks us though is how they feel they need to constantly insult our college. They are actually hurting the reputation of our home here in New Brunswick with their words."

"Sounds like a discussion about pride," Leggett interjected at this point. "As we all know it is a true poison. It is a vice, one of the seven deadly sins, for a reason and that is because it can tear others apart and harm them."

"Spoken like a true Reverend, William," George said. "And you can see why we need to do something about it right away."

"Careful, George. That pride enemy can destroy men on both sides of the equation."

"Believe me William, it is the boys down in Princeton who have started it. And they have done it with the intent to cause harm."

"I do not doubt that to be true. However, when you state right off that we need to do something about it you are heading in the wrong direction. Man's mission is not to boast louder to bully the other fellow down. No, that is not the Christian thing to do and not something I would want to be a part of."

"But they are working to destroy the very college we attend. It is your school too!"

"It is. And I will pledge to always do my part to build the strength of this cathedral where I can through good deeds and actions that bring a good name to our college. I am a loyal son of Rutgers no different than you. But I cannot condone actions that simply attempt to harm others to enhance my own gain."

George looked at William and studied him for a moment before speaking.

"Let me get this clear. What you are saying is that you would help to enhance the reputation of the school by helping her improve her image in the eyes of the community and the world. All you are against is not joining in any acts that are intended to tear the opposing school down?"

"Yes, that is a fair assessment."

"Interesting."

Again, George went silent as the two walked ahead again. This time it was William who started their chat back up.

"So why your interest in catching me after class and telling me this today?"

"Well, I have seen your outstanding skills as an athlete with this new sport we have been playing lately. You are especially good at that federation football game."

"It is just exercise, George. A workout that is intended to help strengthen the body to help foster a healthier life and mind. I am not sure I am any more skilled than anyone else out there following our professor's direction in those club activities."

"In part I agree," Large cut back in. "It is a game and there are merits to this exercise. But to the point about you being just another participant, I would tell you that is not accurate. Why just last evening the group all chimed in about your skill and ability in that arena."

"And why are they talking about me?" Leggett asked.

"William, whether you wish to admit it or not, you are a skilled athlete. You have, pardon the expression, a God-given talent with sport and this sport in particular. The lads last night brought your name up in the context of the discussion they were having about the incident in Princeton. It came up because we are thinking of challenging them, or accepting their challenge depending on how one sees it, to a contest of skill and strength. The goal is simple. Prove to them that we are if not better than them then at least we are their equals."

"A contest?"

"Yes, a game of this new modified federation style football. The plan would be to take them on in this arena which we have seen is a new and exciting sport. Our hope is that we win this time. Beat them at it and we can boast as having won a victory that was the first contest of its kind!"

"So we plan to counter their prideful actions with one of our own? Not what I would want to be a part of George."

"William, I think you understand that this is much more than that. This contest is about trying to right a wrong that has been perpetuated in the past."

"History is man's writing of the story, George. The only book that matters to me is God's book, the Bible."

"And I in no way aim to harm that legacy in any manner," Large countered before tactfully repositioning himself to extend his appeal.

"But I also know that there are other values of great importance. Values like loyalty to those in your community and willful intent to better what you have been granted here on earth. Face it William. Rutgers is our home and this community is our community. If we do not attempt to stop an attack of this sort on the reputation of these entities, we fall short of what is expected of us. We fail as men. How do you tell the residents of New Brunswick that we did not stand up for them when faced with the insulting stories that can threaten the very fabric of what our college and community are meant to stand for?"

"So you believe a simple game will right all the wrongs of the past and seal the prideful mouths of Princetonians for all time?" Leggett chuckled. "Be serious George. A game like this changes nothing."

"Oh you could not be any more wrong," Large responded.

"Please!" Leggett smirked.

"I will give you this William. A game may not solve all the problems in the world. But in this situation. This setting. This moment in time. This action is what is called for. It is not just a game for laughs and fun this time. This is about holding one's ground that is their ground. This is about defending not just one's honor, but protecting what is rightfully theirs. This is not just about young college lads doing something for their personal pride."

Large began to sound more emotional as he went along.

"This is about establishing a line – and yes a permanent line – that defines the debate with the Princetonians in territorial terms. We will not go away. We will not be dragged under by their taunts and attempts to defame us. We will not be ruined by the efforts of jealous men who failed to secure a land grant or who seek only to establish their own educational place as unique in the state. Rutgers will not only continue to exist but it will prosper in spite of their attempt to end us altogether. Do you know what they suggested again as it relates to our standing?"

"No, but I am sure you will tell me," Leggett answered.

"They brought back up that we should be relegated to Nassau Hall's prep school. That Rutgers, with its inferior foundation and expectations of its incoming student body should be reconstituted as an educational setting that tutors students to prepare to enter the halls at Princeton versus being an academic bastion of higher learning!"

"It is just talk, George."

"Talk that, if left unchallenged, will eventually destroy what has been built here in New Brunswick. Idle chatter of school boys you think William? That idle chatter sets the seeds of thinking of future leaders. Men who look to reshape all that they can control. Believe me, I heard the talk through those Judges and Senators and leaders of industry who felt that what their Princeton youth were bringing forth was the real record versus a story among youngsters."

"I still think it was just talk. Talk that has been around forever."

"I agree. But think of how powerful that talk becomes."

"Just talk George. We should think twice before we become involved in foolish stories."

"So, William, if your goal as a future clergyman is to unite versus divide, think about this. Take Cain and Abel or any opposing army clash in the Old Testament and what do you have at its roots? The human element of trying to raise one up by crushing their opponent. I do not think that this is the case this time. We are the college who sees not the desire to ruin the other institution but rather be the college who finds a shared academic standing and place with her sister school in Princeton. We only can negotiate from a position of power, William. We can only support our President Campbell by giving him a footing from which to stand on with excellence in academia as well as honor."

"I still am not positive that this is for me, George."

"William, you have the makings of being a leader among men one day. You have a skill as an athlete and you have a talent for setting an example others would want to follow. From that you are sure to be a great religious figure one day. But now – today – your fellow College mates here at Rutgers need you to support them and be a part of them. They need to have, as I said, your God-given tools if we are to establish a future place that is provided the respect we should have as fellow scholars and men."

Leggett glanced at the entryway to the Parsell home and the doorway that separated him from his visit with Mary Eva and her brother John inside before turning back to George Large.

"So what are you asking me to do?"

Large saw a light starting to crack through the interior shade of the window of the house and knew that his time in conversation with Leggett was short.

"Look. Simply come to Van Nest Hall this evening for the Philo normal discussion. It is set to take a different turn." Large sounded as if he was almost pleading with Leggett at this point.

"Meaning?" Leggett asked.

"Tonight will not be about establishing our normal papers for debate. Rather it will be an evening where we help shape an appropriate response to the verbal challenge sent out that night in Princeton."

"The contest," Leggett stated.

"And all the language that goes with such an event."

"Why do I feel that you are pulling me into something that I may regret later?"

Large smiled. "I do not see me in that role at all, good sir. No, I see you leading us at some point. Hopefully you take that mantle of leadership sooner than later. This is our chance at uniting our college in a common cause and saving the reputation of both our school and community."

"Master Leggett," the doorman stated as he stepped out on to the landing in front of the home. "Is everything okay? Miss Parsell had asked that I inquire."

Leggett called back that all was fine and that he would be right there. The doorman nodded but remained positioned on the front step to await Leggett's entry into the home.

"Well I guess your lady friend is awaiting you," Large said.

"Acquaintance. She and her brother as well as her parents are all my friends." Leggett corrected him. It had the tone of voice of the warning sound of a man who did not accept any challenge to the integrity of his relationships or to the reputation of the young lady who belonged to a family to which he felt favor.

Large smiled again. "Seven o'clock," he noted as he started to walk away. "Van Nest Hall second floor. Same room as we meet for Philo. I hope to see you there."

Leggett said nothing but simply moved forward and disappeared into the home.

As he walked back down the streets of New Brunswick, Large began to recall the same haunting strands he had heard from summer and as he had ridden to school at the start of that term. The word "purpose" reverberated amidst the sound of marshal music and his mind drifted again to the men standing to honor the Union cause by the bandstand back in his home town.

Large glanced one more time toward the home of the Parsell's.

Positioned on a main stretch, it was just a short distance from the main Rutgers campus. As he turned back up Church Street to get to his destination, he glanced back at the finely kept entranceway and the neatly painted shutters and frame. It was not ostentatious in any way. It was the type of home a family whose father held a respected position in the community would own.

Inside he was sure that Mary Eva's father, or at least her mother, was present to chaperone the visit of the young Rutgers College student. There was no way even the intervention on their conversation by the doorman had been orchestrated by simply Mary Eva sending the servant outside that day.

Large wondered what Leggett would share with the young lady. Large had never met her nor knew anything about her. And Leggett was as serious about his academic time as any student on the campus. He wondered if the young girl would admonish him from pursuing anything beyond his studies or his attentions for her if they did have something special going on.

Large thought about what Mr. Parsell would think. Would he counsel Leggett that this game would be a waste of time? Would he see it as having a purpose? Would he realize the importance of Leggett accepting a role of responsibility with his peers and acting in a manner of leadership?

Or would Mr. Parsell act as so many already removed from college life would and suggest that young William not be distracted by a trivial activity and fail to see it was meant to be in the pursuit of something grander.

Large thought about his own father and the voice that would probably opine the same way. Time is money and the business of man is business. These games are not about money and they produce no viable product for the well-being of a country so therefore it does not qualify as a business.

If his father were in the mix Large was sure his father would confront the staff at Rutgers, maybe even the President himself, to demand that the young men not idle their time away on distractions of this kind.

Still, Large could not separate his thoughts about how important his contest may actually be. It served a purpose, he kept repeating to himself. Sometimes it is about the game.

As he moved away from the Parsell's residence he thought once more about the personality and qualities of William Leggett.

Leggett was an excellent athlete, no question. Leggett was a quality individual with strong religious values, no question. Leggett possessed that natural skill to lead others, no question. But would he join the cause?

Large knew that Leggett's reporting to Van Nest that night would mean there was a chance. He walked away unaware of what was transpiring within Leggett's head inside the Parsell household.

Would Leggett even consider what had been raised?

16
New Brunswick

Leggett was intrigued and he wasted no time in telling Mary Eva what had just been discussed.

Like so many other young college men away from their homes, he had felt lonely and estranged at times. Leggett was no different from the others who sought out the company of locals to fill the void of friends left behind as they arrived in distant college towns. While academics were the rationale for the experience, life continued and the social growth and development was intertwined with the regular basic curricular instruction.

He met Mary Eva Parsell shortly after his arrival in New Brunswick. She was several years younger. But she and her brother, John, had become like family to him. Both let him into their family circle and he had enjoyed meeting her father, Major Parsell, who also was there for good counsel.

While Mary was younger, she was full of energy and always anxious to hear anything William would share about his studies or thoughts about life in general. True, she was a female and most males sought male companionship for matters of the mind. Still, she was a good listener.

Their initial chats had felt "comfortable." Their relationship clearly had developed as they spent time together. He enjoyed the company of her family as well. They were welcoming people who were happy to support the youth who journeyed in each year to New Brunswick for the College.

Eventually, Mary Eva had become a trusted confidant for him in this New Brunswick community away from the schoolboy dominated environment of the campus. The advantage many Rutgers students shared was that, while they did not live in one common dormitory like many of their peers down in Princeton at Nassau Hall did, they were able to interact on a different level with the locals as borders within the homes of the community.

"So they are back at it again." Mr. Parsell who was home when Leggett arrived shook his head. "You know, I heard the conversation about the cannon escapades and thought to myself at that point, one time we need to get that thing back here!"

"Oh father," Mary Eva stated. "Don't you go joining the next hunting party and go and get yourself arrested."

"Oh they wouldn't catch me," the senior Parsell laughed. "Too sophisticated to get caught up actually being there versus cheering our lads in action."

"So what do you think of the game challenge?" Leggett asked Mr. Parsell. "Do you see it as a waste of time for young men who are supposed to be engaged in their studies?"

"I guess I am not exactly sure about the sport itself," he answered. "From what I have seen and heard, it is a kind of a physical group activity that resembles bedlam versus a gentleman's sport like rowing or horses."

"It is rough. I can attest to that. But it is a true team sport," Leggett clarified. "It does bring a group together in a way that an individual contest often divides even members of one's chosen side."

"A lot to be said for that," Parsell stated. "Especially in light of why they seem to want to play."

"I think it would be fun." Mary Eva joined back in with no hesitation, a rare social action on her part due to the fact that she was a girl in her father's home. "All that rushing about and being able to be called the victor."

"I guess if it is just that, it is not something I would wish to do," Leggett said. "But the idea that it helps solve the fighting between the schools. My classmate George Large had predicted that such a contest could end the evil bickering and growing hatred with the lads in Princeton. I do like the thought of that accomplishment."

"Personally, I do not see an ending to the squabbles between communities or any of the boastful habits of men," Mr. Parsell responded.

"At least not from a game or any singular battle. Unfortunately whatever caused the original divide is rarely erased."

His military background often played out in the words he selected when speaking with anybody and especially when he was around young people. It was this common habit that led most to still refer to him as "Major" when they saw him in the community.

"As I well know from my experiences, wars do not end internal feelings or original desires between combatants that brought them first to do battle. But these fights do have the potential to draw boundary lines between sides. And like you said when your fellow classmate enjoined you, a contest on this level could restore a level of confidence within the victor. I also believe that when fought well, there is even a new found respect for the opponent who lost. However to ensure the change you want, the key is always to win."

"I agree you could get respect by how the game was actually played," Mary Eva stated. "There is honor even in a loss when the efforts are seen as valiant. Think of the story of Sparta and the Battle at Thermopylae."

"Sounds like the storylines in the books you have read are expanding," her father smiled at her. "There are times when I believe the greatest thing I have ever done as a parent was encouraging you to read."

"So you think I should participate in this game?" Leggett asked them both.

"I hope for more than that," Mary Eva started. "I would hope that you would follow the request of George and lead your classmates with a high level of chivalry and possibly even to victory."

"I agree with my daughter. Oh what I would give to be there and feel that energy. There is something beautiful about the camaraderie of soldiers on the field of conflict. And, as Mary Eva has already said, if offered one should always agree to take the mantle of leadership."

"I agree with my father. I hate how the people of Princeton have spoken about the college here in our town. New Brunswick has so much more to offer when compared with a little village like Princeton."

"I think you misunderstand the motive," Leggett cut back. "If we play it is not to try and do harm to Princeton or even the reputation of the College of New Jersey. The point is that we engage in a contest to re-earn their respect. In winning they see how we foster a common bond in the future toward a better pathway for both communities."

"Spoken like an amazing future clergyman," Mr. Parsell stated and patted the young man gently on his back. "But I would keep in mind as it pertains to your troops currently enrolled at Rutgers here in the present;

the leadership they are seeking is one that helps build up that challenge so that others they compete against feel the importance. In turn, this is what develops the character of your men. They are needing the skills of a leader where he ignites the passion of his teammates to want to give more when they are weakening."

"True. True." Mary Eva agreed.

"But more than that," Mr. Parsell continued. "The good people of New Brunswick, like myself and my daughter here, would both love to see our lads at Rutgers establish themselves in a manner that no one in Princeton in the future can ever say we are any less than them!"

As Leggett walked along the grass pathway up toward Van Nest Hall that evening the words of Mary Eva's father repeated again and again.

Step one, as outlined by the old military leader from a war so recently fought, was very clear. Leggett as a leader needed to help establish a challenge that would leave no question in the mind of the opponent that this competition had meaning.

Leggett took a quick glance skyward. It was his regular habit whenever he communicated with his divine leader and shared a hope that this would not be seen as an act not in God's favor.

With that, Leggett stepped into Van Nest Hall.

He knew this action would signal to all those present his willingness that he would do what was being asked of him. There would be no backing out now.

Immediately he was greeted with a cheer by his fellow Rutgers mates who were assembling there.

"William Leggett, are we glad to see you!"

George Large stepped forward and offered Leggett his hand.

"Welcome to the meeting, Captain."

17
"Challenge Defined"
October 11, 1869
Princeton

"Have you read what it says?"

The question was asked again to no one in particular among those present in the room at Nassau Hall.

Several young men huddled closely around each other. They leaned in toward a single figure who was seated at a table in the center of the group. This student held three sheets of handwritten note paper tightly with both of his hands. These sheets of paper, in turn, were tilted toward a candle on the table next to him in an attempt to get the best light available to read within this cramped dark room.

"Yes, and hush up so that I can repeat the part that I think we need to hear again."

"*To those who think they represent the good state of New Jersey because they have been called the College of New Jersey think again. They call you this only because of the old age of your building.*"

"Seriously!?!" A different voice cut in, having already memorized the taunt written within the opening phrase of the letter sent to them from these upstart fools at Rutgers College.

"Shut up and listen!"

"Let him read!"

"*We hope you do not feel too feeble or incapable of partaking in a contest of skill and physical rigor as well as one of endurance that can help shape the standing between our colleges in a fair setting as co-institutions of scholastic excellence and learning where great minds are developed and the common purpose of both our colleges can be praised-*"

"What does that even mean?"

"Is it an insult or some type of a request that we take them seriously?"

"Feeble or incapable?"

"After we have demolished them or beaten them at any opportunity?"

"As if they could even stand a chance?"

"To think they think they could ever be considered our equals?"

Big Mike stood within the group circle and hunched forward. His large body always commanded a presence wherever he went and all eyes focused in on him. He put up his open hand and instantly the group's chatter paused to allow him to speak.

"Look, regardless of the trash that is clearly placed in this letter to make us angry, the question has been called about whether we are up for a challenge."

There was collective cheering from "Hell yes" to "Damn right" throughout the room.

"So the question, as I see it, is not whether we care about their infantile attempt at insult but rather whether we want to accept their terms to play."

Instantly there was a chorus of objections about allowing Rutgers College to dictate the terms of the contest.

"Why should we do what they want?"

"I don't think they should dictate anything!"

"I don't think we should have to travel to play them there for this first contest if they are the one's issuing the challenge."

"The rules they list do not match how we have been playing this sport. What about the free kicks?"

"Do we really agree with that scoring? The game won't last long enough and they'll want to make the score higher to qualify as a win while they are losing."

"Really, it doesn't even sound like we get anything out of this."

"They want to play us to regain their pride? Let them come here and try to do it!"

"I disagree," Gummere's voice cut in.

Everyone there turned back to face the dissenting opinion. Gummere was still seated at the table next to the candle that had given him the light when he had read the letter.

"Let's take a look at what was written at face value. They want to be our equal. They want to be considered as good as us in some way. If our purpose is to prove that they are not, then we accept the challenge as presented, on their terms, and we destroy them once and for all by beating them on their own terms. It fits with our own College President McCosh's message to us. Stand up and prove all others wrong by our actions. Do it because of who we are and not by some trickery or pretense of our past laurels."

"I agree with Gummere," Billy Buck announced. "After we crushed them in baseball the first thing they came up with were excuses about the layout of the field and the way the membership of the teams were arranged."

"Billy is correct. They whine about that game even today years later."

"Probably because they cannot forget such a beat down!"

"My vote is what Gummere said. Beat them now on their terms and there are no excuses they can make afterward."

"Losers always make excuses."

There was scattered laughter but slowly the side chatter stopped and the objections to competing whittled away.

"So we agree to play as they requested."

"We respond in a humble manner," a voice suggested.

"Men from Nassau Hall are never humble," Gummere stated back. "We will be cooperative and in this case amenable to their request to be given a chance at redemption. But we still remain true to our standing. We stay true to our position. We stay true to our place as THE College of New Jersey as the best, and in most eyes, the only true college in this state."

Several in the group cheered the boast.

"I say we elect Gummere to be our leader!"

"Yes, Will for team captain, in this venture!"

"So young Will Gummere becomes our captain and we accept the terms. Do you think we should go over one more time what they are actually suggesting so we all know what we are agreeing to?"

"Yes. Yes. Back to the playing rules again," Charlie Darst stated and took the paper from the table where Gummere had placed it and he began to read what was in the letter.

"Proposed rules of the game..."

He proceeded to read out loud the rules, one at a time, after noting that there were roughly ten in all.

What the listeners quickly learned was that each of the rules included several particulars. It started first with the playing field which was outlined with the size of the field at 360 feet long by 225 feet wide and two goals on each end spaced 8 paces apart. The letter next set each team at 25 active participating players on each side.

Game play itself was to consist of ten segments or periods and each one ended by a score with a short break to follow. There was no time clock or time limitation. The first team to six scores would end the contest itself and the team with six scores would be declared the winner.

"Or it could just say, when we reach six we simply declare them the losers."

"Those Rutgers chaps are already a bunch of losers!"

This was followed by a loud round of laughter from the group assembled there listening.

"Gentlemen, back to the rules of the game," Darst brought the group to order to get their focused task completed. He then started to read through the letter with the rest of the rules.

There was an explanation of how the ball could be batted by hand or kicked and dribbled. There was also a clear explanation that no one could catch the ball and then throw it forward again. While full contact was allowed there was to be no intentional tripping or holding of an opposing player from behind when he did not have the ball. An out of bounds rule, when the ball escaped the field of play, indicated how it would be put back in play.

To start the game, an opening kickoff after a coin toss would take place. In addition, a kickoff would be held after each score to the opposite team. There would be six officials in the mix with two designated as referees and four as judges.

When the reading of the rules were completed, a silence fell over the group while they let it sink in.

Gummere was the first to speak up.

"It sounds pretty standard to what we have already been playing here."

"I agree," Darst added placing the papers he had just read from back on the table next to Gummere. "I would say it is much the same as we have been doing here in our college during our intramural recreational activities with the exception of the free kicks we noted earlier."

"I see some differences," Big Mike stated. "But you know I sort of like that where we have unopposed attempts with kicks they are suggesting that we can plow straight into those little buggers and run them right over into the ground."

"And I can see you being the one to run them over Big Mike!"

"You bet you will," Big Mike answered back, flexing both arms to show off his muscular frame to the group's delight.

"So while there are some technical differences, the general consensus is the rules are similar," Gummere summarized their thoughts.

Heads nodded in agreement.

"So, what is our first step now?"

"We tell them we accept the challenge they proposed to our challenge."

"How do we accept the challenge?"

"In a way that makes them know we are ready, willing and able to beat them down at any time, any place, and in any manner they so choose to be beaten!" Gummere declared.

"I say we go up there and nail it to the door just like Martin Luther and pronounce our intent to all at Rutgers College that we will decimate them at any time, with any game, and at any place just like we have done in the past."

"Whether we nail it or mail it, we need to write our response to this first," Gummere said as he held the Rutgers letter high in his hand.

The group cheered and the serious work of putting together a first draft of their letter with accepting the challenge was begun.

18
October 14, 1869
Rutgers Campus

"So now what?" George Large asked.

He stood with William Leggett outside the steps of Old Queens building. His voice had a sense of frustration in it as he spoke in a quicker tempo then he normally would.

"He was supposed to be there last week when we were in training and he was not. We go ahead and send the message to Princeton, mind you, without my desire to do such. We have not alerted any faculty here before we did it to get approval. We all say, no problem, Professor Doolittle will support us. Now we find out he is not available for another week?"

Large moved around now and started pacing. He pounded his fist into the open palm of his other hand.

"This is bad, William. This has the potential to be very bad!"

"Look George," Leggett finally replied in a slower and softer voice while patting his classmate's shoulder in an attempt to calm him down. "You know I agree with all you are saying. It would have been better to have gotten word to the faculty before today."

"Today?" Large semi-exploded. "Today is late in my view and you know that! They probably have already read what we sent and are formulating a response. What if they tell their faculty first and our faculty gets word after that. How will that seem when we never told them?"

"I understand, they will be angry."

"Angry? Do you think William?" Large's pacing turned more to an anxious stomping about now.

"Look George, what is done is done. We need to figure what we do next. Backward thinking only builds regrets. We can offer an apology but we cannot change the past."

"Lovely William! Just lovely," Large spit out. "Bottom line is that this can all blow up in our faces if we do not get to someone on staff now. I cannot even think of the embarrassment if our Rutgers faculty comes back and tells us that we cannot play after the men in Nassau Hall agree to take us on. You helped write the letter. We both signed it. You know what it said!"

"And I also agree that to not play will be a blow to our school's reputation from which we might never recover," Leggett cut in. "But jumping up and down out here gets us nothing. The fact is Professor Doolittle is out of town. He is not returning for a while. Hence, the simple solution is to tell someone else."

"Again, William, that sounds fine in theory. But who other than Doolittle do you trust would support us especially knowing that most of the others that we see every day appear to be against anything that would cause us to deviate from our studies?"

"You don't know that," Leggett stated.

"Seriously, I think that I do. How about Dr. Cooper or Reilly? Want to ask either of them what they think?" Large offered.

Leggett took a deep breath to stay calm in the midst of the human meltdown in front of him.

Large was correct, most of the staff in the Classical Section to which both he and Large belonged, tended to be on the conservative side of things. Doolittle had appeared as an exception from both of their experiences in the classroom.

But Leggett refused to believe that. Simply because they did not know the true feelings of the others on the staff from how they performed in the classroom, it did not mean that they might not be sympathetic to their cause. Surely there had to be someone who they could approach and feel a sense of common bond with a proposal that would enhance the reputation of the school.

"How about Reverend Campbell, the President himself?" Large's comment broke into Leggett's thoughts and brought him back to the immediacy of his environment. "I cannot even imagine walking into his office and requesting a meeting. Let alone, can you imagine asking him what he thinks a about a game with another college at this time?"

"Easy George," Leggett tried to calm him down. "You and I both applauded for him when he spoke about the cannon decision in this very hall."

"And then he sends us on bended knee to Princeton to apologize!"

"I'm not saying that he is the right man to go to. All I am suggesting is that we calmly try to look over our options without bursting like a firecracker."

"Hey guys," a voice called out to them.

It was Robert Adrain, a fellow student in the Classical Section and a friend of both Large and Leggett as a well-known baseball player on campus. He was accompanied by a second student, John Herbert, who neither Large nor Leggett knew very well.

"Hey Robert," Leggett was the first to respond. "What are you up to today?"

"I am coming here with John to meet with Professors Cook and Murray," Adrain stated. Then turning toward his companion he introduced him to the other two students.

"Pleasure to meet you," Leggett said as both he and Large shook his hand.

"The same," Herbert answered politely back.

"The famous Professor Cook," Leggett repeated, as if pondering the name for some further purpose. "I hear that since he built that new home of his and then comes here and climbs the steps of the observatory, no one sees him anymore."

"Oh that is not true," Herbert immediately defended the man. "He is always available to the students. He just happens to be highly engaged in so many different projects he can be hard to track down at times. But he is by far the most intelligent and inspirational man in his field that you could hope to meet."

"So what is the reason you have to come back to meet with him today?" Leggett continued.

Herbert took a step back. He did not even know this fellow student and instantly he appeared to be spying on his very actions. Still, there was something warm and inviting about how this fellow Leggett spoke.

So, instead of blowing him off, Herbert replied, "Basic delivery of some information that he had requested. Nothing special I assure you. He needed some numbers that related to a field survey and he had indicated he would be here in a meeting with some staff today."

"Interesting," Leggett appeared to be processing as he said it. "And Dr. Murray is there too?"

"Yes," Herbert said. "Or so that is what I had been told."

Leggett glanced over at Large who seemed to fully understand suddenly where Leggett's questions were heading. Large shrugged back in his direction with the body language suggesting, *Sure, what could it hurt?*

"I know it may seem a little forward but, do you mind if we go with you? I mean, would you be okay if we go and see the good professors as you go deliver your survey materials?" Leggett asked.

It was now Herbert's turn to look at the student who had accompanied him on this task.

"I don't see why we would care," Adrain answered, looking at Herbert as he spoke. "Any special reason you would want to do that?"

"Well, to be honest, as we always should be," Leggett began. "George and I were looking for a faculty member to whom we could share some information today and he is not available. Hence, we feel that the information that we need to share still needs to get to someone on the faculty and we were not sure who else we could confide in that we knew."

Picking up where Leggett had started, Large joined in. "Professor Doolittle was to be our point of contact today. But he is out of town. We were hoping to speak with him as he is known as one who has a reputation for having a more sympathetic ear toward student daily life issues."

"And both Professor Cook and Dr. Murray, while I do not know them personally, have the same reputation on campus as being men who envision the future versus staff who may be more bound by convention and rules." Leggett paused for a moment while he watched Herbert let the words sink in.

"You are not planning some kind of revolution or prank, are you?" Herbert asked.

"Prank, no," Leggett smiled. "What we wanted to speak to them about was more about a formal contest and getting the faculty's permission for such an event."

"And if you do not mind my asking, if this is a contest like some classical society debate why would men like Cook or Murray even care?"

Leggett did not hesitate to respond. "This, John, is not a classical debate but rather a competition of physical skill. We have sent a challenge to Princeton for the students in the college there to play us in a football game. Rutgers College versus the College of New Jersey."

"It has as much to do with trying to restore pride in our own school from those who feel it is their position to stand and mock us at this time," Large added. "It is an attempt to change the dialogue that is running rampant in the streets that we, here at Rutgers, are in some way inferior to those same age lads who attend classes in Nassau Hall."

"You see, John. This is less a game between two colleges and more a battle to earn the respect that we, as fellow scholars and young men building the future in a common fashion for this great nation, feel we deserve." Leggett placed a hand on Herbert's shoulder as he finished speaking and added one last question.

"So -- are you okay with that as a reason we join you in your meeting today?"

19
Rutgers

"Well young Master Adrain, I have to say it is a pleasure having the opportunity to meet with you today. Your grandfather still stands as the foundation from which this entire Rutgers College math department rose from. You know we all owe him a debt of gratitude for putting us on a pathway to excellence."

Professor Murray continued to shake the student's hand as he spoke.

"I consider his work as a great example from which I have fashioned my own career."

Robert Adrain nodded at the compliment for his relative. Several decades earlier his grandfather had been a mathematician and professor at the original Old Queens College and again after it changed its name to Rutgers College. Robert was often told about his grandfather's ability as a writer and how often his research was referenced by others as Murray was doing this day.

"You know, Robert's grandfather gave the first proof of flaws with Gauss' Distribution in Probability Theory showing that errors where distributed in a bell-shaped curve. Never gets the full credit but there is no denying that he was the first to do so."

"Interesting factoids," Professor Cook smiled from his chair.

"Truly a legend in mathematics," Murray praised the elder Adrain to his grandson.

"Interesting to remember he also taught at a time when he had to teach all the higher level courses. He also left Rutgers just in time to go to Columbia as this very building was turned over to the Dutch Reformed Church to be converted into both a dormitory for a Reverend from the Theological School and a boarding corral for a cow they owned," Cook laughed.

"Okay, Okay," Murray waved his hands at Cook. "I get the message. Too much history and too much hero worship. Still your grandfather was a great man," Murray smiled at Robert.

"Agreed," Cook stated. "So, dispensing with the past, what is it that we can help you respectful young scholars with today?"

"Well, Professor Cook," Herbert began again after the interruption from his introduction of his companion Robert Adrain. "We delivered the mineralogy reports we had discussed. We also have a folder here with the information sent to me from my father alerting you to the civil engineering points you had asked about in his area of the state."

"Excellent work, son."

"Robert and I also ran into these two fellow classmates here as we were entering to deliver this to you. They requested a moment to speak with you and I am sorry that we did not ask first if they could come along."

Herbert now nodded toward Leggett who took his cue.

"Sirs," William Leggett stepped forward. "Let me start by apologizing by bursting in on you unannounced in this manner. In no way did we plan to interrupt your day and would not have done so unless we did not have what we feel is an important matter that should be shared with a member of the faculty."

The tone was serious enough that Cook sat straighter in his chair as he asked, "And who are you son?"

"I am William Leggett, sir, Rutgers Class of '72. This is my fellow classmate, George Large. We are both in the Classical Section so we have not had the opportunity to actually meet you before in any formal manner-"

Before he could continue, Professor Murray broke in.

"George Large? So you are the young chap who John Voorhees was visiting when I ran into him back on campus a few weeks back," Murray announced. He looked pleased at being able to match a face and a name.

"Yes, sir," Large replied somewhat surprised by the revelation that the professor was aware of any prior interaction he would be having on a social level.

"How is the young lady he spoke about? Mr. Voorhees indicated he was sharing a package with you on her behalf," Murray asked.

Leggett immediately shot a look at Large. The visual look carried no verbal statement but it clearly transmitted a clear message that would have said, "You chided me about my personal relationships and yet you have girls of your own on your mind?"

Large, trying to ignore Leggett at his side, answered rather sheepishly to the professor, "She is well."

"And a good woman friend I would say having Mr. Voorhees carry that item all the way from his place of business for you," Murray added.

Large felt Leggett's eyes burning on him.

"She is actually my sister, Dr. Murray. Her name is Hannah Mary and she is married to Mr. Voorhees. John is my brother-in-law."

It was now Large's turn to smirk in Leggett's direction.

Leggett shook his head as if trying to clear it from the information that had just been shared about Large and redirected his attention back to the matter at hand.

"Well sir," Leggett explained. "Our purpose today was to alert someone on staff about an action several of our Rutgers students, George Large and myself included, have engaged in."

"Do tell," Cook implored him to go on.

Leggett's voice was clear and confident as it walked through the divide that engulfed the two colleges and threatened the well-being of the future for their community.

"It appears that the students at the College of New Jersey have started a campaign to attempt to ruin our reputation here at Rutgers. In their deliberate actions they have brought about statements and writings which they have gone to great lengths at sharing with all who will listen that the quality of the student at Rutgers College is less than desirable."

"In their remarks they have highlighted historical stories that I know did not show well with the recent exploits of several of our fellow students in their failed raid down at Princeton in attempting to re-secure the cannon."

Leggett continued to outline the prior history that had built this rivalry.

He then shifted gears to focus on the animosity that now seemed so prevalent between the two colleges. He even included the work that both professors present had played such an integral role in, the Morrill Act grant, as a part of this current tension.

"So many of us feel that this jealousy has spilled over to where the conversation between students and the dialogue between communities is no longer healthy in anyone's estimation. It has turned to intentional hurtful acts on the part of those in Princeton to defame us as individuals and, collectively, as a college."

"Hence the near altercation reported back from the social event at Judge Olden's that night in Princeton," Dr. Murray stated.

"That is correct sir," Large chimed in.

"You are well aware, I would think, that our faculty was there and witnessed first-hand the interactions that night." Murray's comment was directed to Leggett.

"So what is this critical message you are asking to share?" Cook asked, shifting the conversation from a historical recounting of events past and toward the actual proposal the boys had intended to discuss.

"That evening, in Princeton, there were students as you know from Nassau Hall who confronted our lads. The conversation was not just taunts about historical events of cannon ownership or lost baseball games. The talk was more of a threat with a statement that they would continue to beat us at anything in the future," Leggett said.

"They essentially put out for all to hear that not only had we failed in the past we were now too frightened to accept any challenge from them again in the future," Large clarified.

Leggett moved a step closer to his classmate as he spoke to give a unified perspective.

"So together, students here at Rutgers have processed what they said and they have deliberated on what we should next do. George here, helped me see that to not respond in some viable manner left us in a position where the divide would become even wider. To fail to act now could create irreparable harm to the reputation of our college."

Large took over.

"A small group of us met first. Then more students were added. The basic goal was to find an action that we could take which would show the boys back in Princeton that we were their equals. The plan was simple. Get them in an environment where we could provide the lesson that Rutgers students were not to be messed with any longer."

"So you have planned to go fight them?" Murray asked.

"Not exactly," Leggett responded.

"Although the thought did cross our mind that first night we were reviewing options," Large admitted.

Leggett went on to explain how the contest format they selected was football.

He detailed that they had picked the sport for several reasons. First, it was a new sport. It was just evolving and a head to head show down would not have any prior conceived notions that someone had beaten the other at this before.

Secondly this was a very physical game. Thinking of what Mary Parsell had stated when she first heard of the contest and her reference to the Spartans Leggett added that when over, regardless of the outcome, no one could challenge the other's manhood if they had held their own on the field of battle.

Third, short of war, it allowed for aggressions to be carried out in a manner that through the exertion of energy no further physical fighting afterward would needed.

Finally, this was truly a team sport. Instead of a single athlete standing for an entire college, like a boxing match, this provided a forum where two large groups were there for their school. Together and united this group did represent a bigger part of each college population on the field of play.

After Leggett finished explaining the dynamics of why the sport was chosen, he outlined the process in which the challenge had been written down and sent on to the students already at the College of New Jersey.

Leggett then provided their closing remarks.

"While we still do not know what the reply would be from Princeton or if the lads at the College of New Jersey even have the desire to accept the challenge or not, we are worried that the faculty here might upon hearing this not let us follow through with this contest. It has dawned on us that Rutgers College staff may not see this contest as appropriate in some manner after the prior events in Princeton and the faculty may forbid us to play."

"Such an action of having to withdraw our intent to participate would be more than embarrassing for the individuals involved," Large emphasized.

"Our greatest fear," Leggett concluded. "Is the message not playing would send about the entire college. It would be seen as if we are afraid of the College of New Jersey after all. And that, good sirs, would mean the end of our college as we know it."

Leggett's final words were met with a protracted silence.

Both Cook and Murray looked at each other as if they were thinking the same thing.

How often they had heard similar themes coming from their own faculty meetings. How often they had heard the missives from President Campbell himself lamenting both that the relationship between the two

New Jersey colleges appeared broken and, even worse, that the college in Princeton for whatever reason was seen as the true College of New Jersey and that Rutgers College was always perceived as the "other" college in the state.

Professor Murray was the first to speak.

"I respect the passion gentlemen," he began. "And what did you say you were studying for again, Master Leggett?"

"I would like to pursue theology, sir."

"Such a waste," Murray blurted out before correcting himself. "Such a waste for science, I mean. Obviously God needs great soldiers in the war to save men's souls. But the field of science could also use that passion and reasoning you just displayed."

"Thank you sir."

"Well gentleman," Professor Cook rose from his chair. "I am, like Dr. Murray here, duly impressed with your passion and skill as orators. I am also pleased to hear the feelings you share about our college. As for your proposal, be sure to know that we will share this in some capacity with others on the faculty in the immediate future."

"So," Large asked. "Does this mean we need to wait for some formal response?"

"Honestly," Murray replied. "I do not see a reason why you should not continue on your current path with the expectation of participating on your chosen dates. As long as this is scheduled when no student misses classes or chapel and it does not interrupt anyone's study schedules, I do not see how anyone on the faculty would intervene."

"Still," Cook added. "We will bring it forward and share with others on staff. The faculty do need the opportunity to express their thoughts about such an activity between colleges. While my colleague here sees no obstacles to approval, I think we need to give the rest of our esteemed instructors a chance to review and agree before we speak for them."

"Fully understood," Leggett nodded.

"Good then," Murray smiled. "We will bring it forward for the faculty's formal approval."

"Thank you both," Leggett shook their hands. Large followed in the same manner.

Adrain and Herbert said their goodbyes and headed out the doorway toward the exit. Leggett and Large started to follow them.

"One other thing," Murray called out before the students left the room.

"Yes sir?" Leggett and Large turned back to hear what was being asked of them.

"It would be nice if you beat those lads from Princeton when you do take them on!"

Murray and Cook were both smiling as the students left the facility.

"I don't know David," Cook stated as they watched the boys walk away. "Sometimes I wonder if you and I are not at the very center of the reason this controversy is growing to such a pitched battle."

"You sound like Campbell there," Murray replied. "Better be careful with shifting too close to his line of thought though."

"Seriously, they can babble about cannons and little athletic contests all they like. But you know as well as I, that what is bubbling up right now all comes back to the hostility on the part of the souls down there at Princeton who had their feathers ruffled when we were awarded that grant versus them."

"Indeed I am aware of that."

Murray paused as he looked back around at the older furnishing that adorned the room. Hardly an impressive set of trappings for a group of men engaged in the state's highest level of academic work.

"In the end, my dear friend, I do believe that it does all come down to the money," Murray observed.

Cook patted his friend on the shoulder and prepared his exit from the building for the day.

"Whether it is the wealth of the many or the few, the reality is that money always gets equated to power. Power likes to be perceived as being on the side of the winner. Colleges need financial supports to exist. It also needs those financial supports for the expansion of future research. Let's hope this little scheme these lads have planned help turn the tide to those with money once again having the faith that our students are winners with a college worth investing in."

"Agreed," Murray nodded. Then, as if remembering the last thing he had spoken to the two students about, he looked at Cook and asked, "So you really do not think there will be any objection from the faculty with the boys playing in this contest against the lads in Princeton?"

"Why would anyone object?"

Murray shook his head. "I can think of some who might not want us mixing with anyone in Princeton again after the most recent events for fear that it could soil our reputation further if the lads were seen as acting poorly in another public display."

"Hopefully they will carry themselves as fine sportsmen," Cook countered.

"Some might see it as an interruption to their studies," Murray added.

"Pure poppycock," Cook blew off the thought. "They need time to develop both their minds and bodies and what could be better than an event like this that would be an exhilarating contest of skill and strength for two sets of college students."

"I suppose," Murray responded in the face of Cook's confidence.

"Oh there may be those who will doubt and will object to almost anything. But to get this off the ground for them, it is really all about timing and how it gets presented to the final decision makers on this one. But nothing new about that, Dr. Murray, as you know that is always the main strategy to get anything accomplished which one wants in life."

20
October 15, 1869
Rutgers Campus

Murray sat with President Campbell in his office at the President's House and looked over the letter that had been shared with him.

"You can see why I would be irritated, can you not?" Campbell asked.

"Without question, sir."

"There are times where I think we are making headway and then – this!"

"The language is clear. There can be no mistaking what is written here. At the same rate, do we really know if that is the intent of this letter on his part?"

"I think that is just as clear Dr. Murray. His way with that phrase—"

"Ugly and at the same time provocative," Murray analyzed.

"Nicely said." Campbell stood and lit his pipe. The action of the smoke pulling through him and into his lungs seemed to have a calming effect on his whole demeanor.

"So David, what do you think we should do in reply?"

Murray looked over the letters again. The phrase, *we feel pity in how your current state has befallen you and wish that there were some way that we could assist in helping at least prop you up temporarily while you figure out some new plan for your future*, spilled out with the venom it was intended to deliver.

McCosh's first reply to President Campbell's correspondence after the Olden incident had been met with a simple written answer which had been delivered without delay the next night.

In that letter Campbell had attempted an olive branch approach. The goal was to appease the squawking from those in Princeton and specifically try and appeal to the honor of the sister college to move ahead and leave the past animosities behind.

This written reply now, from McCosh, had been delivered by post on the same day train.

Murray looked up at President Campbell.

Campbell was a good man with a kind heart and was at his very soul a gifted Reverend. As the eighth president in the history of Rutgers College, he was seen as the very model of the moral fabric that the Board of Trustees hoped all the Rutgers future graduates would emulate.

An experienced practitioner in his craft, he had served as a pastor in New York and taught and worked as a school principal. Originally enlisted at the theological seminary in New Brunswick to teach oriental languages, his connection to Rutgers College started while still in that capacity. He served as the professor of belles letters, his skill with elegant literature and his ability to review the artistic quality of student writing endeared him among the experienced faculty at that time.

He had then been appointed seven years earlier to the position of the President. He immediately embraced the work of Cook at that time with the development of the Scientific School and, with the assistance of Murray, through the application and selection of Rutgers with the Morrill Act Grant forged a new relationship with the State.

Still, there were lingering issues that plagued the college like lower enrollment counts, which Campbell had been unable to find a suitable solution for.

Financial arguments appeared endless and the need to find gifts from donors to support additional courses in fields like the sciences were both essential for the continued academic future of the college as well as the infrastructure of the institution itself. Those very "new" science-related courses that interested men like Cook and Murray also caused consternation for men like Campbell who were saddled with the task of securing the funding to make them real. No wonder Campbell at times could be heard to comment that he longed for the older curriculum that required less funding and allowed for more time in academic thought and reflection versus expensive disposable manipulatives.

It was also no secret that Campbell shared with those close to him that he yearned for a shift with the trajectory of his career from the college setting and back to his personal foundation with the church. Faculty who worked with the financial planning knew that Campbell's hope was to one day secure the gift of the estate from Mrs. Sophia Astley Kirkpatrick and establish a chapel right on the college grounds. Some thought Campbell saw this as his life's true spiritual mission on earth and that this was the final incentive that motivated him to remain at Rutgers College.

While he heard the talk, Murray felt he knew the man well enough to believe that Campbell stayed not for some personal connection with a new edifice but rather for a personal honor code which he lived by. Murray had heard Campbell say, he had given his word when he accepted this role and his own standard for himself was a level of commitment to see this job through for the future generations who would attend.

Still, Murray worried about the man's health. Campbell's eyesight seemed to be giving him a personal daily battle while the forces around him always seemed to be conspiring to bring the energies of President Campbell down and, with him, that future of Rutgers College.

"Sir, again I am no man of letters like you are," Murray offered Campbell. "But I respectfully disagree with you. Even an artistic turn of a phrase here cannot create any other reply. You cannot avoid a stern and direct reply to counter the basis of what President McCosh intends and tell him if it comes down to it, Rutgers will prevail. This is a threat and the underpinning of all that he has written is that there is only room for one college in this state. And with this letter he leaves no question in announcing that the one college that is left is not Rutgers but rather it should be the current College of New Jersey in Princeton. He must be put back in his place and told if we drop a college it should be in Princeton. He has left no room for any other type of answer."

"I simply do not agree," Campbell said back.

"That my interpretation of what McCosh is saying is wrong?"

"No David, I think you are right on mark. I just do not believe that the state only has the ability for one college and that this one college needs to be anchored in Princeton."

"So what do you suggest the reply should be?" Murray asked. "Do we now sound the trumpets for battle and hurl ourselves headlong into some pitched confrontation to beat out resources for our school while they attempt to hoard all future funding?"

"No," Campbell replied, the use of his pipe keeping him calm as he thought through the process. "I believe the course of action is still to take the higher road. McCosh may be right that given the correct motivation state legislators and financiers may prefer only being billed from one college to sustain itself to save them money. However, I feel that we need to change that dialogue to where we both are seen as necessary. It needs to become apparent to all that both are worthwhile investments for the future success of both the state and the nation."

"And that is done by?"

"It begins with me responding again back to President McCosh and making sure that he understands our point of view and intentions." Campbell paused for a second before adding, "At the same time, Dr. Murray, I acknowledge that I need to elevate our tone to demonstrate our willingness to muster any troops to stem the tide of his attempt to wipe us off the map. Instead we must establish our place in this academic world so deeply that we cannot be challenged."

"It sounds noble sir. But with all due respect, how is this actually accomplished?"

"It involves us all, David. You and your colleagues in the research world creating new areas of discovery that bring us glory. Those of your peers writing scholastic papers with published language that marks our place in time. It involves our alumni believing in all that we stand for and not allowing them to see any weakened front that would give them pause in supporting us in the future. It involves getting to those who create the avenues of funding to see that we are the best investment and that our output meets or exceeds any other and assists in their pursuit of gathering wealth."

"And this starts with-"

Campbell continued before Professor Murray could finish his sentence.

"It starts with the very students here on our campus. We have to continue to provide the highest quality education experience for them. But even beyond that, we need to foster within their own ranks a renewed pride in this place and what they are now a part of. They need to believe in Rutgers. They need to see us as the answer and the hope for the future. That needs to become a part of their being while they are among us and before they exit our halls and join the rest of the world. It needs to happen for them, now, so that they can use their influence later when they assume positions of future power and influence and become those who direct the resources to wherever they will eventually go."

Campbell paused for a moment as he took his key and adjusted the tobacco in his pipe before re-lighting it. He stopped to inhale the smoke and calm himself back down.

When he started again, his perspective caught Murray slightly off guard.

"You know David, President McCosh is not entirely wrong with his line of reasoning."

"How is that sir?"

"He knows that resources are limited. The recent events with the Panic and the subsequent talk coming off Wall Street demonstrate just how fragile the entire funding stream really is. If the reports are accurate and the likes of men like Gould or Fisk can manipulate men with ranking positions connected to the United States President in their schemes to make themselves rich at the potential ruination of not only other people but our nation as a whole; this world just became a scarier place. Is the consolidation of wealth into the hands of just the elite now close at hand?"

"And that relates to McCosh being correct, how?"

"Think about it. Those resources on which we all depend can easily be transferred to be controlled by just a few men if there is nothing to limit the centralization of wealth. Once that happens, the odds of having multiple points of view supported (like backing two colleges versus just one) becomes vastly reduced. Unless the same men who are motivated by greed can suddenly be convinced to pursue altruistic ways, even with the Lord on our side, there are bound to be winners and losers among that format."

Campbell now moved back to his chair and sat down before he continued his analysis.

"The trick, and McCosh understands it, is to try and influence as many men as possible ahead of the belt tightening that inevitably evolves through normal economic cycles. He sees that convincing them about the value emanating from Nassau Hall is so great it should be prioritized whenever financial fates tumble and the axe befalls allocations. Building their base is what politicians call it. One does it by lining up and doing favors so that when a ballot day rolls around they grant you their one vote."

"So his plan is to either make his college look so good that it is the victor in any cut back battle or make us look so bad that men are already thinking about our elimination when cost cutting time appears," Murray summarized.

"Only he is positioning to do both. Elevate where he is in Princeton. There is no question that he is attempting to build an amazing education institution there."

"Agreed."

"But his Princeton workers, David, are also tirelessly undermining our good name. They are sowing the seeds of discontent and placing questions of our worthiness out there so our reputation is trampled. Their strategy is to suggest, well in advance of the next financial tumble, that maybe Rutgers College is not really an essential element in the future plans of our state after all. Maybe this is a surplus that is not needed for the good of New Jersey."

Murray paused before asking the question. He was pretty sure he already knew what Dr. Campbell would say although he was not positive he believed it.

"And the motivation?"

"That was what I asked you when you first read the letter," Campbell said as he now held the pages of it up in his raised fist from where Murray had placed it back on his desk.

"And your conclusion?"

"Maybe it is an honest belief that hard times are coming and he is doing all he can to gain the best position for his college to survive cuts that are on the way. Maybe it is because the work at the College of New Jersey is not progressing as he had hoped and there is fear that we might be gaining and he is just trying to get back up to speed with us. I must tell you though, I have trouble believing that second one though knowing of his confidence levels in himself."

"It could be that he is just an evil man," Murray suggested.

"No," Campbell sighed and smiled. "Of that I simply do not subscribe."

"President Campbell, there are evil people out there whether you wish to believe in the good in all men or not."

"David, I am not naïve. But I also know President McCosh. In his heart he is a good man too. His way of doing business may be vexing to us but he does not do this out of an ill-willed devilish spite."

"So, again President Campbell, what do you think is the motivation for his tactic?"

"In the end, I am gambling that it may just be his push to compete. He has this desire within him to win that each of us harbor. Of this I am not concerned. However, I gather from talking with him, he may want to win at any cost which is something I do fear."

"Because?"

"That energy could be so better utilized building up the mission and inspiring us all. The mission is more and not less higher education options for students. And the audience for all includes our politicians, legislators, and wealthy businessmen. People who are in a place to donate and others who cast votes that influence others on what they should do. I truly believe that, together, we can help foster a better culture where they see the value of higher education as being inseparable from the national welfare. This would be a shared vision where it is understood that this is an arena that needs everyone's support to grow and not shrink. That with more minds engaged in looking at the essential questions of our time and the essential questions of all time we can find solutions in making life better for everybody."

Murray smiled. The man had a way with putting the positive spin on anything.

"David. While the reply is my responsibility, one thing I do need is someone to hand deliver this response versus looking to send this by the post and wonder when it arrived. Is there anyone you can think to spare who can take a trip down to and back from Princeton tomorrow?"

"I will send for one of the tutors now," Murray answered.

"Good. Whoever you are sending might need a little warning to change their personal daily schedule to prepare for this full day trip on such short notice."

"And what do you plan to write, if you do not mind me asking sir?"

"Whatever I write, I guarantee you, will have a little less flowery speech in it much like you first suggested. It might not bite the reader like a viper, but my letter will announce the fact we are up to any challenge to find a way to co-exist as professionals to the benefit of both our futures."

Murray nodded and stepped out to send a note for one of the tutors to come by the President's office right away. Before he left he turned and added one last thought for Campbell to keep in mind.

"For what it is worth, President Campbell. I have been speaking with some Rutgers students recently who I think share your desire to respond to the folks at Princeton."

"Not talking about another cannon episode I hope," Campbell groaned back.

"No. This is some type of athletic challenge to settle things with their peers at Nassau Hall. Not too clear on the details but it appears a safe way to work with their perceived adversaries within the context of your messaging to the staff at that college."

"Interesting," Campbell replied.

"The point though, sir, is that I do think we are building current scholars who care about our college here. To hear their passion in setting up this contest was, well, refreshing to say the least. It gave me hope to hear it that day and I do believe it fits exactly with what your plan is."

"Good to hear, Dr. Murray. Good to hear."

21
October 16, 1869
Princeton

The meeting dragged on longer than he had intended. The staff, he knew, would love to debate the merits of the Classical Curriculum forever if given the chance.

McCosh struggled to hold back a yawn as the designated faculty leader droned on.

"So we look to add only the expanded segments in Latin?"

"There is no greater skill we can provide beyond what is embedded within the framework of the theme writing as long as we require that the expectations of quality with each of our students is kept."

"I support the position that all seniors continue to be expected to complete examinations in Latin, Greek, chemistry, and political economy. In addition the essential analysis applied to the ethical and moral reasoning theme of the balance between religion and the pursuit of science must also be continued. Adjust these foundational requirements would reduce the prestige and value of their entire program of study."

"So you are suggesting no examination that pertains to literature respective to our own British heritage? How can we justify this continued omission?"

"The faculty council has already ruled on that. I know your desire to incorporate Tennyson or Chaucer but there is just no space for this more recent literature at this time if we are to do justice to the other academic domains."

And so on it went. Details on what Latin passage to translate and what grammar rules deserved the greatest weight. Debate about the level of specificity needed interpreting the Ancient Languages and the link to the historical context from which the Greek, Latin and Sanskrit key words had evolved.

As McCosh listened to each of their perspectives, he continued to be amazed at how little credence they gave to the importance of the contemporary world in which their graduates were about to enter. They were learned men, considered by their peers among the most brilliant in the country at what they did. It was not that they did not value or care about the futures of the young men in their charge. Quite the contrary, they truly believed that what they were doing would far outweigh any other benefit the students could derive from a different approach or point of emphasis. It was just that the term relevance in areas like future invention never crossed their tongues.

McCosh found the debate related to mathematics the most interesting.

While each man praised the work in this field and emphasized the importance of what study in areas like algebra and calculus could do for their young scholars; they also did not see how some students would benefit with furthering their study in this field versus what would be gained from a traditional approach through the Classics.

McCosh winced as he heard one on the staff proclaim that the students, if they could not show proficiency in mathematics before their senior year, should not have been moved on to senior status to pursue "higher level academic study" in the first place.

Eventually McCosh completely tuned out the voices knowing the discussion on this topic would follow the same path it always had. Today was not the day to fight this battle between Classics and the need for relevance within the context of the territory these professors felt the strongest about.

His mind drifted to the letter that had been delivered from Rutgers to his office earlier that day.

President Campbell had been deliberate in his response. There could be no question about that. The man's prose was filled with gushing words of praise and effusive language about the wonders of all that the College of New Jersey provided young men in the way of building moral character and an educated society.

How these faculty members would have loved to read that, as they boasted their credentials each time they proposed the next examination iteration using as evidence the preaching of the ghosts from the past. No need to feed the staff ego any further today, McCosh thought to himself.

The conclusion in Campbell's letter was the part that McCosh felt compelled to read over several times to try and find the real intent of his counterpart twenty miles northeast of him.

The rest of the text had been clear. Both schools served an important purpose in linking students to the traditions of the past while building a higher level of understanding to solve the problems the world would face in the world of tomorrow. Nice sentiment, but too verbose for McCosh's taste in reading material. But the conclusion was somewhat puzzling.

So that our places of higher learning never fail to support each other, I agree that it is time that we elect to compete directly with each other in any field of intellectual or physical combat with shared expectations on how we both will benefit. We are beyond games of apology or the patience of listening to insult. Instead we will see that our students, faculty, and community at large are afforded the same professional courtesy and respect of common mission to which we have so provided you and those in your charge within the confines of Princeton's college. We compete, and can show this, on all levels and together we succeed.

Was Campbell trying to jump on to the attack here? What was the intent?

McCosh reviewed his last correspondence sent to New Brunswick. He knew it would strike a nerve, as it was intended. He knew that his purpose, to make it clear that the College of New Jersey was the only place for investment in the state, would irritate those at Rutgers. State leaders and to those in the business and professional community who financially gave to the growth of college programs needed to maximize their monies for the College of New Jersey mission. To divert any funding to another college like Rutgers was truly a waste of taxpayer and fundraiser dollars when resources were scarce.

Be abrupt and forthright. These were two principles that he found were the best tools when competing for external support and funding. Be direct and be taxing. This set the best tone in any letter sent to the competition for those desiring legislative support and financial backing.

A day did not pass when he did not hear about the failure of the College of New Jersey with the fight to secure the funding from the Morrill Act. Not a day passed, as he listened to his valued staff in the Classics, he did not ponder if his own staff had not in some way sabotaged these resources for fear of the potential undermining of their hold on the college's traditional set curriculum.

It bothered McCosh that it was only right that the college with the designation the College of New Jersey should have been given the legislative support and money that would have come with the grant. The path to regain the upper foot with Rutgers College and tap into the resources that, in his way of thinking, had been misappropriated would require his full attention. The steps to get there would require a full on assault of those who had been given the funding instead. His strategy along with the future plan with Nassau Hall, would require the dismantling of Rutgers itself.

While the bricks would never burn, a school's reputation could be tarnished to such a point where it could cease to be relevant and, in the case of state funding supports, lose the ability to function. No state legislator or Governor would dare send dollars to a school where the prevailing thought among a state's citizens was that the college was inferior or its demise already in motion. No alumni, even those entrenched in high ranking political or business positions, would be able to divert the funds from an institution that proved itself beyond repute to give it to a college that was seen as failing in its mission as well as its very purpose as a college.

To get there McCosh understood that the school in Princeton had to prove itself worthy. He had confidence that would not be an issue. To get there McCosh also understood Rutgers, which was in possession of the state grant funding at this time, had to be erased.

He saw the events with the cannon and the failure on the competitive front between the students as unnerving the folks in New Brunswick. This was perfect. Frustration with any failure often leads to further failure. All that was needed was someone needed to fan that fire and create the tension which would cause more turmoil and a rapid diminishing respect for those learning along the Raritan River at Old Queens.

McCosh did not mind the jousting with sharpened points that went with such a venture.

He did not pause in the challenge to still have the Land Grant funding transferred over to Nassau Hall. The goal was not to eliminate existing funding but rather redirect it. He did not stop building the reputation of those in Princeton. He also fully understood that in order to accelerate this process it would be enhanced by a collapse of the belief in the Rutgers mission itself.

The invitation to Judge Olden's house had been to serve a purpose. Bring them on their apologetic knees and expose the weakness of Rutgers in the public eye. Promote the stories of competitive failure and the school and community in New Brunswick becomes a standing public joke. Highlight Princeton's academic standing over what could be offered at Rutgers at every juncture and the college in Princeton would become the college for the state and not just due to its name.

It was this last thought that made him look back again at his faculty engaged in this tedious talk today about the finite points with exam questions. They always saw their job as one to push for more academic rigor and difficulty. In turn, they felt making student assignments closer to impossible equated to an elevated ranking for the college.

McCosh had to admit it was true that the college had earned its reputation from previous graduates who had struggled to survive with the workload thrown at them when they were students still enrolled on campus. Upon graduation, their tales of horror at how hard the coursework had been supposedly enhanced the college's standing.

He looked back again at the letter from the Rutgers President.

If Campbell was readying their troops for some kind of battle, this was probably not the best time to create any further discontent within the ranks here in Princeton. He crumbled McCosh letter into a small ball of paper in the palm of his hand.

With that, McCosh dismissed his initial plan for that day which had been to argue the merits of integrating a more progressive curriculum with his firmly embedded Classics staff. Instead he smiled at the group as they talked about ramping up, once more, the technical difficulty of the examination.

A smile came to his lips as he thought to himself about the added ammunition this provided in his attack on Rutgers.

He would write Campbell back. The man was starting to sound as if he were on edge. One more push and…

22
October 16, 1869
Princeton

Adkins paused outside the shop.

While the streets were nowhere nearly as busy or congested as they would be back in New Brunswick at this time of day, there were still bodies everywhere. Remembering the advice of his colleague and friend back at Rutgers, he looked around at these people moving about. Clearly, he thought to himself, they appeared just as interested in his personal business as they were in their own.

There was no way he wanted to bring undo attention to himself or to the affairs of the millenary shop with those who were inside.

The last time he had seen her, as Elizabeth and her mother had driven off to the train, she had thrown out the challenge to him to find a way to make contact with her next. While he had debated sending a letter, he had not been able to find the right words to help him compose anything that did not sound too forward or wanting.

His friend had looked over the many drafts and laughed at his lack of skill in matters of the heart.

"You are supposed to be a college educated man engaged to tutor others and you cannot fashion a note of your own?" He had taunted him with every draft. Still, even when his friend had helped, the letters sounded no better.

Hence, no letter had been sent. As the days passed by, Adkins began to worry that Elizabeth had probably begun to believe that he was no longer interested or, even worse, she may have tired of him.

Then President Campbell had called him into his office yesterday. There, with Professor Murray at his side, he requested that Adkins take the morning train to Princeton and hand deliver a letter to the President of the College.

At first he had felt somewhat insulted.

"Courier," had been the word used by both Campbell and Murray as they directed him to this task.

"Can you believe my role has been reduced to this?" he had asked his friend upon returning to his building that evening.

That was when his friend pointed out that, with this errand, it was his chance to go and see his Elizabeth in person.

They had talked about it all evening. This was perfect. He felt much more confident talking in person versus writing a possibly misinterpreted letter as a sign of love.

This way he could see her face and her reaction as he asked her to attend the function in New Brunswick at the end of the month. In person, if she said yes, they could discuss the logistics of transportation and whether she would prefer for him to arrange for a room that night to stay or would she prefer to return to her own home.

He also, with a slight twist of the truth, could explain the lack of posting a letter sooner and provide the explanation that he had been awaiting this assignment to be in Princeton so they could talk.

It all seemed to be a perfect plan.

That was until now, outside the shop.

What if she did not appreciate gentleman callers while she was working? What if rumors started because these "nosy" people walking the streets of Princeton elected to gossip about the comings and goings of the shop?

Stop making excuses, he said to himself. You know why you are here waiting versus inside talking. You are scared.

But what was there to be scared of?

He had made a big enough fool of himself that first time he had met her. And yet she still spoke with him at that event. Then, that afternoon at New Brunswick, she had scouted him down. Not that he had minded this in the least. Finally, in leaving, had she not requested that he contact her in the future?

No, it was not the gossip mongers or the inconvenience of social visits during a work day that stalled him. It was the same problem he had encountered when he had attempted to draft the letters. He liked her and what if she did not yet share his affections? Or even worse, what if she had simply decided to move in another direction?

He took a deep breath. Only one way to find out.

A small bell above the door rang as it was opened. Adkins stepped in to a small show room.

He looked about at the items displayed for shoppers who might enter. Hats were artistically arranged with all sorts of bows and feathers as they were perched upon small box stands on tables positioned to be seen both within the store and also outside the large shop glass window by those who were passing by.

"Can I help you?" came a soft, somewhat distracted female voice. He turned to see Elizabeth walking into the room from behind a cloth draped curtain that separated the showroom from the workshop behind it. She was carrying three large hat boxes and could barely see beyond the outline of these shapes.

"Miss Warren," Adkins began. "I hope you do not mind but I decided to stop by to see you today unannounced."

"Mr. Adkins," she responded back, twisting so that the boxes were no longer in her direct line of sight. "What a surprise!"

"A welcome one, I hope," Adkins answered.

"Most surely," Elizabeth replied. "Just give me a moment and let me put these things down."

"Can I help?" Adkins asked, stepping forward.

"No, thank you. I do this all day."

Elizabeth gently maneuvered around the small display room and placed the three boxes out of the way from the current display. She then turned and, brushing back a lock of hair that had come loose across her face, she smiled. "So what do I owe the honor of this visit today? I do not suppose you are here to purchase a ladies hat?"

"Oh no," Adkins chuckled. "Even if I was buying a hat I would have no idea where to start."

"Well it is really not all that difficult. Each one has a personality and a look all its own. You take a moment and see what first catches your fancy. Then you take it and review it to see if it has the actual features that you desire. Is it positive and fun? Does it match what I think it should have? Is it colorful and full of life? Will it add to your life what you hope you want added?"

"And if I feel that it does those things for me, Elizabeth, what next?"

"Why, Mr. Adkins, then you take it out of this shop and see if it likes you back!"

"You make a hat purchase sound like a match making activity between two people."

"I suppose it can apply that way too," Elizabeth smiled knowingly at him again.

Adkins felt himself blush.

There was something about this woman that made his head spin. She was way more forward compared to the other women he had previously met. But her confidence that generated through her as she spoke was endearing and energizing at the same time.

"So," Elizabeth asked, cutting into the void of silence that his lack of quick response had caused. "What again was the purpose of your visit today?"

Adkins cleared his throat and attempted to sound both mature and in control as he spoke. "Well, as I am sure you recall, when you and your mother visited me in New Brunswick-"

"We were there on business that day, Mr. Adkins. Please do not confuse the chance meeting with the actual intended purpose on our encounter there."

"Right," he regrouped. "Well, at the end of that day after we had an opportunity to tour the grounds of the campus. You do remember that, do you not?"

Elizabeth held back a small laugh. "Yes, Mr. Adkins, I do remember that."

"Well, at the end of that tour, and before you departed by train that day, you suggested that I make the next contact with you."

"And I must declare!" The voice came from the backroom as a second body emerged from behind the drawn cloth curtain and into the show room. "With no letter arriving yet I am sure my daughter was wondering if you ever planned to follow up with that suggestion?"

"Mrs. Bell," Adkins responded.

Surprised, he turned his attention in her direction. He was actually glad to see this woman whom he believed liked that he has shown an interest in her daughter.

"What a pleasure getting to see you today."

"And the same to you, Mr. Adkins," she replied, also carrying a hat box into the room. "Pardon me dear," she stated to her daughter. "I was just bringing this one forward to make it available to Mrs. Aston when she arrives in a short while."

"How thoughtful and convenient, mother," Elizabeth stated. She stared at her mother the entire time as if she were intruding where she did not need to be. "I will be sure to give it to her if she is to show."

Silence descended over the room.

Mrs. Bell looked about and straightened a few things. Sensing that the conversation would not resume while she was present, she excused herself and disappeared again behind the curtain.

"So Mr. Adkins, you were saying?"

"Yes, well, I am sorry that I did not get word to you sooner."

"There you go apologizing again," Elizabeth reminded him of his habit.

"A regular pattern it appears whenever I am with you, ma'am," he acknowledged.

They both laughed.

He started again.

"Well, apology or not, I fully realize it would have been more polite to send notice ahead instead of just showing up today. But, when I got word that I would be traveling to Princeton on Rutgers College business for President Campbell I instantly thought what a great time to see you. I honestly could not craft a message at that point worth writing. So I decided that, instead of sending some impersonal letter at all, I would simply take my chances and come by to see you in person."

"How nice," Elizabeth responded with little inflection in her voice. "I do appreciate the gesture."

"Oh please understand that this planned day has the intention of being more than just a casual visit to stop by to say hello while I was in town," Adkins moved on.

"So what were your intentions today?" Elizabeth asked, sounding more intrigued.

"Well, I assumed you may be too busy to do anything of a social nature here today. And I especially understood that the suddenness of my appearing here would conflict with your full day's work scheduled. I really came with the hope of delivering a personal invitation for you to return for a fun social event later this month back in New Brunswick."

"And that event would be?"

"They have a special evening that corresponds to All Hallows Eve that elicits chills and thrills for all who attend," Adkins explained, his voice growing more enthusiastic as he went along. "There is a tour that we could go on together, if you would like, that moves us through the ghostly stories of the town and features a party intended to protect us from the dead."

"Sounds interesting. Tell me more."

Elizabeth sat and watched as Adkins talked about everything from the tunnel tour underground below the streets of New Brunswick to the evening he had hoped they could share with several other couples afterward at one of the households of a Rutgers staff member.

She smiled at his awkward manner as he outlined options that she could consider for such a visit. He promised he would help with the details as it related to protecting her reputation with night time housing and coordinated transportation eventually back to her home.

She had to admit, beyond the natural physical attraction, his energy and genuine heartfelt way of expressing things to her had caught her fancy.

She thought back to the last several days.

Since they had left Adkins that day in New Brunswick, she had complained as her mother had checked for a letter daily at the post office. Why make a big deal? She had kept telling her mother not to get all wound up over something that may not materialize.

But secretly, as she had admonished her mother for her over anxious behaviors, she dearly wanted to hear from Mr. Adkins too.

While she had not given up hope, she had not expected seeing him there in Princeton that day.

Now here he was talking about this event in New Brunswick. Obviously he had spent a great deal of time working out the logistics and putting this plan in order.

He obviously cared.

So he was a little late in following up and contacting her. She had fully expected a letter by now. But this visit today – this was even better.

"So, are you asking me on a date, Mr. Adkins?" she asked him directly, when he came up for air.

"Well," he stumbled for a moment. "Yes. I am."

"Well then, Mr. Adkins. My answer is yes. While some of the details that you just outlined will obviously take a little time and some planning on my part, I can wholeheartedly tell you, yes, I would enjoy your company that evening in New Brunswick."

"That is wonderful," he heard himself reply before she quickly added.

"There is one thing I need to tell you about myself and my life here in Princeton before we elect to move ahead though with this social engagement, Mr. Adkins."

"And that would be?"

Before she could answer an elderly customer entered the shop. The older woman was followed by two other women who were younger in age. The older woman immediately moved past Elizabeth asking only, "Will I find your mother back here?"

Elizabeth answered in the affirmative and while this woman vanished behind the curtain, the other two women requested Elizabeth's help with the order their older companion had obviously placed.

Elizabeth excused herself while Adkins nodded and took a chair closer to the window.

Adkins watched as Elizabeth moved two boxes forward for them to see.

She had said yes, he repeated to himself as he drew in a deep breath. He was finally able to relax for a moment from the anxiety and pressure of the anticipation awaiting her reaction.

He looked about the shop. It was a cute business nestled neatly in the main market area of the town. While not overly large, it clearly had the signs of being successful with fresh paint and nicely ordered furniture here in the display room. He knew, from surveying the building before he had entered, that it also had a much larger part of the structure screened behind the curtain, most likely for a work space and storage.

He glanced again toward the curtain where, behind that curtain, he could hear the older woman who had recently entered clearly engaged in a friendly social conversation with Mrs. Bell.

23

As the train moved along the tracks on its way to New Brunswick, Adkins felt his heart still racing.

The day had gone by so fast. It was still mostly a blur.

She had said yes.

Of this he reminded himself several times. She had not even seemed to hesitate to have to think about her response to him! She just said yes!

He laughed as he thought about what Hasbrouck had said to him before he had left New Brunswick. Hasbrouck had stated that he thought this lady appeared a little forward to him. Beware an overbearing woman, he said. Hasbrouck had warned him that if she appeared way too anxious to see him when he arrived, she may not be the type of woman that would be good for him.

Then that meeting in the hat shop. Elizabeth appeared genuinely pleased to see him but in no way did she seem desperate.

"Beware the spinster," Hasbrouck had coached him. "They make lovely first impressions but they are alone in most cases for a good reason." Hasbrouck was the one who had suggested a group outing.

Adkins smiled as he thought now about how he hoped that Halloween night would progress. It was the perfect activity to have with friends and others about in case he did end up with a case of the nerves when she was there.

Still, he had felt so much positive energy around her that day when she last visited New Brunswick.

"Smitten," Hasbrouck had said. "Just like some school boy."

He had taken offense to that. It sounded like a challenge to his manhood.

Yet, as he looked out now at the dark farmland as the train passed it by in the night air, he had to admit to himself; he was totally entranced by her.

There was something exciting about her that he could not define. A mysterious air that seemed to draw him in even when he fully believed she was being coy with him.

She definitely did not come across as the traditional female he had read about in literature books or had seen so often in public settings. Those women were so reserved that he often wondered if they had emotions or feelings or were capable of intellectual comment.

True, he had to admit, the social rules and mores of the day handcuffed them from opening up like a man could. Still most women he had met seemed recalcitrant in sharing higher order thinking on any topic.

Suddenly Elizabeth, with her constant jabs, came into his world. Yes, there was a physical attraction but he could not deny that there was instantly something so much more. There was her ability to talk simply as a person and not as a second class mindless entity as so many women thought was their place in society when they were around men. There was her fearless corrections of his own statements and her willingness to point to his social flaws without him ever feeling insulted – that was a skill that was rare.

Then again there was the news she had shared with him that day. It had come as something of a shock.

Starting with his sitting in Elizabeth's shop he replayed the day over again in his head.

Elizabeth had stepped off to the farthest portion of the rear of the workroom used as a storage to tend to the customers who had entered for a purchase.

"So what about her children?"

He had heard the voice of the older woman say this as he had sat in that chair within the shop.

When he had turned around, he saw that the older woman customer was speaking with Elizabeth's mother, right by the drawn curtain. The curtain was tilted to the side of the doorway just enough for him to see where the two women were conversing.

As a social courtesy he had glanced away. However, as they spoke the volume of their speech and the context of their talk made it next to impossible not to eaves drop in.

That conversation was now etched in his brain.

"She and I have discussed it Haddie!" Mrs. Bell tried her best to whisper but to no avail. Her voice carried forward into the display area of the shop where Adkins was seated. "She understands her responsibility."

"That is what she told you?" Haddie asked.

"That is how she lives. Elizabeth is a wonderful mother first. I told her she needs to step back, if even for a short while, to rejoin the rest of the human race. Her children will be fine with me watching them. Go and experience some of the fun things that all other people her age still enjoy."

"No one would have said that in my day."

"Oh Haddie, you are younger then I am and I know there has never been a formula for things like this."

"Well, I think a woman picks her day and actions and is bound by those choices – good result or bad!"

"First, you are now talking about my daughter so you better behave yourself if you still value our friendship. Secondly, those two little darlings are angels sent by God himself. My daughter does not see that gift as a consequence of any kind."

"I know. I know. We all love her kids, Anilee."

"Then you know that Elizabeth has created a home that is warm and loving and filled with everything that is good in this world. That said, it does not mean she is sentenced to a prison term that says she is not allowed to enjoy herself as a person again or that she is not allowed to pursue a new romance-"

"Mother!"

The word had rung back out across the shop.

Adkins could not help but to look up. The loud scream had startled him from his seat. His eyes had caught Elizabeth, aghast, standing in the doorway to the shop and instantly realized that she knew he had heard what her mother had been talking about. Elizabeth's mother suddenly realized it too.

Everyone had frozen in place for what, to Adkins, had seemed an eternity.

Elizabeth was the first to gather herself.

She looked down at her seated mother. Elizabeth asked that she remove Ms. Haddie to the rear area of the shop with her companions. With that and without further comment to her mother, Elizabeth had stepped through the curtain and into the room with Adkins.

Mrs. Bell had started to say something to Elizabeth but, thinking better of herself, announced to Haddie that she would need to leave the shop through the back exit.

The older woman, who to Adkins appeared to be the type of person who only tended to use a front door, did not object. Quietly all other parties, besides Elizabeth, seemed to disappear leaving the two of them alone.

Elizabeth had walked forward. She appeared cautious at first but she was not embarrassed or sheepish in any way. As Adkins thought about that moment and replayed that scene in his mind, he recalled that Elizabeth had been very calm and very much in control.

"Well, Mr. Adkins, I suppose you heard some things that you now have questions about. Please know that is not exactly the manner in which I had planned to approach this."

"No need to apologize," Adkins had worked out of his mouth, searching for what to say in this awkward setting.

"Oh, I never see a need for apologizing for my children, sir," Elizabeth had said without a blink of an eye.

"I didn't mean—"

Before he had gone further, she raised her hand and asked, "Would you care to take a stroll? The air in this shop has suddenly gotten very stuffy."

As the train continued now along the tracks toward New Brunswick, Adkins replayed every word she said to him while they had walked through the town of Princeton that afternoon.

She had talked about her relationship with her own family and the events with Mrs. Justice. She went back and highlighted her courtship with young John Warren and their marriage. She went on to talk about the ravages of the War on their brief, but wonderful, time together. She talked about the shop and her mother and the responsibility with her children.

He listened intently, hanging on each word.

Then the part got even more personal as she relayed how much she cared about her children.

"They were beautiful from day one, Mr. Adkins. Two greater creations God has never made. The boy, Jonathan, handsome and healthy and strong. The girl, Anna, wonderful down to every line of her smiling face and curl in her hair and laugh from her precocious personality."

"They are my life, Mr. Adkins. They are my world."

"I understand," Adkins had replied, honestly believing each thing she said.

"And I have told my mother, for several years now, that this world out here beyond our home and shop doors really is what is awaiting them. I always stressed to my mother that I understood that same world may no longer be awaiting me."

She had paused when she had said this and Adkins detected that she appeared to be fighting back a tear over what might have been those thoughts of lost opportunities. Then she had continued.

"Mind you. I will guard against any evil or harm that could touch them out there. But also know that life for me is fulfilled just to hear them breathe."

"They sound wonderful," Adkins had answered, unsure what else to say. "I am sure you would go to any length to protect them."

Elizabeth had smiled.

"Of course my mother, who I believe you have by now been able to gather a pretty complete impression about, felt that I still needed to expand my boundaries. Explore what is out there, was the phrase she would say. She was telling me and everyone around me there is a romance waiting for everyone. You just have to take the steps to make it possible."

Elizabeth paused again before adding.

"You know I went with her that evening to Judge Olden's more as a favor to my mother. She did not wish to go there alone and yet she so wanted the social activity her friends were sure to provide. I felt badly when I first told her no, as I did so often. Then she came home that evening and there appeared a sitter for the twins. So off we went."

"Then we met, by chance, Mr. Adkins. And as you know one thing has led to another and now to where we are here today."

"I was planning to tell you about them Mr. Adkins. In the shop today before that customer came in I was getting ready to inform you, although I realize now you may not believe that. I also never planned on having you learn about the twins from my mother's lips in a conversation with a lady who was a total stranger to you."

"I do believe you," Adkins had replied.

"Good. For what it is worth, that does matter to me. Anyway, I know how sudden and overwhelming this information can be. I fully understand if you get on that train—"

"The train!" Adkins had announced. He remembered how he had instantly glanced at his time piece as he had stated, "I almost forgot. I do have to run."

Adkins remembered how she stepped back when he had said this.

He remembered exactly how she had looked, as she politely smiled at him, and said, "I understand."

He also remembered clearly the look on her face when she spoke again after he had asked his question.

"So how do we get the details straight for our – date – on All Hallows Eve?" he had asked.

"Pardon?"

"Our date? Maybe I shouldn't call it a date if you feel it should just be called a night out at a social event. But we didn't get a chance to finalize the details before."

"I am not sure?"

"How about I write you?" he had asked.

"If you are serious about this, how about I write you this time with the plans?" she said with a happy laugh.

"Of course I am serious. And you writing first, yes that definitely works for me," he had responded.

Then, as he started to leave he added, "I do look forward to meeting both Anna and Jonathan at some point in the future. Maybe not that night in October as that is really just for you and me. But definitely sometime in the future."

Impulsively she had stepped forward and placed a soft kiss on his check.

He had touched his hand to his check, smiled, and turned to start jogging toward the station to catch his train.

Before he had lost her from his sight he had called back one more time.

"I look forward to getting your letter!"

Adkins looked out again at the landscape on the dim, but visible horizon. He put his hand to his cheek and touched where she had kissed him earlier.

There was something special about that girl. Even the news of her having children did not seem to matter at all. All he could think about was that smile when he had last turned back. He already yearned to see it again.

Maybe Hasbrouck was right. Maybe he was "smitten."

The train pulled him quickly back toward his world of work. It was a world of work that now, with this impending date, would have to find time for a new type of social event on the calendar.

24
October 22, 1869
New Brunswick

"So you look quite the sight this evening, Master William!" Mrs. Fannie Parsell made her observation as Leggett stood in the foyer. "Hardly appear ready for an evening rehearsal with a church choir."

Leggett's clothes looked as though they had been dragged through the streets of New Brunswick under the feet of several horses. His face still showed signs of where he had attempted to wipe the mud away and instead the water used had only smeared the dirt around. His hair was rumpled and matted to his head, small strands of dead grass appearing entwined on the back side.
"Yes, ma'am," he responded, unsure what else to say.
He understood how his appearance was totally unlike his normal, formal, look he always attempted to maintain when visiting the Parsell household. He tried to arrive most days without a hair out of place. This was especially true if her husband the Major was there.

Mary Eva and her brother John entered the room and had a similar response. Mary's face scrunched tightly as if she had just picked up on the scent of a skunk.
Seeing her reaction, even before she could comment, Leggett felt the need to explain.
"Mary and Mrs. Parsell, I do apologize for the way I look this evening. I fully appreciate that my attire is less then what should be expected for such an activity. I apologize to you Mary and understand if you do not wish for me to accompany you and your friends to the choir practice in this manner."
"Oh stop being so formal and feeling like you need to apologize to my sister," John said.
"Where were you? Out tending to horses in the barn?" the girl asked.

Before he could answer, Mr. Parsell entered the house. Home from work, the Major took one glance at Leggett and remarked, "My lad. You get caught up in a tussle with some other fellows in the street?"
"No sir," Leggett now turned to look directly at him. "I just did not have time to stop and change after attending our football practice today."

Mr. Parsell's voice changed instantly. "Oh, wonderful. Glad to know you lads are out there practicing full steam. I would hate to think that you are not fully ready to take on those chaps from down in Princeton."

With that, he moved out of the doorway and past Leggett, kissing his daughter, tapping his son on his shoulder, and then kissing his wife on the cheek.

"Are we having him over to hose him down and clean him up before our supper, dear?" Parsell asked his wife.

"No," she answered. "He appeared at the door two minutes ahead of you with the intent of taking Mary Eva and John to the community choir practice in this state of distress."

"Yes sir," Leggett added. "I was just apologizing and saying that I understood if Mary Eva and John wished to attend without me this evening."

"No such thing," Mary Eva cut in. "I partially believe you did not wish to attend the choir rehearsal and came here like this with the hope it would play as an excuse not to go. Well I am fine with it as long as you stand downwind the whole night when we get there."

The door knocker clicked on the door and the maid, standing aside since Mr. Parsell had entered, moved to open it. At the door were two young ladies, both Mary Eva's age, and a young male. Besides the fact this male was cleanly dressed, he looked much like Leggett.

"Good evening," all three seemed to say at the exact same time as they entered the now crowded foyer. Instantly Leggett's appearance was the first point for comment.

"What happened to you?" the male in the group called out. "Were you beaten by some street thugs on your way here?"

Mr. Parsell saved Leggett from having to respond and interjected in grand fanfare.

"I would say not! Master William here just joined us fresh from his practice with the other lads over at Rutgers College where they are preparing to whip the loud-mouthed and arrogant youngsters down at Princeton. He is working hard to bring honor back to New Brunswick."

"Do tell," one of the young ladies exclaimed to the grand announcement. "Are you planning to go fight them?"

"Not exactly, Kathleen," the young man who just entered responded. "William here is helping lead a team of our students to victory in a game of this new soccer style sport called football." Then, turning to look at

Leggett he added, "I heard the game was rough but I did not realize it would leave you looking like this today."

"Just a great deal of running and bumping on that dirt field. Believe me, I suffered no injury beyond the tear of my shirt here and the stains of grass, dirt, and sweat from exertion."

Before William could continue, Mary Eva noted the time.

She then stated for the group, "We must be off now."

With quick good-byes to her parents, Mary Eva and her friends exited the household with her parents' instructions about expectations with walking without a chaperone and timeliness about returning.

The group proceeded up the sidewalk. The three girls chattered with each other as they walked ahead. The two males spoke with Leggett as they walked at his side.

"So from the looks of things, you had a major workout today," the male guest commented. "Still, could you not take a moment before coming out to wash yourself off?"

"Look, Cornelius, I did wash myself off at the corner fountain. I soaked my hair to get the grass out and my face and hands to try and get the dirt off."

"Too bad it didn't work," John laughed.

"To tell the truth, you would not have recognized me at all if I had not stopped to wash up. And if you saw my shins, they are so bruised you would think my skin is actually a purple pair of trousers."

"It does sound like the game is rougher then I had heard."

"You should come out and join us," Leggett offered his fellow college mate. "I will not tell you it is not physical but I will tell you I have to admit it is fun while tough at the same time."

"Oh, I prefer a game of skill and cunning versus one that just has men beat on each other to make a point," Cornelius answered. "Any way, I would think you have your team fully selected by now."

"There are twenty-five to a side," Leggett explained. "At the rate we are going, I am not sure that after we finish practicing and even get to the game we will have twenty-five to choose from!"

"Dropping like flies?"

"More like shot clay pigeons," Leggett clarified. "Two of them ran full steam into each other's head at practice today. When I left I am still not sure if you asked them they could recall their own names."

Cornelius laughed. "You make it sound so inviting."

"Seriously, it is good fun," Leggett circled back. "And it is interesting seeing Kellogg, Atherton and Hasbrouck hovering around us and making us work."

"They enjoy beating you do they?"

"Kellogg with his army talk. All this let's fight and time to dig in. You would think we had enlisted in the army instead of getting ready for a sports contest."

"Again, you make it sound so enjoyable."

Leggett chuckled.

"Sorry, Sorry. I will stop complaining and tell you it also is great when you do score or when you outrun your opponent. All that is refreshing and exciting in so many ways. But it is the bigger goal that I enjoy going after, Cornelius. I think we are getting better with practice and I do hope that this contest is able to prove to all of Nassau Hall once and for all that we are their equals in any field of combat that they select."

"Are you boys even planning to speak with us at all this evening?" Mary Eva called out as they came to an abrupt stop on the path.

"So sorry ladies," Cornelius bowed as he apologized. "What is it you wish to discuss?"

"What is the prediction? Are you going to beat the boys at the College of New Jersey?" the girl earlier identified as Kathleen asked Leggett, seemingly ignoring Cornelius and John altogether.

"Yes. And when is this great challenge going to take place?" the other girl, Rebecca, not waiting for Leggett to answer jumped in with a similar level of interest.

"I hope you beat them to a pulp," Kathleen replied, also not waiting for him to reply. "Those students down in Princeton think so much of themselves as if they are better than everyone else out here. Really, what have they done in the past to prove that they are deserving of such high praise?"

"Unfortunately," Leggett answered. "They have beaten us badly at a few things before."

"Still, Mary Eva was telling us about how they challenged you as if you were not even men here at Rutgers College. I know that my father and his acquaintances all were fired up about that cannon thing and how the Princeton men all feel it is their birthright to steal our property from New Brunswick," Rebecca charged in.

"I agree," Kathleen added. "They really need to be taken down a peg. Whip them like Sherman did the rebels down in Dixie during the war.

Hard to walk around so high and mighty after you are humbled by a stunning defeat. Don't hear them tooting any horns anymore!"

"Wow, that is awfully strong talk from some ladies," Cornelius interjected. "You act like you are the one out there doing all the fighting."

"Well you certainly are not," Kathleen held her head up as she spoke. "So do not go cheering all the merits when you do not even don the battle attire to begin with."

"Easy," Mary Eva broke in. She stood next to Leggett and pointed to his tussled hair, torn shirt and grimy face. "Do you really think we want all the men at Rutgers College looking like this?"

"I could play if I wanted," Cornelius stated defensively looking back at Kathleen and ignoring Mary Eva's call for a truce. "I have just chosen not to play, so far."

Leggett, hearing Cornelius' comment and the potential for another recruit stepped right in. "And it is not too late to join us. As I told you, we are starting to fall short on teammates and could use some more bodies. Anyway, you are a great athlete with skills that would translate so quickly to this sport."

"Cornelius running into and hitting others? Really?" Rebecca asked.

"I can do that," Cornelius shot back.

"No, we really need skill players. And Cornelius has shown before that he has that. We have several of our mates who feel compelled to just ram into each other. What we really need to win, in my mind, are players who can actually coordinate their body in a way that allows us to move the ball in an effective manner."

Leggett put his hand on Cornelius' shoulder.

"Ladies you should see this man when we play baseball. He is by far one of the best. I tell you, Cornelius, you could translate that skill to this game and be amazing at this too."

"We would come out to cheer you on!" Kathleen said, suddenly warming up to the idea of her male friend engaged in the contest.

"I would definitely come to see you too," Rebecca stated.

Feeling the pressure of all eyes looking directly at him, Cornelius shrugged.

"I guess I could take a shot at your practice, William," he said. His voice lacked any level of enthusiasm.

"Excellent!" Leggett slapped his male friend on the back not taking a chance that he would back out. "Our next practice is tomorrow after studies. We are at the field between Sicard Street and College Avenue. Be sure to bring an extra shirt."

Mary Eva moved to walk between her brother, John, and Leggett. The other two girls now circled around Cornelius.

"This will be so exciting!" Kathleen stated.

Cornelius seemed to enjoy the renewed attention and the group started forward again to the choir rehearsal destination.

"So what music were we supposed to practice for today?" Cornelius asked the group as they walked. "It is hard to concentrate this early on Christmas caroling in October."

"You know there is only time for two rehearsals a month," Mary Eva argued. "That is barely enough time to get ready for the annual event if we wish to not sound like fools or goats."

A fool or a goat, Cornelius thought to himself? Only a few rehearsals until the event? Just like this game! It was hard for him not to translate that statement immediately to the football game he had barely ever played before. And it was already being promoted as the most important activity at Rutgers College that year and sure to draw a crowd to see the players, and him, possibly fail.

How many practices would they have before they played the College of New Jersey? If he barely knew the sport, how would he make sure he did not look like the goat in front of his teammates?

Then, as he looked at the girls on either side of him he thought; how do I not look like a fool in front of these spectators?

He already began to regret that he said he would give it a try. Practice and not be good enough to play? What would they think of him? Participate and appear to be the worst one out there when he played?

His stomach started to hurt. Oh how this evening had taken a turn for the worse. And he had not even made it to choir rehearsal yet where he knew he did not have any ability to sing.

"Great to have you on board," Leggett called out to him, obviously still happy to have trapped another student into playing.

"Thanks," Cornelius answered back.

How he did not share Leggett's joy in his participation.

25
October 23, 1869

Trenton, New Jersey

As they walked the small area between the shops, Gummere called in a loud whisper over to his group of friends who had joined him on the trip to his hometown of Trenton.

"There, see that one?"

He pointed at the tallest figure in a group that were standing about outside of the market area.

"I bet she would be about Big Mike's height," he continued on in a loud whisper.

"No girl for so long Big Mike. We all are beginning to wonder if you will ever catch one. Maybe worth paying her to be your beau," one of the guys teased while the others chuckled.

"I imagine she could be my type," Mike said looking over at the figure in the distance that Gummere had identified for him. "Just watch me work and see how a professional does it," he added as he started to move toward that person to introduce himself.

As soon as Mike reached that other group and started to talk, his friends started to howl with laughter.

The figure in the flowing cape, when that person turned to face him, was actually a man with a full-faced mustache. While the French mannerisms may have come across as refined and womanly, it was abundantly clear about his gender.

"That's not a woman," Frank Burt called out. "You fool, that's a man!"

Mike's face whitened and then turned a brilliant red as he quickly retreated back to his college mates.

"Sorry Mike," Chaunce squeezed out between breaths. "That was probably your last chance. Looks like you should have taken that giant ape back at the zoo in the park when you had the opportunity."

Big Mike, with arms that many had observed were as thick as trees, grabbed Chaunce by the neck. "Let's see if you find it funny when I break you in two!"

"Easy Mike, easy big fellow," Gummere coaxed him as he and three of the other Princeton youth circled him and each started to pull Chaunce away from Mike. "You know we only joke with you because we love you."

Mike backed down and the six of them regrouped.

"It wasn't funny!" Mike fumed at Chaunce and Frank Burt. "Not funny at all!"

"Sorry Mike," Chaunce offered. He paused before adding, "But yes it was."

Gummere cut Mike's attempt to get back at Chaunce and helped guide him forward as they walked on ahead with their adventure.

They moved further downtown and closer to the river where the commercial might of economic trade flexed itself beside the political voices in the New Jersey state capitol building.

Trenton's industrial and merchant footprints were clearly well beyond what they encountered each day in Princeton. Business existed in Princeton in less of a manufacturing sense and more of a service format. The shops were smaller and typically employed only several employees. The warehouses and smoke shooting from chimneys in Trenton could not hide the sheer volume of people needed to run such a series of production operations.

For the students from the college in Princeton, this excursion was a wonderful diversion from the rigid oversight of their daily lives. The expectations in Nassau Hall were clearly outlined for the students ever since several student expulsions took place for starting fires in the dorms years before. No dishonorable behaviors were tolerated. While the town of Princeton had taverns and students did try to sneak out at times and enjoy themselves, it also represented a real challenge in that the townspeople in Princeton too often shared gossip about the goings-on in town with the college staff. As such, attempts to cut loose in the town were very difficult.

Then this symposium was advertised for today. It had provided a scholarly rationale to leave the college campus behind and head to Trenton.

The six of them had dutifully boarded the train and attended the morning speaker's session with their staff chaperones without fail. They each took notes as the speakers talked and listened as expected within the sight of the three faculty chaperones who had accompanied them on the trip.

As the final morning speaker made his concluding remarks, one of the faculty with them leaned over to explain to young Gummere and the students that plans had changed. The staff members had just been invited to visit at the State House and they would not be present with the students for lunch or with them to visit the city during the planned afternoon session.

"I fully expect each of you to demonstrate the upstanding moral character of a young man representing the College of New Jersey. While you will be on your own this afternoon, know that any misbehavior will certainly be reported back to us and will be dealt with severely."

Gummere and the other students nodded respectfully as the faculty walked away with their hosts leaving the young men behind and on their own.
When the afternoon break was taken the students exited for lunch.
They had first planned to visit at Gummere's father's law office and then return to the grounds to read over the documents that had been referenced in the morning lectures.
Then the reality of several hours to kill while on their own in this large setting where they could be themselves became too powerful an elixir for the young men. Together they decided against visiting at Gummere's parents' office and house and instead toured the city with a swagger to match their new found independence.
Gummere knew the streets well and acted as their tour guide.
Trenton had a population six times that of Princeton. Its wharf along the Delaware River provided a depot for goods headed west into Pennsylvania while the train yard linked New York and Philadelphia cross state travelers.
Burlington had once competed with Trenton in an earlier day due to each being in a pivotal spot with Philadelphia across the River. However, with the critical need for a manufacturing point in the western part of the state, Trenton had flexed its muscles and produced work in everything from iron to glassworks. This moved industry and then money into and through the city. In turn, businesses continued to grow and the smoke from plants filled the skyline as furnaces blasted away all day six days per week as products were shipped across the country.
Row houses lined the streets near the shops and factories. The wealthier part of the population lived in more sophisticated Victorian homes on tree-lined lanes which dotted the landscape of key approaches to the downtown portion of the industrial city.
The greatest activity was nearer the bank of the Delaware River. Here everything from warehouses and plants mixed with small shops and houses of ill repute. The State Capitol building was strategically situated slightly north of the workhouses near the wharf but close enough to daily activity to give the feeling that it was in the hub of this growing city.

The students followed that natural pull to where life appeared to be happening.

Eventually they wandered near several taverns and smaller homes south of Market Street but just north of Ferry Street. Tightly packed structures pushed together. These buildings obscured any of the more pastoral view that would have surrounded the students each day at the college in Princeton.

String music from a banjo and hard hitting keys on a piano rolled out into the street. It pulled the group toward the festive sound.

"Let's go in here!" Chaunce Field announced as he heard the strands of the song. "I love this tune, *The Man on the Flying Trapeze*!"

A group of men could now be heard singing along with the instruments. As they entered the room, they could clearly see that the focal point was a woman. Her legs extended, pushing out she was swinging back and forth on a small legless wood bench suspended from the ceiling held up by two ropes. There were flowers entwined around the lower part of the ropes and it was obvious this contraption was supposed to represent an outdoor tree swing.

This woman, as she rocked back and forth, sang out with the men. In turn they cheered as with each kick of her legs, the swing went higher.

"What'll you have?" a gruff voice yelled out at the lads from Princeton from behind the bar.

"We are actually here to try our hand at the billiards table my good man," Lawrence Joueur responded, pointing toward the tables in a side room.

"You come in here to this place you drink first," the man growled back. "You drink, you pay. You pay, then you can play!"

Finding it hard not to accept the invitation, all six of the students ordered up at the bar. At two bits for a beer, they divided up the tab and separated the mugs between them.

They took their drinks and headed over to the billiards tables.

Several men were already at the tables when the College of New Jersey students came over. These large, rough bodies were fresh from an extended night shift down on the docks transporting and unloading goods or working in the iron furnaces.

"Able to get a table and into a game?" Joueur asked.

"If you have the money to place a bet," the man with the billiard cue in his hand replied.

"And the going rate?" Joueur asked.

The man paused, stood straight up and looked Lawrence Joueur over. Then he did the same for the other students in the group before smirking and spitting on the floor.

"Well the way it works, your young highnesses, is that you put your money per game here," he pointed to the spot on the edge of the table as he spoke. While the comment and tone were obviously meant to be insulting, Joueur looked on as if totally engrossed by the explanation.

"Then you put your betting money on the table here. Twenty five cents per player goes to the house. The betting amount is up to you. Anyone wishes to match a bet puts their money next to it. Two sets of bets and you play. You win the game, you get the money and first shot at the next bet and game. You lose and the money is gone and you decide if you want to place more on the table and, in this case today, keep losing it."

The eight or nine other men who had been playing or hanging around the two billiards tables had stopped to watch the interaction. They laughed as the man finished his explanation on how bets were placed.

"You finely dressed young lads interested in a game?"

Joueur was the first to speak.

"Well, I would be willing to give it a shot. I played a little four ball billiards in the past. Not sure I will be the best at this 15 ball pool but I always wanted to give it a try. Is this where I place it good sir?"

The man nodded and the black grime on his teeth dimmed any hint of a smile.

Placing a dollar bill on the table, Lawrence Joueur asked, "So I just wait to see who wishes to match it to play? Correct?"

To several of these men who worked the furnace as an iron molder a dollar was the equivalent of half a day's wages. For the iron molder helpers, it was a bigger part of their day's pay then that.

Each of them eyed this well dressed young lad who looked as if he had just come from a formal society engagement.

"I'll take you on, lad," a tall man with a thick neck and an even broader chest pushed forward with a body that made Big Mike appear average in size. He placed a dollar on top of the one Joueur had placed on the table. "Just better not find out you are some kind of hustler or anything."

Joueur looked at him and smiled innocently.

"Me? As I said, I just wanted a shot at playing a game."

The game began with each player taking a shot to even the break. Joueur then missed hitting any balls as his first shot went wide.

The big man laughed. "Watch and learn."

"Watch and learn?" Joueur repeated slowly back. "That felt so, I would say, insulting."

"It is what it is."

"Well, if you feel so confident." Joueur took another dollar out and placed it next to the one he had placed earlier on the table. "Care to double the wager to back up your words?"

The big man looked about at the group. Clearly he was hesitant to place that kind of money out on a game of chance.

"Anyone else feel that this man here will be the clear winner and want to match my money for him?"

A mixture of the obnoxious manner in which Lawrence Joueur spoke and the desire to beat someone out of pride drove a dollar on to the table from the man standing next to Big Mike.

"Here," he said, placing the dollar on top of Joueur's other bill. "My money's on Talmadge," he said. Then nodding at the big man playing against Joueur he added, "Now kick his fancy wise ass!"

The older man took a shot at the balls along the rail and sank two numbered balls for points before strategically shooting and blocking Joueur before Joueur went for his next turn.

"Just to be clear," Joueur asked. "We get the points from the balls we sink. The order of the balls, from low to high, is the order that they must be sunk. You knocked in the 1 and 2 number balls so you have three points. I sink the 3 ball and we are tied, correct?"

"That's how it's played," the older man growled out the words. "And with money now on the table squirt, I am done teaching you with any more words. Your next lessons are all based now on watching me play!"

The play now went back and forth on the low point balls with Joueur appearing to struggle before commenting that the older man was getting a pretty big lead.

The older man's friends were now laughing and told him, sorry kid, that's how it goes.

Joueur paused for a moment before responding, "It is?" He then winked at his college mates before adding, "Well time for me to see what I can do about that."

Joueur smiled at the group and then sank seven straight balls leaving the highest point ball at an odd angle on the table. Joueur walked around the table twice whistling to the song playing up on the musical stage as he sized up his shot.

He walked back to the far side glanced up at the older man and smiled.

Then Joueur calmly knocked in the final ball with a double-banked shot and tallied the final points to win.

Instantly furious and salty language came out of the mouths of several of the man's companions who stood around them and who had joined in to place bets.

"First time player?" Talmadge physically moved so his large frame was up against Lawrence Joueur as he stood next to the money on the corner of the table. The anger in his voice was crisp and clear that he was about to erupt.

Gummere watched as Big Mike shifted position, as did Parker and Wier, besides the local men. It became very clear they were all preparing for a brawl that was apparently about to break out.

"I never said that," Lawrence Joueur stated without any sign of nervousness. "All I asked you for was a chance to play a game."

"A hustler," one of the men from behind Joueur who had placed a bet grumbled. "I knew it with his fancy clothing and fake and innocent talking!"

"No, my good fellow," Joueur responded as he averted his eyes from Talmadge for just a moment. "A hustler worries about taking your money." Lawrence Joueur now picked up the money in his hand. As Talmadge glared at him, Joueur counted out the twelve dollars, placing it in two neat six dollar stacks.

Next, Joueur distributed six of the dollars on to the table in the direction of the dock and iron workers who had wagered and gestured for them to pick it up.

Slowly, each man who had placed a bet took their money back, a quizzical look upon each face.

"And Mr. Tallmadge," Joueur said flipping another dollar from his own stash to him. "This also belongs to you for your willingness to, how did you say it so friendly-like at the start of our game? Teach me something."

Lawrence Joueur stepped back and placed his jacket back on. "With that gentlemen, I want to thank you for providing me the opportunity to play and I wish you all a good day."

The dock and iron workers stood and watched as Lawrence Joueur moved as if to head out.

Joueur stopped and turned back, pausing to look at the men for a moment while the room stayed quiet.

"As my friends and I take our leave, I do provide you this one last thought."

"And?" Talmadge asked, rolling his money in his hand.

"No," Joueur remarked. "I really have nothing to add. Lessons apparently have been learned."

With that Joueur moved toward the door without running. He stepped with confidence and sense of a purpose to exit the hall. The other five students from Princeton moved out too, right on his heels.

As soon as they stepped back into the fading light of the afternoon, they broke out in a loud round of laughter. The students started bantering back and forth and pushing each other as they burned off the energy and steam they had built up from coming that close to a major bar fight.

"Joueur. That was insanity!"

"That was amazing," Gummere noted.

"I truly thought they were going to fight us!"

"I thought that too and just hoped we were ready if they jumped us."

"I was ready to break some of those old timers in two!"

"Boasting, boasting, boasting," Gummere noted. "Glad we didn't fight. Those old-timers would have kicked our butts!"

"Seriously? No way! I will go back there right now if you do not believe it!"

"I do believe you would have fought. You won't now. And we have to get going," Gummere announced.

They followed Gummere as they headed away and while the excitement was sustained with the manly pronouncements continuing, the physical pushing and shoving slowed down as the adrenaline faded back to normal. This stage was replaced by various stabs at humor. They joked and laughed at each other the entire way as they headed back for the train to take them to Princeton.

Seated on the train, the group relaxed and enjoyed the ride. Slower, calmer, small talk began to fill the air.

"You know, you really were taking a chance back there with those dock workers and iron thugs," Parker said directly to Joueur. "You know, unlike you, they had nothing to lose."

"Without the risk, there is no fun," Joueur replied.

"It was crazy," Gummere noted. "But I loved your risk taking and confidence."

"Promise you that every time. That is how I always am. You guys should sneak out with me more often to enjoy the fruits of this world before you grow old and are not able to do it any longer."

They laughed.

"I am not lying. You walk with me any time and you will find that the wild activities of the cowboys out west are tame compared to the adventures one can have in the city. I am not boasting when I say I can make you winners in this game of life and nobody can stop me now."

"I'd love to see you have that confidence when we join together as teammates against Rutgers. That game will be here before you know it and we need that kind of spirit to teach them a lesson about life. I am happy to hear you bragging now about all you can do but just bring it when we head north to New Brunswick in two weeks," Gummere advised him.

"We all plan to bring it!" Big Mike promised his roommate as he pounded his fist into the open palm of his other hand. "Do not worry about the beat down at Rutgers."

"It will simply be another sorry Rutgers outing!" one of the others on the train called out.

"One more day to say goodbye to their college!"

Gummere loved their enthusiasm and confidence.

It was something he shared with them. It was not just a love of his college or a desire to win in any challenge that was presented. It was a genuine belief that they were destined to be the best of the best. It had been drilled in to each of them by their families and now through the pronouncements of staff at the college in Princeton and those who supported it.

Still, deep down, Gummere knew that with every contest one had to actually play it and win it before you could boast that you were victorious. And in the case of the competition in New Brunswick, like his peers, his goal was not just to win but rather to crush their opponent.

Unbeknown to him, that desire was equally shared by a key person back in Princeton.

Unfortunately for Gummere and his classmates, that man was soon to be lectured by powerful men who were very active in shaping life within the Princeton community. They also happened to be men who were more interested in supporting a part of the faculty which favored the historical image of the school and they endorsed the concept of fully enforcing fundamentally defined moral values. They expected this practice and principle to be applied to the student body at all times. They were not interested in any type of activity that could tarnish the image of the college. And, to the detriment of the college president's office, they listened to and tended to believe any complaints or rumors that college staff were willing to share.

26
October 28, 1869
Princeton

"So let me see if I am clear on what you are asking."
"You are looking for some form of symbolic discipline immediately to be imposed by our college leadership to make an impression on our young charges. Then you wish this to be extended to additional punitive measures to limit any freedom for student actions beyond lecture and study time. On top of that, you are telling me that you do not want us engaging with anyone at Rutgers College on any level. This restrictive behavior would be targeted to include me, staff and students and encompass any form of activity or professional endeavor?"

McCosh gripped both hands tightly on the arms of the leather chair to contain himself. He knew he could not allow what he truly thought to escape from him or words be uttered that would be perceived as if he had lashed out at these men seated in front of him.

The insanity of it all! The sheer stupidity!
Word had been leaked about the ongoing communications between him and President Campbell at Rutgers. That was obvious.
That text of what had been exchanged could be interpreted differently by any reader. What he had written could even be seen by these visitors as good or bad. Obviously, for the moment, they were interpreting his bold statements toward the Rutgers President as done as too aggressive. Unprofessional was their basic review while still taking a moment to support his position that Rutgers was a second rate college.
What had caused the greatest consternation though for McCosh was the fact that it was most likely one of his staff who had shared it externally with this group in an attempt to discredit him. That was not good. There was still clearly a play for power in his own ranks.

Then their sharing this anonymous, mysterious complaint about the missed study time for students. Most distressing was how they relayed it. "Misguided" was actually how they had phrased it. They expressed their displeasure with the audacity that he had displayed when, as the college president, he had moved forward without full staff approval and Board review for his new practice of allowing the students the time to deal with their strengthening of body and physical fitness activities.

It was no surprise that his faculty had been opposed to his program initiative. The staff had openly balked at his assertion that this was the next great thing for expanding young minds. They had instantly rebuked the work by Dr. Hitchcock up at Amherst College in this field of Physical Education when he had proposed that this was what they should be following here now in Princeton.

His instituting it over their objection had ignited fireworks over what they felt was lost "real" study time in their minds when he started to put the assigned wellness time on the daily schedule. He knew it was also about deeper competitive interests that drove their passion. They simply saw it as prioritizing the financial cost that a new gymnasium would impose on the college. In turn, that would take away money from the work of other departments.

As to the topic of student behavior, there had always been the random public comments about questionable public behavior by several students when out in the community. Again, what bothered McCosh the most though was an undertone that this information came from staff. The way these men explained it today from what they had heard, this noticeable angst about any boyish hijinks was a further sign of the erosion of daily control within the confines of Nassau Hall and a lack of leadership which was adding to the moral decay among their youth.

When McCosh asked for specifics all they had offered had been cast in the context of a new revelation about an incident by one student in particular who had left campus on a jaunt. These men sounded just like the faculty would have when hearing about an allegation of illegal involvement. They demanded accountability and immediate disciplinary examples be made. All purely punitive, and highly public, actions.

As he was forced to sit and listen and answer for himself, McCosh knew it was not unusual to be chastised and directed on how to behave by any of the ruling bodies that oversaw the administrators of any college. Such was the life of a college president.

This visit, though, appeared so much more than the typical "play nice" speech to which he was so accustomed. Instantly he began to wonder how many "inside voices" had panicked the Trustees to cause such a visit by these two self-described distinguished gentlemen today.

"Look, Dr. McCosh. You are planning on heading out on a multi-state visit. That is to be followed by an international tour in search of donors and to spread the name and reputation of this great college. While this will cause great expense to undertake, I do appreciate what that may also bring back in return in new enrollments and financial support. In addition, I am thrilled at the prospects that exist with how this trip may succeed in advancing the name of this college."

"However," the second man cut in. "The very image of this college hinges on the traditional framework that it was established upon. No matter the new audiences we bring our college to, there is a fundamental basis that should not be shaken or tainted by any speech or action on the part of the faculty, students, or the administration."

Again, McCosh had to physically summon his strength to control himself before responding to either of these businessmen. McCosh was all too aware that financial fortune had turned them into legislative leaders and self-proclaimed higher education experts and not their knowledge of how to run a school.

It also did not help his impression of them that both men flaunted their personal wealth in their clothing choices. In many ways it was symbolic of their common bond among all men who saw themselves as those who should dictate to all others because of the amount of inherited coin they had secured in their family-based wallets.

Still, McCosh cautioned himself. Beware of these legislators, seated here now smoking cigars in such a pompous manner. They were now entrenched in these positions due only to connections to those with power in this collegiate conservative structure and disagreeing with that element on campus would have inevitably put them at odds with McCosh.

However what bothered McCosh the most today was the way in which men like this spoke. Superior in wealth? Fine. Strut your money any way you prefer. But to consider yourself an intellectual equal to the scholars like himself on this campus when determining what those at the college should or should not do on a daily operational basis? In no way could that not make McCosh bristle.

Again McCosh warned himself to keep his wits about him and speak with them in a calm and respectful manner. These men hold access to power in both legislative and financial domains. Whether it is through their own purse or through legislative spending of others they vote with, you may need support from them in the future. Watch your tongue!

"So what is it that you would like me to do?" McCosh finally asked for their directive.

"I do not feel that is my role," the heavier man lied, before pausing to take a long drag on his cigar for effect.

McCosh almost impulsively filled the momentary silent void with a, "Then thank you and have a good day!" But he pinched himself and he held off.

After filling the air of the room with his smoke puffed out in bold fashion, the large man eventually shared what he envisioned for the future.

"Some would point to the recent events with what they are now calling Black Friday as an example of the cause of the subsequent economic pinch we are feeling. I hate men who preach that position. Too many always ready to blame their financial distress on others in my mind and looking for a handout without the work. Not that I personally like either Fiske or Gould, but it is that kind of willingness to take investment chances that had made America great. Those two rascals understand what so many others continue to fail to grasp. There are fortunes still to be made. And there are mounds of money out there for those with the skills and intestinal fortitude to fight to acquire it."

"However, in answering your question, I feel I must make my position abundantly clear at what caused this predicament in the first place and how this gets solved. Let me add, this is a viewpoint that is shared by many other important men and you will take this to heart, if you get my drift."

"That recent War dwindled the resources of this college. We are very sensitive to that loss that you may not fully understand as it preceded your arrival here in the States. You see, so many of the good wealthy southern families who sent us their gentlemen scholars before the troubles broke out have obviously shifted away from our doors. That loss took away young men embedded with private tutoring when they were children. That loss took their intellectual starting point not often shared in the mindset of our local Jersey boys from lesser means. Worst of all, with their exit also went with them their fathers' financial contributions."

"That was before you arrived and really is of no fault of your own. We do not blame you for that," the other man re-stated.

McCosh nodded at the obvious. It was hard to hold him personally accountable for the actions of others before he knew who they were or even before he had set foot in Princeton.

"But we are now under 300 students enrolled," the man went on. "That is a reality. We need additional students who pay to attend to support the bottom line of operations at this place. At the same time, I fear that if we do not reinforce the integrity of the school, we will not get future desirable students with families to contribute. To be clear, we cannot afford to fall any further."

"Think of it this way, Dr. McCosh," the second man spoke to him as if he were an expert and McCosh a child on the ways of the world. "Why not attend Yale or Harvard if our college in Princeton fails to be seen as molding the morals of our own through the rigors of hard classwork and discipline?"

"And, again for clarification, sir," McCosh choked on the words as he said them not really wanting their input. "What is it that you ask we do?"

The first man responded aggressively without any hesitation.

"Simple. Stop all interactions where our students are seen by anyone in the community as being undignified for a higher moral standing in society. No more blemishes that tarnish the school's good name and reputation. Step in and bring an end to any of their juvenile non-academic shenanigans!"

In a calmer voice the second man added his thoughts about direction.

"President McCosh, step one to me is very obvious. Support your faculty here in matters of academic rigor and classical studies. Let them help steer this ship. While you may feel it is not my place to tell you how to do your job, as I would hope and expect that you know how that should be done, you need to promote the elite intellectual property this institution has entrusted you with. Like my colleague said you need to get rid of the foolish acts that undermine our elite position that is our birthright as a college and community!"

McCosh watched quietly as both men simultaneously tapped the end of their cigars to extinguish the burn on the arms of his chairs leaving blackened spots behind. Formally, they pulled on their lapels and stood. He knew this was a signal they were done with their meeting.

The personal aide, who had stood at the side of the two men the entire time without speaking, now gathered their capes for them which they wore in as a formal top coat. Pulling them from the rack for each legislator, he placed the capes over their shoulders. He buttoned each under each man's chin while handing each of them their walking canes that were used by them as purely ornamental in purpose.

McCosh rose with less formality as the legislators went through these paces and moved toward the doorway with them to support their exit.

"Well then, Dr. McCosh. It was a pleasure speaking to you today," the first man said. "While it did take from our time, I hope what you heard and the work now outlined for you to do does move the college forward."

"Be sure you take to heart all that we have shared," the second man added as a cautionary warning. "There are many who would hate to see this communication today not carried through with. Do not confuse this visit with a social stop. We are calling for action."

The first legislator, already heading to leave, stopped and turned to provide one final word to Dr. McCosh for the meeting.

"Immediately!"

With that, they nodded and McCosh bid them a good day. They exited with what had by now become their standard pomp in a choreographed flourish. The aide followed closely behind escorting the two men straight to their carriage seats and closing the door for each before moving the foot stool to the rear for future use.

McCosh watched from a window as that carriage vanished from sight down the street in front of the President's house. He knew it would then move past the small business shops that lined the way into the center of Princeton proper. He also knew they would most likely not even glance out at these lesser locals as they moved back to their world of the wealthier environs of the affluent who had secured a place from which to rule.

McCosh turned and looked over the state map on his wall. The Jersey land itself was tinted in a bold pink and blue over a tan canvas background. It was finely detailed and showed the historic boundary lines that had once separated the eastern and western portions of colonial New Jersey into two distinct regions. He always marveled at how the first 1687 boundary, known as the "Keith Line," might have shifted Princeton from its western membership and into the eastern domain instead.

The 1743 line on the map though, grouped the people of New Brunswick separately from those who resided in Princeton. To those east of Princeton that division had been engrained in the geography of the political landscape that had been there since the colonial founding.

McCosh had learned from his research that New Jersey as a whole was a land bounded by two major American cities. Philadelphia to the west and New York on its eastern border each played into the economic and social dynamics which divided not only loyalties but also the financial livelihood of so many.

This current division of Princeton and New Brunswick may have been averted altogether had the railroad which now served as the primary mode of transport for goods existed first. Instead, waterways were the original economic transportation kingpin. As a result, a region's identity was forged by its proximity to either the Delaware River or to the Hudson River.

The negative relationship between communities, by the linking of New Brunswick to New York City and Princeton to Philadelphia, exacerbated so many other factors due to this split. For McCosh, he knew it resonated in the minds and actions of men like these legislators who had just left his office. The base rivalry also clearly echoed in the halls of Nassau and Old Queens where there were even greater reasons for a divide.

After the Great Awakening, the move to create colleges within New Jersey was a shared vision for both the Presbyterian group who became the founders for Princeton and the Dutch Reformed Church group who eventually were the founders at Rutgers College. The Presbyterians had a Scottish influence that had spread to areas like the rural community of Princeton. The Dutch Reformed Church, with its historical center of power in the United States in New York, was more closely aligned to New Brunswick.

The Civil War strife, to which his recent visitor had alluded, was due in many ways to that Presbyterian connection to households in the pre-War South.

Young men who had attended classes in Nassau Hall came in large numbers from Virginia and North Carolina due to this religious commonality in Princeton. The Rutgers footprint beyond the states of New Jersey and New York had been minimal. With the previous southern representation on the Princeton campus the War had caused tensions that, at least to this date, had not been completely repaired.

The rift between Princeton and New Brunswick had a fundamental element which McCosh believed he could exploit to Princeton's advantage. Unfortunately for Rutgers, to make the college in Princeton look better, they needed an entity to play the failing role. He needed a scapegoat to build up his college's reputation and support in his plan and Rutgers was the perfect foil.

The physical view, which McCosh enjoyed each day outside his door, was a pastoral landscape around Princeton. A rural framing of farms hinted at an agrarian base. However, instead of a future with small tenant farmers, McCosh saw a future with advancements that would allow for large gentlemen farmers who were not bound to toil in the soil each day. Instead, he foresaw men who ran their property as an extension of their other business interests they were engaged in. The advantage of this was that it meant there was great potential for increasing localized wealth that held political power versus subsistent farming poverty.

McCosh truly believed that Princeton was the perfect setting for scholastic work. He saw this as the environment which was better prepared to allow for focused academic study without the diversions of an urbanized society that brought with it the economic pressures toward a daily base profit for survival. Any economic downturn in an urban village could spell collapse if a factory closed. Here, research work among the faculty could be removed from having to stand each day with urban planners and a political city manager anxious to see immediate returns on any of their personal investments.

In contrast, Rutgers College sat in the center of a major population expansion around the campus. What was becoming the city of New Brunswick had grown to almost five times the size of Princeton. The campus sat in a community which had shifted to an industrial and manufacturing focus. This change for Rutgers now prioritized any decision there that needed to be made in regards to topics ranging from land availability to simple quality of life. In his last visit to New Brunswick, McCosh would have been hard pressed not to define this as an urban environment. It was the opposite of what he saw as the ultimate for a college community and for what existed in Princeton.

Yet, while McCosh saw the benefits of the Princeton setting, he also saw the potential future challenge from Rutgers. The campus, with local industrial ties and big business dollars in their neighborhood, could bring to bear legislative pressure on future school funding allocations for Rutgers and against their college in Princeton if this game were not played correctly.

The failure with the Morrill Act had demonstrated this risk so clearly.

Rutgers, not the College of New Jersey in Princeton, was seen as the practical school that gave an immediate return to the business world. McCosh believed that Rutgers was selected simply because it looked more like a place where an investment, in the eyes of the state leaders, more closely aligned with the future growth of wealth versus an agrarian study of the past.

So McCosh had engaged on his initial attack on Rutgers College. Reduce the reputation of Rutgers in the hope that the men with the money and political power would want to back a winner and shift their support to Princeton and future success.

McCosh was also aware that this could not be a stand-alone local strategy.

His plan, which had just been approved by the Trustees, was to embark on a major promotional tour of key cities. He planned to go oversees to extol the virtues of the education the youth received in Princeton. A world-wide advertising tour of his college.

His mission was to be aimed at the growing Presbyterian populations wherever McCosh encountered them. There were many loyal parishioners who had moved into positions of wealth and influence and whom he would recruit to pledge their financial support for a college built on their religion's foundational stones. He would also take the opportunity to recruit the sons of the wealthiest donors as future students. In this way he would try to build a future alumni base that would be flush with inherited cash to contribute, he hoped, to Nassau Hall as they graduated with a new found college allegiance.

In this manner he also felt that he could out-recruit and gain financial pledges that would never be matched at Rutgers. Rutgers did not share as large a historic religious foundational base. Rutgers could not build their endowment through a similar strategy.

McCosh rolled a pencil in between his fingers and breathed deeply to calm himself. The debate within his own mind had led to a huge question from which he was unsure which direction would be best.

On the one side, he did yearn for the funding, as well as the program recognition that the Morrill Act had provided Rutgers College, with a shift to grow a scientific program of studies aligned to industrial and business research needs in the broader economic setting.

Unlike the majority of his fellow Princeton faculty, he did see the sciences and industry as the future of college study. It did not mean there was a need to eliminate the Liberal Arts approach. He felt there would always be a need for that area of studies, especially with his Christian-based recruitment plan.

No, it just meant a college would take an enhanced approach which expanded the quality of the education options with a practical aspect. That shift, McCosh knew very well, created a better look for future investment versus just an altruistic component of building a better educated society as a Classic Studies curriculum preached for its value added.

Rutgers was poised to move in that direction. In that way it was a real threat to be dealt with.

On the other hand, McCosh reasoned, maybe his real energy should be at giving Rutgers the College of New Jersey "title" for their school. Justify the name change with the Morrill Act Grant and allow it to saddle them at Rutgers in a way that being a "state" school actually diminishes worldly prestige. Having a "state" name for a school was hindering the image of his college in the eyes of President McCosh.

McCosh knew his approach to attract students and donors from across the country, and especially across the Atlantic, was harder to sell due to the narrowed state association.

Having the label as a state's college did not cleanly translate to verbiage about a national or universal mission and appeal. He saw how names like Yale and Harvard projected an independent and global image which suggested the highest level of scholastic research and student learning.

Why not name the school "Nassau College" after the historic building? Or name it after the highest giving new donor? McCosh had wrestled with the opportunity for revenue that option might bring if he could connect it to a fundraising effort with naming rights.

McCosh was not even opposed to calling the school "Princeton College." The community of Princeton was undeniably, in population size and layout of the grounds, connected as a college town. And it would no longer sound like a state institution but rather a historic grounds like naming it after the building would hold the prestige of a historic site.

This was all rolling around for McCosh when he was interrupted by a knock on the door.

"Dr. McCosh," the housekeeper announced. "Your one o'clock appointment is here."

Instantly, he was drawn back to the day to day logistics of running the college and the issue at hand.

How would he fulfill this "demand" of the Trustees to only emphasize the Classics and the Spartan restrictive student lifestyle they favored?

For some of his faculty, he knew, they would cheer such a declaration about teaching only in the Classics manner.

McCosh chuckled as he imagined how happy and smug their faces would be on hearing such news. They would love to see their President McCosh told what he could and could not do!

Of course, McCosh reminded himself, those faces would be the same ones that would belong to the staff who would elect to march in to his office whenever they felt any outsider was attacking their own academic freedom.

McCosh debated his next steps. He was not positive on all the details he would share at this time on merging where he hoped to direct the college and where he needed to yield. Still he knew this meeting would require that he communicate the message given to him today on to those in his charge in some manner. He also knew it would require to have some action take place immediately.

And then there was this dealing with the current disciplinary matter at hand?

He looked up at the housekeeper.

"Thank you. Please show him in."

27
October 31, 1869
New Brunswick

While light from the scattered street and home lamps flickered off spots directly around them, for the most part, this section of New Brunswick was very dark. Without the glow of an overhead moon, the roots and rocks that were randomly dispersed on the pathways would have made navigation by foot nearly impossible.

Elizabeth could sense the excited but nervous energy in Adkins. It made her smile. She also appreciated his penchant for organization as he took care of every detail in an attempt to make sure this visit would be a success.

As she thought back on it now, so far this day from the moment they had met late that afternoon at the train station had all gone just as previously planned.

Together they had taken her bag to the lodging house that he had secured for her off of Hamilton Street. It was close to the train station and located in what appeared to be the central part of New Brunswick.

Used as a boarding home to earn money for the owner as well as a personal household, the place she was to stay in was a nice, clean residence. The woman who ran the home rented her rooms typically only for longer staying boarders. By chance, Adkins told her, a room had come open and since it had not been rented yet the owner had agreed for it to be used for this one time as a one night rental.

The owner was very polite when she greeted them at the door. It was obvious to Elizabeth that the woman had arranged the rental with Mr. Adkins before based upon the ease with which she spoke. She escorted Elizabeth to her room and pointed out the wash basin and clothing hooks before exiting back to her post.

At first glance the room itself was small but Elizabeth felt it would suffice for one night. She placed her bag on the bed and looked out the small window that opened on to the street below. The view beyond that was of trees and several small structured wood frame buildings across the way.

After freshening herself up from her trip, Elizabeth closed the door behind her to her room as she walked out to meet with Adkins who had waited for her in the main doorway to the property.

At first she had thought it might be awkward meeting the group of people from Rutgers College who Adkins had said they would be joining that night. But now she actually felt a sense of relief that she would not be alone the entire time while they were on their date.

"Date."

The word gave her pause as it rolled over and over again in her mind. How odd a term and yet how fitting in its use this time around considering all the logistical work that went into planning this day. They had arranged the date and time of this meeting and plotted the details in written correspondence.

Adkins had proven to be very thoughtful in asking about what she felt most comfortable with. She was grateful that he took on each task, including securing her room and her pick-up at the train station, in such an organized fashion that she felt she knew exactly what to expect in the way of the itinerary from the time of her arrival until the time of her departure back to Princeton.

They had exchanged letters each day since his departure from Princeton.

The obvious main purpose for writing had been organizational in nature. But while that function about the date was within the letters; this correspondence had also allowed for a natural opportunity for both her and Adkins to ask and provide more details to each other about their own lives.

She was very aware of the magnitude of her announcement about having two children. She could just imagine the weight it must have placed on his mind after Adkins rode away that day from Princeton. If the expression on her mother's face later that day when she had found her mother afterward back at the hat shop was any indication; the average person would have seen that parent of two children revelation for any future social meeting as a deal breaker for any man.

"He is still going to see you?" Her mother half shouted out in disbelief and then danced a small jig in her exuberance over the news.

"Yes," Elizabeth confirmed. Then she corrected her mother. "I have actually agreed to see him!"

Still Elizabeth understood the implications of her situation.

Many men would have politely turned tail and headed off never to be seen again rather than start a possible relationship with a previously married woman with two young children. His reaction that day had crystallized in her mind what she had instinctively felt about him from the start.

He has a kind heart. Yes. He likes me. This now appears to also be true.

Elizabeth had met only a few men after the death of her husband. Each man knew her story about her life in Princeton. She had wondered what their real motivations were to engage her in any conversation. Not that there were a great many men available. Really there had only been three who had been serious in their intentions toward an actual relationship at all.

Two of these men had been war veterans. Each one had claimed to have felt for the loss of their comrade, her husband, and told her it was their duty to come and comfort the widow of a man who had given his life for his country. They both may have been genuine, but she couldn't help but feel they were there for some idealistic purpose. At no time did she gather from their actions it was because of something they had seen in her. Instead they were acting out of loyalty pledged to their dead friend.

Another gentleman was introduced to her by her mother's friend Ms. Haddie. He had virtually spent more time the one afternoon they had met discussing the profitability of the hat shop instead of looking at her. He had walked the storage and work areas as if measuring the space to assess the value of the business. In turn he appeared to do this to help him determine if it was worth the investment of taking on Elizabeth and her two children as part of his personal portfolio. Elizabeth summarized her impression of his assessment of a marriage to her when she spoke later that day with her mother. "Nice shop where you can earn a livelihood and you get the gal too!"

Elizabeth was polite but firm with him.

Thank you for visiting but, no, I am not interested.

Haddie had told her mother at the time that man was probably Elizabeth's last hope when he angrily walked away. Elizabeth had told her mother to tell Haddie that if that man was the definition of hope, she did not want to have any.

That had stopped the local attempts at match-making for a while among her mother's friends even if it did not slow down the everyday gossip among these same women of Princeton.

Thinking about it now, Elizabeth realized he was the last man she had spoken with in connection with any type of "social intent" before Elizabeth had encountered Adkins that night at Judge Olden's home three months later.

She knew that the gap in time without any male options was also why her mother had sounded so instructional in her speeches to her about how to attract a possible spouse.

This was the voice Elizabeth heard from her mother after they left from their encounter on the campus with Adkins in New Brunswick several weeks prior. Her mother had explained then why she should keep her children a secret from him.

Her mother had repeated to her several times that the risk of telling Mr. Adkins about the twins was too high. For any relationship to bloom, she had coached Elizabeth, if he ever did write her she should not reply back about her current status as a mother of twin children. Such news would create a fear in him that would cause any hope of a meeting to end before it ever took place.

This had created a mighty fight within their Princeton household. It had also created a daily battleground in the shop. Her mother was unable from keeping any topic out of the gossip circles with her friends and sought their advice about not telling Adkins about the children. The local women echoed this strategy to Elizabeth each day.

She knew her mother's love for her was genuine. She knew her mother's love for her children was never in question. Still, she couldn't help but quarrel over the constant advice she was being given.

"You need a chance to see if he cares for you first," her mother would say.

"I do not want to start any relationship on a foundation of lies," Elizabeth had replied.

"It is not lying," her mother had defended her position. "If you write him a note about the children only one of two things may happen. First, he may vanish altogether. I've known many a heroic figure who would take to flight at the mention of children – especially someone else's."

"They are a part of me, mother. Better to know now versus later," Elizabeth had countered. "I would only want to start a relationship with a man who has met and already adores my children. They are wonderful and they both deserve that."

"And more lovely children have never set foot on this earth," her mother conceded. "But having a man fall for your children first can also be a problem for you dear. You know, I would think a smart young lady like yourself would see that."

She took the bait. "What do you mean mother?"

"Say he is the paternal type and meets the children. He sees himself as the father right away. Those children could capture anyone's heart. If he is that kind of man, maybe he decides to join with you just to be with them."

"Are you inferring that he wants to steal the kids? That is as crazy a thought as you have ever had!"

"No, I am not saying he would steal the children. God forbid the thought! However, I am suggesting that if he has eyes as a father first, then you may be bound to a man forever for the wrong reasons."

"What?"

"Look dear, you are my daughter. I love my grandchildren and you know that. I want everything in the world for them. But first I want your life to be fulfilled. I want you to be happy. I want you to find love. I want you to say, yes, this is the man for me! Do not settle for taking a man simply because he fits a role as a father figure for your children. I want you to love him and him to love you first."

Her mother had taken her hands as they spoke. When her mother approached discussions with her like this, it was hard for Elizabeth to argue with her even when she was meddling in her personal affairs.

"Mom, I appreciate the thought. I do thank you for caring so much about me. But you also know you have to let me make these decisions myself. I will not, if he does write, let the issue not be shared that I am the mother of two children. That fact about my life is too critical. The reality is that, if a man is to turn and run upon learning this, then so much for that man and good riddance anyway. And if that man meets my children and falls for them first; well that would be something I would have to decide what I would do and not someone else."

"So when he writes you plan to write him back and tell him?"

"Mother, he hasn't even written yet."

"Oh he will, Elizabeth. I saw it in his eyes and I am an excellent judge of human habits and character. While I cannot tell his full worth as a person yet without further investigation, I can tell you he is definitely attracted to you and he will contact you."

Elizabeth laughed at how with each passing day when no letter had arrived, her mother's confident prediction had sounded so less convincing.

Elizabeth remembered how her own mood had shifted too. It was not that she believed there would be no other chance for romance in her in her life. She was too positive a thinker to believe in that type of fatalistic ending. No, her personal conflict was that she could not shake off that special attraction she had felt from the first night when he had bumped into her. Though she tried to ignore it, she had to admit to herself there was something in that Mr. Adkins that she had found appealing. Meeting him had stirred feelings within her that she had not felt in a long time.

What the "it" was; she refused to give it a name.

But now, tonight, as Elizabeth stepped down the stairs to the doorway and then out into the evening air with him on the streets of New Brunswick that Sunday night, she knew that the feeling was one that seemed to give her a new joy in life itself.

This all played through her mind as she heard Adkins speak and bring her back to the present.

"So the three couples we are joining are all great people," Adkins stated.

His voice had that distinct hint of nervousness rising as the small talk between them had faded and the reality of the scheduled event approached.

"I am sure that they are," Elizabeth assured him even though she had only the faintest knowledge of who they were about to meet and only from what Adkins had shared in his letters.

They crossed over Hamilton Street at Hartwell Street and then turned to walk up the less crowded Robinson Street. Two carriages rolled past them moving quickly to wherever their passengers were headed.

Adkins had intentionally elected to walk and talk.

First, as with the last two times they had met, he found that this mode of transport had allowed for casual conversation. It also provided another opportunity for Elizabeth and himself to get to know each other better. Rather than race to a site to awkwardly wait for the rest of their group to arrive, this stroll along the calm street gave him a chance to feel more relaxed in her presence.

Why was he so nervous?

Adkins had played over the details of the evening so many times he no longer had to read it from the paper on which he had outlined their day.

They were now on the way to meet with the three couples at the designated tunnel entrance where their tour would begin. And they were right on schedule.

One of those in the group was Rutgers professor Dr. Cook who was seen as one of the most celebrated members of the staff at Rutgers. He would lead the tour and hopefully his credentials would help impress Elizabeth with the type of man that Adkins associated with.

Adkins had predicted this tour should last slightly over an hour and end right on the campus grounds.

They were then scheduled to go with the three couples back to the Cook's home where they had been invited to dine. Then they would enjoy the company of other invited guests from New Brunswick that the Cooks knew for their Halloween social. Adkins felt that being with a group at a social party might ease the stress of finding things for himself to talk about with his date.

That social would end later in the evening and due to the hour of the night they would immediately take a carriage ride back to the boarding house he had secured for Elizabeth. He would leave her and then return in the morning for them to go for a breakfast at his favorite tavern. He would then escort her to the train for her ride back to Princeton before he had to head back to the campus to be at work.

It seemed like the perfect plan limiting any awkward down time of not knowing what to do.

So why the nerves with the details so clearly all in order?

In his heart he knew the answer had nothing to do with the tactical logistics at all. Those factors he could control. No, what he had worried about and were the real reasons for his anxiety every day since she had agreed to attend were those intangibles.

What if she did not like the people they were spending the evening with? What if she did not like the food or the room she was scheduled to stay in? What if he ran out of things to say?

What if she hated the actual tour they had planned? The underground tunnel and ghost tales were so appealing to him but what if she really did not like it? What if she was that certain type of lady who, when she saw where the tour would take her, might refuse to go? If Elizabeth did that, would it set a tone that then ruined the whole evening and end their chance for a relationship altogether?

Her written response to the evening itinerary he had outlined in the last letter had not hinted of anything wrong. But was she just trying to sound polite?

Still, as he saw the small group waiting up ahead that they were about to meet, he remembered what had made him the most nervous about the entire night.

What was he supposed to do when the evening came to an end and it was time to drop her off?

Was he to shake her hand, like two strangers passing in the night? Was he simply to verbally thank her for a wonderful evening and walk off? Or was he supposed to kiss her goodnight? What was going to be appropriate and how was he to know what to do without looking like a total fool?

He hated himself for thinking this way but he could not help it. He felt just like one of those young school boys he was being paid to tutor and prepare for life. When does this social uneasiness ever end?

"Mr. Adkins!" He heard a male voice from the group up ahead yell out at him.

"So kind of you to join us. We were worried you may have decided to do something else."

Assembled on the gravel path were the two professors, Dr. Cook and his colleague Dr. Murray. At their sides stood each of their wives, Mary Cook and Martha Murray.

Next to them, having just called out to him, was his friend and fellow tutor Isaac Hasbrouck. With him was his wife, Lucy. They were all cast in an eerie light from two lanterns, one of which was held aloft by Dr. Murray and the other one by Dr. Cook.

"Sorry for any delay," Adkins offered back to the entire group.

Then, turning to Elizabeth at his side, he introduced her to the other six in front of him.

"It gives me great pleasure to introduce you all to Elizabeth Warren of Princeton."

"Ah, the Lady Warren of Princeton. Master Hasbrouck at your service," Isaac bowed toward Elizabeth and Adkins as he poked fun at the formality of Adkins' introduction. "Tis an honor."

"Isaac, do not act the fool all night," his wife Lucy admonished him for his behavior with this stranger to their fold. Reaching out her hand to Elizabeth she smiled, introduced herself, and added, "Please excuse the childish behavior of my husband. There are times I wonder why he is allowed out in social settings."

Immediately the other four stepped forward and politely welcomed her while introducing themselves.

As the last person said their hello, Dr. Cook held up the lantern and made an announcement to the assembled group.

In a voice that was all at the same time friendly, authoritative and with a hint of mischief about the supernatural in it, he officially started their tour for the night.

"I am so glad you have all elected to gather here with us on this evening on the festival of souls."

"As you may or may not know, worship of this night is reported from ancient times back to the pre-Christian Celtic festival of Samhain. People once lit fires and huddled in collective masses every year on this date as it was purported that the dead returned to earth on this very night."

"In an attempt to incorporate the popularity of this traditional pagan festival into their worship, the Catholic Church merged this night into a day to honor the saints on November 1. Hence All Hallow's Eve was born."

"However, while exploring the grounds below us tonight it is important to never forget that the attachment to those who had died remained connected through many types of rituals. If all is right we may be witnesses tonight of one of those spectral events with the steps we are about to take."

Waving the lantern toward an impression in the ground before him, Dr. Cook continued.

"I never thought that what I am about to show you was actually possible. I am a true man of science. Through my studies I felt that science could explain everything in the world around us. I have lived my entire life by that creed. This was until one day, while on assignment here in New Brunswick with a simple mineral rock study, I came upon what I am about to show you tonight which changed my foundational belief in all things being absolute for science."

At his request, Mr. Hasbrouck next lifted a patchwork grate from the ground.

When Cook held the lantern over the top of the newly opened hole, a dark tunnel which had been hollowed into the ground below them became apparent to all there.

"Below the surface where we now stand and all life up here on the streets, I encountered a singular voice from within the depths of this very opening." Cook's voice was very serious as he spoke and pointed toward the exposed dark space in the ground before them at their feet.

Then Cook turned to look directly at his wife.

"My dear," Cook said to his wife. "This is the place that you have requested to see first-hand from the stories past that I have told. As you know, I have feared too much to allow you the risk of such a journey when you have asked to go before. I offer you again, this one last time, are you sure you wish to enter?"

"If you survived, my good George, then so shall I."

"Then follow me, my love, below the earth's surface. I will lead the way into what was once a mine but had years ago fallen into great disrepair. Forgotten over decades of non-use, it supposedly became the perfect hiding ground for some who were hoping to escape from oppression to their promised land."

With that, Dr. Cook handed his lantern to Hasbrouck. He sat on the edge of the cut in the ground and then lowered himself feet first with a cautious jump into the dark hole.

A thump could be heard as his feet hit something solid, he was shoulder deep with only his head within sight of the rest of the group above the ground level. He paused for just a moment to look into the darkness at his feet beneath him before looking back up at the group above him. He looked about at the group as he passed on the directions for their descent.

"That is the most difficult physical part of the entry, I swear. It is an awkward first step down."

Then, pointing toward the darkness of the surface below him he continued.

"I am now standing on a platform that has a small hand crank here at my knees that I can turn to lower myself to the next level beneath us in the earth. This first drop is a short way down and this platform stops to rest at an area that was carved into the land beneath us to form that miner's entrance to the tunnels they created."

"Once down here you will see that this small shaft opens itself up into a horizontal tunnel space carved into the ground below. When I get there, I shall exit this platform and the pulley which causes the lift to fall and rise can also be controlled from the bottom. I will send it back up to allow each of you to follow me down to the underground."

Hasbrouck handed Cook the lantern back.

"Gentlemen. Please assist the ladies one at a time on to the platform. Call to let me know they are on it and I will lower it down myself to the lower surface. Then, once they are down below, you should follow. Dr. Murray," Cook instructed. "I request that you remain as the last to join us below with your lantern to keep it lit up here."

With that they could hear the creaking sound of the platform lowering as Cook turned the hand crank. Cook's head disappeared from view but a moderate light still flickered from within the ground as he lowered himself down. Four full minutes passed before a shout from below was heard that Cook had successfully reached the bottom of the shaft. A series of cringing scratching metal against metal sounds could now be heard as the lift rose back up.

"Who would like to go first?" Murray asked the ladies.

"Like to?" Mrs. Cook replied sarcastically. "After my husband's warning who would want to go?"

"I will, if no one else wishes to start," Elizabeth offered, stepping forward.

"Be our guest," Mrs. Murray answered while gesturing toward the hole and smiling. "Just be sure to holler loud if we should think twice about following you."

"Oh, I will be sure to do that," Elizabeth smiled back. She placed her one hand to the ground and pulled her skirts in tight with the other hand. She then scooted her feet over the edge of the ground and into the hole.

"Here goes," she stated as she hopped in. Her feet hit the boards of the lift with a sudden thud. When she straightened up her head, unlike Dr. Cook's, did not reach the surface. But looking straight up into the lantern light in the hands of Dr. Murray her eyes could be seen framed by her white face by the rest of those standing above her in the group.

"Are you okay?" Murray politely asked.

"I believe so," she responded.

Dr. Murray then hollered out "all aboard" for Dr. Cook to know to start the pulley system in motion. Instantly Elizabeth's features vanished into the dark void below.

Adkins partially gasped out loud as his date disappeared from sight.

Hearing him, Isaac Hasbrouck teased his friend. "I guess that's the last you'll see of her. Quickest end to a date probably in the history of mankind!"

Lucy instantly hit Isaac in the arm admonishing him for his taunt. "That was not very nice of you to say to Christopher. You know this is his first date."

"I know. All I was pointing out was he had a short date," Isaac said nodding toward the dark hole in the ground before breaking into a chuckle at his own joke.

The thump of the wooden lift against the restraints caught all of their attention. They watched into the darkness as all appeared quiet and still below them.

"Come on ladies," Cook suddenly hollered up from below. "Miss Warren is fine. It is wonderfully simple just as promised! Just a swaying ride down. No work on your part. All Aboard!"

Adkins looked at Isaac. "Sounds like she is just fine!"

"I hope the same is true for me," Mrs. Cook announced as she moved to sit on the ground next to the entryway to be the next person in.

Slowly, everyone in the party moved in the same manner from the street surface through the narrow shaft in the ground to the tunnel carved out below.

When everyone was safely underground and Dr. Murray's lantern had been added to the existing light with Dr. Cook's lantern, Adkins got a clearer look around.

During the descent, part of the fall had been in total darkness and his eyes did not get the opportunity to adjust and see what he was passing. The darkness also confused the actual distance he was traveling at that time. As such, it was hard to tell what the depth of the tunnel was below the street surface they had just left but his instincts told him this was a great distance underground.

Now out from the tight shaft and in the tunnel itself he could see that it moved out in two long directions. As he looked down the tunnel and into the darkness, he could see the sides and floor were squared off. The sides of the cave rose perpendicular to the ground. However the ceiling above them had been carved in the rock as an arc and this gave the tunnel a cross-cut view that almost looked like the shape of the liberty bell.

Relics from the men who had once worked and walked these grounds were still present in small cut-outs where rusted hurricane lamps could be seen poised to help light their way while they had been here years ago every twenty feet.

"This was originally a copper mine," Dr. Cook explained to the group as they each tried to adjust their eyes to the mix of darkness and the dancing lights of the two lantern flames against the cavern walls.

"We estimate that carving started well over a hundred years ago. The mine was in operation years before the War for Independence from England was ever even conceived."

Cook pointed back toward the hole they had just come down.

"That entryway was known as Shaft Number Two. It was one of the seven or eight major drops to get the workers down here. We are going to rely on lanterns this evening and we will not be exiting the way that we entered."

"Oh thank goodness," Mrs. Murray exclaimed. "I think one drop in a long hole a night is enough. I look forward to walking out and back to civilization up on the streets through any number of steps versus that rickety ride down."

"I apologize my dear for any confusion about the modality as we will need to use a similar method to exit," Cook clarified. "I only meant that since we will be walking eastward, out toward the Raritan River, we will exit by rising through a different shaft and not returning again to this specific spot in the tunnel."

Mrs. Murray looked at Dr. Cook but said nothing.

Cook pointed toward the eastward part of the tunnel and suggested they should start to walk very slowly in that direction as the ground was slippery. Carefully, everyone in the party stepped over the rock surface. He took this silence to continue his narration of their tour.

"As you have no doubt noticed, the ground below your feet is puddled and the majority of it is wet."

"It is hard to believe that rain can even get down here," Lucy said.

"True," Cook replied. "But while some pure rain water is sure to seep in to any location as it runs off the streets above, the reality is that much of this water comes from a man-made pond that links to this tunnel."

"And the pond leaks water this way when it rains?" Elizabeth asked.

"Actually the pond was carved in the ground to capture water from a natural creek-bed so that there was a standing pool of water. A type of gate, or what they called a sluice, was built at the tunnel entry. The mine operators would periodically lift this gate to allow the base of this tunnel to flood enough so that materials could be transported by small boat."

"But why would the water from that gate be here if you said earlier that the miners have not used this tunnel for that purpose in a long time?" Elizabeth cut into Cook's speech.

"Very observant," Cook replied.

"As with any man-made device, things wear down or break. Hence the danger factor you notice with the water below your feet is that the old sluice gate has cracks in it and, at any time, the water pressure in that pond pushes through."

"So it leaks?" Mrs. Murray asked. "Or if it accidently opened, would it flood the entire tunnel?"

"Unfortunately, yes," Dr. Cook responded. "But on the positive side that has not happened. At least recently."

"Recently?" Mrs. Murray now sounded more anxious.

Cook ignored the intended question and went on describing the tunnel itself. "Scientific and historic research studies showed that the work here was never completed as initially planned. You see, we believe the original goal was to carry the raw materials all the way down the slope of the tunnel to the Raritan River docks."

"It doesn't go all the way there now?"

"We have not been able to show that it ever did make it to the Raritan," Cook answered. "We are not sure if part of it collapsed at one point or if it was intentionally closed off for some reason. But we do know it currently runs off in three directions from its starting point and each path comes to an abrupt end. One of the theories on why it stops is that the mine was not profitable and the venture simply ended. I personally believe the carving work at trying to extract copper was halted before the tunnel was complete."

"And the other theory on why the path just ends?" Elizabeth asked.

"It may have been sealed off intentionally after some disaster or by someone to make sure no one could exit that way again."

"There is a way out?" Lucy now asked, suddenly equating the end of a tunnel exit with a walled in cave.

"Yes," Cook smiled. "However, as Martha was disappointed before, the only way out is up through a shaft using the method we came down. Of course, that is, unless we elect to swim through the pond at the west entranceway to the tunnel."

"Now, to get your bearings, we are walking below Hartwell Street right now. We are headed toward where the path of the tunnel crosses under Guilden Street heading toward College Avenue."

"It is strange thinking about all those people who are living right above us. They have no idea we are walking right underneath them unseen and unheard like mice in a basement," Elizabeth whispered to Adkins.

She put her hand in his hand as they walked. "I hope you don't mind if I use you to help steady my step while we walk."

"Not at all." Adkins smiled.

"Now, before we get to the deepest part of the mine, roughly below Easton Avenue, I have a few details I wish to point out. While I will talk about technical items this evening to include explanations about the water and the entry spots and I will review some of the history of the tunnel, I believe you will soon discover why our adventure is so unique tonight."

The group continued to walk in step closely to Cook who continued in the lead. The acoustics of the old copper mine made hearing him easy even while they moved on at the same time he spoke.

"Like I said, the water gate releases water into the mine from a pond that resides just to the west. As noted before, it actually was designed to allow for water transport below the ground. The trick with the gate is that it cannot be raised too quickly or too high. If that happens the tunnel will flood and anyone in it would instantly drown."

"So we really could drown?" Martha Murray now sounded even more worried.

"Now you have my attention," Mary Cook announced. "And remember that if you drown me tonight we have children you will be responsible for ruining their lives."

Cook went on, paying no heed to his wife's comment. "You will possibly hear some strange noises down here tonight that we will not be able to explain."

"Noises?" Lucy asked.

"Yes, strange noises," Cook repeated.

"Define strange?" Lucy responded instantly.

"Before I explain a noise, let me share one more story. This involves that gate securing the tunnel from the pond. In this tale it was reported that the mine operators were trying to hurry the work along one day. In an attempt to get the workers to work faster the tunnel operator may have accidently allowed too much water in at one point. As the water raced in it would have flooded the large area where we are now walking and where the workers would have been standing."

"Could they have escaped up in the shafts?" Elizabeth asked.

"No. The workers would have been swept along with any current and the water pressure from such a rush of water would have pinned them down under. The reality is that it would have drowned any miners in its path," Cook explained.

"But what does that have to do with strange noises?" Lucy brought the earlier comment back up.

"Well, I have heard some insist that this event is what accounts for the sad howls that some say can be heard in this tunnel."

"Sad howls? What does that mean?"

"There are those who believe that there are strange noises which cannot be explained from the ground down here. Some claim it is the miners themselves calling for help before they were claimed by the icy waters that encircled them from the flooding and caused them to drown. Souls trapped in a watery grave."

"Really?" Martha exclaimed.

"Others claim it is not the cries of the miners but rather the mournful cry from their wives. One tale talks about the wives yelling down the shafts from the ground above while waiting for the water to recede hoping that their loved one was still alive. Whether it is the call to see if her spouse is there or the wailing that ensued when no survivors are found, the eternal call is what some say makes up the strange noise that can be heard down here in the darkness."

"Seriously?" Isaac laughed.

As soon as Isaac laughed, everyone in the group was startled when a deep, long and mournful sound seemed to flow past them where they stood.

"What was that?" Martha was the first to ask with a sound of panic in her voice.

"Okay, now I am getting a little scared," Lucy acknowledged wide-eyed in fright and moved closer to her husband, Isaac, for support.

Isaac now said nothing.

They all looked about unsure of the source of the noise and alert in case the sound repeated itself. When no additional sound followed for a full minute, Dr. Cook turned and motioned the group to continue forward. They each walked for a while in silence. The pace of every step quickened either from the slight incline drop of the tunnel floor or from the fear of staying in this place too long and being separated and left behind.

Cook stopped after moving several more yards up the tunnel and appeared for a moment to be looking around to get his bearings.

At this point the group had covered roughly two city blocks. Underground it was difficult to gauge the actual distance and Adkins could only tell that they were moving forward.

Cook held his lantern up toward the ceiling of the cave. When the lantern light bounced off the ceiling rocks, another shaft hole could be seen to have appeared above them in the dark.

"This is the deepest part of the mine," Cook announced. "We are at this moment at that point in this tunnel where we are the furthest under the ground."

"Wonderful," Adkins heard Lucy say to no one in particular.

"Okay, now we need to stand and listen for a moment to see what else we can hear as this is typically where reports of strange noises have come from."

"Are you telling me you did not hear something earlier?" Lucy asked.

"Please be quiet," Cook whispered back.

Without the clicking of their shoes on the rock ground or any talking between them, the tunnel became very quiet.

At first, Elizabeth swore she could hear each person breathing. Even in the dark and not knowing anyone there that well she felt she could predict who was where just from the sound of their panting.

Then, suddenly, she thought she heard a noise that was different from the sound that anyone in their group would make.

It was more like the sound of a low-pitched whistle.

"What was that?" she heard Lucy ask out loud, obviously tuning in on the same thing Elizabeth had heard.

"Shhh," Dr. Cook whispered directions to the group. "Quiet!"

Again, collectively, they strained their ears to listen. After a few seconds of silence the whistling noise started to appear again. This time the noise was even more audible.

To Elizabeth, as she tried to categorize the sound, she thought it resembled a child's whinny cry. To her it was as if that child were in pain in some far-away room in a house.

Suddenly a cool breeze passed by them, breaking the stillness in the cave air. Elizabeth swore she felt that the cold wind separately flicked her check and then tousled with her hair.

She felt herself shiver. It had felt like fingers.

"What was that?"

This time the question came from a scared sounding Martha Murray.

Cook turned and pulled the group toward him in a huddle.

"Look, I am not sure I believe the miner story," he spoke softly to the group.

"Then why did you scare us with that tale?" Martha asked.

"I told you because there are some who do believe it," Cook responded before providing his explanation on why he felt it was not true.

"People have looked back on the history of this mine. There is no written record of an event such as the one that I described to you. This is not to say it couldn't have happened. Any company would not have wanted an event like that to be recorded and left behind as their legacy. However, as any good scientist asks for evidence, I have found none to support it."

"So no ghost?" Martha asked.

"I didn't say that either," Cook replied.

"So you believe there is a ghost?" Martha spoke up again.

"There are no ghosts," Isaac answered. "He is about to tell you about science and science does not support superstitions like ghosts."

Cook looked at Hasbrouck without speaking before going on.

"In asking about this tunnel below the New Brunswick and Rutgers grounds, I uncovered another story the locals shared about the events that may have happened down here from the late 1700s and even into the early years during the Civil War. These events are more likely to be authenticated if even through the oral history they get traced to."

"So this took place in our current decade and not just long, long ago?"

"Yes."

Elizabeth was listening intently as Cook spoke. But she did look away and toward the darkness of the tunnel as she swore she heard the same howl sound again, fainter, off in the distance. As she glanced to her sides it was evident to her the others in the group had heard it too. She watched as they all instinctively inched closer toward each other as if they would have better protection within a tighter circle.

"If you know me then you are aware that I firmly believe that the greatest crime as a nation which cannot be vindicated, even with its eradication as a legalized entity through war, was the institution of slavery. It is a sin on our land that will haunt us for as long as our nation exists. And I stress the word "haunt" when I say this," Cook enunciated as he looked at each of their faces before continuing.

"It is no secret that many people, before they finally took up arms, had decided that slavery should not continue and they played an active role in helping some of those enslaved escape to freedom."

"The abolitionists," Hasbrouck called out as if he was answering a question in a class.

"Yes," Cook acknowledged Hasbrouck's comment. "But I am more specifically referencing those who worked what became known as the Underground Railroad. It is not a surprise to find out that an escape route to freedom came right through New Brunswick as this is a critical point on the way to New York and points north."

"Slaves escaping through Philadelphia came here. Sadly many in New Jersey, even though it was a Union state, still supported slavery until the War ended it. The worst part was that slave hunters and their spies also understood that an escape route had to go through here and were able to find locals who were willing to assist in their work. This group of henchmen set up along the banks and hid within the town waiting for any escapee to arrive. For money they would share information to the hunters themselves while the hunters, in turn, would try and catch the escaping slaves and bring them back for reward money in chains."

Elizabeth clearly heard the howling noise again and was sure she felt that same cool swish of the air as it had touched her before. Like the rest of the group, she did her best to keep her attention focused on what Dr. Cook had to share.

"So when as a scientist I looked for evidence about this, I located a source to the oral history of this very ground. I have heard the stories from the preaching of Camden's Reverend Thomas Clement Oliver. He is a passionate man who tells how he and his father with many other brave souls helped as conductors, a term used for those who guided men, women and children past the evil men and on to the dream of freedom. The local story goes that when conductors like Oliver got the fugitives to the outskirts of New Brunswick, they always sought the help of a man named Cornelius Cornell to try and foil the spies within this city intent on trading back people for cash."

"Now Cornelius' role was to determine if the vermin who worked as slave catchers were on watch and, if so, where they were located. If he felt their presence was too intense on the Raritan River crossing he would shift them southward toward a different safe station. Typically this was within the state at Perth Amboy with the likes of the now well-known Sarah Grimke to help."

The next sound was a clear howl. It was loud enough that even Cook looked up and about along with everyone else in the group. He cleared his throat and called the group's attention back to him before continuing.

"No one has ever figured out who this Cornelius Cornell was. One source shared with me that this very tunnel that we now are crouched down in may have served as both a hiding point and as a way to sneak the fugitives closer to their next step in the journey to cross the Raritan under the spying eyes of those intent on stopping them. This Cornell fellow was supposed to have used it at that time."

Cook stood straight up at this point.

"This tunnel, where you stand, was then the hiding spot before overcoming the final obstacle between being returned to slavery or on to the passage north to freedom."

Pausing for only a second, he looked into the face of each person there.

"Those sounds you hear, and I know that you hear them, have no definitive source."

"So what are they?" Elizabeth asked.

"I was with a team of scientists who have checked the acoustics of how the natural wind downdrafts sweep into the shaft and then into the tunnel to see if that was the source. While a simple hypothesis, they could not verify a thing. But if it is not the wind, what could explain that sound that every human who has descended down to these depths has defined as a human cry?"

Almost as if on cue, the sound cut through sharply again and everyone in the group jumped.

"There had to be a logical explanation further eastward up the tunnel." Cook paused. "That is what I told myself as a man of science. That is also where we are heading now."

With that he moved forward, lantern in hand, toward the end of the tunnel they had not yet explored. The group hesitated for only a moment before falling in step behind his quickening pace again fearing the thought of being left behind.

"Are you okay?" Adkins whispered to Elizabeth noting that her hand was gripping his harder than before.

"This is amazing!" she replied and kept moving ahead following Cook's lead.

Cook spoke again as they walked, explaining their location. "The tunnel now moves from the shaft that was near Easton Avenue and we are crossing under Union Street."

Moments later he stopped and held his lantern up. In the darkness it appeared that the walls suddenly appeared to grow wider within the tunnel.

"David, please bring that lantern forward here and walk several paces in that direction." Cook pointed to his left as he spoke to the group. "I will do the same in this opposite direction. Folks, please stay where you are but watch us as the two lights move out in separate directions."

As the two men walked, one to the left and one to the right, from the general direction the group had previously been heading, it became clear that two new tunnels were connected to the main tunnel they had been walking in at this point.

Cook called out to Murray to stop and then to return back to the group. He did the same.

"As you can see, the miners did head off in various directions within this mine creating other tunnels, just like they had multiple shafts extending to the surface. This is not unusual and this large juncture sits roughly half way between our current Union Street and College Avenue running parallel to each. This was the second place that I and fellow scientists studied the unusual sounds down here that I and they had heard emanating from the tunnel. Again, if we pause for a while longer, I predict on this night you will hear the same sound again."

The group dutifully stayed silent and listened. Once again, the howling sound could be heard.

"We made a strange discovery here when I explored the sections to the north and south," Cook said pointing in the two directions he and Murray had just walked back from. "If you go down each of those tunnels to our sides, you eventually hear nothing. So the source, somehow, runs the direction of east to west but not north to south. But how? Why? Again, I was convinced as a scientist that there had to be some evidence to support a practical answer."

He looked over the group and could tell that several of them, including his wife, were starting to tire from the length of the walk and the pace they had been keeping.

"Almost at the end," he told the group looking specifically at his wife and smiling at her to encourage her to keep moving along.

Again, talking as they walked, Cook pointed to a shaft as they passed underneath it and noted they would return back to this point momentarily.

"Why go past if that is the point of return to the street above?" his wife asked.

"Just stick with me, Mary. We will stop just ahead," he replied and did not slow as headed east.

True to his word, he stopped the group a few moments later and pointed to a steep change in the incline of the ground ahead.

"We just crossed under College Avenue," he began. "In front of us the slope increases to a point where, tonight, I fear that it may be too dangerous to go on."

"However, from this point where we now stand, I will ask you one last time to remain silent to attest to the fact that you can hear that same cry we have heard several times before and I ask you to determine if you think it is louder or softer. I also ask if you feel a breeze, from which direction does it approach you?"

Again they listened.

Again the howling sound started and was clear to all in the group.

Elizabeth listened too and shuddered as she felt that same icy brush from the breeze upon her face. Looking about at how the others in the group touched their faces or hair indicated that they had felt the same disruption to their body too.

"Now," Cook began softly. "I will tell you that the sound appears at the end of the tunnel which is down the slope ahead. It is even louder there, although it defies reason as to why that would be."

"Why?"

"With an echo, the sound is louder at the source of the sound. In a tunnel that would mean the closed end should be softer then the opening where the sound was being made. If it were a directional breeze causing a howling sound, it should be blowing in the opposite direction away from the closed end of the tunnel and not the other way. If you felt a small wind go past you just before, I believe you will tell me it was headed toward the closed end of the tunnel."

"It was in that direction," Lucy agreed.

"So for scientists who argue that the sound can be explained by a hidden shaft that is beyond the wall of rock that can no longer be accessed the breeze makes no sense. At least," and here he paused for a moment.

"At least what," Elizabeth was the first to ask.

"At least unless this is not a wind. Unless this is a phenomenon which cannot be explained by science."

"A ghost standing behind the walled off part of the tunnel?" Hasbrouck chuckled. "Dr. Cook, as a man of science and not a professional actor on a stage I know you cannot believe in such things."

"As a scientist, Isaac, I would agree. But if you know the history of how this mine was no longer in use and the desperation on the part of those trekking toward their freedom through an unforgiving land and what they may have encountered here? I am not sure that there are answers that science may be able to provide. We might learn that only providence may explain it."

"So where do you think the sound is coming from?" Martha asked.

"I tell you I am not sure," Cook answered back.

"So what do others say?" Elizabeth interjected.

"Well I have told you there are stories about the slave catchers setting up spies in the most populated parts of New Brunswick. At that time that would have been due south of here. Then you realize that the shaft we are about to exit from is near a spot where there was less traffic and lower chances of those spies catching you by accidently seeing you. With that escape route logically in place, I do believe that it is possible this path we have crossed over tonight had so many footprints from those attempting to flee that their story may hold the answer to that sound."

Cook stroked his beard and slowly the group followed him back to the shaft where they were to take the lift to exit out.

"Could some unique cut in the rock have been made in a closed off end of the tunnel that we have not yet detected that emits the louder sound and helped guide those escaping in darkness through the exit of the tunnel? Possible?"

"So is that it?" Lucy asked.

"I do not know. However, this is why we came tonight and the strangest part of the tale. While sounds have been detected at other times, it is only on this night each year, when we remember those who have died, that the sound seems like a cry that I know you all heard. I remind you that tonight is often seen as the night of the dead by many cultures."

"Some ask, could it be the cry of someone who did not make it left behind in the tunnels? Could it be the cry of a call to freedom's door? Could it be a cry of someone hoping that someone else was still coming? Martha to your earlier question and Lucy about what is it; the answer is I just am not sure."

For a moment they all remained silent. The weight of his words and the sorrowful sound and its possible meaning causing all to give pause.

"Well, I still believe there has to be a scientific explanation," Isaac spoke out first.

"Then why louder tonight?" Lucy asked her husband.

"George, we really must get going," Mary stated softly to her husband. "Our other guests will be arriving soon and we have yet to feed our current group here."

Cook pulled the chain to engage the weights and pulley and lower the lift from above.

As the lift lowered toward them, Cook explained to Murray and Hasbrouck that this lift and shaft, twice the width of the earlier one, would allow two to go on up at once. He pointed out that as the lift reached the top of the shaft they should duck their heads slightly until they were able to lift the metal plate that covered the hole from above. Once they stepped out holler all was clear, lower the lift and he would then lift the next folks up.

When the lift arrived down on their level, Hasbrouck and Murray climbed on. Before Cook lifted them back to the surface, he called for the group's attention again.

"Folks, know that Isaac is probably right. It is only an unproven scientific explanation that I have failed to discover."

"It always is," Isaac replied.

"Maybe," Cook stated caustically.

"Sir?" Isaac came back sounding slightly confused at Cook's retort.

"Until I have proof of something else, I think I will give more credence to the tale that was explained to me by a man who had escaped by way of the Underground Railroad years ago."

"That man told me that the voices kept calling him and his family to safety through his entire journey north. Those voices kept guiding him to freedom. Those voices on nights when it was too dark to see and all hope was lost appeared to provide direction no matter where he was on the track."

Then Cook looked straight at Isaac before glancing around at the whole group and concluded his talk.

"The last thing he told me was that he believed those voices still called out looking for other lost souls who never found their way home. So until science proves me wrong, I say that sound is the cry of all women and men's souls calling out in sorrow for a crime committed against humanity. I say it is a cry to remember the past. And finally, I say it is a cry to remember that there is always hope that we all one day will be found."

With that Cook shifted the chain to allow the weights in the system to first move the lift with Hasbrouck and Murray, and then the rest of the group, on its rise back to the street level.

28
October 31, 1869
Later that same night

It was a short walk from where the group had emerged from the tunnel along College Avenue to their destination for the remainder of the evening.

The gas lamps illuminated this segment of Seminary Place and gave it a finished look compared with the often Spartan landscape of homes in other areas. Elizabeth paused for a moment as the group came up the walkway and she smiled at what she saw in front of her.

The residence she saw felt right in place even as it rose between the emerging campus structures. The house, named *Riverstede*, sat grandly in its position. It was a fine stone home. When one looked at it they felt that welcoming energy of those who occupied it. Brand new, the Cook's had just recently moved in and somehow instantly given it a homey, personal feel.

"That was incredible," Elizabeth confided in Lucy as they sat and cleaned off the muck that the tunnel and streets had caused to become caked on to their shoes.

They had just finished brushing off the dust from their dresses, a practice more common for women in households near city streets in the summer when the manure dust flew about after drying all day in the hot sun.

"I was totally amazed at the story in the tunnel. I swear I thought I felt the ghostly spirits that were calling actually touch my face and hair. And I cannot believe how smart Dr. Cook is. His overall knowledge of so many things was truly impressive."

"Oh that was nothing," Lucy said with the shake of her head. "The man is one of the most brilliant people I have ever had the pleasure of meeting. As you heard from that story tonight he has an amazing heart for others too. I will also tell you that Dr. Murray is not far behind him in both the brilliant and caring departments."

"But the story was so down to earth. It was so much about people and life. I guess when I think about a college professor I think about someone who is detached and so caught up in theory and research that they have no knowledge that others even exist on this planet."

"Not Dr. Cook," Lucy said. "He has never forgotten his roots or that in order to matter in scientific research you have to make life better for others, not just write papers."

"He sounds impressive."

"If you want to hear more about him, take some time and talk with Mary, his wife. She is a lovely lady too who is also rightfully proud of all that he has done."

"I will," Elizabeth promised herself, as much as she was answering to Lucy.

A well-dressed young man escorted Elizabeth and Lucy into the dining room. Adkins was already standing there with Isaac waiting for their arrival. Each man pulled out a seat for their female companion and all were then seated.

Mrs. Cook explained to the group, almost apologetically, that she knew this looked like a light supper being served and that they were all probably famished. She promised though, when the remainder of their guests arrived, there would be many additional refreshments for the planned larger social part of the night.

Seated next to Dr. Cook, Elizabeth asked him about his years prior to joining the staff at Rutgers College. She then plied him with questions to have the full opportunity of getting to hear as much as she could about the background of this fascinating man.

Cook took her all the way back to his early years in Morris County and his childhood in Hanover. He spoke quickly about his first work as a civil engineer and surveying land for the Catskill and Canajoharie Railroad. He explained that like many others with a first job he found that this role had convinced him to try something different. He studied at Rensselaer Polytechnic Institute in Troy, New York. This was where he met a man named Amos Eaton who Cook said would become his most respected mentor.

"In the world of academia you never realize until later how important those intellectual contacts will become."

Mrs. Cook cut in to tell Elizabeth that, as she made a glance toward Elizabeth's date Mr. Adkins, her husband upon graduation had started as a tutor just as Mr. Adkins was now. He then worked his way to teacher and professor. His role at Albany Academy was also fortuitous in that he followed in the steps there of Dr. Campbell.

"This is the same Dr. Campbell who would eventually become the current President at Rutgers. This was also the setting from which my husband would meet Dr. Murray who also served at Albany in that prior educational administrative capacity."

"I also am supposed to say that Mary and I married around that time frame, whenever we reminisce about the good old days," Dr. Cook added.

"How many years ago?" Mary immediately asked to test him.

"Twenty three years ago dear," he answered without a pause thus successfully passing the quiz.

"We also started to build a family," Mary followed in with the personal life details. "Both our Paul and Sarah were born in New York."

"When did you return to New Jersey?" Adkins inquired trying to gain a foothold in the conversation and, with it, hopefully some of the attention from Elizabeth just as Mrs. Cook had originally attempted to do for Adkins with his date.

"Oh that would have been in about 1850," Dr. Cook puzzled about the actual year out loud. "I believe I was back in New Jersey before I left on that research trip to study in Europe for the State of New York. I was allowed to go only due to them honoring that it was a prior commitment to work on a project for them related to their manufacturing with the salt springs."

"They had already named him the Assistant Geologist for the state in New Jersey before he left though," Mary pointed out.

"That's right. Back in the day with old William Kitchell," Cook answered as if remembering a distant memory.

"Is that when you fell in love with marl?" Dr. Murray smiled at Dr. Cook as he said it from across the table.

"Ah, the other love of my life besides my beautiful wife seated here with me tonight!" Cook toasted the memory by raising up his cup.

"Marl?" Lucy suddenly joined in, curious but trying not to sound too naïve or uniformed. "You fell in love with somebody else after meeting your wife? I thought you just got married? Is that a person I am not familiar with? Was it a scandal all across Europe?"

"Marl is not a woman," Adkins stated before continuing as if he were delivering a classroom lecture.

"Marl is not a person rather it is a substance found in various places in the world. In simple terms it is a clay and lime mixture that, when the balance is correct, can be an incredible soil conditioner. Blue marl is among the most common found here."

The group was totally silent and each person around the table looked directly at Adkins as he finished rattling off his answer.

"Very good, Christopher," Dr. Cook finally stated. "I am impressed. I honestly did not know you shared an interest in the field of geology."

"Yes sir. Thank you sir," Adkins said in a more self-conscious and humble tone, realizing that his commentary about the definition of marl had sounded like he had been trying to show off.

"Keep an eye on this one David. He has potential," Cook announced to his colleague Dr. Murray.

"You really ought to hear his talks about topographical maps," Hasbrouck interjected, winking at Adkins.

"Railroads, maps, geology, marl. I think we have had enough technical talk and definitely enough time spent allowing my husband to dominate the conversation all night. Why George I cannot imagine why these good people would ever wish to return here again the way you have been going on so much about yourself," Mary Cook chided her husband in an attempt to steer the conversation in a different way.

"Mary, I was only answering some questions," Cook replied.

"I fear it was my fault," Elizabeth defended him. "I know I was the one who prodded Dr. Cook for all the details. I just found his tales in the tunnels earlier so fascinating and his background equally impressive."

"See," Cook gestured toward his guests as he spoke to his wife. "I was just trying to be a good host."

"What I see is a young lady trying to be polite and you carrying on forever," Mary stated without missing a beat. "And now, about that tunnel thing. Is there really a ghost? Or was that all a tall tale in an attempt to scare us all into not sleeping when the lights go out tonight?"

Everyone in the room turned to look at the great George Cook to see what he would say. For a moment he appeared to be thinking of an explanation to bring together all the sights and sounds they had experienced under the ground that night.

Instead he responded with just one word.

"Yes."

"Yes what?" Lucy asked. "Ghosts or tall tale?"

"Yes, you all saw what I saw and heard what I heard. Now you need to form your own conclusions."

Instantly the group broke into a conversation about the night's adventure. This led to a spirited debate about the in and out of the supernatural world, religious faith, and then things that are physically provable in the world in a scientific manner versus those that are not.

Eventually, the topic shifted to other social and world event things and the laughter increased.

Elizabeth had barely noticed the maid, hired for the evening, when she appeared at the door. She whispered something to Mrs. Cook and then turned and silently left the room. Mrs. Cook rose and announced that several other guests had just arrived.

She then directed her dinner guests from the dining area through a covered arched doorway with heavy curtains separating the two spaces as the group retired to the larger family room to meet the new arrivals.

New guests continued to enter this area where the Cooks were set up to entertain. The guests broke up into smaller social circles and carried on conversations while taking cups filled with a punch from a bowl that had been placed on a table in the center of the room.

Adkins took the opportunity to move about the room, with Elizabeth at his side, and engaged the various folks from New Brunswick whom he had heard of but never spoken with before to hear whatever they had to share about themselves.

A local member of the water commission in New Brunswick talked about Dr. Cook's connection with this group. When Adkins and Elizabeth spoke about the water that ran under the streets through the old copper mine they had seen earlier that evening the man seemed equally informed. He reviewed the history of the tunnel more in terms of the health hazard though and how coupled with the awful stench it might contaminate the Raritan River itself.

When asked about the ghostly sounds, he looked puzzled. He explained that while there were supposedly legends of a ghost told by others he did not believe in such things.

He concluded his thoughts on the matter by stating, "I personally have been in that old copper mine investigating many times and I have never once heard a thing."

Adkins recalled later how Elizabeth had squeezed his arm when the man had said this.

It was an unspoken communication between the two of them about something they had shared. It was a sign, in his mind, that they were coming closer together. It didn't matter to him if the ghosts of the past were real or not. To Adkins, it symbolized something was building between Elizabeth and himself.

Another guest reviewed an upcoming trip to Europe speaking of how enchanting it was to be abroad. As the guest spoke, they even mentioned how this would be similar to where Dr. Cook would be heading. To Elizabeth it was further proof of how extensive the life of this brilliant man was and the footprint he had in so many areas.

Mary Cook happened to sweep by as they were talking.

When asked by one of the guests she confirmed that, yes, Dr. Cook would be off in the next year to again study abroad.

As the other guests in the small talking circle watched, Mrs. Cook shifted the topic to Adkins and his date.

"Do you ever wish to go abroad Mr. Adkins?" Mrs. Cook had put out there first.

Then, without waiting for Adkins to answer, she turned and smiled at Elizabeth. In a tone that was mischievous and demonstrated she understood she was putting Elizabeth on the spot, she asked her what most single women would consider a very forward question when on a first date.

"What would you think, Elizabeth, about being escorted on an overseas journey to visit the world with our Christopher here being your host? If you were willing to go, where would you visit first in the world?"

The question startled the other ladies in the group as they realized that responding to such a personal question was totally awkward regardless if one said yes or no.

Adkins felt his eyes rise in shock at the unabashed match-making efforts of Mrs. Cook and how they were now playing out in front of him. Did she realize how awkward this would be for Elizabeth?

He was too nervous for her to even glance in the direction of his date. How could he even rescue her from this embarrassing social etiquette moment brought on by their host?

As it turned out he had nothing to fear. Adkins grew even more amazed at Elizabeth in how calm she was in her response.

"Oh, I am not sure where I would pick first," Elizabeth had answered without any angst or physical sign of a blush.

"There are so many exotic and historic places to be seen. I have only read or heard people speak of foreign lands. So as to where I would travel first I am not exactly sure. But I will tell you that after the short while I have been with all of you and observed what an amazing group of people you are; who would not want to be in the company of you personally and brilliant men like my date tonight, Mr. Adkins, Dr. Murray or Dr. Cook on such a journey."

"How true," Mrs. Cook replied demurely.

"Personally I would love to hear Christopher or your husband providing narration of any such sights for the first time. I can only imagine the knowledge and the excitement they would add to that experience."

"I am sure Mr. Adkins would be a wonderful narrator," Mrs. Cook said as she winked slightly in his direction.

"At the same time, like you, I feel that we can also bring so much to any conversation. As long as we also engage in reading and absorbing all this world has to offer, we too can add so much to it. For example, I am sure from how you carry yourself you have read about the world travels of one of the newest American writers, Mr. Twain, when his pieces were published through the newspaper. His journey in the Holy Land and in other ancient places were both humorous and informative and gave such a different perspective. I understand that his letters have been placed now in a book, *The Innocents Abroad*."

"That is true," Mrs. Cook sounded impressed at Elizabeth's knowledge about this subject as well as her desire to read. "We have just purchased a copy and begun to read it."

"Hopefully it helps provide you insights about your future world travels even if your husband is not able to be with you on a given day to help as a guide," Elizabeth replied. "I find that to be an important skill for every woman."

"Well said, my dear," Mrs. Cook nodded back at her and smiled. "This one is a keeper Mr. Adkins. I like her!"

With that, having granted her verbal approval of Adkins' date, Mrs. Cook moved on to entertain her other guests while another in the group presented a follow up question to Elizabeth.

"But your first site to visit in the world? You never answered."

"I do not know," Elizabeth thought out loud. "I suppose the more ancient sites like those in Egypt or a more exotic locale like the Far East if I could only go abroad in life once. The news of the that new canal in Egypt, the Suez Canal, finally being completed does make one contemplate what new sights can be seen and treasures found."

This answer had led to a comment about the wonders of the island of Japan as a Far Eastern destination someone else longed to see just as Isaac Hasbrouck had wandered over and into their conversation. In turn, Hasbrouck provided an introduction to the next guest they were to meet.

Again, Adkins was amazed at Elizabeth's mixture of charm, ease with conversation, and her natural intellectual curiosity which she displayed in each of these meetings.

There was her confidence which he admired as he felt he lacked the same social skill. Yet it was her natural warmth and genuine witty manner which drew him to her. He found he was enchanted with her every word and comment.

From across the room Mrs. Cook tapped her husband on his arm.

"I would say that your young Mr. Adkins is smitten with his date."

Dr. Cook looked over to see Adkins and that he was mesmerized by Elizabeth's presence.

"Who wouldn't be," Dr. Cook agreed with his wife. "It appears that your work in trying to set the two of them up for a successful evening is done."

"And to think when I first heard that Mr. Adkins was bringing a date that I felt sorry for him because I thought you old professors would bore any young lady to run away and ruin the evening with your endless talk," Mrs. Cook exclaimed.

"Appears you were wrong again," Dr. Cook stated matter-of-factly.

"Wrong!?!" Mrs. Cook shot back about to argue but stopped as she looked at her husband and saw that he was smiling back at her.

"You know I am never wrong dear" Mary now calmly remarked. "I told you they looked like the perfect pair as soon as I saw them approaching us this evening before we started our underground tour."

"Of course you did, dear," her husband replied as they both turned their attention back to the others at their party.

The next guest introduced to Elizabeth was a young man who was a native of Japan. He was currently attending Rutgers College. From what was shared, this young student turned out to be an acquaintance of both the Murrays and the Hasbroucks.

Elizabeth stumbled over herself to get his name right when he was introduced.

"Kusakabe Taro," he enunciated. Elizabeth repeated it several times back to him until she got it exactly as he had pronounced.

"I apologize for butchering the way your name sounds. I have just never heard that name used before. Is your name a common name from where you come from? Or is your name a type of family name with a story to it?" Elizabeth had asked.

He went on to explain that his name was actually linked to an original Samuri family name. He clearly articulated the name "Yagi" for Elizabeth to understand. The Japanese student then spoke about the family name's relation to where his family lived in the domain of Echizen.

Hasbrouck told both Elizabeth and Lucy that Kusakabe Taro had come to Rutgers as a continuation of the exchange program that had started between Japan and Rutgers through the religious connection of the Dutch Reformed Church mission years earlier.

The first young males came to study at the Rutgers Grammar School to learn the language and the culture of the country. Then, nodding toward this student, Hasbrouck added Kusakabe Taro had demonstrated an incredible proficiency in mathematics and science. As a result they had brought him to the college and he now came over to study at Rutgers on a regular basis.

Elizabeth appreciated when the Murrays joined their conversation.

They opened the discussion with a thought about studying feudal traditions and how the part that Rutgers hoped to play with Japan was two-fold. They explained that these students who attended here had the ability to bridge a cultural divide. The immersion among American students were envisioned as altering the preconceived notions by American students and staff about their perception of the entire Asian region. In turn, several from the Rutgers staff would go on to various assignments in Japan to share what was being taught here in the United States.

Dr. Murray excitedly explained about how he saw his place in the Rutgers exchange. He was being provided with an opportunity to go over to Japan to teach the Japanese about the concept of an open educational system. He hoped to show them the advantages for a nation when you designed a free education structure which gave an opportunity for all young children to learn.

Kusakabe politely explained that while the Americans saw their mission as training the Japanese how to live differently, he hoped that in America they may take these lessons to heart in how they deal with various people too.

Adkins smiled as he saw that even Dr. Murray was awed with Elizabeth when she offered a connection between what Kusakbe had said and linked it to the treatment of the American Indian in the United States. Her point was how it was possible to see the American Indians status in the west in the same way the Japanese central government was creating one authority over all. She posited how this nation, in many ways, saw the Indian people as living in independent feudal kingdoms and that our government was working to bring them under one national form of control.

"That is very perceptive," Dr. Murray noted without the slightest sound of being condescending as so often happened when a professor heard someone telling them about their area of study.

"I fear that many where I live in Japan fear the central government is looking at their subjugation and loss of freedom," Kusakbe noted.

"I believe many Tribal leaders would see this the same way in the United States," Elizabeth had offered back.

As Murray and Hasbrouck jumped in and the conversation started to get deeper into international roles and about challenges of ethno-centric superiority behaviors in the actions of one sovereign nation to another; a sound interrupted the discussion.

There was a pattern of hard knocking on the front door.

This noise caught the attention of everyone in the room and the socializing quieted as Mrs. Cook stepped out. A moment later she returned and with a wave of her arm, all the guests were encouraged to accompany Mrs. Cook back to the front door.

There, in the doorway, stood a rough looking group in ragged clothes with make-shift masks over their faces. They yelled out in deep Irish accents about needing something in exchange for their good graces or there would be devilish pranks played on this household this night and no one would escape harm or future damnation.

At first, Elizabeth did not know what to make of this.

Adkins saw her confusion and leaned over to explain this urban-style tradition being played out tonight. The pranksters were typically youth of the streets. On an average day they were most often ignored by the "regular" people of New Brunswick when they were down by the docks or the wharf area. For the most part these youngsters were even invisible working their jobs in the growing factories.

"How can they be invisible while they are working?" Elizabeth asked.

"Ignored might again be a better word," Adkins answered. "They serve a purpose in doing the odd jobs but most elect to look the other way and pretend they do not exist on the streets when they pass them at any other time."

"But you know they are there?"

"Yes," Adkins admitted. "And in some ways we do feel guilty knowing their lot in life. Part of that guilt, I suppose, is why we play along and provide this outlet in charity on this evening."

Adkins went on to explain that they engaged in this ritual each year.
While sounding threatening, these street urchins visited from home to home dressed in costumes in a playful game. In exchange for food and hoping for some financial tribute to them, they would agree to pray for the household's relatives who had died. If the household failed to provide some form of treat the likely result would be a prank of some sort with all souls getting cursed.

"What kind of prank?" Elizabeth asked, noting that this looked like a rough crowd.

"Oh, I've seen them throw rotten eggs or lumps of manure at doors. At times they light bon fires in the street and scream to scare the inhabitants further. Sometimes they toss in a wooden handrail from a walk or tear down and burn branches off a tree in a person's yard. Typically nothing too bad, although there are stories of pranks that went too far."

"What is Mrs. Cook handing out?" Elizabeth pointed toward the small paper packages wrapped with string being distributed to what Elizabeth was still sure were street ruffians.

"She calls them soul cakes, the traditional name. They are actually just sweet breads baked ahead of time as a favorite item handed out as the tribute. Typically they include a coin or small toy inside."

"And why are they called soul cakes?"

"Think of this night again, and the idea that the dead return on this evening to again inhabit the earth. While we often mourn the dead the reality, like our earlier talk of ghosts, is that most living people are not anxious to engage with anything other than the living."

"Agreed," Elizabeth noted.

"For each household that shares a gift of a cake, these masked street youth claim that they will communicate with the dead on a family's behalf. Once given their tribute they pray for the good souls who have given it to them and they supposedly have the power to inform the souls departed to leave this family without harm."

"As soon as the gift is exchanged, the group just leaves?" Elizabeth asked.

"Watch," Adkins suggested, pointing out toward the group that was congregating in the street in front of the Cook household.

The masked hooligans stepped away from the front entrance to the home and now stood by the curb calling out something that Elizabeth could not understand.

"What did they say?"

"They are telling all others that this home has been visited and has proven worthy and that if anyone attempts to bring harm to this home tonight they will seek them out and harm them."

"That is the message for the dead souls?"

"No, that is the message to the other masked prankster street groups patrolling the streets tonight," Adkins answered.

"And the others all stay away?"

"Sometimes."

"How sweet," Elizabeth jested.

"Keep watching," Adkins told her.

At that point, the group broke out in song. The words were soft and had a pleasant rhythmic melody to them, much like a song one might hear from a church choir. Even Elizabeth had to admit that as dirty and ragged as this group appeared with their weirdly masked faces, the songs they sang were beautiful and fun to listen too.

"They sound like a choir," Elizabeth exclaimed.

At the end of the choir-like song, the group turned their voices to some type of chant. This chant was accompanied with what looked like stomping and banging of sticks. They then broke into what clearly looked like wild dancing. Then, with another wild scream, the entire group took off running away from the home and down the street, soul cakes in hand.

As they ran away, the members of the household broke out in applause and cheers.

"What did you think?" Adkins asked.

"An odd twist on Christmas caroling." Elizabeth smiled. "Not what I am accustomed to seeing on this night back in Princeton. But I did enjoy it."

Back inside, the party resumed its previous pattern with small groups socializing.

Adkins sighed to himself as they had re-entered the room. He finally felt less anxious and began to relax. Elizabeth and Adkins both spent some time with David Murray and his wife Martha.

The Murrays had just married one year earlier. Martha spent some time highlighting the virtues of her brilliant husband and his work with petroleum and land surveys. Together they told the tale, much like Dr. Cook, about how Dr. Murray had been at Albany Academy and was brought to Rutgers. They also noted the pinnacle of his work with Dr. Cook had been in helping secure the Morrill Act Grant from the state legislature in New Jersey for Rutgers.

"You know I hear people talk about that event in Princeton," Elizabeth offered.

"Sadly, it was a competition that has left a great deal of hard feelings between our two colleges at this time," Dr. Murray said. "There is so much promise about what can happen when college faculties collaborate. I hate to see any animosity that has the potential to stall further exciting gains in so many fields due to an argument over the past."

"I hate that a competition exists too," Elizabeth agreed. "Everyone here seems so amazing."

The social activity began to wind down after cake and coffee had been served.

As the guests all started to leave, Elizabeth hugged Mrs. Cook and thanked her for having included her in the evening's activities.

"Thank you, my dear girl, for being so polite to listen that long to all my husband had to say earlier," Mary Cook replied.

"Thank you both for being such gracious hosts," Elizabeth added.

"She's a keeper!" Mrs. Cook called out to Adkins as he walked away.

As they stepped out into the street Elizabeth heard Isaac, who had exited with his wife ahead of them, call back to get Adkins' attention.

"So Christopher. One last Hallo's Eve tradition for good luck?"

Adkins looked at Elizabeth.

"Interested in one more activity before we call it a night?" Adkins asked his date.

"What is the activity?"

"A visit to a cemetery?"

"Are you both coming?" Lucy called out to them. "If you want we can share this carriage?"

"And we go to a cemetery why?" Elizabeth asked Adkins.

"Like Isaac said, it is another superstition about tonight that has become something of a local tradition here for good luck. Still, it does mean going into a cemetery at night and walking among the dead buried in the ground beneath you and you hope not to take the wrong step in the dark. If you would rather not go, I understand," Adkins told her.

Adkins saw a devilish grin appear on Elizabeth's face.

"Thank you Lucy. We are coming. We wouldn't want to miss it," Elizabeth called to the Hasbroucks as she took Adkins' hand and started toward the other couple. "Hold the carriage for us."

Halloween had always held a night filled with superstitions and traditions. This was another one that had been shared among the city folk with a visit to read the graveside stories on the tombstones just before midnight in a cemetery.

Once in a cemetery, you were supposed to read the grave markers until you found a poor soul who had died in some way that deserved praying for. The act was supposed to help soothe the soul of the departed while bringing a blessing on all who partook.

The carriage they rode moved along George Street until it arrived by the crossroad at Livingston Avenue. It stopped at the entrance gates to the Willow Grove Cemetery. The two couples stepped out of the carriage and walked into the dark cemetery.

Isaac had brought a small lantern with him for this purpose of attempting to navigate the grounds and hoped the light would be bright enough to still be able to read the grave stones.

"I can barely see," Lucy complained.

"Stay in the carriage then and have a year of bad luck," Isaac replied without sympathy.

Lucy elected to stay with the group and stumbled on at Isaac's side.

"Good luck," Lucy grumbled to her husband as she fought to keep her balance. "I thought you were the one who did not believe in ghosts earlier this evening."

"I figure it never hurts to get luck out of any tradition," Isaac answered back.

Adkins reached out to hold Elizabeth's hand just as she had asked him to do earlier for walking support when they had been on the uneven flooring in the tunnel. She took his hand but this time wrapped it under her arm, looping their arms together.

"I think I may need a little more support walking here, if you do not mind," she told him.

"Not at all," Adkins smiled back.

The darkness made each step difficult as the lantern gave off very little light to see clearly.

"You able to read anything?" Adkins asked the group.

Elizabeth squinted at the marble and granite markers struggling to make out a trace of any message of a deceased memorialized name or story.

"All I can see are some random names and dates," Isaac announced in a frustrated voice.

Off in the distance Adkins was sure that he heard loud voices approaching. While the neighborhood hooligans had been somewhat controlled earlier around the homes enjoying their games, Adkins was not as confident that in this setting they would not revert back to some type of thuggish behaviors. They might attack whomever they encountered on their turf to take whatever the strangers had.

"Maybe we should get going," he suggested, thinking about wanting to keep his date safe and bring her back to her boarding house that night without any physical or emotional harm.

"Look! Here!"

Elizabeth pointed at a marker. Small, but visible in the lantern light, it had the name of one William Van Arsdale deceased now roughly thirteen years. What she saw was a small notation indicating that he left behind a wife and six children.

"Van Arsdale," Isaac repeated the name. "I believe that is the name of the New Brunswick police department officer who fell through the ice of the canal one night while on patrol and drowned."

"That is sad," Lucy added.

"Folks know the story because when they went looking for the man, all they found was the hole where he fell in and his hat was there, frozen on top."

"That is terrible," Adkins agreed.

"Let us join hands," Isaac stated to the group.

They circled around the grave marker and joined hands. Hasbrouck spoke as if he were a preacher at a graveside service.

"William Van Arsdale. We tonight are here at Willow Grove cemetery to pray for your memory. We hope that the sadness that your soul has felt due to the unfortunate series of events that night finds you now have relief and that your family has found comfort."

Isaac then kneeled down beside the grave marker and placed a few small coins next to the grave.

"Four coins, one for each of us here tonight, as a reminder that we have prayed for thee. Now, we ask that you use the heavenly power of your soul to provide us with some divine blessings for this next year.

Please do this as a sign that you have accepted our prayers for you and we shall send our prayers and well wishes to all who still feel the pain of your loss."

The noise appeared to be coming closer.

"Is that it Isaac?" Adkins tapped his friend on his shoulder.

Isaac looked up and suddenly seemed to hear the same approaching voices that Adkins had heard earlier. Hasbrouck quickly came to the same conclusion that these were probably street ruffians and that no good end would come with meeting them here.

"Yes. Now we can leave."

Isaac said this as he rose to his feet. He took Lucy by the hand and hustled her back to their carriage with Adkins and Elizabeth right behind. Instantly the driver urged the horse on.

As the carriage turned the corner a group of city revelers passed on foot. They yelled out at the horse demanding that the large animal give them all a gift.

It was hard to distinguish if this rowdy group in the dark were the same prankster merry makers from earlier. They did look older and Adkins knew they were more likely the regular night street ruffians intent on harm versus young rascals out for fun. Regardless, Adkins was glad they were no longer in the cemetery about to find out which group they actually were.

The carriage dropped the Hasbroucks off first. They said their goodbyes.

Adkins and Elizabeth then rode on in the same carriage with the driver getting directions on where to drop her back at the boarding house. They arrived at the address and Adkins stepped out of the carriage. He then helped Elizabeth down. He escorted her to the door of the building while the carriage driver waited behind.

"It was a wonderful evening," Elizabeth said as they came to the door.

"I hate to see it coming to an end myself," Adkins replied.

"Your friends were amazing. The tunnel adventure is one I will never forget. Dr. and Mrs. Cook were such gracious hosts. Thank you for all you have done in setting this visit up for me," Elizabeth said.

"It was my pleasure." Adkins held her hand in his, her arm swinging gently with it.

Elizabeth turned to knock on the door as she had been instructed, expecting it to take some time to receive a response. Instead, the landlady at the boardinghouse immediately opened the door.

"Right on schedule," the landlady announced. "I like that when there is no chaperone."

Elizabeth let go of his hand and smiled back at Adkins as she stepped forward, toward the woman waiting for her at the door.

"I had a wonderful evening Mr. Adkins!" Elizabeth said.

"As did I," Adkins agreed. "But please call me Christopher."

Elizabeth smiled again, fully understanding the humor intended. Elizabeth nodded at the woman holding open the door and then took four quick steps back to where Adkins was standing.

With her hand on his chest, she leaned forward and gave him a gentle kiss quickly on his lips.

"Thank you, Christopher, for a wonderful evening," she whispered this time, so only he could hear.

She turned and returned back through the door in one grand sweep. She moved past the woman standing there and into the boardinghouse without further comment. The woman guarding the door looked out at Adkins who appeared like a statue totally incapable of any physical motion.

The landlady called to him, "Good night Master Adkins!" Then she stepped behind the door and closed it, the sound of the lock immediately clicking tight.

Adkins slowly walked away and got back into the carriage. He gave the driver his address and the horse lurched forward. As the carriage pulled away Adkins glanced back at the large wood frame structure and saw a lamp, just lit, suddenly brighten up a room on the second floor.

"I send you my heart," he said softly to the lady in that room behind the dark curtain.

He then joked to himself out loud. "You fool. You have no idea if that is her room. What if that was the room of the landlady?"

Not realizing how loud he was or that his voice had carried, Adkins was startled when the driver called back to him.

"Not to worry, lad. Been in that place several times myself and that room is not the room of the inn-keeper there."

Unsure what to say, he simply replied, "Thank you." Then, alone in the darkness of the seat of the carriage, he began to replay the entire wonderful evening over again in his mind.

29
October 31, 1869
Princeton Dorm Room

"This is insanity!" Billy Buck yelled into the faces of the two messengers. "This has to be wrong!"

"There is no question about what was being shared," Jerry Sharp answered back at his college mate defensively in an equally loud and animated voice. "Dr. Westmoreland could not have been clearer in his pronouncement."

"I agree," Lee Nissley, the other student messenger added. "We both heard him clear as day. His opening words and closing words were delivered as absolutes on this topic."

"Tell us again what he said." Several equally anxious voices sounded off in chorus around the room.

Sharp tried to calm himself down before speaking. He took a deep breath and paced a few steps in each direction to try and gain his composure. Finally, stopping in the center of the room with Nissley at his side, Sharp looked out at the assembled group to speak. All eyes were fixed back directly at him in total silence.

"Lee and I were out in that open field behind Geological Hall. You know, the field nearer to where the West College building is located."

"We were just kicking a ball back and forth, Jerry and me, and telling a few jokes," Lee jumped in.

Sharp then went on to explain how Professor Westmoreland, walking with two others, came upon them. After greeting them and rhetorically stating that he wondered why two young students would be out here playing instead of studying at this time of day, Professor Westmoreland had informed Nissley and himself that they had just come from a meeting of the faculty. He very clearly stated that it was at this faculty meeting where Dr. McCosh, the President himself, had announced that they were taking immediate steps to restore social order among the students on campus.

Nissley said when he had respectfully asked what that meant, Professor Westmoreland had explained that word had come back to members of the Princeton community about the antics of a young man representing the college. They believed he had been out cavorting with men of lower society, drinking and gambling and bringing embarrassment to the college and the community.

Westmoreland stated that evidently several key community members and the Trustees were outraged and had approached Dr. McCosh. That group had echoed other concerns including the general behavior of all college students that night at Judge Olden's house. They had told President McCosh in no uncertain terms that he needed to immediately tighten the reins here. Dr. McCosh was told to redirect all student energy back toward the real goals and purposes of the college.

Sharp pointed out that Professor Westmoreland clarified for Nissley and himself that in the future students would have no more social outings. There would be no more activity where students could foster an image that was unbecoming of the college where the very mission was to raise scholars who respected the moral teachings of the church. It was time to be focused entirely on students only partaking in their studies.

Westmoreland had added that even this simple activity he observed of kicking a ball between Nissley and Sharp during free time was not going to be tolerated without formal supervision by a faculty member. There was to be no more unstructured time that generated too much youthful error.

Sharp then quoted the final words Westmoreland had shared.

"The faculty is going to ban all general social activity beyond two basic things. One will be the direct local work with the church. The second will be college endorsed service projects for the well-being of the local Princeton community."

The silence after his final comment lasted for less than five seconds as several furious voices roared out from around the room.

"No social interaction with students on any other campus?"
"No competitions of any sort in public places?"
"No part in the life of the community beyond charity work donated through a church sponsored group?"
"What about our debate and speech societies? They are going to be chaperoned too?"
"I can't believe this is happening!"
"Calm down!"

The sharp directive came from Gummere. He cut into the noise with such a forceful manner that the assembled mass stopped to await his next words. In turn, Gummere looked around at the group that had gathered in Big Mike's and his room. Crowded together, these students represented a significant portion of the team.

"There has to be an explanation for this before we start letting our imaginations run wild."

"This is serious, Will!" Big Mike was the first to comment. "What about our game with Rutgers?"

"I hadn't even thought about that!" another student exclaimed. "Can they take that away too?"

Again Gummere halted the voices before they got out of control again. Holding up his hand as if to prohibit any other student from speaking, Will first glanced back at Mike.

"Yes, the Rutgers game was the first thing that entered my mind when Lee and Jerry first entered the room with their news," Gummere stated. "And, yes, you know they can stop us from playing Rutgers." Then, turning his attention specifically to Lee Nissley who was still standing in the middle of the room with Jerry Sharp, he asked two direct questions.

"Nissley, first, did Professor Westmoreland tell you how this announcement was going to be shared with the rest of us in the student body or when we would be told?"

"No. I do not recall him saying anything like that," Nissley stated.

"He just gave us the impression that it had just been decided and that we would all hear very soon," Sharp added. "It was like he couldn't wait to deliver the bad news by talking with us."

"So to be clear, there were no details of this and there was no explanation about the timing of when this so-called formal action would be imposed?"

"No," Nissley repeated. "He just made it sound like it was inevitable."

Chauncey Field suddenly entered the room slamming the door behind him. Before Gummere could get further clarification about what Nissley and Sharp had heard, all eyes immediately turned to focus on Chauncey as Charlie Parker said loudly, "What in the devil is wrong with you?"

Chauncey looked shaken. His face was flushed as if he had been running and there was a strange, frenzied look from his eyes as if he had just been chased by somebody. Chaunce stepped forward as it was obvious that the hush that filled the room upon his entering was going to remain until he reported why he was in such a state.

"Chaunce, what's the matter?" Gummere tried to coax out an answer for the group.

"It is Lawrence Joueur," Chauncey finally spit out. His voice was quavering as he looked about and he suddenly spoke now in a rapid speed. "I couldn't believe it at first. They just came in and pulled all his personal things and dragged them out of our room. I asked them to stop. I asked what they thought they were doing. They pushed me aside and told me to mind my own business. They laughed as they said that Joueur had been expelled and will not be returning."

"What? Expelled?" gasped out one student.

Chauncey Field ignored the comment and continued on.

"They didn't say much else. They just bagged up items that didn't fit in his trunk and carried them out of our room. Walked right out past me with all of his stuff. So I followed them right out the door. As they exited the building, I just kept asking them what they were doing. All they kept saying was to shut up, mind my own business, and just know that Joueur got his."

"Joueur got his what?" a voice in the room asked.

"They who? Who is this they?" another voice chimed in.

"It was one of those officers we all hate from town," Chauncey answered back. "He was there with two of those guys who work around the college here. I have seen the other two around here helping do chores for Dr. McCosh. I am not sure of their names but I think that one guy is a footman when he works McCosh's carriage. The other guy is the one who is related to that farrier in town."

"Did you try and stop them?"

"Stop them? No! I couldn't stop three of them."

"Why not? What if they were just robbing him and stealing Joueur's things?"

Chauncey stopped speaking as questions were being called out to him. When the questions seemed to slow and then stop, Chauncey stood there silently, as if in a trance, until Gummere spoke.

"Is there any more, Chaunce?" Gummere asked him in a calmer tone.

Turning to face Gummere directly, Field added to his story.

"I did follow them up the street, Will. Eventually they came to a parked carriage. They tossed his things on board. Then Lawrence appeared. He walked out the door from the President's office. He was escorted by his father who I recognized because I have met him before. They were followed behind by two other police men. He didn't even look up as his father forcefully took his arm and led him into the carriage. The officers mounted their horses. Then they just followed on horseback as the carriage left and pulled off up the street and off the campus."

Chauncey paused for a moment again before continuing.

"You know it happened so fast I didn't know what to do. So I stayed around on the grounds after the carriage left. I stayed there basically hidden and out of sight by the President's house for several minutes before I saw four or five of the faculty walking out."

"I decided to follow them and I remained behind them as they moved back toward wherever they were heading. They did not see me but I was close enough to hear one of them tell their group what I had heard from the men in the room before. It was repeated that Lawrence Joueur got exactly what he deserved. That same voice then said something about how the actions of one rotten student should not be able to spoil the reputation of an entire college. Then someone else said that they need to get rid of a few more apples who have also caught the rot from the likes of Joueur."

"What did they say he did?" one of the group there asked.

"All I heard was one of the faculty say something about I hope he appreciates the rigors provided to him behind bars as he obviously did not appreciate the scholarly structures we had safely put in place for him while he was here."

At this point Chauncey shook his head slowly. He looked exhausted.

"And that was the last thing I heard said," was the last thing that Chaunce uttered.

"This is beyond crazy," Parker was the first to speak. "First the announcement from Nissley and Sharp and then this from Chaunce?"

"It has to be connected," Sharp said. "What Professor Westmoreland shared with me and Nissley and what was seen happening with Lawrence must have been at about the same time."

"Of course it's connected," Billy Buck announced. "Why else would the faculty here at the college suddenly put a ban on the rest of us unless something had taken place?"

"It just seems so draconian," Parker huffed. "One student does something and we all get punished as a result of that person's actions?"

"I still wonder what he did?"

"You don't think it had anything to do with when we went to Trenton, do you Will?" Mike asked the obvious question which was on several of their minds. "Those guys there were pretty peeved at the way that Joueur played them that day."

"Heck, if it is about Trenton do you think they are coming for us next?"

"Maybe we should be back in our rooms checking on our stuff!"

"Look, do not go jumping to any conclusions," Gummere said. "Like I told you before when Jerry and Lee were speaking, if you let your minds start spinning out of control over what are little parts of some bigger story you are going to create rumors that could lead to worse outcomes."

"Will is right. And besides, Joueur didn't break any laws that day in Trenton," Buck added.

"What could have been so serious that they haul him off without a chance to say goodbye? Is he really going to be put in jail?"

"Chaunce, think. Joueur loved to brag and you were his roommate. Did he ever tell you he was going to do something that you think would possibly get him arrested?" Gummere asked.

"I don't know. You all know Lawrence. He was wild and a little crazy. He loved to have fun. But no, he never told me he was doing anything anymore illegal then the rest of us might have done at some point. A drink here. Place a bet on a card game there," Chauncey replied.

"He obviously did something though."

"And whatever that something was I'll bet is what makes it appear necessary to the faculty and President McCosh to serve a consequence the rest of us."

"I could see them shutting us down from any activity if he murdered somebody," Big Mike offered. "Then I would understand that the rest of the world might be scared of us for a bit and want us to stay away from them. But what could he have done that would impact us in this way?"

"I agree with Mike. Why penalize us for something Joueur did?"

"And what do you think those blokes up at Rutgers are going to think if we don't show up to clobber them this weekend?"

"I can't even imagine what they will say and how they will make fun of us based on their big mouths!"

"Who knows if any of this is even true? Just like Will said earlier, we could be over reacting over nothing!"

"Still, someone has to find out if this ban on our future activity exists!"

"Someone also needs to find out what happened to Joueur!"

"It really isn't fair though if this turns out to be true."

"And I can't believe we might miss destroying those fools on the field up in New Brunswick because one student here did something wrong and the rest of us get banned from playing."

"And if we suddenly don't show up to play them that day? Do you know what they are going to think?"

"I can tell you what they will think. They will think we were afraid to play them if we don't show up."

"And worse, I can tell you what they will say. They will tell everyone that we chickened out."

"And what's even worse than that is that we know we would kill those Rutgers boys just like we have always done at everything else!"

Again, it was Gummere getting the conversation under control by calling the group back to order.

"Gentlemen," Gummere began in a very serious voice. "Charlie is right. We may be over-reacting right now. However, based on what has been shared so far, it will only be worse to find out later in the week we cannot go to Rutgers and we do not even have a chance to tell them we are not coming."

"I can't even think how that will look. Them standing there waiting to play and us not showing up like we were scared of them or something!?!"

"So what do we do Will?"

Gummere calmly replied to the group. "We elect a representative from among us to go and speak directly with President McCosh to ask him to clarify what we have heard."

"I say that should be you," a voice called out and the sound of agreement filtered through the room.

"Fine," Gummere stated.

"And what happens when Dr. McCosh tells you that what Nissley and Sharp have heard is accurate and there is a ban now in place?"

"I ask him if we can still go to Rutgers to play," Gummere answered without a pause.

"And when he tells you no Will? What then?"

"Well then, gentlemen," Gummere summarized. "We send one among us directly to New Brunswick to carry our message asking first for a delay in the date and, if not agreed upon, to simply tell them that at this time our college leadership has prohibited us from any competition."

A collective "ugh" could be heard from each student there.

"I see no other way," Gummere announced and no one disagreed.

"Whoever gets that task of going to tell the Rutgers lads that the game is off and we are not coming is going to have to be someone who will not blow their cool. They infer that we are afraid of them. They start laughing at us and saying we are scared of them and continue insulting our good name in every way they can. Who will not start yelling back? Really who is capable of being that messenger?"

"I would not want to be that person"

"Nor I!"

"I'll tell you one thing if it comes to that, It's not fair to have Gummere do that too!" Big Mike cut in, defending his roommate. "If it comes to that, I say we draw straws and the short straw goes."

There seemed to be agreement as the young men nodded at the suggestion.

"Let's not get ahead of ourselves," Gummere commented. "Let's just see what President McCosh is willing to share before we take any other action in that direction."

"And what about Joueur?"

"What about him?"

"Do you really think McCosh is going to say anything about Joueur right now if there is some kind of case or legal investigation going on? I cannot think that McCosh in his formal role is allowed to talk on why a student has been expelled, if that is true"

"That is a good point."

Chauncey Field looked out at the group. "If it's all the same to you, I really would like to know what happened to my roommate."

"You can always write him for his story, if he will answer you. You were his roommate and he might be more open to you versus anyone else."

"He is still a friend of all of us," Big Mike reminded the group. "We probably should just keep our ears open for our school monitors talking between themselves. Just like Chaunce overheard the faculty earlier, that might be the best source out there."

"It sure is faster than having to wait for the post to deliver a letter back."

"Look gentlemen," Gummere proclaimed. "I promise I will give it my best with President McCosh."

"When will you go see him, Will?"

"I suppose there is no time like the present."

With that Gummere turned to chat with the two students who were right by his side. The other students started to filter out of the room as the larger group conversation appeared to be over.

Eventually it was just Gummere and Big Mike in the room. Mike asked the question again that had been on his mind and bothering him the entire time since Chauncey entered the room.

"While I know I asked your thoughts about this earlier, but what if this is all about our day down in Trenton? Joueur was a little crazy that day. Those day laborers were all pretty mad at how he tried to pull a fast one over on them even if he didn't take their money from them. Maybe they did report him being there and had some contacts to make things happen. Maybe Joueur even confessed and told McCosh we were there with him? What if they just haven't had a chance to speak with us yet and we are next?"

"Calm down Mike," Gummere advised. "If it had anything to do with Trenton then I am pretty sure we would have been called in as quickly as Lawrence. Figure, they had to know about this for a while if his father was able to get here to pick him up already. Anyway, besides being there while he was gambling, the rest of us did not do anything the police would be interested in."

"I didn't even mean the getting arrested part, Will," Mike replied. "I was referencing what Sharp and Nissley had shared from what Professor Westmoreland told them. What if this ban on activity is based upon the fact that it was not just Lawrence out doing something that broke the law. What if the overall ban is because they learned from Lawrence when they questioned him that many others, including us, were out and about drinking and doing things the college would frown upon?"

"Then, my good friend, I suppose we suffer the consequences. And you know what Mike? When I go speak with President McCosh, if that is what he shares with me; at least we both know we had a great time that day in Trenton!"

Mike smiled. "That we did."

As Gummere pulled a scarf around his neck and moved to get set to leave on his errand, Mike called out one more time to him.

"So what do you plan to tell him if Sharp and Nissley are right?"

Gummere paused in the doorway for a moment before replying.

"I guess I try to appeal to his sense of pride in our college. I will explain the damage we perceive by not showing up would cause our school's reputation. I suppose I emphasize that when a man from the College of New Jersey gives his word that he will be somewhere, that pledge should be honored. Beyond that, I am less afraid about what I will say and fear more what his final edict may be."

"Good luck."

"For you, me and the men on our team at our college too!" Gummere added.

With a wave of his hand he was off to request an audience with the college President.

30
November 2, 1869
New Brunswick: Rutgers campus

"She must have written that letter on the train when she was on her way back for it to arrive here that quickly," Hasbrouck stated as he watched Adkins examine the neatly folded paper addressed to him.

"Who cares when she wrote it or how she got it here so quickly. All I know is that I am happy to hear from her without having to wait another day," Adkins told him.

"Our young love-struck tutor," Hasbrouck joked. "How will you ever concentrate today until you get to read it?"

"Read what?" Dr. Cook interrupted the two young men speaking.

"Nothing sir," Adkins answered. "Just a letter from Elizabeth."

"Lovely young lady, Christopher," Cook noted. "I truly enjoyed her intellectual curiosity and willingness to play along with the group on our Halloween jaunt."

"She told me she fully enjoyed it too."

"Excellent. Excellent," Cook replied. "I would think she is a keeper, young man. You don't want her to slip away. I also know that Mrs. Cook saw your lady friend the same way!"

"No sir," Adkins nodded, feeling a little awkward at the discussion of his personal affairs in this setting.

"Now gentlemen, we do need to get back to the matter at hand. How do we get the surveys completed in a fashion that is both expeditious and accurate without disrupting the rest of our responsibilities here on the campus?" Cook started back in.

Adkins forced himself to listen but, as Hasbrouck had predicted, the letter that he twisted in his fingers caused a major distraction from focusing on what Cook was sharing. Cook's mantra was the same as it had been each time before and Adkins now knew it by heart.

Cook respected the work of the many in his field who pursued both the pure science and the research approach as their focus. However, Cook's passion and the plan for this project circulated around applied practical science. Cook repeated this continuously as they outlined the next plan along with how they would need to be true to the scientific method. His point of emphasis though was how without the ability to adapt to make it a tangible process for people in the field, the work would fail to meet its mission. That was the challenge for this team.

This is what led to a discussion on how they would get farmers to come to a remote site and visit the agricultural lab they had in mind. They could not expect farmers to leave behind their farm for any length of time so access to the rail for transit speed was essential. Still, they could not allow their project to look more like a business venture versus an institute of learning for the farmers themselves.

They talked about control features. This shifted back to the need to complete the surveys just to get the land plotted in order to determine if the project was even feasible on any scale large enough to deliver a statewide change.

In usual Professor Cook fashion he announced that it would have to work. And with that, they all had their official charge.

As the meeting ended, Adkins bid Hasbrouck an abrupt good-bye. Adkins then sped as fast as he could to a corner bench to be seated and to read his correspondence in private.

The opening salutation of "My Dearest Christopher" actually caused Adkins to pause. He swore he felt his heart flutter. This is crazy, he thought to himself. Cook is right, I can't let anyone who can make me feel this way ever slip away.

Clinically he saw that the rest of the letter fell into three basic parts.

The first part was a review of the night they spent together with Adkins' friends and to those connected to the Cook family. She explained how much she enjoyed every facet of that day. It was also filled with her fondness for the way that Adkins had treated her on that trip.

The second part of the letter shifted to her thoughts about her hopes that if Adkins also saw this as a budding relationship between them it would not be harmed by the distance they lived from each other. As he read this, it appealed to him how her writing spoke to the way others had overcome challenges of geographic locations when the prize to do this was the heart.

The final segment of the letter was what gave him another reason to pause. He then read it over again several times to make sure that he understood what she was proposing as the next step in their relationship.

In writing this, I hope you do not find me too presumptuous, but I do wish to provide an opportunity most immediate in which you may meet my two children. While I shared with you that my first goal was to get to know you first, I also wanted to remind you that these two jewels are fully bound first to my heart.

As such, I am seeking to find out if you are willing and able to allow us the pleasure of a visit to New Brunswick this coming Saturday to have a chance for me to see you again. This may also be arranged so that you may meet my twins. I fully understand if you feel this is too rushed. I will respect a reply that says that you do not yet feel that we have known each other for enough time for this to be appropriate. Still, as I have always been honest with you from the start, my life in this way cannot move forward in any manner without knowing that the man I am seeing also finds that he too may share a love as an equal, if not as powerful as mine, toward my children.

I shall wait to purchase our tickets until I hear back from you. If the answer is yes, we shall arrive on the morning train this Saturday to spend the day before departing in the evening back to Princeton. We would be available any part or all of that day if you have the time free with which you can see us.

Please know, I also understand if your answer is no. I will feel none-the-less for you from such a response if you honestly feel it is just too soon for you to take this next step. While I would be heart-broken, I also would respect an honest reply if you feel that the children make our future together as a family one that you could never embrace.

The letter was then closed off with, "My heart awaits your reply – as does my appointment book with a date to visit or not to visit the station to purchase tickets on the rail."

He read the final words out loud. "Fondly, Elizabeth."

Adkins, refolded the letter and tapped it on his thigh. She was direct.

"Lost in thought my friend?"

It was Hasbrouck's voice who had come up upon him.

Looking at his colleague, Adkins was sure this was not a meeting of chance but rather one of pure curiosity in what the message was that the post had recently delivered him.

"Get a chance to read your letter?" Hasbrouck asked, fully aware that this was what Akins had just been doing as he could see the open letter in his hand.

"Yes," Adkins replied without sharing another thing right way. He watched as Hasbrouck twisted himself down to be seated on the tree stump that rose just several inches off the ground next to the bench where Adkins was seated.

"So, tell and do not make me wait or beg you for information. What word does the fair Elizabeth send ye'," Hasbrouck stated in his best romantic Shakespearean sounding acting voice he could muster.

"She wrote to thank me about the night and told me how wonderful my friends were that she met."

"I would expect nothing less considering that she had the opportunity to meet me," Hasbrouck kidded. "Anything more though about you and your future with her together?"

"There was," Adkins answered, knowing that his nosey friend would not let it drop until he shared some additional tidbit about himself. He also knew that Hasbrouck wanted this information so he could run home that eve to inform Lucy what the latest gossip was. Whatever he shared would surely be discussed between the two of them that night.

"And?"

"And, she expressed her hope that we will get to see each other again soon," Adkins responded without adding any indication of the possible weekend rendezvous with Elizabeth and her children.

They chatted for a while about this topic with Hasbrouck giving all his advice about how a romance should begin between a man and a woman. Eventually the conversation shifted to what Cook had discussed with them earlier.

"So do you want to carve out any time this weekend to go over and review the layout of where we will need to draw the project schematics from?" Hasbrouck asked.

Quickly, Adkins deflected the possibility of any work or meeting with Hasbrouck to Sunday. He did not want his colleague's schedule to possibly interfere with any potential plans he might set with Elizabeth on Saturday. He also was looking to allow himself some time to mull over what his reply to Elizabeth should actually be.

Hasbrouck appeared content to let the week go by without a formal time being set now for their venture across the Raritan River to the site suggested by Cook for an agricultural experimental farm and the future operations at that station.

"Okay, well let me know when you can be more definite," Hasbrouck stated as he rose and dusted off the seat of his pants and he prepared to leave.

"I will," Adkins promised.

"And do not forget to give my regards to your sweetheart in the letter I am sure you will be penning and sending back to your darling Elizabeth," Hasbrouck added with a smile, patting Adkins on the shoulder. "Ah. Nothing as beautiful and wonderful or sickening as young love!"

With a laugh Hasbrouck was off leaving Adkins to return to his task at hand; deciding on what to respond with to Elizabeth.

He paused to think about it for only a moment. Then Adkins reached into the small satchel which he always carried while on campus and pulled out a sheet of paper and a pencil and began to write.

"My Dearest Elizabeth," he stole her salutation. "I cannot wait to see you and the twins this Saturday…"

31
Later that Same Day
New Brunswick: Open field off College Avenue

"I am totally bruised up," Gilmore stated as he looked at the black and blue welts rising on his arms and shins. "A few more of these and I may be too sore to play this Saturday."

"You are playing," George Large shot right back. "We are already short men and there is no way we are letting you not show up due to some old lady pains."

Rutgers Professors Kellogg and Atherton along with Tutor Hasbrouck stood on the far side of the field reviewing the tired student bodies from the work-out and the paces they had just put them through.

Neither of the professors understood much about the game that the young men were about to play. But both men were firm believers in military discipline and the fitness level expectation for each man. To this end, they had been eager and persistent in carrying out President Campbell's initial edict that the young students be engaged in more physical activity.

The younger Hasbrouck, on the other hand, had tried to support the students with tips on skills and strategies to be used when they actually played. The reality was that even he knew little about this new hybrid of a game and what he shared had as much to do with rugby and soccer style play versus what the students were calling football.

Initially all three had not been aware that the students had sent a challenge down to Princeton to engage in this football contest. The three staff members were simply in the process of working the students out at what they saw as a critical component with student fitness standards. They also saw this activity as student consequences for their actions in September with the Princeton community. When they learned later about the actual game, none of these three men objected. They liked the competitive idea and how the challenge would motivate the boys to work harder. At the same time the conditioning did not end. Atherton and Kellogg firmly believed that the disciplined workouts were what were needed for all men and would help them with any task in life.

The numbers of actual players attending was well below the whole Rutgers student population which had first been required to participate in the drilling. But those who remained appeared dedicated and the students pushed themselves hard at every workout.

It pleased all three men to see that the students were taking seriously what was being asked of them and mattered little if the true motivation was the opportunity to participate against Princeton in this matter. While the drills they had run with them did not necessarily focus on the fundamentals of that game, they truly believed that any exertion was better than sitting about and doing nothing.

As the contest date drew closer, they were also pleased when the students themselves had requested to take time to work on the nuances of the football sport itself and the students took on leadership roles within their own ranks in developing a regimented practice routine to include scrimmaging for game practice.

Hasbrouck was also relieved when he saw the students researching for their own knowledge of the sport. For while he supported their endeavor and wanted them to be successful too, there was little to be found in current readings that he had been able to locate to help provide them much insight into how this game was supposed to be played.

"Progress," Kellogg had told both Atherton and Hasbrouck. "Marked progress."

Kellogg now called out to the students on the opposite side of the field to "take ten" before they would do their final drills for the day.

The young men slumped to the ground or leaned on the three rail wooden post fence that ran the length of their side of the otherwise open field.

"Leggett!"

Leggett turned at the sound of his name and saw the student who had accompanied Robert Adrain the other day approaching him.

"John Herbert," the student reminded Leggett of his name as he reached out to shake hands to greet him when he got to his side.

"I do recall," Leggett answered. "What can I do for you?"

"Well, I am actually here because Cornelius heard I was headed in this direction and he requested that I deliver a message to you."

"Oh, good. I was wondering why he had not shown up for practice yet. Did he say when he would be coming?"

Herbert shook his head. "Well, not exactly."

"What do you mean, not exactly?"

"Cornelius told me to share with you that he has just not been able to carve the time out of his schedule after classes to join you. He fears that his commitment was made first to this year's new student publication and he cannot leave his work there to participate in your practices."

"So he is not coming?" Leggett feared what was about to be clarified.

"That is correct," Herbert answered, almost apologetically. "However he did say that he would try to make it to the game on Saturday to cheer you and the lads on."

"Wonderful," Leggett said sarcastically. "How sporting of him."

"I am sorry, William," Herbert said. "From what I can make of it, it sounds like you were depending on him to participate."

Leggett nodded yes and then explained why.

"I believe without him now we may be short a player for our game. We have lost two others with injuries and one to his studies."

"Well," Herbert suggested. "Would you like to see if I can give it a go in his stead?"

"Really?" Leggett asked. "Do you know much about the game?"

"No," Herbert answered honestly. "Actually I do not know anything. But I would be willing to give it a try if it means that much to the college like you had explained when we last met. I listened when you shared the purpose with Dr. Cook and Dr. Murray that day. Honestly, I was impressed."

Leggett smiled. "Well, the truth is that most of us are just learning this sport too," he began and pointed toward the far side of the field.

"Professor Kellogg and Professor Atherton have been working us out to ready us for any kind of physical combat. The truth is that even they know very little about how this football game is played and really have been preparing us as if we are getting set to charge up a hill in a battle against the Confederate soldiers."

Herbert laughed. "Well, I can try to charge into something as well as the next guy."

With that, Leggett introduced Herbert to the other teammates. They greeted him warmly, happy to see any fresh warm body join their ranks.

"Let's get ready for the next charge!" Kellogg yelled across the field.

"May want to toss your jacket aside," Large called over to Herbert, as the group took off in a sprint toward where Kellogg and Atherton had been standing.

As soon as they reached the point where Kellogg and Atherton were standing they were met with an immediate shout. "And again!" rang out from Atherton.

Instantly they turned and sprinted back across the field to the opposite side. There they caught up with Herbert who had finished taking off his coat and tie and was now preparing to join them.

"Is this all we do?" he asked as he ran alongside one of the other players.

"Yes," was all that player could wheeze out as he attempted to keep up with the group.

"Really?" Herbert stated out loud.

"Yes," another player answered back. "Just run and shut up please."

When the group had completed a series of five sprints across the field, Kellogg called them together.

"Listen men," he started. "A good regiment works together as a unit and a single man helps guide that unit and that unit follows the orders without fail. Am I understood?"

"Yes sir!" came back the call, startling Herbert who was still trying to figure out what Kellogg had just said.

"As I have told you before, you can always win when you attack with full confidence and full force but this only works when you attack as a group and not as an individual," Kellogg continued. "Am I understood?"

"Yes sir!" the group called out in unison.

"Good. Good. While it appears some of you were slowing down on that last run, I remind you that preparation now is the only thing that makes you ready when your day of combat arrives this Saturday. Am I understood?"

"Yes sir!" echoed out. This time Herbert joined the call to fit in.

"So we fight together. We fight as a unit. We listen to the commands. We do not question that command but rather we act upon that command. Am I understood?"

"Yes sir!"

"Okay we have rested long enough. Do you think the enemy is going to let you catch your breath?"

"No sir!" The group called out together although Herbert almost said "yes" just from what he had just started memorizing as the chant of the group.

"Then rise, my men of Rutgers. Rise and continue on with greater heart and greater determination. This time, on my call, two forward rolls then stand and run for twenty paces. Then you hit two forward rolls and stand to run for twenty and repeat that pattern again. Are we ready?"

"Yes sir!" they yelled out and each student hunched ready for his signal to start.

"Go!" and they tumbled forward and ran.

After twenty minutes of this running and tumbling and gliding sideways and hustling backward, Kellogg called out for a five minute rest. As they crumbled against the ground and fence post again Herbert, breathing hard, moved next to Leggett.

"Is this all that we do?"

Before Leggett could reply another student cut in.

"Mostly," he laughed. "But with the next and last part of practice we toss out the ball and give chase to that instead."

"Really?"

"Leggett!" Hearing his name yelled out to him from across the field, he looked up and saw Atherton standing there with the ball in his hand. "Are you the captain of this motley crew?"

"Yes sir," Leggett yelled back.

"Then come and take this ball and let's get your team practicing. Call out their orders and get them moving. Dark is approaching and there is only so much time left before you take on your foe!"

"Yes sir!" Leggett answered while running across the field to gather the ball.

As Leggett moved the other students rose and, just as if they had followed this routine many times before, sprinted to various spots on the field.

Herbert watched from where he stood on the side unsure of where exactly he was expected to go.

"Herbert!" Leggett called out. "You stay on that left side, back a bit, and punt the ball forward if it comes your way."

"Yes sir!" Herbert yelled back assuming this was the appropriate choice of words for a reply. He jogged over to the far corner and figured that, if he was lucky enough, he would get a chance to watch for a while to learn what to do before the ball would come his way.

Half the team faced the other half of the team. From what Herbert could ascertain, the group on the other side was given the ball along with the order to charge at his half of the players on the opposite side. The purpose appeared to be with putting the ball through two sticks posted near the end of the field. His job, he guessed, was to not let them get the ball there.

Leggett yelled, "Charge!" Off they came in a head-long run at Herbert's group.

The first player had kicked the ball forward past one of those on his side and the rest of that group came racing toward him, punching and kicking the ball ahead of them.

"Punt the ball forward." Herbert replayed the instructions Leggett had given him as he watched the other players approach.

Suddenly the ball squirted free and bounced awkwardly toward Herbert. Instinctively he ran forward to kick it back in the opposite direction.

With one giant sweep of his leg, Herbert attempted to boot the ball as far as he could.

He missed the ball completely by a good three feet. As he realized his error he turned to recover the ball but was instantly pushed in the back and to the ground by one of the players who was charging down the field. As he attempted to rise he was pounded again into the ground by the forearms of another player coming in the same path.

Herbert watched from the ground as the other group kicked the ball in between the two branches stuck in the ground.

Without any fanfare, the players jogged back in the other direction. It was announced they would do the same thing again.

This went on for the next half hour. The players charged down the field. The other group tried to stem their charge. Surprisingly, Herbert's group booted the ball away several times back to the opposite side of the field which signaled a stop in play. More often the ball went in some unintentional direction off to one side or the other causing players to give chase to it for fear the ball would become lost on the other side of the street.

Herbert watched as Leggett gave directions with each drive. Leggett helped tell the players what position to shift to and where to send the ball.

The game did not seem too complicated. It looked a lot like soccer to him which he had played the previous summer with some friends. There were several big exceptions from soccer though. For example, you were encouraged to use your hands and physical contact was encouraged and you were not penalized in any manner for pushing another player down to the ground. You were actually expected to tackle the opponent to get him to stop and to get the ball away from him and back for your team to use.

Unlike rugby, which he had seen played once before, you were also not allowed to just pick up and run any which way you wanted when you got the ball. The game had more of a set control to it from what he remembered.

He was sure there were more rules, but watching this day, he just was not certain what they were.

Eventually Kellogg yelled for the students to come back to where he was standing on the side of the field.

"Good work today men. Now do you think that you did good work today men?"

"Yes sir!" they yelled back.

"Well I lied," Kellogg snarled back. "And if you thought that was good work you will grow complacent. You will grow weak. You will not convince yourself that you must work harder. Now, again, was that good work today men?" he shouted.

"No sir!" they yelled back.

Kellogg nodded to Atherton who now stepped forward.

"We have done what we can. Professor Kellogg and I do believe in you. We believe that what we have shown you, when applied correctly, can bring you success against your enemy this Saturday."

Herbert arched his back, suddenly realizing how much pain he was feeling from having been run over several times. Atherton continued on using terms like "loyalty" and "fortitude" while Herbert began to wonder if he had joined the military versus a sports club.

"And so, as you walk away from here tonight," Kellogg had now taken back over. "I hope that you remember that you are stronger together then when you act alone. In the same way, when you as an individual decide not to give 100% toward your effort, you undermine the whole and fail your team!"

"Leggett," Atherton barked out. "Do you have anything you wish to add as the captain before we call it a night and end our final practice with you?"

"Yes sir. Thank you sir," Leggett replied and stood to face the team.

"Mates. First I thank you for your effort over the past few weeks. We face our foe on Saturday. I do not have to remind you how much this contest means to both our school and community of New Brunswick which supports us. Your play that day will help shape the way we all are seen here at Rutgers College."

Leggett's voice now grew more animated as he spoke.

"When I say all, this includes those on and off the field of battle that day. All means for future generations of Rutgers students who have yet to be born. All means a legacy that shall not be forgotten. How you play that day will be the story that is told. Be weak, men, and we will be remembered forever as failures. Be strong, men, and people will remember us across all times as the loyal sons of Rutgers who brought her school's name fame and glory!"

"Hurrah, Hurrah, Hurrah!" the students chanted three times in a loud cheer.

"While we thank our professors for their time and energy in helping prepare us, the task to be successful has now fallen to each one of us. The game is but a few short days away. While their formal practice with us ends today, I challenge each of you to meet with me each afternoon for the remainder of this week to join in team practice to help sharpen our skill to the very end. Who is with me?"

"Aye!!!" was collectively cheered back. Even Herbert, new to the team, was swept up in the response.

"On to victory Rutgers!!!" Leggett yelled and the group repeated the call.

Slowly, the group dispersed after collecting their personal belongings left at the side of the field. They headed their separate ways back to their boarding locations.

Leggett took a moment to thank both Atherton and Kellogg for their work with the group and for trusting in him with the leadership role they had approved.

"Your teammates selected you," Kellogg reminded the student. "We believe they chose wisely. Also know, Master William, their vote of confidence in you is a great responsibility in that you can push them to be better than any of them believes they can be. Do not forfeit your chance to do this if the time comes."

As Leggett joined the other students walking away, Atherton and Kellogg also started their walk back to their respective rooms for the evening.

"So how do you think they measure up? Atherton asked.

"When they started, as I told you back then, they appeared soft. They were very raw recruits," Kellogg replied.

"And now?" Atherton followed up.

"They are in better physical shape. They are definitely better organized. I think they are beyond what Dr. Campbell hoped we would be able to get them too by this date in time," Kellogg observed. "And what think you, Professor Atherton? Where do you see them standing in a fight against their peers?"

"The game appears to be a violent and physical one," Atherton began. "This group, as I look around, are not overly physically large or big by any man's standard. But they certainly gave a full effort to all that we have asked them. Those still standing and here today have committed to giving it their best. I love the fact that they play with all the heart that they have. In simple form, I love their grit and determination to be the best."

"I would be proud to take them to war with me, Mr. Atherton. Many a man went in to battle with so much less. I know you saw the same. It is that heart of the warrior that matters most and, I am proud to observe, they have that warrior's heart within them."

"I agree. I just hope they find it this Saturday against those lads from Princeton and come Sunday we all can boast about how proud we are to be sons of Rutgers."

32
That Night
Rutgers Campus

They crowded together again at the room in Van Nest Hall. Like their past few meetings, there was little discussion of anything beyond the upcoming encounter with the College of New Jersey.

"Look, we need to get these final arrangements out to them or they may not even show up!" Stephen Gano paced impatiently back and forth in front of several other students seated at the tables.

It had been a long day and now, with this task at hand, it was getting even longer. Four days to go until the contest they had been preparing for. It was about to happen and they still had not agreed to an itinerary for that day. Simple logistics based upon train schedules would determine the arrival time of the lads from Princeton as well as the time they would need to depart. The desired activities of feeding them when they arrived and before they departed were expectations for anyone when looking at the rules of etiquette. Still, the biggest point of contention had still not been clarified.

"So how long does it take to play a game?" Gano half-shouted the question again. "How can we not know that?"

"You know as well as we do that it could take hours or be over in minutes," Lasher responded, equally tired and frustrated to still be engaged at this task at this time of day.

"Look, I just say we pick a random time to set the other events. We keep the game time as 3:00 p.m. and let the chips fall where they may."

"And if the game takes three hours instead of two; what then? We don't feed them before they go back?"

"So we don't feed them! Who cares?"

"We should care. We are the hosts!"

"I agree. We will look like idiots if we can't get the general setting for the day settled regardless of the outcome of the game."

"You all know there is no way to guarantee what the length of the game will be. A team wins by besting the other out of ten points. If we win by scoring six right off the start, the game ends early. If it takes us all ten goals to get a winner, then it lasts a lot longer."

"What does happen if the score goes five each? Can there be a tie?"

"I guess so."

"No there can't."

"Well we need to figure that out before we start playing!"

Tempers were getting heated and the words caused an escalation of anything that was said. Leggett knew it had to do with them being exhausted as much as anything else. When Charles Pryun and Douwe Williamson started yelling back at George Large and Thomas Clemens who were reminding everyone about the need for a team cheer or song, he knew it was time to wrap it up.

"Seriously, why would we need a song?" Charles asked.

"Look. I was in the fife and drum corps at age 14 with my brother after he took me and joined the army," Clemens announced. "Music stirs the spirit and gets one charged up to fight!"

"And I did not say it had to be a song. It could be a cheer of some sort. If it is written right and we learn it correctly it could boost our spirit and build team morale!" George explained.

"It could also make us look foolish," Willliamson shot back. "Standing there and singing while they are beating our butts into the ground! Stick to designing plays and practicing on the field!"

"We could also look like we failed to prepare if they have one and we are just standing there watching without anything to respond with!"

"Okay guys, easy." Leggett broke in. "Save some of that energy for the team from Princeton later this week! We need to get back to drafting this letter and getting it out in the post!"

With audible grumbling each of the teammates present took a chair again around the table. Half of them sleepily placed their heads on their folded arms upon the table.

Leggett started.

"Okay, let me try to make this as painless as possible. We all agree that a good time to start is 3:00 p.m. that day. That allows for any unforeseen issue with their ride on the rails in the morning here and does not give them the feeling they are being rushed into playing as soon as they get here. We also all agree we should serve them dinner afterwards. Ideally we have time to socialize and share some fellowship with each other before they have to depart back on the train. We all agree that the best place to accomplish the postgame is at Northrups Tavern. Anyone object to any of these details?"

No one said a thing, so Leggett continued.

"So, what I propose is that I will draft and get this letter posted tonight. George has volunteered to remain here with me should I need any help."

"I did?" George sounded dumbfounded.

"You did now," Williamson joked.

"Anyone not trust me with what I put into it as long as I follow the details I just reviewed?"

"No," Clemens stated. "But please be sure to send them one last point of emphasis that we are not scared of them and plan to beat them that day!"

"Here! Here!" several in the group chimed in.

"Good enough then. Go get some sleep," Leggett directed.

"I still have to study tonight," one student called out followed by several others who also moaned about the fact that they still had to endure doing schoolwork.

"Well do that now and get some sleep right after. And do not forget," Leggett added. "Captain's led practice at the field right after classes tomorrow!"

The group dispersed slowly, half of them giving the appearance that they had been in a battle. The room emptied without much talk leaving Large and Leggett behind.

"So now what?" Large asked Leggett.

"We write."

Leggett roughed out the start of a rough draft and he handed it to Large to edit. He then moved on to draft a second page that incorporated the challenge statement the teammates had requested he include.

"Looks pretty good," Large handed the page back.

"Any changes needed?"

"I think you have it perfect," Large replied.

"Care to look over the second page?"

"Not really," Large honestly replied.

"It is short. How about I read it and you tell me if anything needs to change?"

"Sounds good to me." Large leaned back in his chair, his eyes also looking heavy as the day's workout had drained the energy from him too.

"With the end of dinner, I know our team will be happy to escort your team back to the train station for your ride back to Princeton. We will seek to arrange carriages be readied in advance so that you are not detained should the festivities after run long and the time to get to your train is short."

"Good so far," Large stated.

"I do hope your team will find that they have enjoyed their visit to New Brunswick even if the outcome is not what you had hoped from the contest. We also will alert the conductor and station master should several of your players find it difficult to walk well enough to get on the train. We will ask they announce the stop at Princeton in case your hearts are so heavy from your loss your teary eyes make it difficult to see the signs for when your stop back in Princeton has arrived. Hold strong, our rivals, in knowing that to have fought and lost to us that day is better than being too frightened to have fought us at all! Sincerely, the Loyal Sons of Rutgers."

"I love it," Large summarized. "I would not change a thing."

"Excellent. Then let me run to get this to the post and off in the morning train. I fear if it does not get off tomorrow they may not get it in time."

"Thanks," Large said. "You know I think we did a great job in picking you to be our captain."

"Thanks George," Leggett smiled.

"One observation though, and take the advice and use it any way you want," George began.

"Go ahead," Leggett replied.

"Looking around at our group tonight they looked pretty exhausted and beat up. I would hate to think that they are defeated on Saturday because their bodies have not been able to recover from our own practices."

As Leggett hustled to get the letter to the morning post, the words that Large had shared played over again in his head. He, too, felt sore and tired this evening. The workouts, he truly believed, had benefited them all. But George was right. If they were too hurt to play on Saturday all those practices would be for naught.

He passed the letter off after paying the postage and headed back toward his boarding house. He was definitely going to re-think what they did for the next few days. Maybe less violence with hitting and less pounding with running on their legs. Maybe going through more of a walk about with an emphasis on strategy would be a better way to prepare.

Leggett tossed the idea back and forth as he headed away.

Behind him, Master Leggett had no way of knowing that his letter plopped into a mail bag on top of another letter bound for Princeton. The destination of that letter, instead of heading to Nassau Hall, was the household of another Princeton resident, one Elizabeth Warren.

33
November 3, 1869
Princeton

As Gummere headed toward the President's office within Dr. McCosh's home, he glanced about at the bare leafless trees around him. The weather had turned cold early that year and coupled with rain on a night with frost, small icicles had formed on the small tree limbs. November had just started but it already felt like the dead of winter with a damp wind blowing in his face.

Of course, that empty feeling winter brings a man could also be explained by the events this week on campus and his impending meeting with the President of the College.

He thought back on that evening.

Three days earlier the news had first been shared about what his fellow students had heard relating to a ban of all social activity. He had hoped he would have been able to speak first with McCosh. In his mind he had played out exactly what he wanted to say and he felt that if he was able to place an appeal immediately there might be a chance to stall any decision.

But McCosh was not accepting visitors that night. Gummere was informed he would need to make an appointment. He had asked for the first available time and had cringed as the front secretary flipped calendar pages to give him a date three days hence.

In the interim, rumors had spread like wildfire among the students in Nassau Hall. Oddly enough, there had been no official proclamation or even an explanation about the ban or the missing student who had been reported as arrested and expelled. Word did not leak from any confirmed member of the faculty. It was as if the Princeton staff had been told not to discuss the matter with the students.

However, as so often happens in the absence of real information, various stories circulated and tales of what one student heard were tracked back to the source only to discover it was not an official with actual knowledge of the events.

One thing was clear. Lawrence Joueur was not on campus and he, along with his things, had been removed post haste.

On the issue of a general consequence of eliminating any non-church or non-charity activity from the regimen of all students; there appeared to be more of a hesitation on the part of the students from doing anything, versus a stated ban. The past two days saw poor weather conditions which did not encourage anyone to attempt to go outdoors for anything beyond required walks on errands or movement to assigned classes.

Tuesday afternoon, students who were in the choir, went to churches without anyone saying a thing. That evening, students in each of the societies converged to hold their weekly meetings. It was at that meeting where Gummere met with several of the players to discuss the status of their upcoming game. There the day's rumors were also shared.

Charlie Barrett explained that he had overheard a conversation stating that President McCosh was to give his edict before the weekend on Friday just before any free time would take place for students.

Dave Mixsell concurred that he, too, had heard about this coming announcement. Only his sources said it was supposed to be coming out later the next day.

Frank Burt said that the hall monitor had shared with him and another student not to make personal plans because the President was going to be calling all students together late the next day with an announcement of some sorts. When they asked for details he relayed that the hall monitor had been smug and simply stated that he was sure we already knew what was coming.

Chauncey Field said that he had inquired of everyone he knew about the status of his missing roommate. He had even gone to see the President to ask for details on Joueur's whereabouts only to be told that McCosh was not available to see him at this time.

One detail that possibly confirmed Chauncey's report about the expulsion took place when a townsperson came by Joueur's previous room the prior evening and had been there with an official from the college. The two men asked Chauncey if there were any other items left behind that Chauncey was aware of that belonged to Joueur and may not have had taken as he would not be returning.

Chauncey said he listened in while the two men looked about and exchanged small talk about Joueur. Chauncey said that, if they were accurate in what they knew, Joueur was supposed to have brought money to a meeting at the Princeton train station to settle some gambling debt.

As the two men talked the best he could make out was that supposedly a person from back in his hometown of Jersey City had been scheduled to arrive on the train to collect the debt. When Joueur went to meet the train there were two people, a man and a woman, who he accompanied to a room they had rented in the tavern. What happened next was totally unclear.

Chauncey said that the townsperson simply said the cops were in on it. They grabbed the boy out of the room in the tavern and now he had several charges against him versus just welching on some illegal bet he had made.

Still, Chauncey cautioned them all. This story was not substantiated by anyone official. He noted the townsperson may have been as prone to rumor mongering as any of them on campus.

Gummere had rallied his teammates around him not to give up heart.

At this point, no one had told them they could not play. All information shared, even the details that Chaunce had provided, were still secondhand and none carried the ultimatum of no activity to their doors.

Gummere redirected the attention of the group toward thinking through the strategy of the game at hand. He discussed the need for a solid effort on the part of each individual. He emphasized that when everyone was giving their all on the field they would be successful as a team.

Finally, he went over the plans for the day as he understood them while they awaited final confirmation from Rutgers about the actual logistics with where to meet and when they would eat. All were reminded that they were to take the second train out of Princeton that morning and, since there was still this lingering doubt of if they would be allowed to go, he suggested they wait to buy their tickets until that morning at the station.

Gummere had to say he felt a surge of confidence that the warning from Nissley and Sharp may have been overstated and that Professor Westmoreland may just have been predicting future expectations if he had been privy to the impending arrest and expulsion of Joueur. He went to bed that night feeling better than he had about this issue in two days.

That confidence was shattered that morning when he awoke. Word had already spread that Dr. McCosh would most likely be addressing them later today at the dismissal time after classes ended.

The message had worked its way through Nassau Hall and East and West College buildings and he could feel the stare of each and every border in his dorm as he exited for his morning meeting scheduled today before classes were to start.

Now, as he approached the front steps of the President's home, he took a deep breath and replayed in his mind what he needed to say. He knew he had just this one chance and, if a decision had already been made to ban all activity, then at least he was being given the opportunity to propose a delay.

He glanced once again at his feet before knocking on the door. An awful gulp trailed down his throat as he thought about how hard a pill it would be to swallow if he were the one who would be telling the lads at Rutgers College they could not come up to play.

He was escorted into the office of the President.

Dr. McCosh was seated when Gummere entered the room and was reading through several pages of a text at his desk. Dr. McCosh continued to read after Gummere was ushered in. He flipped through the final few pages without comment, closed the book, and finally looked up at Gummere.

"Please, Master Gummere, be seated," McCosh said pointing to a chair on the opposite side of his desk.

The meeting started with small talk about the weather and a question about how Gummere felt his personal studies were going. Gummere answered each in polite fashion. The small talk continued until Dr. McCosh asked him directly about why he had requested this appointment.

Gummere explained that three days earlier students had been approached by one of the members of the faculty and been informed that they would no longer be allowed to participate in general activities outside of the domain of their scholastic studies. He then shared that one of the fellows at Nassau Hall had come to tell them that one of their classmates had been taken out of the school and his belongings had been removed from his room already.

Gummere did not disclose any details about who had shared this information or about the depth of the rumors that had persisted after the initial talk. Instead, he then alluded to the pending meeting that was being reported about an important message to be delivered to the student body today. He feared what the content of that message may include.

"Dr. McCosh, I do believe you may be aware of our sports contest this coming Saturday against the college at New Brunswick. When I was attempting to reach you on that first day, there were rumors going around that still exist even today. I am hoping these rumors are not true

289

and, if they are, then I wanted to share with you the importance of this contest and hope that nothing will impede our ability to compete."

McCosh said nothing for a moment and averted his eyes from Gummere as he appeared to be weighing his words.

Truth be told, McCosh had known about the competition and would traditionally have backed such an event without any hesitation. The very concept of having the students in his charge out there proving their metal through physical challenges appealed to every fiber in his body as it related to how to educate the whole scholar.

However, with the events of the past several days, this contest had slipped from his mind and no one on his faculty who had been speaking with him had ever brought this item up in conversation to remind him. They had been way too busy extolling the necessity of bringing the college youth back under control.

He understood how the incident with Lawrence Joueur in the town had been the final push for the conservatives who desired to gain control over the future mission of the College of New Jersey to exert their influence. In no uncertain terms, he reminded himself, the directive to him had been the college leadership was expected to contain these young men and lock their growing minds into classrooms with the Classics. This was what had given the college its stellar reputation in the first place.

Still as he looked at this student, young William Gummere, here with him now he also remembered why he had accepted this position in the first place.

"So tell me Master Gummere, why is playing this contest on Saturday so important to you?"

Gummere sat forward in his chair.

"Sir, I would answer you that it is about honor. And when I say honor, I mean it on many levels. But perhaps the highest level though is that we gave our word that we would be there."

"I understand you gave your word, young man. But this contest was never sanctioned by the faculty."

"Sir, I apologize if there was some approval or protocol we failed to follow in our ignorance. However, to the students at Rutgers College and I am sure the people of New Brunswick, I believe they would not separate our word we have given to participate from the word of our college at this time. I believe failure to show up on the appointed date would diminish the reputation of us all."

"And how do you see that?"

"Because I believe it would bring to question in the future on whether one can trust the word of Princeton men. One's value is always defined by whether they honor their word."

Gummere continued on, emphasizing how this item should not be negotiable.

"You know every young man is now looking beyond the War that engulfed our past. With a nation in full reconstruction, those battles are now a part of our history. Sir, it is that future which has the eye of every student in this college. How fast the world is changing. Imagine, a train that now can take you at lightning speed from one end of our continent to the other with the hammering this year of one golden spike. What possibilities are out there for our tomorrows?"

"But regardless of that vision of which so many of my peers now dream, sir, there is one thing we all agree should never change. And that is the importance of a single man's word. This is a lesson that you and the professors have instilled in us here. Holding to that promise is often all that separates us, through our character, from any other form of wild savage on earth.

McCosh rubbed his chin.

"I feel you also need to understand, as a young student, that there is a bigger picture which also guides our hand. That bigger picture requires times where we must reorganize to ensure that expectations on behavior and scholarship are being met."

"Dr. McCosh. You told us to stand on our own two feet. Let no other man who encounters a student from Princeton ever walk away from that meeting without feeling that he has engaged a man of integrity. Sir, those are your own words."

"I did say that and still believe what I said to be true. And I understand your comparative parallel to this situation. But please know, Master Gummere, there are many others who feel that as a group you are too young to be making life decisions on your own. That a more sheltered approach on this college as it relates to your free time and your free will is necessary to attain the desired outcomes with your education experience."

"With all due respect, sir. Just four years ago young men my age and men the same age as my classmates were thrust into battle and asked to defend our very nation in a great Civil War. If that War were still in progress we would most likely be there, in a field of battle, far away from the security of the social structures here on a campus. And in that capacity, as was shown in the past, many of my younger peers would be in a position where they are making life and death decisions each day and asked to lead men, many older than ourselves, into the eyes and fire of the enemy line."

Gummere's passion drove his statements on.

"I request you, or maybe it is those among you who are directing you, to give us that same level of understanding Generals gave their men in that field of battle. We ask to earn your respect and trust through our choices and actions when we are engaged in conflict in the larger world arena. We ask for the opportunity to participate and not just be spectators to life. I do value the heroic tales of great historical figures who took on challenges and through that were shown to be worthy. Our readings show that many of those same classical figures we are compelled to study were younger than us."

Gummere slowed at this point but his words were just as passionate. "Please sir. Allow us that forum to prove our worth and carve out a name, in the future historical ledgers for the college and the community of Princeton, to which all can be proud."

McCosh had initially been ready to rebut Gummere as soon as he had started. There were limits to what he, even as the President, was supposed to do in the face of directives from those above him. But something about Gummere's ability to point out that he was just following directives caused him to pause. He was the President, he reminded himself. He was brought in to make hard decisions and not just follow orders.

McCosh knew that the mission of this college was also to develop young men to be leaders and not just to become followers of orders. What example was he setting if he did just that?

When Gummere finished speaking, McCosh sat for a moment without responding back.

Then, without speaking directly to Gummere, McCosh rose and called out to his house servant to come to assist him.

Gummere watched, in silence, and wondered if he was about to be escorted by this house servant back to the dorm to collect his things and then to become the second student dismissed from the college this week for being so direct and outspoken with the President.

Instead, when the personal secretary appeared first, McCosh walked with him toward the foyer. McCosh then stood and gave him directions in such a manner that Gummere knew they were being stated so that it was clear for him to hear.

"Please make plans to have my bags brought down and taken right out to our carriage. I have decided to cancel the afternoon meeting with faculty and students so I may take an earlier train on to Albany."

"Yes sir."

The house servant disappeared and returned a few moments later and laid the bags by the door. McCosh had not left the foyer and Gummere had not risen from his chair.

"Please keep in mind my itinerary," McCosh started again with the secretary. "It will keep me from Princeton for approximately two weeks."

"Yes sir."

"As I will not have time to communicate with the faculty before leaving, please be sure they are made aware that I will not rule on banning our students on campus from participating in any event. I will make a decision on our position when I return and after I have had appropriate time to consider any objections to such an action and what it would entail. Until them, make it clear to the staff, the students may participate in activities as they have been permitted previously and, if they elect to travel beyond our campus borders to another town for an athletic competition, they are welcome to do so."

The personal secretary helped McCosh with his top coat while the house servant pulled the bags to assist McCosh to the door and on to the carriage which had just appeared on the drive by the home.

Before exiting McCosh emphasized to the personal secretary, but actually turned to look back directly at Gummere as he spoke, a reminder on what to do once he left.

"After you get me to the carriage, please be sure to show our student in there out. Apologize to him that I am not yet able to rule today on if a ban will be put in place."

Then before exiting, and still looking directly at Gummere, he added one final point.

"And please emphasize to this student that if he and his classmates elect to go to their contest this weekend to play, they had best defeat Rutgers!"

With that McCosh headed out the door, down the steps and on to the waiting carriage. The carriage, as soon as the bags were lifted on, took off at a slow trot.

The personal secretary re-entered the house and moved into the office where Gummere was still seated in the chair. As he was about to speak to repeat what Dr. McCosh had spoken to him, Gummere raised both hands and stated that he appreciated the message but he had heard clearly what Dr. McCosh had said.

"Very good, young sir," the secretary stated. "Let me give you your coat."

Gummere took the coat but stopped as he was about to exit the door and turned back to the secretary.

"I do not know if you or another person on staff is expecting to write President McCosh, but if you do write could you please share this message with President McCosh. The message is simple. Please write him that his loyal students of the College of New Jersey will do both him and the college proud!"

Gummere exited.

His step was much more energized than when he had first entered the home even though he knew he was about to head to six hours of class lecture. Regardless of the academic task ahead, it was the message he carried back that now turned his quick step to a sprint.

"Game on!" Was all he shared when he encountered his classmates and then watched as they let out a collective cheer.

34
November 5, 1869
Rutgers Campus

The clouds had created a dreary overcast sky outside and the darkness crept into the rooms of the Old Queens Building where the students were seated awaiting the second part of the lecture to begin. The chill of the November air twirled in with the wind that always seemed to find each crack where the window frame held in the panes of glass. The students were hunched at their desks fighting off both the desire to drift off to sleep and the incessant cold.

The final session on every Friday always felt longer than the rest of the classes and this class today was no exception. While George Large appreciated the historical perspective Professor Doolittle was driving into them, he also wished for a respite from the ancient text and an opportunity to prepare for their activity tomorrow.

The practices had been lighter the past two days.

The Rutgers players had emphasized passing the ball to develop their individual skills and teamwork in place of slamming into each other. They had emphasized where to stand about on the field to create true angles from which to receive a pass and they emphasized where to stand on the field to defend against an opponent's charge.

The teammates all were pleased when two of their tutors, Hasbrouck and Adkins, had met them on their final practice the afternoon before. Hasbrouck had shown up with suggestions about the angles and a level of analysis that appeared to make sense in supporting their skill strengths.

He had joked with them, along with Adkins, about their less then overimposing size and physique. But he also worked on their confidence by saying he could not recall students who had been able to run faster or move quicker across the field.

They also appreciated the short talk Hasbrouck gave them at the end of the day. He tied their experience in winning a great contest with his own experience as a Rutgers student himself as a graduate in the Class of '65, just four years earlier.

Adkins, who had also been with the group that night when they had been confronted by the students in Princeton at Judge Olden's place, spoke about how one can summon great strength from prior experience. He urged them not to dwell on the insulting feelings they felt when they exited Princeton that night. Rather he encouraged them, instead of feeling helpless by events in the past, to use that negative memory energy now to correct a wrong.

George Large thought that much of Rutgers appeared to be behind them as they left practice yesterday evening and went back to their beds for the night.

But today, all day, he felt the energy start to drain from him as he sat in lecture after lecture. Maybe it was the rain. Maybe it was the cold. Maybe in was the material that his professors were covering or the style in which they spoke. Whatever it was, he feared that the positive energy he had felt the day before was now almost completely gone.

The Professor in his classroom, Reverend Doolittle, continued on about the theories of David Hume.

Doolittle emphasized the contrasting points from works by John Locke. The Mental Philosophy course, while giving weight to the importance of the Age of Enlightenment and science, still had a decided anchor in the religious tenants of the Dutch Reformed Church which was the foundational cornerstone at Rutgers. So while Doolittle went on about his skepticism with Hume's actual acceptance of any traditional religion, he also alluded to the existence of the Divine at every chance he could.

The basics of the lecture were no different from the ones given before

Like most lecturers, Reverend Doolittle often appeared to be delivering the material to the walls above the students. In many ways, the slumped figures and shapes before a lecturer might not even have been present while they spoke.

The expectation was for the student to listen and the professor, as the font of all knowledge, to spew forth all content information often reading quotes from texts or prepared thoughts from hand written notes. Rarely was the professor challenged while he spoke. Rarely was a professor expected to respond to questions or repeat himself in this setting.

However, this day Doolittle shocked them all when in mid-sentence he closed the cover of the thick text slamming it shut on the lectern before him and simply stated one word.

"Now!"

The students, some caught daydreaming, scrambled in their chairs in case the Professor had been directing some line of reproach at them.

Instead, Doolittle stepped in front of the podium, a position rarely seen in this classroom. As he did, the long robe arm swung almost majestically along with him.

"Now," he repeated the single word and then did it again. "Now."

The classmates looked at each other unsure of what to make of it.

"Gentlemen. The word today in this lecture hall is now. We talk so often in these halls about the past and we hope you can find a means of taking these words to tie them to your future. But today, I want us to take a moment to think about what this one word, now, means to us all."

Again the students, not accustomed to saying anything beyond recitation phrases and rote memorized response answers, sat there in stunned silence.

Doolittle stepped forward and moved to where the students were seated. Then he began to move about them as he would when proctoring a written exam. Only this time, Doolittle spoke as he walked.

"You have heard me speak of Hume and Locke. You have heard me speak of the great moral reasoning that goes on with concepts like freedom and trust. You have heard me speak about the debate of economic motive and man's divine responsibility to his neighbor. You have heard me speak about the constants that guide our universe and then the men who have come to challenge those constants."

Doolittle paused and looked about the room.

"In each of these lessons, I am sure, you felt I only spoke of the past."

Then looking into their eyes, really for the first time during a class lesson, he asked, "Am I correct?"

There was some slow nodding of heads in agreement.

Doolittle smiled.

"Well gentlemen. Today is a good day to stop and give reflection on the material covered and apply it to your own moment in time. It is well known that many of you have elected to join together to form a team that will face off against your fellow students from Princeton at that College of New Jersey."

He looked over at George Large who was providing him his full attention.

"It is to be a contest of strength and skill. It is to be a game of chance and planning."

Doolittle moved completely to the back of the lecture hall as he spoke and all the students had turned in their chairs to face him.

"But it is also a test. It is a test of will. It is a test of who has prepared the best and of which team works as a unit together in a manner to defeat their foe. Like a great battle it features two opposing forces who enter a field of conflict and only one emerges a victor."

Doolittle's voice had risen louder as he spoke.

This time after he paused and started again, his speech returned with a softer sound. But the words still rang with the passionate tone of a man who had an important message to share.

"I need not tell you how we share in the hopes of those of you who enter that field. We all pray that you will emerge victorious. I am sure you are aware from all the talk that everyone within these college halls support you. We all want the best outcome. But I do wish to ask those of you who are playing to pause and ponder this. When you enter that field of battle keep in mind that while we root for a win, only you carry the knowledge on that day of if you gave it your all. What will be the answer to the question when you ask yourself, did you not let down your teammates, your school and yourself by never holding back?"

Doolittle stepped toward the windows at the side of the hall and stood before them.

"Let me tell you. Like all men who walk this earth, one day you will work for a wage. Adam Smith would tell you that wage is what motivates all men. And in a daily world of work, this is often true. Tomorrow, you will play in a game. There is no financial reward to be found in playing a game. The gold is not tossed to you for doing better or worse."

"But in that contest there exists something which is even greater than a day's pay. And that, my young men from Rutgers, is the ability to walk away with the knowledge that what you have done has restored the honor and reputation of a college and a community when those around us have challenged us and tried to diminish our very being. You can write the script not only for how you hold your head high but for how the world sees Rutgers College and New Brunswick."

"Is this a war? No. Not in the traditional sense with the use of weapons like guns and bullets and with fatalities to tally a victor. As I say this, I hope you all remain blessed to never have to fight in a conflict of that kind in your lifetimes and that our great nation, so recently reunited, never faces that horror for our young men ever again."

"But this game is a type of war nonetheless."

"This is a war of existence. For those who are not aware, there are foes who would sweep this great college off the face of the map. There are men who would like to steal our mission of scholarship and independence and trade it down to Princeton with a rallying cry that only one college is needed in a state and only one college makes more economic sense."

"These same people point to wins and losses in any venue as ammunition for their point. They compare schools and count the tally. Numbers enrolled. Entrance scores. Perceived difficulty of required course work. False rumors that students at one college are better equipped to face both mental and physical challenges in life. And some say that school in Princeton outscores us on any scale."

"Well now is the time to prove them wrong."

"We teach you about the divine power of man and a greater mission in life. Tomorrow, for those of you that are in that game, please know you carry with you the spark of hope for all people in New Brunswick and for all the loyal sons of Rutgers."

"Today, our time spent talking about the past is done."

Doolittle now pointed to the land beyond the window.

"Gentlemen, go out there now and write a new history for our Rutgers College that becomes our story for tomorrow. Go out now and defeat those lads from Princeton! Go out there now and bring honor and glory to our college, our home, our common bond forever. Go out there now and win for Rutgers!"

With a grand flourish he swirled his academic robe as he moved across to the door and he exited the lecture room.

The students, still in awe by the suddenness of this activity, were totally silent for a moment.

George Large felt the words burn a new spirit into his heart. Quickly it replaced the emptiness that had crept in with the energy to compete he had feared he had lost just a few minutes earlier. He remembered again what had been there that had started the cause. He remembered why they had practiced and all that they had gone through. He remembered why this was so important to him that first day and why he would not allow himself to forget why it was important to the school and his classmates the next day.

Instinctively he stood. Immediately he started to clap his hands.

Around him, the rest of the class stood to follow his lead and applauded.

Cheers of "Rutgers" rose within the room.

With feet stomping in a military marching sound the noise began reverberating in the halls. To this stomping beat the students exited their lecture room and in unison chanted cheers of "Down with Nassau Hall" and "All glory to Old Queens."

"Told you we needed a spirit song!" Clemens, marching next to him, tapped George Large on the arm and they laughed as they were both caught up in the excitement of the moment.

Others ran into the hall from various rooms and for a moment watched in wonder.

Then, like they were captured by a contagion spreading fast, the students from these other rooms started cheering along in the revelry that comes from the desire men have for belonging to something greater then oneself. They joined the ranks and marched together out of the building. They marched out onto the grounds. They marched into the streets of New Brunswick united in a common bond of a love for their college.

"Rutgers!" shouted out.

"Rutgers!" yelled back.

Away they left, one great swarm screaming their school name to all.

"What was that all about?" Reverend Meyer asked, a flustered look on his face as he watched the students disappear over the hillside.

"Just a quick send off to our gallant lads with a wish for the best in their challenge tomorrow," Professor Doolittle smiled.

"Glory to Old Queens, eh?" Meyer said.

"Glory to Old Queens," Doolittle repeated.

Together they walked back into their academic building to prepare for the scholastic work ahead.

Beyond them the sounds could still be heard of a new energy building among their youth. It was still echoing loudly to those across the community no matter where they stood. It was heard even as the students moved off in the distance repeating their vibrant living cheers. Every ear picked up on the message of joy these young people called out. It was a voice that held both the promise of today and the hope for victory to bring honor back for their school through victory tomorrow.

35
November 6, 1869

It was a cold and blustery day with the chill from the damp wind making the morning air run right through one's bones. The dark and overcast sky made it feel like it was still the dead of night as the first of two trains prepared to pull out of Princeton that Saturday morning at 8:00 a.m.

On the train platform, there was a great deal of activity as passengers joked about the events that would be taking place later in the day up in New Brunswick.

Random cheers and yells went out when a young man from the College of New Jersey happened to come by to purchase his seat for the train that was scheduled to depart later for the ride east.

Elizabeth had bundled her two children with hats and scarves as if preparing for a winter journey to the Arctic north. Beyond the basic grumbling of being too warm when the clothes first went on, both children now complained not a lick as the reality of the cold morning air hit them and they shivered inside their layers of clothes wishing now they had put even more clothing on.

A train ride was always an adventure for the children as it was a rare treat. They watched out the windows with unbridled excitement at the passing landscape which appeared to fly by.

It was definitely magic in the minds of every child, and still many an adult, at how fast a train could move over the ground. The rumbling noise and rocking sensation of the car added to that feeling and each time the whistle roared, the two children jumped with surprise.

The other passengers were a wide mix of young and old with each one heading to various points on this cold Saturday morning. Some were catching connecting trains to visits in New York City while others were simply riding on their daily excursion to a work point that did not allow them to take the sixth day of the week off for frivolity. Elizabeth tried to pick out the ones around her who might be headed to the contest later in the day in New Brunswick.

Word had circulated quickly throughout the Princeton community, as it typically did, about the goings-on at the campus this day.

She had heard constantly the previous day on Friday in her shop from women coming in and talking about their views on how the Princeton lads were just so better mentally conditioned and physically prepared to be the victors in any contest. They wagered that the students at the College of New Jersey would win all competitions they entered whether it be a challenge of might or mind. They bragged about how the student of their college was superior in every way to the less talented young men who had the unfortunate lot of having to attend Rutgers College.

Elizabeth had to laugh when she overheard her own mother repeating the score of a baseball game played between the two schools on an earlier date. She went into a detailed overview explaining how that was another perfect example of how mismatched in ability the two colleges were.

"Have you ever seen a baseball game?" Elizabeth asked her.

"No," her mother responded. "But I know when a score is that lopsided you do not have to be a news reporter on the scene to be able to state that the other team is a big loser."

"And do you even know if the young men who participated in the baseball game are the same ones playing in this new sport game this weekend?" Elizabeth had countered.

Frustrated at being challenged by her daughter in front of her friends, her mother huffed and simply stated, "Does it really make a difference? I would think that the weakest of our lads here In Princeton against the strongest of their poor lads at Rutgers would easily beat them on any field and with any sport selected!"

Then, turning to her friends, her mother continued with the dismissive, "I do not even know why our boys bother to travel up there knowing that they are so far superior that it is bound to just be a waste of their time and day!"

Elizabeth loved Princeton. But she also never backed down when she and her mother were discussing things and she felt her mother was showing her ignorance. Elizabeth slung back at her the comment that drove all supporters of the College of New Jersey wild.

"Well, I suppose that is what gets shared in Boston and Hartford when the lads at Harvard and Yale think about us here in New Jersey."

You could see steam rise from her mother's head as her eyes and face appeared to turn a brilliant red.

"Oh that those fancy-dandies were to come down here and try to beat our lads at anything! Besides having an earlier date on which their colleges were originally founded, there is no one man alive can convince me that anyone at Harvard or Yale has anything over our boys in Princeton!"

To a chorus of "Here! Here!" from the three older ladies socializing with her mother, each of the four women turned their heads away from Elizabeth and refocused their attention on their personal chat. It was a signal to Elizabeth that they no longer had any interest in entertaining her input in their affairs.

Riding now on the train to New Brunswick, Elizabeth could hear the same little snippets among those seated around her. Talk about how simple a school Rutgers College was and how deficient they were in so many ways. Chatter went on about the learned men who were the professors in Princeton and how they trained those in their charge not just to be solid scholars but also leaders of other men.

The pride in the college within their community was strong.

A college was the anchor, in so many ways, to the small town life. It provided that elitist feel among the townspeople that they too, in some way, were superior by just having this highly regarded college in their midst. Not that the locals in this place were so highly educated or aware through their own upbringing or their where-with-all in the ways of the world. Their lack of knowledge about true libertarian societal news was commonly visible and that small-town mindedness appeared too often.

Elizabeth still bristled at one of the worst public spectacles from years earlier and the way that the citizens of Princeton had treated Lucy Stone when she had come to speak with her husband at her side at Mercer Hall. To a chorus of boos and whistles, their ignorance and small town fears had been on full display that day. There was very little of the knowledge of the world the lads in the college were supposedly inheriting through their lessons that had rubbed off on her neighbors. These were the same loud-mouthed louts who basically ran Stone out of town at the time. They were aggressive toward her speech for simply making a few suggestions about equality and suffrage for all people. And they had even hissed at basic comments about incorporating the concept of rights for women in one's daily life.

And it was not just their prejudice toward women or outsiders either that bothered Elizabeth. Princeton, like much of New Jersey, had a lurid past with its roots in slavery. While the college boasted intellectual attainment and freedom, it had also been populated before the Civil War with many sons of southern planters with their attachment to their own set of off-base moral principles. Along with the agrarian base in the southern part of the state, life there was dangerous for freed African-Americans as it was in many areas in the south. Men and women escaping the evils of slavery in the south often found that the passage to freedom through New Jersey was fraught with peril due to these very people who resided here and who were as likely to support the evil institution as to oppose it.

Not that Princeton in 1869 was unique in her prejudices.

As for women's rights, much of the nation was as backward Princeton. Fear that a woman's suffrage would cast an evil spell over a male dominated society kept the idea of female liberty and the right to vote far at bay in many communities. Influenced by the routines and cultural traditions, many women even bought into and espoused the institutionalized practices that kept them from being equal partners in life with their male counterparts.

In regards to the status of the end of slavery, beyond the economic realignment after the war, newly emerging struggles were increasingly apparent with those who harbored ill will toward equality for all.

To an avid reader like Elizabeth, their ignorance and actions in Princeton about topics like social equity and world matters could make a person scream.

Still, there was something charming in the manner in which they would defend the college in Princeton against all detractors. Provincial without question. But they were fierce and ready to fight off any outsider who dared challenge their home turf. Claws out, it was as if they were the mama bears protecting their cubs.

Elizabeth chuckled as she recognized this same emotion in herself and how it played out whenever she heard Adkins bragging about Rutgers.

At that moment, Elizabeth felt her son tug at the arm of her coat to get her attention.

"Is this our stop?" he asked as the train slowed and the whistle started in again.

"Yes," Elizabeth answered back, glancing at the sign of the approaching station platform. "You both stay right by me as we exit and do not get separated!"

Pulling her bag over her shoulder so it would remain positioned there, she straightened her own hat atop her head and then reached down and grabbed the hands of each of her children.

"You look pretty mommy," her daughter's voice came to her.

She glanced down at that smile and those eyes. Angelic!

"Thank you sweetie. Now, again, stay close by my side."

The passengers surged off the train as soon as it lurched to a stop, each person acting as though they were on a sinking ship and feared they would not be able to escape. Elizabeth held her children back with her for a moment as their bodies were about to be swept up in this swift current exiting the train.

Slowly they moved from their seats, once the mad rush had gained some forward distance, and walked through the train door and down the steps to the landing of the station below.

"Elizabeth!"

She heard the voice call to her and recognized it instantly as Adkins. He came over to them in a quick jog, smiling as he dodged past the other passengers on the platform.

"Hello!" he announced when he was directly in front of them. He then hesitated for a moment as he assessed the manner in which their relationship should allow a formal greeting.

Elizabeth let go of her son and reached forward with her gloved hand, palm downward. Adkins carefully took her hand and kissed the back of it, holding it for a moment afterward and giving it a gentle squeeze before releasing it back.

"Mr. Adkins, may I present to you my two amazing children, Anna and Jonathan." Elizabeth let go of her daughter's hand as she spoke and took a step back so that Adkins was now directly in front of both children with their mother behind them.

"Pleased to meet you," Adkins leaned down and shook Jonathan's hand as if he were a young man.

Then, turning slightly toward the little girl, he took her hand in the same fashion he had held her mother's and gently kissed it. "Charmed," he stated as he gently bowed toward her as if she were a royal princess.

Looking up, he could see Elizabeth was smiling.

"Well, no reason to stand here in the cold. I have a horse and carriage all set for us and a day full of activity planned." Looking at Elizabeth for approval Adkins announced, "Anybody hungry and desire a bite to eat first?"

"That would be wonderful," Elizabeth replied.

"Excellent!" Gesturing toward her large bag over her shoulder Adkins asked, "And would you care for me to carry that for you?"

"Thank you but I am quite capable," Elizabeth stated. She stepped forward again between her children and, taking each by the hand again, moved toward Adkins' side. "Well lead on and we shall follow."

Adkins took the cue and instantly began to guide the trio through the people still bustling around the train platform. He moved them off to the roadside where he had a carriage waiting.

He glanced over several times as they walked to size up the two children at their mother's side. They were clean and well attended children. Each child had an innocent look about them. He could sense that they may take a little time to warm up to a stranger in their company. And Adkins was very aware, he was clearly a stranger to them. He only hoped that what he had planned would help break the ice as the children squeezed themselves onto the same side seat of the carriage where their mother sat and left Adkins to sit alone on the bench opposite.

As they now sat in the carriage, Jonathan saw a large skeleton head of an animal on the floorboard by Adkins' feet. It was directly beneath the seat where Adkins now sat facing them.

"What is that?" he whispered behind his small cupped hand which he held up to his mother as he spoke, but loud enough for Adkins to hear.

"This, my young man?" Adkins grandly announced as he reached underneath his seat and pulled up the two foot long skeleton's skull.

"This is just a sample of one of the magical things you will get to see today when we visit the storage area later in the basement of the new observatory!" Holding the skull above his own head for the children to get a clearer look, Adkins added, "Have you ever heard of dinosaurs?"

Both children shook their heads slightly side to side as the glare of their eyes never left the aloft skull.

"Well a long time ago, way before even your mother and I were born, there were giant animals that roamed all over this very land. They were huge beasts."

"Bigger than buffaloes?" Jonathan asked.

"Much bigger than buffaloes," Adkins smiled back.

"And we are going to see them?" Anna asked.

"Sadly, no, we cannot see them anymore. You see they have all vanished from the face of the earth. These huge animals one day just disappeared before any people even had a chance to see them." Adkins shook his head as if he were disappointed at their departure.

"If no one ever saw them then how do we know they were ever here?" Jonathan asked.

"Great question! Men may not have seen them with their own eyes but they have clues they were here. You know like when you are outside and leave a footprint in the mud when you leave? The next person who comes on by sees the footprint but not you. Even though he cannot see you he sees the footprint and realizes that you had been there. That is called a clue."

"So you saw their footprints?" Jonathan came back with his next question.

"Well our clues are that we have found bones and things called fossils that tell us that they were once here. The men I work with have collected many of these bone clues to help us better understand what these dinosaurs may have looked like before they vanished."

"Doesn't that sound exciting?" Elizabeth interjected.

Both children nodded and Adkins put the skull on the seat beside him before providing clarification about their plans for the day

"So first we get something to eat. Then we take a carriage ride around New Brunswick so you can see some of the large buildings and churches we have here. Then we go to the college and visit the observatory where we will start by looking up at the sky to see the stars. Then we will go down in the basement where we get to see the old, giant dinosaur bones," Adkins summarized the agenda.

"And will we still get to see the contest?" Jonathan asked his mother.

"Contest?" Adkins looked back at Elizabeth to translate for him.

"All Princeton has been a flutter about the students coming up here today to take on the sports challenge over a boast made by the students at your Rutgers College. Anna and Jonathan have been hearing about it all morning so far on the train," Elizabeth explained.

"A boast? A contest? You mean the student football game?"

"That's it," Elizabeth replied. "This new sport, football. First time it is ever being played between two different schools. Supposedly the Rutgers students think they have finally found a challenge they might win at and have written a boast to provoke the lads in Princeton. Of course this has fired them up down in Princeton where they feel there is no contest that Rutgers could ever pose in which the lads in Princeton would not end the victor."

"Well, I suppose they already have forgotten that the New Jersey legislature gave Rutgers College the Morrill grant money instead of Princeton's College of New Jersey when both competed head-to-head for those largest funds ever given," Adkins responded defensively.

"I assure you I have not forgotten that one positive about Rutgers," Elizabeth answered, her short reply sounding as if she had been insulted by his remark.

"And a boast by the Rutgers students? Really? It is the boys in Princeton who are notorious for making prideful boasts in the face of others. They are famous for their arrogance and smart comments insulting others. Need I remind you of that night at Judge Olden's?" Adkins exclaimed.

"So you are now putting down Princeton, Mr. Adkins?" came Elizabeth's retort. "I just hope you feel that after the students at Rutgers lose their contest again today you have equipped the young students with a broad enough vocabulary to be able to explain away yet another defeat much like their lost cannon and, what was the score of that baseball game between them again?"

"You are defending Princeton and that college there?" Adkins sounded genuinely surprised. "I thought you found the people there in Princeton uninformed compared with the likes of New Brunswick men like Dr. Cook and Dr. Murray when you spent the night being entertained with them here? Have you already forgotten that?"

Elizabeth bit her tongue before spewing out the first words that would pop into her head. Were they actually arguing?

Before Elizabeth could reply back, her son tugged at her coat arm and asked, "Wow! What is that giant building and all those clouds?"

Both Elizabeth and Adkins paused their discussion and looked out at the large factory alongside their passing carriage. Smoke was billowing out the top of the chimney stacks.

"That is a factory dear," Elizabeth replied.

"It is enormous!" the young boy observed.

"Mr. Adkins, is that building even bigger than your dinosaurs?" Anna asked.

Adkins chuckled at the young girl's question. Instantly he was warmed by her willingness to speak with him directly. Maybe the stranger image was already starting to fade.

"No darling," he smiled, his voice calmed from the previous interchange with Elizabeth about the Rutgers and Princeton reputations. "Some dinosaurs were bigger then horses but nowhere as big as that building."

"How can you be so sure if they have all vanished and you can't see them anymore?" the young girl came right back at him.

Adkins looked up at Elizabeth who was looking at him with the expression of, now what do you tell a child?

"Well," Adkins stumbled to find the words to answer this and unfortunately fell back upon his scholarly analysis versus what would make sense to a child. "You see science is based upon the evidence men collect. Based upon the initial discovery or a thought, men create what is known as a hypothesis. The scientists work to find out if that way of thinking has evidence to support it. Then, after they get all the evidence they can find they draw conclusions from that evidence and announce what they have found out. From that work with fossils and bones there is no evidence to support a dinosaur that size."

Both children had a stunned look on their faces as the cab in the carriage became silent. Adkins froze. He looked back at both of them uncertain what to say next.

Elizabeth broke the silence.

"What Mr. Adkins is saying is they just didn't build anything that large back in those time."

"Oh," the child answered, sounding happy enough with her mother's simple explanation where Adkin's response had not been able to reach her.

"Are we going to eat soon? I am getting hungry," Jonathan announced.

"Yes. Yes!" Adkins now stated, anxious to divert attention from his previously failed attempt to communicate with the children. "Our stop is right up here in just two more blocks."

The carriage stopped moments later and the group stepped out of the cab. Adkins spoke with the driver for a moment and then joined Elizabeth and her children for them to enter the establishment to eat.

"So," Elizabeth asked him as they opened the door to enter the eatery. "I am curious if we will we be stopping by that contest today at all?"

"If you and the children wish. I am sure I could try and arrange that," Adkins responded cautiously, not wanting to start another heated conversation on the topic.

"I only really want to go if you feel there will be no strong animosity if the boys from Princeton deliver another victory over Rutgers again."

Adkins felt his temper start to rise. When he looked at her, Elizabeth was smiling. He realized now she was just teasing him.

"Oh, I assure you that will not be the case," he replied, almost sounding apologetic.

"Good," Elizabeth answered.

"Because there is no way that Rutgers plans to lose today!" Adkins quickly inserted.

Elizabeth's head jerked quickly to the side.

As she looked at Adkins he was now smiling back in a manner that said he was simply reciprocating.

"Well played, Mr. Adkins," she smiled back. "Yes. Well played."

36
November 6, 1869
New Brunswick: Noon

It was a noisy group that got off the train two hours later.

The hands of the clock on the platform were getting closer to reaching toward noon. The jovial spirit of those in carriages that surrounded the station at the arrival of those who rode to New Brunswick with the players from Princeton by train generated a level of excitement not commonly seen at this site.

"Are you ready to win?" a voice called from one of the carriages toward the young men as they disembarked from the train.

"Hail victors!" came another voice launched in their direction.

"Are we ready boys?" Gummere yelled back to his teammates.

Instantly there was a collective "Hell yes!" that rolled out, shocking some of the more refined and pious folk within earshot.

"And how do we plan to do it?"

"Blow them apart!"

"And how does that sound?"

They used a cheer stolen from the Union Army's 7th Regiment called the sky rocket. In unison, as they had obviously planned and practiced, the players loudly chanted out the words.

> *Ch-ch-ch! Boooom! Ah!*
> *Hooray! Hooray! Hooray! Tiger!*
> *With his ch-ch-ch! Boooom! Ah!*
> *Fol-de-rol de riddle-diddle de*
> *Ch-ch-ch! Boooom! Ah! Rahhh!*

Immediately there were yells and applause among the young men and neatly dressed ladies with gloved hands holding parasols aloft. They stood on their carriages and on the train platform and continued to welcome their team to New Brunswick.

Watching as they waited to go and help direct their Princeton guests to the afternoon events to be hosted by their college; both William Leggett and George Large now wondered how much harder a task truly lay ahead for them.

"These guys are huge," George Large stated to Leggett looking the group over. "And they look like they are made of steel!"

Leggett, patted the shoulder of his companion. "No sense worrying about that now my good man. Big or small, right triumphs over all!"

"Nice rhyme, but they still look huge!"

Together they stepped forward.

Leggett and Large introduced themselves to the first players they came up to and were then directed toward Gummere. He identified himself as the team captain and Leggett did the same.

After shaking hands and a few simple pleasantries, Gummere instantly turned back toward his 24 other teammates and shouted, "These are the lads from the losing team here to welcome us."

The pro-Princeton crowd roared in laughter.

"Sorry, just having a little fun," Gummere turned back to the two Rutgers students and smiled at Large and Leggett. "So what fun do you blokes have planned for us here this afternoon in New Brunswick to kill some time?"

"You mean before beating your football team?" Large stated sarcastically as he stared at Gummere.

"WOOOO!" people in the crowd close enough let out collectively as Large's statement sounded like fighting words to their energized ears.

"Just having a little fun back," Leggett winked and stepped forward in front of Large as Gummere gave back a harder stare. "Okay now, why don't you follow us up this way? There are few more of our guys up there ready to give you a tour of the area. Then we'll get you back to a meeting place to do a short lunch before we head to the field later for the game."

Gummere nodded and the group followed behind Leggett and Large as they walked up a few blocks to where several more of the Rutgers teammates were waiting for them.

Leggett told Gummere that he had a few options for the pre-game period and, before saying anything further, Gummere called out to the straggling line behind him.

"College of New Jersey men. Pull in here together to get the directions from this fellow from Rutgers."

As they grouped around Leggett he explained how they would break the group up with a Rutgers student acting as a guide to walk a few of them about to see the campus and some of the town.

"Do you have any billiards parlors?" one of the students from Nassau Hall called out.

"Do we have billiard parlors!" a Rutgers student announced in a boastful tone.

Instantly Gummere cut in.

"I do not need to remind you gentlemen. Our purpose here is the contest later today. To that end, no fooling around and getting yourself in any trouble. I can just imagine how these folks in New Brunswick will treat us if they perceive we are acting out of line here today. Your tail sitting in a jail while your teammates are playing without you is not the sight we would want to see."

"We'll still beat 'em even if we are a few bodies short, Captain!" one of the Princeton group joked.

Large clenched his teeth to not comment back. Leggett ignored the comment and continued.

"Break off in groups of roughly five and two Rutgers students will get with you. Then we will break these smaller groups out in different directions so you are not tripping over each other as you walk the streets."

Slowly, each group dispersed in sets of five or six and headed out onto the streets of New Brunswick to use up some time before lunch.

Leggett and Large watched as the clusters left and then headed back toward Van Nest Hall. This was where they had left a few others behind to help set up the area in that building to allow the Princeton group to eat lunch before heading over to the field.

Mary Eva and her friends had agreed to act as hostesses for the lunch and they had secured donations of home baked chicken, rolls, gravy, and apples for the midday meal. They were busy at Van Nest Hall taking care of the details with the meal when Leggett and Large arrived.

As Leggett reviewed what else they had to take care of today before the game he was grateful Mary Eva and her friends had shown up. They had volunteered to not only secure the food but also volunteered to set up and to serve and then clean up so the Rutgers players could get ready themselves. It was one less thing to concern himself with that day and he trusted she would handle all things like this well.

"Man they are arrogant," Large stated angrily as they had walked. "I tell you they just make you want to slug them every time they open their mouths!"

"I am sure they feel the same about us. In the meantime, that sound you heard was not just them being pompous boasters. That is the sound of true confidence," Leggett told his friend. "They, to a certain degree, have earned that right to be confident today as they prepare to play us based upon the results everyone has heard about with prior Rutgers' teams and their athletic experiences."

"I don't care what they've done before they still make me mad when they talk to us that way!"

"And I agree that their victory on a baseball field a long time ago has little bearing on the outcome of this contest today. Still, let us not forget our purpose that you originally explained to me."

"And that was?" Large asked as if he never remembered any previous conversations.

"George! Need I remind you of what you told me when you were recruiting me to join you and the team to play today?"

"Maybe I just need to hear it again," Large stated.

"Today may have many moving parts but it still all comes down to one singular goal. That goal has never changed and our focus needs to be to show those lads from Princeton what we are made of and teach them that we are their equals on any field of battle. We need to make them walk away from here understanding that our fight today will be a victory for the glory of our team, Rutgers College and our town of New Brunswick."

"Well said, future Reverend Leggett. Well said!"

"Let's not forget now why this was started. Let us not take a step back down at this time when it is the time to charge forward to show our metal."

"I agree, William. I do agree. But honestly, tell me just one thing."

"And what would be, George?"

"Weren't those guys huge?"

37
"The Contest"

Lunch went by quickly as the College of New Jersey players rolled in and informally grabbed at the food that had been brought for their nourishment.

Leggett and Large elected to leave and not stay for the lunch to watch them eat. They also decided that remaining there was not good for either one of them out of fear that their tempers might also boil over at any ongoing taunts from the players from Princeton.

Mary Eva and her volunteer core were not as lucky in avoiding the constant bragging of their Princeton guests. In their roles they were required to remain and hear the ongoing talk about how great the College of New Jersey was. There were boasts made about the ultimate defeat and then the fall of Rutgers College altogether from the rolls of existing colleges in America.

Mary Eva summarized this after the game had been played.

The group from Princeton, according to Mary Eva when she spoke with Leggett later, appeared to have enjoyed their day strolling through New Brunswick.

They had shared stories about what they had seen and what they were impressed with. Several compared New Brunswick with Trenton in size and manufacturing styles. Others noted the number of churches and a few who had taken a carriage to ride out along the Raritan River had mentioned their surprise at seeing several fine homes. Of course, when they talked about fine homes seen here they were not comparable to the finer homes found in Princeton.

By far, the majority of the early chatter related to the exploits in the billiards halls. From what the Princeton players were saying each of them sounded as if they had entered one of the locales and partook in the games of chance there and that they had played and won their fair share on the tables that day.

Kathleen had even pulled Mary Eva aside at one point after overhearing the talk about the billiards games.

"I thought they were supposed to be pious young saintly men heading all into the ministry from Princeton," she had exclaimed.

"Whatever gave you that impression?" Mary Eva asked.

"I do not know. But I cannot believe all they were interested in all day today was gambling!"

Her prior image of the men of Princeton forever altered, Kathleen went on and kept serving. In turn the Princeton youth who kept eating it appeared to Kathleen as if they had not had a meal in weeks.

Eventually, the players were grouped together under the guidance of the team captain.

He reminded them first of their purpose in coming to New Brunswick that day. Then he went over the basic outline of strategy with the game and the designated places the players would take not leaving any detail out.

Mary Eva had to admit she was impressed with the intensity with which their team captain spoke.

He was in command as he stressed the expectations for how the men were to play that day and how they were to carry themselves on the field. He extolled the importance of teamwork and staying within the rules while always pushing oneself for the benefit of the whole.

She felt chills as he spoke about honor and respect for a code that they never should break. He emphasized a pact that they must remain loyal to; one that they had entered into by belonging not only to the College of New Jersey but for being men from Princeton.

Mary Eva looked at how the players listened without interruption. She had to admit that his ability to make a large group of same-aged students follow him in the manner that he did was amazing.

Eventually they collected their things and prepared to head over to the field for the contest.

Mary Eva pushed her group to clean up the tables behind them as quickly as possible not wanting to miss the contest across the campus herself.

Thankfully there was no left over food to wrap or to process as the young men had eaten everything down to the last bone. However, Mary Eva and the New Brunswick girls did have to collect all the materials, like forks, plates and cups, and get those in a basket to return these items later to their appropriate homes.

She also grabbed the material they had put out to protect the college tables from spills. Tossing this material in a large basket with her winter cap knitting project, she carried this full basket out the door with her in case the game proved boring to watch. At least, she reasoned with herself, if that were the case she would get some knitting done.

Amazingly, as the College of New Jersey students did not appear to be in a rush, Mary Eva and her friends were actually able to get out of the building before the players from Princeton left the Hall.

This field on which the two teams were slated to play was located a short walk just a few blocks from Van Nest Hall where they had just finished eating. It was situated in between College Avenue and Sicard Street and extended out in a rectangular shape.

The land itself was mostly a mixture of dying rye grass and wild weeds holding bare patches of dirt in place from running away with each rain. A wooden rail fence ran the length of the field on the two longer sides and over a portion of the short sides of the field. As one walked over the field it was evident that dogs, horses and goats had felt free at times to use this stretch of earth for their own purpose be that for food or as a spot to relieve themselves.

On the far end of each side of the field were two tall stakes driven into the ground. On closer inspection, one could see that they were actually recently cut thin young trees. They were no more than twelve inches around and at most eight feet tall. The stakes had been placed about twenty feet apart from each other on both sides.

As Mary Eva and her friends approached the grounds they noticed that there were people milling about seemingly waiting for the start of the contest. A cool breeze had started up again and the afternoon air was getting decidedly colder than it had been when the Princeton players had first disembarked from the train at noon. Several of those awaiting to watch the contest had huddled around the back side of buckboard wagons. Small little campfires could be seen now burning. These were strategically placed so that they were away from the line of sight of the horses that had drawn the vehicles there.

A few had lowered the tail end gate board of their wagons. They all appeared to be happy and relaxing, eating and drinking while seated on the flattened wagon backs.

Walking past one of these groups Mary Eva observed that they were roasting small sausages on sticks over the flames, keeping them held high enough so as not to burn them. She also watched as tin mugs were passed from hand to hand and clinked ceremoniously to small salutations. Each canister most likely held either watered down burned coffee to stay warm or, in some cases, beer to lift one's spirits.

Oh how the pious in the local churches would be frowning upon that, Mary Eva thought to herself. Out drinking in an open public place.

There was no doubt if someone else saw it this would be brought up in tomorrow's sermons in churches across New Brunswick. All these revelers sitting about eating and drinking in this manner. People just sitting on the tail end of their wagons, gate boards down and feet dangling. Beer in public, oh my!

Sin and impropriety in our fair town. She could hear now how the minister would start admonishing those who participated as well as those who allowed it to happen.

The number of spectators who dotted the fence line was not large, but they were spirited. It was difficult to tell where their rooting interests might lie as the cold and windy day now had folks wrapped up in blankets over their shoulders disguising even the best dressed among them. The one exception to this degree of financial anonymity were several fancy lady hats that would pop up here and there exposing the wearer as some type of socialite.

Mary Eva and her friends walked to the far side of the field, along the path of Sicard Street, and secured a spot by the fencing there.

"Could it be any colder?" Kathleen whined as a hard breeze filtered leaves past their faces.

"I recall February days much warmer than this," one of the Rutgers students who was not on the team agreed. "Still, I do want to see a little of this contest."

"Me too," another onlooker agreed. "From what I hear this is supposed to be better than a prize fight."

"It will only be interesting I fear if our lads from Rutgers can take a beating like I predict is about to come. Did you see the size of those players from Princeton earlier today?"

Mary Eva watched as the players for Rutgers started to approach from the various individual sites they had just left. Unlike the team from Princeton, they had not formed as a unit ahead to prepare together. Instead, in no set pattern for arrival, they slowly walked on to the field and eventually started to gather together on the far end of the field, to Mary Eva's right.

A few minutes later she saw Leggett coming and, as he neared, she called out to him.

Leggett waved back and gestured that he would come over to chat with her shortly as he joined the groups of Rutgers players who had arrived on the field ahead of him.

Each of the Rutgers players kept on their coats and hats to help weather the cold as they talked about the upcoming game with each other in a small semi-circle.

Suddenly, from out across the other side of College Avenue somewhere on the Rutgers grounds between Van Nest Hall and the field itself, voices could now be heard. It came across as a sort of chanting with a rhythmic sound.

"*Hah! Hah! Hah! Hah!*"

It echoed, deep and slow, much like a train starting up from its stalled position on the track.

All who were seated on the fence or were engaged in small group conversation stood to look toward the approaching sound.

Mary Eva watched as the group of players from Princeton marched toward the field. Heads seemed to bob up and down as they walked. They chanted with each step.

As they came closer, the people who had come to support the College of New Jersey also seemed to take up the chant by clapping at the same pace that the team roared out its cadence.

"Hah! Hah! Hah! Hah!"

The words started to increase in speed, as the team members crossed College Avenue, giving the appearance of the train starting to accelerate.

"Hah! Hah! Hah! Hah!"

Eventually the individually enunciated words seemed to bleed together into one fast rhythmic sound – a train rolling at full speed.

As the players stepped onto the grass field, the team captain raised his fist in the air and shouted. "Men of the great College of New Jersey, circle about!"

With that command, the twenty-five pulled into one large circle with arms linked over each other's shoulders and they started the chant over again.

The Princeton players began to sway from side to side in slow fashion. The words came bouncing out slowly and then started picking up pace repeating over the slow to faster acceleration sound of a running train.

"Hah! Hah! Hah! Hah!"

Again, the supporters from Princeton clapped to mimic the player's chanting.

The Princeton captain called out to the members of his team. Without fail each one of them replied each time in unison.

"Are you ready?"
"Yes!"
"Are we ready?"

"Yes!"

"Then for God. For country. For college and the love of Princeton. Let us take all the glorious names of our past on to the field of battle as we honor all of them with our performance today!"

Gummere then trotted out of the circle from among his Princeton teammates and halfway across the field of play to await his Rutgers counterpart.

The Rutgers players were all standing and watching, unsure of what to make of this organized energy.

With a roll of her eyes at Leggett, Mary Eva gestured toward the middle of the field as if instructing him to get to the Princeton player immediately.

Leggett chatted for another moment with his teammates in a voice too low for those beyond his immediate teammates to hear. Then, as if he had done this many times before, he walked slowly with the hope his calm demeanor provided no hint of fear toward the opposing captain from the organized spectacle of massed unity they had just witnessed.

Six students, three from each school, also walked toward the center of the field at this point. Each one of these students was fully decked out in tall stove-pipe hats and each carried with him a walking stick. They held the walking sticks like they carried a shillelagh set for a fight.

They were dressed this way to distinguish themselves from the actual players on the field. They had been selected to help guide or officiate the play and step in if there was a challenge by either side about who got to control the ball or if there was an issue on if a team had scored. Two were designated as referees to manage any questions with the field of play. Four (two from each school) were to position themselves by the opposite goals and would be considered the judges on if a point had been made.

At center field the two captains again met. When one of the judges suggested that they run over the rules one more time since neither team had ever faced the other before, both captains elected to have seconds from their teams join them in case there was a rule with which one side or the other might not recall or agree with.

The basics were reviewed.

There were to be no more than twenty five players per team on the field and playing at any one time.

Both captains nodded in agreement.

The judge who was speaking continued.

"You each have two men who are to be appointed to stand and remain by the opponent's goal. They are to be known as the sleepers or captains of the enemy's goal. Is that understood?"

Both team captains nodded yes.

"Okay, then please announce who these captains of the enemy's goal are to be and have them report now to that assigned position so all know who they are and there is no question about their position at a later time. Mr. Gummere, who are your men for this task for the College of New Jersey?"

"Boughner and Billmeyer!" Gummere called out to his side of the field where his players were standing. "Report to your positions by the Rutgers' goal."

There was light applause as these two students from Princeton jogged to the field.

"And Mr. Leggett, your two captains of the enemy's goal for Rutgers," the Judge requested.

"Dixon and Gano!" Leggett copied Gummere's call. "Report to your positions by the College of New Jersey's goal."

Once these four players were in place and everyone had seen who they were, the judges continued with the review of the rules.

One part of a team was to be designated to remain in set positions around the field. They were to be known as the protectors of that part of the field or simply as the fielders or defenders. They were to remain in their specific part of the field and not chase the action up and down all the way across the field. A dozen men were given this task.

Eleven other players were designated to be allowed to run the length of the center of the field up and down with the movement of the ball itself. They were not restricted on where they could go, like the fielders were. Instead, they were to push the ball through the opponent to get it to the enemy's goal to try and score. They were also expected to deter their opponent from moving down the field and toward the goal their team protected when the opponent had the ball. They would be called bulldogs.

A player was allowed to catch the ball and bat or punch at the ball with their hands and fists to move it forward. However, a player was not allowed to grasp the ball and hold it for any extended length of time or attempt to carry the ball in their hands up and down the field with the intent of attempting to throw it between the posts of the goal.

Moving the ball by kicking it or using any other body part to move the ball was allowed.

No man was to be granted free areas on the field from which he could kick the ball or attempt to move the ball without being challenged or possibly hit by the opponent. The exception of this rule was to be at the start of each game. At that point a player on a team would kick the ball as far as they could toward the opponent's goal in an attempt to race down the field and gather the ball in an attempt to score. This was to be called "bucking" the ball and was the only time an opponent could not contest the ball on the ground.

The contest was to be divided into ten games, each one ended when one of the teams scored a point by getting the ball over the line of the opponent's goal. The game would re-start with the other team kicking off the ball in the direction of the opposite team.

The captains looked around the field and at areas where the ball might roll out into one of the four streets beyond the fence-line. A reminder was made that the ball after it was finally found and recovered would be rolled back into play on a horizontal line and no attempt to advance the ball forward could be made when the ball was simply being returned to restart the action.

While full contact was part of the game, there should be no attempt to simply trip an opponent who is running on the field or any attempt to hold an opponent from behind or down on the ground if they have fallen to the grass unless it was a part of earlier contact.

The Judges then announced that there would be two coin tosses. One would allow the team to have their preference as to the way the wind was blowing. A second coin toss would decide who would kick the ball forward to start the game.

The first coin toss allowed Rutgers to have the wind at their backs. The second coin toss, won by Princeton, saw them select to kick the ball off into the wind.

"Let us have a good game gentlemen! We start according to my time piece at exactly 3 p.m. and that is in exactly ten minutes. Any questions?"

Both Gummere and Leggett shook their heads that they had no additional questions.

"Then may the best team win."

Several of the rooters for the Rutgers group had moved from the fence positions and closer to where the players had been seated.

The Rutgers players were now pulling their coats and hats off and tossing these items to the side.

On the far side of the field, the players from Princeton were doing the same thing and had even adjusted suspenders to act like belts around their waists to support their trousers as they readied for the violent tussle.

As Leggett walked by Mary Eva, who had moved to the area where the Rutgers team was preparing, she called him over to her side.

"Mary Eva, I really do not have time to stop and chat about anything. We are getting set to go," Leggett said. "I am sorry I must be so short with you but there is little time and you and the other young ladies need to stay by the fence."

Mary Eva nodded and brought to his attention a collection of cloth strips that she now held in her hands.

"Your players may want these."

She pointed to the scarlet pieces of cloth, some of which had recently helped cover the tables at Van Nest Hall on which they had prepared the afternoon meal for the players from Princeton. She also had in her hands the several similar colored stocking caps that she had previously knitted and she had intended to be handed out as gifts at a later date to some of the college boys who she and her family had become friends with.

"I don't understand," Leggett replied.

"I saw how spirited they were on the Princeton side with their songs and chants," Mary Eva started.

"And?"

"Well, I thought it might be spirited over here too if we all looked more like the same army and carried the same colors, as my father would say, into battle," Mary Eva responded.

"That is nice. But those scarlet pieces of cloth and those knit caps are hardly a flag."

Leggett was more abrupt then normal and harsher then intended.

"I know, but maybe the players could wear these around their necks like scarves or on their waists as belts if they do not wish to wrap the material around their heads," Mary Eva suggested.

"I fear they would simply be torn off as soon as play started. I do not think you realize how physical this contest actually is," Leggett explained.

Then, looking at Mary Eva and seeing how she now looked hurt at his declining to take her advice on this, he offered, "How about I still pass these among the players and let them decide how they might wish to use them."

"Excellent!" Mary Eva smiled. "And it might even help those of us watching to figure out who is playing for which college!"

Leggett smiled at her and then left to call his players together as they were getting set to start to offer a prayer.

"We play today for Rutgers College and the good people of New Brunswick who support us. We always act each moment of every day in God's glory and we hope that we resemble that image he envisioned we portray through his divine light. Be the men that He created us to be today. Let no opponent drag us under where our moral or physical being was intended. In God's name we pray and play. To His glory we shall dance at game's end for having been blest to share this day!"

"Amen!"

"Men. I give you a touch of scarlet to represent our college, Rutgers. Wear it proudly on you today as we join together as one team united to bring honor to our school."

"You know, this may actually help us see quicker who is on our own team in the middle of any scrum out on the field where everyone is mixing it up."

Leggett nodded and passed out the scarlet cloth in various lengths and the stocking caps to each of the players who reached for them.

Each man took one with many electing to wrap the scarlet cloth around their head in turban-like fashion in an attempt to keep the sweat off their brows and their hair out of their eyes as they ran. Several of them looked like helmeted warriors as they finished adorning themselves with the scarlet cloth on their heads. The common color made it clear to each player that he was a member of a team.

The players from Princeton resounded again with a "Ch-ch-ch! BOOOM! Ahhh!" cheer and ran onto the field of play.

"Man they look huge."

Leggett looked at the Rutgers' player that made the remark. He then looked around at his team as several of his teammates glared out at the Princeton group now on the field stretching to get started. They were drawn in by the sheer size of the opponents and Leggett could sense they almost appeared scared versus being ready to match skills with this team.

"I think that guy's arms are as thick as trees!"

Before Leggett could say anything, he heard Madison Ball snap back at the last remark.

"Look when that big boned buffoon comes around the corner we smash him. Smash him right where he stands. No way he can be allowed to just roll over us."

"Madison's right," he heard another Rutgers player state. "Guys, you have to think this out. It is not about the size of our opponent. It is about the better strategy. You know, just like a chess match."

"Chess Match? When was the last time you remembered getting hit by an enormous opponent and spitting out blood during a lousy chess match?"

"I agree this is nothing like a chess match. This is war."

"No it isn't and, no, war is nothing like this," Madison scolded the group. "Don't you novices go telling me what war is and isn't. They don't give you a break in between the shooting to catch your breath. There ain't no rules and you don't get to say stop as some Johnny Reb comes running at you with a bayonet or swinging some rusty sword—"

"All I know is that big guy might start kicking our butts around the field and we gotta stop him or we are gonna lose this thing here and now."

"Man I can't even hardly breath already just wondering how its gonna hurt when he hits us."

"Can't you stop complaining?"

"Oh so now it's my fault!"

"Enough!" Leggett called out.

"Yes they are huge. So what? This is why we have to play together. We have to outsmart them. We have to use what we have to our advantage and not just get pounded by their brute force. We cannot play into their hands with what we are doing and we have to change it up."

"So what do you want us to do?" one teammate asked.

"Just don't call it a damn chess match. I can't stand chess!" another cut in.

"Okay- no chess match," Leggett laughed.

"Thank goodness!"

"And Madison, I won't dishonor the Union dead by calling it a war."

Ball silently nodded.

"But this is like a battle and every battle needs a plan – a strategy – to be successful."

"I say bring out the bayonets and then wave the bloody flag," one of the players stated and Madison glanced at him with a stern glare.

"No bayonets, but clearly we wave the flag. And when they have the ball, we do charge at them full steam to slow them down," Leggett announced. "As a unified team!"

"So what is the plan?"

Leggett looked around at the faces of his teammates all anxiously looking back at him for some form of specific guidance.

"We rally at the same point and lock arms when we have the ball. No one man gets hit by himself. The ball follows behind us and we charge in mass toward their team as a team. When they try to take us down as individuals we run over them as a group," Leggett explained.

"When they have the ball we go charging into them with three more guys to hit 'em all at once. We do not back down!"

"I guess it's a plan."

"At least it's not chess!"

"Men of Rutgers, let's circle in here," Leggett directed.

"What now?"

"Shut up and get over here."

They slowly moved into a rough human circle, heads facing in. They turned toward Leggett.

"Gentlemen—let's remember what we were feeling when we heard about the challenge. Let's remember those who were going to play out here today but couldn't. Let's remember those who laughed when they saw the Princeton players step off the train today and sized them up against our smaller frames. Look—I do not know about their character but I do know about ours. It may not be a war, Madison, but this is a battle. It is a battle for us to prove once and for all that we are better than those loud mouthed opponents from Princeton. Oh, one day we may lose a contest in the future. We may lose a fight in a bar or lose a gal to some other fellow. It happens. But today – this is for the championship of a brand new contest. A contest never before played on this land. And to emerge victorious today – that title stays with us forever! So shake off the cobwebs out of your heads and tough it up and stop whining about some sore ribs or broken finger you may get and prepare for honor."

"Today we do it for Rutgers. Today we do it for every man in a fight where the odds were stacked against him. We fight for the underdog and the belief that on any given day good may triumph over their oversized enemies like these boys at Nassau Hall who think that always winning is their divine right. We play to be champions today men."

"Who is with me!?! Who will follow the scarlet in my hand to victory!?!" Leggett called out.

Leggett waved his scarlet bandana in defiance of the Princetonians assembled and watching for the Rutgers team to join them.

"Look, he's waving the bloody flag," one of the Princeton men joked. "Thinks he's leading Sherman's troops through Georgia."

"No, you arrogant asshole. We're signaling your team's demise!" one on the Rutgers team yelled back at the Princeton group.

"All talk," the player from Princeton shot back. "As usual, all talk and no play."

"We'll see about that," another Rutgers player chimed in, defending his teammate. "Let's see who carries the girl home tonight!"

"Enough talk. Let's go!" the referee called out.

"Scarlet! Scarlet! Scarlet!" the Rutgers team chanted as they moved forward to assume their line.

"Let's make 'em shut up," yelled a player from Princeton.

"Like you could!" the Rutgers player snarled back.

The Princeton team lined up with the Rutgers team in front of them. All was now ready to make the opening kick of the first football contest in the history of the United States between two college teams.

38
"The First College Football Game – Ever"
November 6, 1869
New Brunswick: 3:00 p.m.

The crowd quieted as the player from Princeton set the ball up for the long kick by placing it on a small mound of dirt he had scraped together with his hands. He used this to provide a slight elevation for lift on the ball from his foot gliding under it.

He paused and looked to either side of him.

His teammates nodded back in his direction.

Slowly he stepped forward and swung his leg. His foot connected with the ball and it lifted off.

The game had begun.

The ball, after being "bucked" as they called it, swirled off to one side. Instantly the players on the Rutgers team raced in the direction of the ball to try to recover it first.

The boys in the group from Princeton moved after them in a full sprint but a Rutgers player pounced on the ball ahead of them.

"Circle to protect him!" Leggett cried out.

Quickly his Rutgers teammates ran around and circled the Rutgers player who now had the ball in his hands as the Princeton players slowed down as they approached the massed group.

While one Rutgers player stepped four feet to the side of his teammate, the rest of the Rutgers offensive players formed a human shield in front of the player with the ball and the player at his side.

"Lock arms!" Leggett yelled, and instantly the Rutgers players linked around the two players with the ball standing behind them.

Together they started to move forward.

Similar to the motion with the pass of a volleyball to a teammate, the first Rutgers player patted the ball to the player at his side and he batted it back. They tapped it back and forth with the player beside them as they moved the ball forward up the field, the rest of the group moving slowly ahead around them as their human shield of protection.

Standing still for only a moment, one by one the Princeton players attempted to break through the locked arms of the Rutgers players in front who had now picked up their pace to a slow jog.

Like a cow on a track encountering a cowcatcher on the front of a train, the players from Princeton were pushed aside. They were unable to manage to get at the ball within this tight human phalanx moving toward them.

Arms raised to their chests, those in front on the Rutgers team wedge flexed their forearms into the on-coming players from Princeton as they zigged and zagged across and down the field.

The Rutgers ball carriers dropped the ball to the ground and kicked it forward in a dribbling motion. The players at his side joined their arms. They locked their arms now at their elbows and formed a single blocking line.

As the Rutgers group moved up the field, a Princeton player would try and ram in to a Rutgers player and knock him to the ground. However, if the Rutgers player fell from the contact, another Rutgers player would slide over to take his position and not let a gap form in the line. Quickly, any fallen Rutgers player would bounce back up and jog to join again in to that shield at the back side to protect the flanks and maintain the arc.

Several Princeton players attempted to push the Rutgers wedge backward but to no avail. It only seemed to slow the movement down but would not allow them to get to the ball behind the line of bodies blocking their way.

It took several minutes but eventually Rutgers had been able to keep the ball secure and move it the length of the field. The action was more like a human tug-of-war versus a run that was made up a field as bodies were bracing against a hit and others were pushing or pulling to move toward their goal.

As the Rutgers players closed in toward the area of the Princeton goal, spectators along the fence jumped up and down and started screaming!

"Get that point!" could be heard across all of downtown New Brunswick. Young ladies, with lads at their sides waving their hats, yelled at the top of their lungs for Rutgers to score.

The visitors from Princeton screamed equally loud for their Princeton lads calling out commands.

"Stop them!"

"Goal! Goal! Score a goal Rutgers!" hailed out from the line of Rutgers players who were not immediately engaged in the offensive attack in front of them. They jumped up and down too, like the fans, as they stayed in their required spot on the perimeter as defenders awaited their turn for when Princeton would attack Rutgers back.

The two masses of players slowed to a crawl as they pushed in to each other, the Princeton players actually getting the Rutgers players to take a step backward.

Just as it looked like the momentum would cause the Rutgers line to falter, the ball suddenly squirted out from the gang of Rutgers and Princeton players crushed in together in the scrum nearing the Princeton player's goal line.

The ball ricocheted to Rutgers player, Gano. He quickly kicked it back to the other captain of the enemy goal for Rutgers, Dixon.

Several Princeton players left the mass of tangled bodies that had pushed down the field to go after Gano and Dixon. Several Rutgers players rammed into the Princeton defenders to keep them away from the two Rutgers players now moving the ball forward the final yards.

As a Princeton player chased after each one of them, Gano and Dixon batted it back and forth. Before a player from Princeton could take it away from either of them, the ball crossed the goal line.

For a moment, no one moved as the ball rolled forward past the end-line and between the two wooden uprights in the ground defining the parameters for the goal.

"Rutgers point!" one of the referees at the goal line shouted out. "They win game one!"

Gano and Dixon looked at each other at first, unsure how to react. Then, energized by their accomplishment and filled with the excitement of having scored the first point, they jumped into each other's arms and started bouncing up and down. Quickly they were circled by the rest of the exuberant Rutgers players who came running toward them to join the celebration.

Nearby, the Princeton players watched this response while they stood around angrily picking off clumps of grass and wiping off dirt from their clothes.

The ball was gathered up by one of the referees and he handed it to the Rutgers players.

"Rutgers now bucks the ball back at Princeton," another one of the officials announced.

The Rutgers players jogged up the field as the two teams switched sides for the next kickoff. Rutgers prepared for its turn at bucking the ball. Imitating the Princeton player, the Rutgers kicker also started building a small mound of dirt from which to kick-off from.

"We are up one game to zero," Leggett stated the obvious to his team as they started to spread out and position themselves. "Remember our plan when we attack and they get the ball. We act as one team to take them down as individuals! Most important, do not let up!"

Over on the Princeton side Gummere was adjusting the team's strategy.

"Big Mike," Gummere quickly explained as Jacob Michael nodded back at his team captain. "Big Mike due to your tremendous size and strength there is no one out there on that team who can match you. Do not forget that! When the ball comes to our side you need to clear out some bodies. Hit them as hard as you can and hit as many of them as you can."

Then, from his observation of the Rutgers linked arm offensive approach of moving the ball up the field and scoring that fast he added, "But more importantly, if they get the ball back you need to lead the charge and smash right into them. You need to run at them like a charging bull and knock them down like boulder hitting into a stack of empty glass milk bottles!"

"Got it," Mike snorted back.

"You knock 'em down in front and we get the guy behind with ball," Gummere clarified.

"Got it," Mike answered.

"Men from Princeton! They do not do that to us again today," Gummere yelled to his teammates from Princeton but also loud enough for the Rutgers players to hear the challenge.

"Here! Here!" they yelled back to him like knights getting set to enter battle.

The energy of the game was ramping up.

The Rutgers player kicked the ball and it went higher in the air then when the Princeton player had kicked it off earlier. It also went way off to one side of the field and away from the massed group of players from Princeton standing toward the center of the field waiting to hit the Rutgers players running up the field toward them.

The ball floated down the field toward the left side of the Princeton team. Several Rutgers players, using their speed, were able to outrun other Princeton players who had watched the arc of the ball to get to the ball at the same time as the player nearest it from Princeton. One Rutgers player gathered the ball, a second player ran straight into the Princeton player and both tumbled to the ground.

Three other Rutgers players raced over to surround the Rutgers player who had secured the ball and started to link arms as they had done before in forming a wall around the player with the ball.

This time tough, before the Rutgers players were able to move forward, Big Mike came crashing into the lot of them. Running full speed and without slowing down, he lurched the entire weight of his body into three Rutgers players at one time. The collision drove all three of them to the ground with Big Mike landing on top of them.

"I just lost a tooth!" one of the Rutgers players yelled out.

No one paused to search for it. The fight was on.

Instantly the contact got more physical. Following Big Mike's example, other Princeton players crashed into the smaller Rutgers players as they attempted to get up from the ground. They were unable to regroup. A Princeton player knocked the Rutgers player with the ball backward and as he fell the ball was knocked away and bounced up in the air.

A Princeton player batted the now loose ball forward to one of his teammates

The Princeton players started to work the ball forward by trying to kick it across the field to gain an advantage. But the Rutgers team was quick and resilient. They circled back in front of the Princeton players who had now regrouped and formed a wall of players around their ball carrier who moved to dribble the ball forward toward the Rutgers goal.

Following behind the Princeton wall, several previously fallen Rutgers players got back up and rammed into the player with the ball and it skirted outward to the side of the field. The mob gave chase and several players arrived at the same place at the same time. The impact threw all four of them off their feet as the ball continued to roll away.

This time a Princeton player was able to get the ball ahead of the approaching Rutgers players and lofted a long kick toward the Rutgers goal.

At first it looked like the long kick might be caught. But there was confusion on the Rutgers side on who should grab at it and that momentary lapse allowed the ball to move through.

"Score!" one judge announced, holding both his arms in the air for effect.

"Tied. One game apiece," the referee in the center of the field added.

This time it was the players from Princeton who were celebrating.

"All us from this point on," One of the Princeton players shouted while beating his chest.

"Did you see Big Mike lay out five of them at once?" another bragged about his teammate.

Several Rutgers players were still wiping themselves off from the clumps of grass that had pressed into their shirts and trousers as the Princeton players started to walk back toward their positions.

"Boy, wait until you see how big that cut is across your nose," one of the Rutgers players said to the teammate next to him who was out of breath and trying to collect himself.

"Wait until you see how both your eyes will be black when you get up tomorrow," his teammate responded back as he dabbed the blood from his nose.

Already aching, the players from both squads lined up for the third kick.

The ball carried through the air and the players raced down the field and directly into each other.

Again the contact was fierce. The tone and the tempo of the game had been set now. It would be a violent battle to the end.

After the next kickoff, Rutgers was able to gain the advantage when a player from Princeton batted the ball with his hand sideways to a waiting trio of Rutgers players. Quickly two more joined and their wedge had been re-formed and they moved ahead this time without Big Mike right there to break them apart.

The Rutgers players spread out wider this time and moved the ball by batting and kicking it from side to side, inching their way forward as they did this.

Slowly the Rutgers team slugged it out and passed the ball, keeping it in their possession and trying to steer the ball away from the punishing hits from Big Mike.

As the ball got closer to the goal line, Madison Ball took possession of the ball. The Princeton players came charging at him as he was out in the open.

A Rutgers teammate, behind him, seeing that he was about to be run in to by the Princeton player called out to Madison to kick the ball back to him. Madison turned to face his teammate, his back now facing the goal he was supposed to be heading toward.

Just as a Princeton player worked his way through the blocking, he saw that Madison was about to kick it toward his teammate. The Princeton player, trying to anticipate the kick and to intercept it, changed his direction away from Madison and toward Madison's teammate.

Madison's leg swung over the top of the ball as the Princeton player moved passed him toward where he thought the ball would head.

Madison's forward action to kick the ball did not see his foot actually connect with the ball. Instead, Madison's leg stepped right over the ball. He then kicked the ball backward with the heel of that boot toward the correct goal line.

The Princeton player, who had assumed Madison was about to head in the other direction was completely thrown off course and could not recover to defend. Two other Princeton players, believing that Madison had simply miskicked, slammed into him just as he had kicked it backward with his heel.

The ball moved unimpeded to his teammate, Dixon.

Dixon immediately took the ball in the open area and put the ball immediately across the goal line.

"Rutgers scores and regains the lead 2 games to 1," an official judge called out.

"Next time, watch the ball!" one of the Princeton players admonished his teammate who had overrun the play allowing Dixon to score.

"Gather up men!" another Princeton player called out. "Don't worry about that one. Now it is our turn to return the favor and the pain!"

This time the kick went to the main contingent of Princeton players in the center of the field.

As a Princeton player took the ball, Big Mike pulled several of his teammates around him. This time they had some momentum as they charged up the field at the Rutgers players rushing down the field toward them. They moved forward as a line. Together, the Princeton players attempted to drive straight into the Rutgers players using their wedge technique.

Screams of pain rose up as several Rutgers players were trampled underfoot with the quick moving line of Princeton bodies with the ball carrier protected within them.

A loud crack, like two fresh wooden bats hitting each other at top velocity, resonated across the field when heads collided.

As the Princeton wedge moved forward a Rutgers player was flat on his back and appeared to have been knocked out cold from a blow to his head. Seated, and holding the front and top of his head with either hand, was the Princeton player who had been in the wedge and had been the other body in the head-to-head crash.

Dizzy, he staggered to his feet just in time to watch as the ball moved forward and Big Mike and his band of blockers rambled through the Rutgers line to put across the second goal for the players from Princeton, Rutgers players littering the trail to the goal line.

"Score for the College of New Jersey and now the wins are tied."

"Rutgers 2 and the College of New Jersey 2," one of the other judges then called out.

As the players looked back to survey the bodies who had been battered on that last drive still laying and seated upon the ground, the singular voice of one of the spectators could be heard from across the way near the fence line.

The voice came from a Rutgers professor who had happened by on his bicycle. He had paused to watch what was taking place on the field for just a moment.

Everyone watched and listened in shock as the professor raised the umbrella in his hand above his head, stood by the fence, and then yelled out at the top of his lungs to all that were assembled there.

"You men will come to no Christian end!"

Red-faced and clearly angry at the violent behavior of the players on the field, the older professor got back on his bicycle and rode off.

The spectators said nothing as they watched him leave.

Eventually someone broke the silence and asked the obvious question. "What was that all about?"

Instantly there was a round of laughter.

While this played out on the sidelines, the players dusted themselves off again, gathered their strength and prepared for the next surge.

39

Elizabeth and Adkins helped the two children from the carriage as it pulled up to a stop along College Avenue. Noise from those assembled nearby could be heard as they approached the site of the game. They stepped forward to where several spectators were already seated on the top rail of the fence watching the contest unfold before them.

Before coming to the field, Elizabeth was feeling wonderful. They had all been enjoying everything that Adkins had planned for them that day. Along with visiting all the sites in the town and walking through the College buildings, the children had been thrilled when they were able to glance through the telescope out at the stars above them.

Even at their age, they were fascinated with what was shared about the dinosaur bones. They saw molds taken from giant footprints found in lower water basins and touched the fossils that Adkins explained he too had been lucky enough to extract out of the Jersey marl.

While it was hard for them to visualize the finds from Haddonfield of a complete dinosaur skeleton that was 8 feet tall and 14 feet long; they loved the drawings that Adkins and two students they met there were able to create. The picture of what they thought was a duck-billed Hadrosaurus may not have been completely correct, but it stirred the imagination of both her children.

They also loved the chance to roll the tooth of a fish-like creature in their own hands and then rub the surface of a jaw bone and femur of a Mastodon that once stood close to ten feet tall. Adkins was able to show an artist's rendering of what a Mastodon may have looked like and his story about modern day elephants totally enthralled his young listeners.

Stopping to get treats from the bakery had been a wonderful surprise and, Elizabeth had to admit, Adkins appeared to be perfect with her children.

While the day had been a joy, the noise they had heard from nearby had kept their awareness of the contest on all their minds and it was the cheering that finally drew them in.

Now, here in front of them, was this talked about clash between the two colleges.

Elizabeth knew that this was actually a little risky as the mention of a win by a Princeton team over Rutgers had struck a nerve in Adkins' body. His reaction, while true to his school, was extremely passionate and she feared that if the College of New Jersey was running up the score and humiliating the Rutgers lads the day could end up badly regardless of its fantastic start.

Just as they approached the fence, a yell went up from the far side of the field.

"What is happening?" Jonathan asked his mother.

Before she could reply, one of the spectators turned around and looked at the small group.

"Rutgers got a point!"

That, to Elizabeth, did not sound good. Clearly from the way that comment was made, the team from Princeton must be destroying the Rutgers team by this time with lots of points if the fan was so excited that Rutgers had finally scored a point.

"What is the score of the contest," Adkins asked the same person.

Elizabeth cringed as she awaited the news.

"Rutgers is beating them 3 to 2," the man answered.

"What?"

The word escaped from Elizabeth's mouth before she could pull it back.

"He said Rutgers is winning the contest by the score of 3 points to 2 points," Adkins repeated. "You appear surprised about something?"

"Wow," Elizabeth tried to recover. "That is a surprise."

Adkins chuckled and shook his head.

"Mommy I can't see," Anna pleaded with her mother.

"That is because they are spread out all over the field dear," she said. Elizabeth calmly lifted her daughter in her arms to look out over the action.

The players appeared to be running all over trying to catch up with an oddly shaped ball that bounced around at strange angles.

On closer inspection, it looked like the men on the field were actually engaged in some mixture of a sport that combined wrestling, punching, kicking and running into each other to make the other person fall down.

At the same time the elusive ball tended to go in every direction with the exception of the direction one of the players wished it to go.

"Look at that," Adkins spoke to Elizabeth's son who had moved up next to him and was now seated on the top rail of the fence. Adkins balanced him there safely from behind.

"What are they doing?"

"They look like they are going after each other," Adkins replied.

"Are they trying to hurt each other?" Jonathan asked.

"That is not the intent. But I can see it can happen that they might get injured when they try to dislodge the ball and take it back from each other."

Just as Adkins said this a collective "oww!" could be heard among those watching when two opposing players again ran straight into each other.

Seeing the two players sprawled out flat on their backs, Anna asked her mother the obvious question.

"Are they dead?"

"No dear," Elizabeth replied without missing a motherly beat. "They are just resting."

Elizabeth continued to watch hoping she was telling her child the truth about what they had just seen.

"Now what are they doing?"

Like a herd of buffalo stampeding, a large number of players took off on a sprint after the ball as it headed toward the fence near where they were seated. Elizabeth's eyes grew wider as she realized they were all racing right at them.

The speed at which they approached startled even Adkins causing him to pull Jonathan off the fence. He held the young boy in his arms, back toward him and away from the members of both teams who were rapidly closing in.

Four of the players dove toward the ball with one reaching out and slapping it on a quicker roll toward the fence. Two players, George Large of Rutgers and Big Mike from Princeton, had not slowed their gait and they pushed and shoved side-by-side as the distance from the fence grew shorter.

With a hard push at each other they both rammed into each other just as they attempted to lunge for the ball. Off balance, they crashed into a segment of the fence boards less than twenty feet from where Adkins, Elizabeth and the children were watching.

The momentum of their force drove them straight through the fence itself, shattering the boards that took on the direct impact. It also threw several of the startled spectators who had been sitting on the fence railing on to their backs and butts.

The spectators howled.

"He hit me!" one young lady yelled, her hat twisted sideways as she sat flat on the ground.

"Watch where you are going!" another of the recently fallen fans shouted out at the two men. "How about a little respect for those who are here watching you!"

There was no movement at first from either of the two players who had collided with the fence. They lay there, still, for a good sixty seconds.

Slowly as they seemed to come back to life and separated themselves from the parts of the splintered fence rail, neither Big Mike nor George Large appeared to see or hear the spectators' moaning that was around them.

Eventually they rolled over each other before pushing each other away.

The game itself though paused for only a moment longer. Another Rutgers player near them scrambled off the ground and to his feet faster. Deftly he recovered and kicked the ball back into the field of play. The bouncing ball was punched forward by another Rutgers player who was standing in perfect position to receive the ball.

Big Mike finally started forward again and moved after the ball.

George Large finally got to his feet and, shaking his head, appeared to be trying to get his bearings after having been unconscious for a full minute before that.

With play resumed, the physical collisions on the field continued. Two additional Princeton players went flying sideways off balance as three Rutgers players formed a mini-wedge ahead of the ball carrier. Eventually Rutgers forced the ball across the goal line again.

"Rutgers goal. That makes the score Rutgers up 4 to the College of New Jersey's 2!" the judge announced.

Adkins cheered out immediately. "Go you lads from Old Queens!"

He turned back and saw Elizabeth giving him an odd look.

"What?" Adkins asked innocently.

"Please try to control yourself in front of the children," she stated through a strict sounding voice used by many a nanny when scolding a child.

The next sequence saw Princeton and Rutgers once again knocking each other about.

"I think that young fellow just lost a clump of his hair!" Elizabeth noted out loud to no one in particular.

"Mommy, why are some of them wearing red hats?"

"I have absolutely no idea," Elizabeth confessed to her daughter.

Adkins took over.

"I think the ones you said are red are actually wearing the color scarlet. They are wearing scarlet color caps and the few I can see with the scarlet tied about their necks like scarves are players from Rutgers. My guess is that they are wearing these colors so they can quickly see where one of their teammates is located in the crowd."

Elizabeth looked at Adkins as he completed his explanation. He shrugged.

She smiled back. That was as good a story as anything she could have created.

"Isn't that chap in the scarlet taking the ball the wrong way?" one of the other spectators asked.

"He is. You idiot! Turn around!" another spectator next to the first one yelled out.

"He just kicked it toward his own goal!" the first spectator stated in disbelief.

Before the Rutgers team could recover from the misdirected flight of the ball, the players from Princeton pounced on the ball and tallied it past the goal line. They danced around at their good luck and the joy of capitalizing on the mistake by the Rutgers player.

"Princeton goal," the judge announced.

"Hurrah!" Elizabeth yelled out before the judge could complete his announcement with the running score of the contest.

This time it was Adkins' turn to stare. "Really?"

"Hey, they scored," Elizabeth came right back.

"What about the children?" Adkins gestured to them both.

"They should be just as happy. It is their home town!"

"Rutgers four and the College of New Jersey three," the spectator nearest them announced, staring right at Elizabeth. "Rutgers is still winning lady!"

Before Adkins could ask the man to mind his manners when speaking to a woman, Elizabeth shot back.

"Not for long, dearie!"

"Elizabeth!" Adkins exclaimed, half shocked at her brazen retort and half equally impressed at her ability to handle herself.

Once again everyone's attention was drawn back to the field. The yelling from both teams had increased after the last score.
The Rutgers players were trying to comfort their player who had taken the ball in the wrong direction. Obviously upset that he had cost his team a point, his teammates first offered condolences but now shifted to outright demands.
"Shake it off!"
The players from Princeton were announcing that the Rutgers players were obviously beginning to tire and make mental mistakes.
"Ride right at them!" one of the players from Princeton called out to his mates.
"Gallop into them boys. Gallop straight into them! They are tired and about to fall!"
To the casual observer, it did look like the Rutgers players stayed focused on trying to give instructions to their own men. However it appeared to be a less organized team when responding after the ball was kicked toward them.
Their reaction was not as quick as before. Hesitation during the kickoff on the part of one Rutgers player caused him to be run straight over as th player from Princeton had implored his fellow players to do.
With force more than speed, the players from Princeton pounded their way through the Rutgers attempt to defend their side.
Methodically the Princeton players pushed the Rutgers team backward and, when the Rutgers players were on their heels, only a few quick lunges on the part of their players defending right by the goal kept the Princeton surge from moving across the line.
"Come on boys," Adkins heard himself yelling out. "No quit in any man from Rutgers College!"
"Come on lads," Adkins heard Elizabeth yell out beside him. "Run those Rutgers boys straight over!"
"Oh now that was hardly original," Adkins said to her after she had called out. "You are just repeating what you heard those other college students saying earlier."
Adkins never got a response.
"Hurrah! Hurrah! Hurrah!" Elizabeth screamed out as she watched the ball with a Princeton player cross the goal line at the same time.

"Princeton goal." The judge announced. "The score is now even at four points each!"

Elizabeth looked over set to cheer at Adkins, but stopped.

He appeared to be irritated at what was transpiring. It appeared to Elizabeth and everyone else watching that the team from Princeton had gained the momentum. With the score tied at 4 to 4 and the momentum on their side, Princeton was now also poised to win the contest.

In seeing him today, she understood that he had so many great qualities. Kind. Mannerly. Respectful. Thoughtful. All these things were incredible character traits that made him a wonderful man.

But in watching him here, excited for the college he was so loyal to, it brought her to the realization of the moment when she knew there was something unique and special about him. Something beyond just being a good man.

It was during that first visit to New Brunswick and the tour they had taken that day. The joy he showed in his eyes with a college that meant so much to him. The way he could make a campus seem like a dream land. His words etching out a future filled with endless opportunity while respecting those who had come before him who created the foundation for him to have this chance.

That was what had drawn him to her in a different way than just wanting to be friends.

It was that passion for something greater that made her feel, she acknowledged to herself, that she was falling in love with this man.

In his cheering even over a simple game, she knew that he was a man who would defend the honor and integrity of all he held dear. She knew, from what she had witnessed, that he would be an incredible defender of a family, and of her, in the same way.

Yes. This was a man she wanted to spend a future with.

Quickly she made a decision.

"How about we leave while the game is all tied up?" she suggested to him.

"What?" he asked, puzzled at first that anyone would want to miss the excitement in front of them.

"That way we have no one who has to lose and we are all winners for having played the game?" she explained.

Adkins looked out across the field. Both teams had gone to their respective areas on the opposite sides to catch their breath and clean off their wounds.

The Rutgers players were now seated and to Adkins, even that far away, it appeared that the spark he had seen when they had first arrived may have gone out of the Rutgers team. Still, as he glanced over at the team from Princeton, while their bodies appeared to be twice the size as that of the Rutgers players, they also looked physically exhausted.

He turned back to Elizabeth to ask her about waiting for one more score.

Adkins froze before he spoke when he looked into her eyes.

She was smiling.

As he looked at her face, the entire rest of the day now suddenly rushed over him.

The hand holding when they could sneak it in around the children. The laughter at the little jokes and their matching happy glances when the children had made cute comments. The quick kisses they had stolen when they thought no one was looking.

He smiled back. For whatever reason she wished to leave, why ruin this wonderful day and not honor this simple request?

"Sure," he said. "That is a great idea."

"Let's get going then," Elizabeth immediately called to her children. As a group they started their walk back to the carriage.

"One day I want to play in a game like that," Jonathan announced.

"Me too," Anna joined in.

"One day you both may, you never know," Elizabeth laughed as she patted their heads.

"And one day you both might be able to go to college here in Rutgers to be a part of this," Adkins added, both children holding on to him with each of his hands.

Elizabeth gave him that look that he now understood about the Princeton and Rutgers rivalry. Words were already no longer necessary as the only means of communicating in the relationship the two of them were building. They had created a new bond. A connection that was stronger than two people passing in the night.

"I really liked their red hats," Anna said as she sat back in the carriage seat.

"See," Adkins said to Elizabeth, as he just couldn't resist. "The future first female Rutgers scholar on the campus here at Old Queens."

40

Leggett looked over the ground where his teammates were stretched out.

There were fresh cuts and spots of blood on shirts everywhere. Bumps were protruding on foreheads. He was too afraid to even look at his own legs and shins for fear of how bad the bruises would appear.

A pail with water was passed around the group as the dipper moved from man to man.

Leggett wiped his brow. It was hard to believe that, as cold and windy as it was out here right now, he could be perspiring this hard.

"Just over four more minutes on your break," one of the judges called out. "Time to get ready to go again."

"Any last words Captain," Large asked him, as he stood to stretch before returning to the field.

"Actually, yes," he said as he looked back at his teammate.

Leggett stood now and walked to the middle of where the players were sitting.

"Well men. I guess the question we need to ask ourselves is, have we accomplished all that we have set out to do today?"

"When this game first began, I am sure that many thought that we had no chance against an opponent so big and with a history of such success in athletic endeavors. But as soon as the game started, all that talk and conversation flew away and it was just us and them here on this field."

Leggett turned to try and maintain a connection with all the teammates seated around him.

"And we have had our successes today. True, within these last two rounds we have stumbled a bit. But that fall is all a part of a grander plan. For once one falls he always has the choice if he will pick himself up and come back with a spirit and determination greater than the one with which he began. That is the test that we have here for us now."

He lowered his voice now so that only those seated near him would hear.

"First, think back to what we did best at the start and where we were more skilled than our opponent. They clearly have a size advantage. They clearly are taller and able to bat down any shots when we take that attempt to go above their heads. So where do we excel? Simple. We are faster. We are more agile. We started with a plan to create a wedge and push them away. They have countered that. So now we adjust again. We use what is our true ability to our advantage and turn this game back in our favor."

Leggett dragged a stick marking the dirt by their feet.

"We spread them out and make them run. We hold in the center but attack now on the flanks. The strategy is no longer to try and create this wedge in the middle. Rather our plan will be to exploit their weakness on the edge. Keep the ball low and sprint to our positions. We beat them with speed and skill versus the reliance on brute strength."

"Two minutes more!" the judge called out.

Across the way, the players from the College of New Jersey were slowly getting to their feet and starting to make their way back onto the field. The Rutgers players started to rise now too.

"One last thing men," Leggett stepped back from the middle of the circle so that all eyes could be set upon him.

"When we started this game it was with a defined mission. That has not changed. But do not forget that in the hardest of times in the dead of winter the man in his log cabin in the wilderness is able to save his family through only one tool. That is fire to bring them warmth. So the way man defeats winter and Mother Nature is by going out and chopping wood."

"Chopping wood? What does that have to do with football?"

Leggett looked back at that player before scanning the entire group.

"It is our mission. Do not quit. Keep doing what we started and what we are capable of doing. Keep on trying and never give in. Keep chopping wood and we will survive this battle and come home with a victory over our foe. It is what they do in the wild. It is what we will do here forever at Rutgers College. Never quit!"

"Chop," one player said.

"Chop," another repeated.

"Keep chopping," one motioned with his arm as if he had a swinging a hand axe.

"Keep chopping," the group chanted as they broke from their small circle and spread across the field.

"You got it Captain! We'll keep on chopping!"

The judge called out. "Let's get started!"

They lined up again. The Rutgers team faced the Princeton team that was now in position to kick off. Dirt, sweat and grime could be seen on all bodies regardless of team affiliation.

Leggett glanced over at his opponents.

True, the players from Princeton had scored the last two. But now, as he looked at their faces, Leggett could see that they were equally tired from the fight. It had been a rough day so far for us all and taken a toll on everyone's body regardless of where they attended college in New Jersey. We can beat them, Leggett thought to himself. He looked at the teammates on his left and right. They still had that determination in their stance and in their eyes.

We can still win!

At that moment, the Princeton player lifted the ball into the air with a mighty kick that outdistanced the fastest of his own teammates down the field and the game was back on.

The first Rutgers player raced to the ball and cleanly fielded it on a hop and swatted it forward to one of his teammates in the middle of the field in front of him.

As the players from Princeton ran down the field and shifted in their direction, the Rutgers player paused for just a moment to draw them in closer. Then, as they closed in, he gave the ball a kick to the wide side of the field.

Instantly, the player who was split out on the end corralled the ball and moved it ahead.

Now the main body of players from Princeton had gone past the ball and were attempting to reverse their path in the opposite direction. Tired legs made giving chase that much harder.

Keeping the ball low, this Rutgers player skidded it forward along the ground.

Again there was a mob rush in that direction by the Princeton players as they all attempted to reach the location of the ball as fast as their legs would carry them.

This time, instead of pushing the ball forward, the Rutgers player pushed the ball straight across the field opposite from the side that the Princeton players had just headed.

The Rutgers player split out on that end of the field now moved the ball straight forward toward the opponent's goal line at full speed, moving with the ball ahead of him.

As he neared the goal he gave it a hard kick and it bounced upward instead of forward. At this point he caught it and batted it toward Gano and Dixon with his fist.

Once again, it was Gano and Dixon skillfully moving the ball between two defenders and across the goal line for a Rutgers score.

"Rutgers goal. The score is now Rutgers 5 and the College of New Jersey 4. "

"That makes this next point the one that decides the game," the other judge announced.

Fans on the rails started asking the obvious question.

"If the Rutgers team scores next, they win six to four. But what happens if the team from Princeton scores next? Is there no winner today?

"That can't be possible!"

"Seriously, how can there be no winning team?"

"I think if that happens, then the team that scored the last time in the game should be declared the winner."

"How can you say that if both teams scored five times each?"

"I agree, that would not be a fair way to gauge the winner!"

"I think it is the best way as the judge said there is no additional play after this tenth point is tallied."

"Correct. This point gives each team a fair chance at being named the champion."

"But the game is not tied right now?"

"Last goal to me signifies the champion in my mind."

And so it went back and forth among the spectators who had invested their time this day in watching the two teams pit all their energies against each other. The folks from Rutgers arguing that a tie would be a tie and the fans from Princeton emphatic that the final scoring team with each side having five points each, should be declared the champ.

The players from both sides, however, were just glad to have a short break to collect themselves before going at it again for one last time that day.

The players from Princeton this time looked like they dragged themselves to the sideline. Clearly winded from having run both down the field and back again, in addition to having to cross the field twice in pursuit of the ball on that route, they felt the pain in their legs as each player complained about the burn in their thighs and calves.

On the other sideline, a new level of excitement stirred among them as the Rutgers players met on the grass there for the final time out between rounds.

The Rutgers strategy shift seemed to work. By moving the ball to the outside and changing the flow of the game from a center-based push with their united wedge approach had just caused the Princeton team to exhaust themselves. In the meantime, the Rutgers players had not been the ones to have fallen prey to the game of chase and catch and now looked fresher than before.

"At the very worst we tie," one of the players announced.

"We do not play to tie," Leggett countered. "They came here today to beat us down. Our goal now is no less than victory."

His teammates nodded yes in agreement.

"Further, keep this in mind lads," Gano chimed in. "If they score last, that is a moral victory for them. In a game that is tied, they will probably consider that the final score mattered the most!"

"That does not seem fair," Dixon countered, echoing the very sentiment that the Rutgers fans were arguing the spectators from Princeton with at the very same time.

"Fair or not, it is what they will say."

Instantly several of the players started to cast their thoughts about this concept of last score counts more than the rest.

"We have the power to end that conversation in our hands right now gentlemen," George Large reminded them. "We score, we win."

"Again, we did not come here today to play for a tie," Leggett added, patting George on the shoulder as the two players stood side by side.

"So Captain, what is the strategy?" asked Madison Ball in a military-sounding respectful voice.

"So now the plan changes as we must kick away," Leggett brought them back to their newly evolving game plan.

The players circled closer to hear Leggett speak.

"We will have to meet them with their strength against our will and determination to stop them. We still attempt to use our speed to our advantage and take away their ability to pull together a full wedge and drive the field on us. We sprint down that field and try to keep them from organizing."

"Keep chopping, right Captain?"

Leggett nodded in the direction of that voice.

"True. That and we also need more physicality this time men. Each one of us must call on all our personal reserves. We must have a mindset that we are blind to any pain. We know that we must win by hitting Big Mike and the others at the point of contact and not pulling back. We do keep chopping, that is a fact. But now we must also attack."

"We're with you, Captain."
This was followed by others repeating the same chant.

Leggett raised both hands and his teammates instantly quieted.

"Gentlemen. Before we take the field of play for the final time today, I just want to tell you how proud I am to call each and every one of you my teammates. You all know we shared in the fact that no one from Princeton gave us any respect before today. Now we stand here ready to rejoin the battle with one last question."

The group remained silent as Leggett stated his final words.

"What is the story we want to create about ourselves? What is the legacy we wish to write about Rutgers, our own school? At this moment in time the ending of this tale is now in our own hands. We control our own fate and that of our fellow classmates. I am a faithful follower of our Lord. But here today, on this field at this time, is what our God envisioned men should be. We are empowered to control our destiny. As we take the field we must do this with one unified purpose."

"What is that one question left to answer? That simple question is, in playing, what did we come here to prove to others today?"

"We play to win!" yelled out Hebert, jumping to his feet as the rest of the team cheered.

"Now let's go prove that to the lads from Princeton!" Leggett answered back to the team.

"Keep chopping wood," one of the players said as the group huddled together one last time.

"Keep chopping," another answered back as they started to split apart.

With a loud shout, the Rutgers players ran out from the sideline and toward the Princeton players now positioning themselves for the last kickoff of the day. As a team, together, they took the field.

There was a smattering of applause from the spectators who had braved the cold and remained to the game's end. "Go Rutgers!" was heard from a voice out by the fence.

The Rutgers player mounted the ball upon a small pile of dirt. He stepped back and looked at his mates on either side of him. Then, with a slight hop in his step he moved swiftly forward and gave the ball a booming kick down the field. The distance the ball traveled was considerable, forcing the players from Princeton to retreat toward where it landed and to regroup.

The Rutgers players ran swiftly down the field. Several of them immediately passed the players from Princeton who had stayed forward to defend against what they had predicted would be another attempt at a short kick off the dirt pile.

The Princeton players were able to eventually get the ball under control and bring three players around the player with the ball in support and to guard against the incoming defenders.

However, this time the speed of the Rutgers players kept the Princeton players from gathering more than three men into their wedge. Standing still as the Rutgers players started to arrive full sprint at the spot where the ball had been positioned, the time it took the Princeton players to get set deprived them from gaining any positive momentum with the play.

Two Rutgers players did not hesitate as they arrived on the spot and they rammed straight into the front players in the wedge and knocked them backward. The force of the contact caused the ball to be fumbled away by the ball carrier and it rolled dangerously near the Princeton players' goal line.

Scrambling back defensively to recover the errant ball, a quick kick by a player from Princeton saved the ball from crossing into the end zone. The flight of the ball now pushed the action forward up the middle of the field keeping it away from Rutgers players, Gano and Dixon, who had been poised for a quick score.

Quickly two other Rutgers players raced toward the ball that had landed closest to a Princeton player who was in position to make a play on it. They crashed into the Princeton player who was not as fast as they were as they caught up and tried to move past. Off balance, the Princeton player tripped and fell precariously to the ground. The ball scooted forward.

One Rutgers player now reached the ball and was able to push it back out to one of his teammates. This player was all the way out near the end of one side of the field and was flanking the last Princeton player defender close to the Princeton goal.

With a solid swat of his fist, this Rutgers player punched the ball back toward another teammate who took it mid-stride and went with an end-around the outside Princeton defender.

Seeing open field ahead of him, as the now non-spherical ball bounced directly up in line with his shoulders, the Rutgers player swept his arm in a giant arc hitting the ball outward and sending it on a long flight as if throwing a forward pass in the direction of the two Rutgers captains of the enemy goal, Gano and Dixon.

Instantly both Rutgers players, Gano and Dixon, scrambled to get under the ball. They raced to get ahead of several Princeton opponents who saw what was now happening and reversed their field at full sprint and closed in on the two Rutgers offensive players. Like a herd of buffalo, they came charging at them now as a unified mass attempting to smash these two Rutgers teammates from existence.

Gano stretched out to catch the ball and control it by his fingertips.

Moving with all the energy each of the players from either team could muster, their bodies met at the ball at the same time Gano was attempting to bring it in to his body.

Again, the human collision caused the group to hit the ground. The ball squirted back away from Gano as he tumbled to the ground and it moved away again from the goal line and what could have been a possible winning Rutgers score.

Each one of the players threw out their arms and pushed themselves back up off the ground without delay to try and get back in pursuit of the ball now bouncing up the field again.

Now an additional surge of players from both teams descended toward the ball that rolled back in the direction of the center of the field.

Several players from each side got there at the same time. Whether out of instinct to prepare for the contact or the desire to simply hammer their opponent, they all seemed to move on and even past the ball and threw themselves into each other with reckless abandon. They met in a huge pile of bodies, screaming out as if they were all madmen, consumed in a wild rage.

Arms flailed in every direction.

Shirttails were pulled.

Punches were thrown.

Hair was grabbed.

Elbows crashed into foreheads.

In this mass there was also a wild struggle as players pounded on each other and tugged at each other to get into position to secure the ball, which was laying just out of reach, one last time.

As more players were pushed onto the grass and dirt, they actually had a better view of the ball now down on the ground near them. Two or three started to crawl on all fours toward it as they seemed to realize that getting the ball was the object of the game versus just beating on an opponent's body.

One Princeton player lunged and tried to push the ball forward by punching it but his effort was stalled when a Rutgers player jumped on top of him, pinned his arm to the ground with his weight, and then they started to wrestle.

Without conscious attention to the ball and what they were now doing, one free swinging arm from one of the two wrestling opponents connected and the ball rolled back again. It went straight toward where both of the Rutgers players, Gano and Dixon, had stood up and had returned to be in their assigned positions as designated captains of the goal.

Instantly Gano batted the ball forward to Dixon and he batted it back as they attempted to cover the remaining yards between themselves and the goal line. Sweat poured from each of their brows, seemingly oblivious to the icy cold wind that was sweeping across the field and freezing everything else. They ran with everything their legs had left in them while shielding the ball from opponents who were now in hot pursuit.

Then, without further pause, they directed the ball between the goal posts in an attempt to score. It sailed across the enemy goal line with no Princeton player able to move fast enough to stop it.

This action produced the sixth and winning point of the day.

"Score Rutgers!" a judge called out.

"Contest won by Rutgers six to four," the judge standing closer to mid-field instantly followed with a second announcement.

"Rutgers wins!" a centrally positioned referee for the contest followed up with a louder yell.

The Princeton players stood stunned. Silently they stared in disbelief at the goal line where the ball had just crossed resulting in the final Rutgers score.

Several muttered curses as reality started to set in. They had just lost.

Unlike the jumping exuberance after the first goal, Rutgers players Dixon and Gano were almost too tired to move this time. For a moment, they too, simply stood and stared at the end line where the final score had just been registered. Dixon smiled and then patted Gano in a brotherly-like fashion on his shoulder. Gano, at his side, repeated the same action toward Dixon.

After a deep breath they both turned back toward their Rutgers teammates. They walked to meet their fellow players closer to where they were currently strewn about on the ground nearer to the center of the field.

"We won," a Rutgers player half whispered as if trying to convince himself of the end result.

"Damn right!" Madison announced, as he stood back up and extended his hand to his still sitting teammate to help him up off of the ground.

"We beat those sons-a-bitches!"

Other voices from the Rutgers team started to join in.

"We won!"

"Hell yeah!"

It came out now with more energy and excitement as the repetition seemed to drive the point home. Reality started to set in. They had defeated their hated opponents from Princeton. No one had thought it even possible, but it had happened. They had won and no one could change that final outcome of the game anymore.

The cheering switched to outright yelling as the tired Rutgers player bodies seemed to forget the pain for a moment as bear hugs and congratulatory embraces were exchanged among each of the Rutgers mates out on the field.

To the side, two Rutgers students who had observed the game danced by the fence rail that they had been sitting on and watching the contest.

"We need to write this one up in the papers for all to read about."

"I know someone at the *Freedonia* paper who I am sure would love to cover this story."

"That is great too. But I think this would make a wonderful first edition piece for our own new school paper, *The Targum*, so every student and staff member gets to read about it!"

"Perfect! I think I remember all the details and will sketch them out just as I saw them!"

A few of the spectators from Princeton and a few from New Brunswick started to exchange words about the outcome and it began to cause a slight stir on the sidelines.

"What do you think about our boys now?" one New Brunswick man asked one of the guests from Princeton who had been bragging about his team the entire day.

"The game? Who cares? We will always be better than you in this stinking town!"

With that there was some pushing and some more angry words exchanged.

"We hated you before and we hate you now!" one fan screamed.

"You are still losers to us!" they came back with.

"We'll make real losers out of you now!"

Again, there was some more pushing and shoving among the fans still there. One young man fell on his butt and there was a call to round up some more New Brunswick youth to teach these guys a lesson. With that, several of the Princeton fans elected to get on their carriages and head right out of town versus being involved in a street fight right by the field.

But the players on the field itself ignored those who were jawing away on the outskirts as they attempted to collect their own thoughts and check their own emotions after the contest.

In stark contrast to the Rutgers players was the sound, or the lack of sound, coming from the lads from the team from Princeton.

For a while they stood and watched the Rutgers players celebrate.

Then, realizing that the game was over and nothing more could be done this day, they started to head toward their side of the field to collect their things.

"Good game Big Mike," one of the Rutgers players yelled out toward Mike and his teammates. "Man you were amazing and I am glad we didn't need to mix it up with you any longer today."

Big Mike smiled, turned around and walked over to congratulate the Rutgers opponent who had called out to him.

"I think I have a few splinters still in my butt from when you and I crashed into that rail fence there George," Mike said as he extended his hand to George Large, his opponent on the Rutgers team.

The other Princeton players followed behind the two of them.

Exhausted, but cordial for a group of young men who had just engaged in an intense physical contest, the players from each team moved slowly back across the field shaking hands with teammates and opponents on a game well played.

"Nicely done," Gummere extended his hand out to Leggett as the two finally met each other near the center of the field.

"Thank you. You know both teams played a game that we should all be proud of today," Leggett said back as they shook hands.

Gummere nodded and shared that he would have rather beaten the Rutgers team versus just getting high grades for trying.

"I do understand," Leggett replied. But you are an amazing Captain who truly made a mark out there on the field of play. I tell you that we will all remember that, victory or not."

Gummere smiled. "That may be true. But in the end, Captain Leggett, I am sure you are more grateful that your team won today versus any personal triumphs."

Leggett smiled back. "Yes, I am."

"You know we will beat you next time."

"Maybe," Leggett responded without lying. "But today is over and we won. That is the simple fact."

"So I guess we head off now to go lick our wounds until we get to play again," Gummere noted.

"There is no time or place for anyone to be feeling sorry for themselves tonight," Leggett replied. "Join us for some refreshments before you leave."

"I am not sure we are ready to get all chummy with you guys here at Rutgers."

"Look, we have dinner and a night of fellowship already planned."

"Not sure we want to hang out all evening just so you can make fun of the fact we lost," Gummere countered. "We probably are better off heading out and leaving this for some other time."

"Captain Gummere, I do hope that today's contest will not deter you from attending. Sure there may be exaggerations about what took place but the reality is that while we were the victors today, there may be no such luck the next time. We do not need to celebrate the score right now. Let's toast the fact that we have begun what is hopefully a new tradition of competition between our two schools."

Gummere looked back over toward his teammates who were collecting their clothing and brushing themselves off from the dirt that had burrowed its way into everyone's skin.

Leggett could see there was still some hesitation on Gummere's part to respond.

"I do not know what you all have waiting for you back in Princeton, but the festivities at Northrop's Resort are not something any of you will want to miss. I can attest to it being the finest party place on the east coast with the best food and plenty of it provided by the owner and his wife there. People forget their troubles there and all have a wonderful time."

Gummere laughed.

"Thank you for the invitation. I will meet you there. And if this place is all that wonderful I would wager a guess that many of the others on my team will be happy to come attend with me. They are usually up for a good party atmosphere."

"Great. Well let's get going then. I know you have trains to catch as the 8 o'clock out of New Brunswick waits for no man and I do not want anyone heading home hungry tonight."

"Sounds good," Gummere answered.

Gummere then left Leggett behind after getting the directions to Northrop's Resort. He rejoined his teammates who were busy getting dressed, the cold wind already starting to cause shivers on sweat soaked shirts.

Leggett stopped and stood with several of his teammates who were all still there and looking over the field as the darkness of the evening started to get deeper, the sun of the day now fading completely from the sky.

A few of them were already recanting their exploits from the day and sharing what they recalled they had seen, although versions of the game were already being slightly twisted as they got retold. The glory of the victory was a wonderful tale to be able to tell and putting a special spin on moments within any major battle was the reward always reserved for the victor of any great battle in history.

Slowly the talk started to slow and Leggett watched as each of his teammates started to disperse.

Many of the members of the winning team could be seen limping from injuries they had sustained that day. However, Leggett noticed, even their limping looked like a happy walk as it was soothed over by the reality of the win.

George Large was the last of his teammates standing there watching the group exit to Northrop's.

"We won," George Large said to Leggett as they stood beside each other and they watched their fellow Rutgers students leave. "It is a great feeling."

"You do not sound as excited as I thought you would," Leggett observed of his friend.

"It is a great feeling," Large repeated the words, his voice still soft and tired sounding.

"You still do not sound all that convincing. Something wrong?"

"It may not look or sound like it Will, but I do feel good inside that we won. Maybe I just need a little while to let it sink in even further though for my mind to register the emotion too."

Leggett patted him on his back.

"You know you fulfilled that purpose you talked about today, George. I do not think after that battle out here anyone will ever say that a Rutgers man is not the equal of any other man in any other college around. And you, George Large, personally made that reputation a reality."

"So true," Large smiled back.

"And this winning is a whole lot better than losing," Leggett added.

They both laughed.

Mary Eva and her group of friends were the last to come over to where Leggett was standing. They had just finished collecting back the scarlet cloth and caps they had shared with the Rutgers players to use to identify themselves in the contest.

"That was amazing!" Mary Eva punched out and playfully hit Leggett in the shoulder.

"It was, wasn't it," Leggett smiled back at her.

"I never saw such raw energy and fierce competition first hand. And you and your Rutgers mates beat them back every step of the way."

"From the bruises and bumps I have I would say they did their fair share of beating back on us today too," Leggett continued to smile as he rubbed the swollen lump under his right eye.

"Oh do not try to tell me what I saw William Leggett. These Rutgers lads were incredible. Tough and fearless. Fast and skilled. They were simply incredible and did not let us down even when it looked bad for a while."

"I will not try to tell you differently," Leggett assured her.

"And you! You were amazing as a leader. Your words so inspirational. Your calm and your demeanor and your ability to bring them all together and make them believe in themselves even when those giants from Princeton walked out for the first time on the field. Your skill-"

Leggett held up his hands and cut her off.

"Enough, enough Mary Eva," he joked with her. "With all the hits I took on my head I can ill afford to let you give me a more swollen one from your compliments!"

"You deserve every single one and a million more, William. You were down right heroic out there today."

"Leggett, let's go!" Large called back to them as he exited the far end of the field. "You do not want to be late to our own celebration!"

"On to Northrop's!" Leggett called to him.

"On to celebrate with your mates," she corrected. Then she added, "I do wish I could go!"

Leggett was about to ask her why she would not be coming before catching himself. There were rules of propriety that dictated what young ladies could and could not do who were her age.

"I am not sure that would be appropriate in the eyes of the Major or your mother," Leggett said, secretly wishing she was able to join him. Her excitement with the game had made him feel even better about the outcome. There was something special about sharing this victory with her that he wished could continue.

"Probably not," she agreed. "But William, that was so exciting. The whole day I mean. I even enjoyed being a part of it with the meal we fed them. Oh the things I will share with you later about what they said about you Rutgers boys while they ate!"

Leggett smiled at her. He could see the excitement of the victory still bubbling up inside her too.

"Mary Eva. I want to personally thank you and your friends and the others in New Brunswick who helped put that together today for the fellows from Princeton. You all did a lot of work to make this day what it was."

"Well, I guess I should get going." Mary Eva turned to her group of female companion volunteers. "We probably need to gather the items we left at Van Nest Hall and get those eating utensils back to their rightful owners as soon as we can."

"It was a thrilling win!" Kathleen called out to Leggett.

"You are the champions!" came a comment from another bystander.

"Hail to Rutgers and New Brunswick!" Kathleen added.

The small group of girls clapped their gloved hands before waving Leggett goodbye.

He watched as the final bodies left the field and the area around it to head on to the night's events. Some took to their carriages and no doubt left to go straight back to Princeton. Others left to walk back to their homes in New Brunswick.

For Leggett, he was glad that he had a post-game appointment awaiting him. He was simply not ready to let the events from this day end yet.

Hail to Rutgers and New Brunswick! Kathleen's words reverberated in his head. And Leggett smiled.

Their victory on this field, while really just a game this day, had surely lifted the spirit of those who had witnessed it. He hoped, as his college mates had prophesized, it would have an equally powerful ability to last and also lift the reputation of the college he loved too.

41
"Post Game"
November 6, 1869: Evening

The atmosphere as he entered Northrop's resort and restaurant was wild and boisterous.

As quiet as the final walk off the field had been, the exhaustion had been replaced with a new energy that soothed the aches and pains. Unfortunately for the players on both squads, they each knew that tonight's fun would not erase the bruising that would be so prevalent the next day.

Players appeared at ease as they were mixing and socializing with their opponents from the opposite college. Some of the general public had joined them and were cheering along as various stories of moments in the game were being retold.

There was a mixture of laughter and admiration as they recounted how Big Mike and George Large had demolished the split rail fencing. There was a sense of awe in the retelling of hard hits and amazing runs. There was laughter at moments like the Rutgers player who misdirected the ball toward his own goal and the Rutgers professor who yelled at them before leaving on his bicycle.

The score of the game itself had become secondary to the tales within the contest that were getting shared by both sides.

The place was packed and people wandered freely about the building. They left the main dining area to roam through the basement level of the structure as well as the upstairs rooms.

The proprietors of the place had the reputation of operating not just the best establishment to eat along Church Street but also as one of the finest resorts in New Brunswick. Food was always plentiful and the guests never left without feeling full and happy. This night was clearly not going to be an exception to that rule.

The beer taps were open full tilt and pitchers and pails filtered throughout the hall and across tables to be deposited in to mugs and glasses which appeared to be in the hands of everyone there. As soon as the vessels were filled, the mugs were raised in various toasts that covered every topic imaginable.

There were toasts for President Grant and a cheer that the war had now officially ended since they dropped the charge of treason for Jefferson Davis. There was a toast for the great new railway that ran across the country and connected the east and west coasts. There was a cheer for the Cincinnati Red Stockings playing their first professional baseball game with the hope that there would be many more games in the future. There were toasts made for exotic journeys to be taken one day to see the pyramids in Egypt and a roar of laughter when one student made a cheer that he was sure one day a United States flag would be planted by visitors from the country on the moon.

True, as the large number of bodies were packed in tightly, the place all smelled of sweat. Mixed with the dirt carried in on the clothes of the players, Northrop's polite public eatery now had the odor one could compare this night with being inside an animal filled door-locked barn.

But nobody seemed to care. It was a festive party. Everyone now was light-hearted and happy.

Laughter bounced off the ceiling beams. Food and drink was being spilled on tables and floors. Jokes were being exchanged with roars of laughter that followed. Smiles were on the faces of the patrons everywhere.

Beyond the torn articles of clothing, facial swelling with bruises, cuts hands, and barely dried blood on recently received scratches; there appeared no vestige that the two groups intermixed here had so fiercely battled and had been hated opponents of each other only a few hours earlier.

Leggett watched as the eating was finishing up when a Princeton player stepped to the piano. Cheers rang out from his mates. He was then joined by a Rutgers College student who was also provided the same vocal encouragement from his fellow Rutgers school chums.

They called back to the crowd that they expected them to sing along if they were brave enough to sit up in front of them and play their instruments tonight.

Then another player from Princeton and one from Rutgers jumped up and stood on tables near the piano and yelled out, "Who wants to sing along with Champagne Charlie!?!"

Instantly cheers came pouring back to prompt them on.

The two college lads, with musical back-up, started into the first verse of the highly popular song. Glasses and mugs were swaying in hand as they marched through the lyrics. *"I've seen a great deal of gaiety throughout my noisy life; with all my grand accomplishments I never could get a wife-"*

Then as they got set to start the chorus both men called to the crowd, "Okay this is your part too!"

With that, the people in the crowd happily joined in and sang along with, *"For Champagne Charlie is my name! Good for any game at night, my boys!"* Their voices filled the building and spilled out into the streets of New Brunswick.

When that song came to an end, loud great cheers went up and a player from Princeton was coaxed up next to keep the spirits light with his version of "Johnny I Hardly Knew You."

At the completion of that tune, several called to Leggett himself to get up and sing. To chants from the Rutgers faithful of, "Captain! Captain! Captain!" Leggett was pulled forward by his college mates.

Standing in front of the group Leggett started by apologizing at not knowing the words of any of the popular songs of the times and with not having a voice that others would wish to hear.

"How about a religious tune to honor our Maker?" one in the group asked him, knowing his future vocation was a calling to be a Reverend.

"Well, I suppose our Lord would not see this joyous day and celebratory moment as any sign of disrespect if we raise one up higher," Leggett announced. "I'll lead. But I fully expect you all to join in right from the start with this song. I've already warned you I am not known for having a pleasant singing voice."

With that the piano player started the music and Leggett led off with the words to "What a friend we have in Jesus." As requested, the crowd instantly sang along.

Next, several of the students who had previously served in the military came up with a few of the New Brunswick guests who had also been veterans of the Civil War and led the group in a rendition of "When Johnny Comes Marching Home Again."

It was at that point, one of the young men from Princeton rose to sing.

He explained that this song, written by Timothy Sullivan a short while ago, was a tribute to Ireland and he understood how feelings on this issue still ran strong. It also had the same tune base as a Union Army song, Tramp, Tramp, Tramp.

Meaning no disrespect of anyone there, he requested if it were okay to sing the version that they had arranged to honor the lads at the College of New Jersey who had brought the town of Princeton such pride.

There were cheers from the guests from Princeton at the mention of their name. Hearing no one from the Rutgers community objecting he, with piano accompaniment, started in with the stirring first verse.

Coming to the chorus, he substituted the words "Ireland" and "Erin" for "Princeton." This instantly brought the cheering and singing Princetonians to their feet.

Realizing that it was just a two syllable substitution, the Rutgers faithful sang the word "Rutgers" each time the song called out for "Ireland" or "Erin" and rose to their feet to cheer their college name.

"God save Rutgers!" and *"God save Princeton!"* now echoed in unison through the building. Fists pounded on tables and mugs banged on the backs of chairs as others stomped their feet in the rhythm to the tune.

"One more time!" the lead singer called out. Again the crowd, now full in throat, enthusiastically sang along with their school name inserted.

"God save Rutgers! Said the heroes; God save Rutgers! Said they all!" came from the Rutgers side. *"God save Princeton! Said the heroes; God save Princeton! Said they all!"* had the whole crowd bouncing in place from the Princeton players too.

As the song came to an end, the cheering was deafening.

Men hugged each other. Leggett believed he even saw some around him with tears in their eyes from the pure emotion that had just been shared. No hatred of the opponent's school right now for this moment but rather unbridled respect and an oath of loyalty to one's own who had engaged together on the field of play.

It was at this point that the final speech making for the night commenced.

The last speaker to share some words was the Princeton captain, Gummere. He rose to address the room to loud chants of "Captain! Captain! Captain!" much like the calls had been shared by the Rutgers supporters for Leggett earlier.

"Today we started as opponents," Gummere began. "Enemies on a field of battle. Both with a desire for victory over the other. Neither side had any further concern for the fates of their foes. But by the end of that great contest of skill, strength, and daring; we each earned the respect, as we see here tonight, of each other!"

Cheers broke out. Gummere then continued when the noise quieted back down.

"Do not back down! We told our lads. Do not back down! They obviously shared this same message over on the Rutgers side too. Teamwork! Personal fortitude! Fight to the end! All these words were ringing true for both teams. This was clear to anyone lucky enough to see this contest today. And in the end, while a score of this first game is now complete, the lesson learned turns out to be a simple one. And that lesson learned is also an important one. It is a message we must carry forth to our leaders and to those in our community we hold so dear. That message, in no uncertain terms is this. Glory to the state of New Jersey! She is a state blessed to have two amazing colleges to call her own!"

Instantly the crowd rose in applause. Everyone there joined in as the chant of "Jersey! Jersey! Jersey!" swirled throughout the room.

Gummere raised his hands to request the crowd settle down and they paused again to listen.

"I do wish to thank our gracious hosts for today. I know my fellow Princetonians had wished for a different outcome on the field."

"Yes. Yes," a Princetonian called out.

"Truth be told, had we simply left after the game all that would have remained would have been the festering anger of a contest lost. A bitterness that we would have found hard to erase from our hearts. But with the fellowship shared here, we leave with such a greater degree of respect of you. Hopefully from this time we have shared tonight and from your observation of our performance at the game earlier, you find in your eyes a greater respect for us. Again, we thank you for providing this forum where that could be fostered."

Polite applause rang throughout the room.

"Now, before our evening must come to an end. And before we exit here in a moment as we also know that no train waits for any one man. We do wish to share with you an opportunity to join us in singing our college Alma Mater. Please know, that like the song earlier, we realize that the lyric may be designed for our beloved institution. But also know, that with the great respect you earned from playing how you did today, we understand how you equally feel about your campus here at Rutgers and no disrespect is meant by the words or intent."

With that, the Princeton players rose and took off any type of head cover they may have been wearing. Placing hands over hearts, they joined together in the words to "Old Nassau."

They ended their song with a yell for their college and a hearty cheer for all.

Leggett and Gummere exchanged handshakes as the Princeton crowd spilled out of Northrop's and onto Church Street and prepared to make the short walk to the train station.

"It certainly was a great day for your lads here at Rutgers," Gummere stated.

"Thank you," Leggett answered back. "There was no quit in you fellows from Princeton either."

"You know I cannot say the day was perfect. But truth be told, we did truly enjoy ourselves at least during this night," Gummere said.

Gummere then turned to acknowledge one of his teammate's shout of "Will, come on! The train is departing any minute. You do not want to be left behind!"

"As did we," Leggett answered out as Gummere started to move away. "It was a great night. And for us, a great day."

Glancing back, Gummere shouted over his shoulder, "You know, while we may respect you a bit more after today, we still do not like you guys up here at Rutgers. In addition, you also know we will most likely beat your brains out next week when you venture down to play us in Princeton!"

"Maybe," Leggett called back. "But forever it will be known whenever the game of college football is mentioned, that we beat you first!"

"Well played, William Leggett! Well played!"

As he watched the opposing team disappear from sight on their way back to Princeton, Leggett suddenly became aware of the large number of people still around him. They were standing there near him out on Church Street looking about and wondering what to do next.

"So now what?" a voice from the group called to those assembled there.

"What a night."

"What a day."

"What a victory!"

"Glory to Rutgers College," a voice then sounded out.

"Glory to Old Queens," another followed.

A low chant then started to ruminate from the group still crowded alongside the street there.

"Rutgers! Rutgers!"

It picked up in both volume and tempo.

"Rutgers! Rutgers!"

Then the chant cascaded into a series of "Hip! Hip! Hurrah!" cheers.

This crowd finally dispersed. Eventually the final stragglers started to filter out in various routes along the streets of New Brunswick.

Leggett could hear various renditions of the song, *The Battle Cry of Freedom*, being bandied about by those now heading up the streets and home. The words they used were the same substitutions as earlier with any critical two syllable word being substituted with "Rutgers."

42
November 6, 1869
New Brunswick: 8:00 p.m.

"The battle cry of Rutgers!" Leggett sang the words out-loud to himself as he walked. The lyrics had a nice ring to them. He smiled as he thought about the earlier excitement.

There was no trophy in his hand as Leggett headed away from Northrop's. There were also no medals or award certificates or adoring fans walking alongside. But he still felt great.

From what he could tell all the other players were gone. The smaller group left behind were basically townspeople who had joined in with the celebration during their regular night out. They too, he noticed, had also started to exit for their homes since the college students had left and the excitement had died down.

Leggett looked about on Church Street. Up ahead he saw the old residence where the Parsell family members had lived before they had moved to a residence off of Neilson Street.

And he thought about Mary Eva Parsell.

He smiled as he thought about how excited she had been today.

She had been right there rooting for the Rutgers College boys. Organizing her New Brunswick friends and working as a volunteer beforehand with the College of New Jersey lads to help them get ready. Then he thought about her excitement as she had come out on the field before the game ever started to hand out those scarlet scarfs and again after the game had been won. No doubt her heart was truly with Rutgers College now forever.

Still feeling some of his adrenaline from the events earlier, Leggett felt he was not ready to call it a day and go back to his room where he was boarding. He took a slight turn up the road. As he walked past the

Parsell's current home, he saw the flicker of light in the main windows and guessed the family had not yet gone to bed.

He thought about how late it was. Would it be appropriate for a young man to be calling at their home at this time of day? But he felt he needed to talk with someone who would share the enjoyment of all that had transpired.

He took a chance and tapped lightly on the door with the knocker and stepped back from the porch. Major Parsell opened the door a minute later.

"Master William!" Mr. Parsell exclaimed. "What a surprise! By the way, that was an amazing victory you boys won today!"

He patted Leggett on his back in congratulatory fashion as the two men stood in the doorway entrance to the house.

"So what brings you by so late at this time of night?"

Before he could answer Mary Eva appeared. With a shawl wrapped over both her shoulders for warmth she bumped her father's side as she joined them there in the doorway.

"I have not been able to sit still since the contest ended!" she blurted out.

"Yes she cannot sit still or be quiet for that matter," her father added. "But we have all enjoyed her regaling us with stories of the day and the game."

"I still feel my head and heart soaring from all I saw. All the girls there were saying the same thing before they left here earlier!" The excitement was clearly still present in her voice.

"Excuse me for one moment, William. I just needed to finish up some business I was taking care of. I need to jot down a note on a calculation I was working on with a pension file before I forget it and have to start all over again. I'll be right back." Mr. Parsell stepped away from the door.

"It was a wild night at Northrop's," Leggett told Mary Eva, anxious to talk about what had been taking place and always appreciating her willingness to listen whenever he needed someone to talk with.

"I just so wish I could have been there," Mary Eva replied. Her voice had the sound of someone who was truly envious of something they had missed. "I can only imagine how that went. I am certain it was wonderful and I cannot wait until you have a chance to tell me everything that took place there."

"I will be sure to come by and fill you in with all the stories," Leggett said. "I just hope you do not ever grow bored from hearing them."

"Bored? Never!" Mary Eva came right back. "Why I will want to hear every detail over again so don't you forget any of them William."

"I'm sure I will not," Leggett smiled as he answered.

"Oh my," Mary Eva said, as if she had just discovered something. "Look at that bruise on your face!"

"I am sure it is nothing," Leggett touched the sensitive spot she most likely was referencing.

"Great game William!" a voice suddenly came from behind him down along the street. It was one of the Van Dorens who lived nearby walking with two other men William did not recognize. "We are all so proud of you and your lads at Rutgers giving those blokes down at Princeton the what for today!"

"Thank you sir!" William called back.

Then, turning back toward Mary Eva, Leggett noted, "That was strange. I wonder how he even knew that we played?"

"Oh it is a big deal," Mary Eva exclaimed. "It may not be world news but I will bet the weekly paper carries a story about it when they get wind of the contest."

"It was just a game," Leggett answered back truly aware that he, too, felt it had been more.

"Just a game," Mr. Parsell announced as he rejoined them in the doorway.

"It was more than a game young man. I know I have told you this from my war exploits. Once you have been engaged in a battle, the testimonials later are always there about the act of bravery or the failure of a plan. From all I have heard this night from Mary Eva and her friends who were present, it was a glorious endeavor that will bring honor to both your college and the town of New Brunswick too!"

"And I can tell you from being there as a witness that you are a hero from all that you did. I tell you that was the vision of you in all of our eyes that were watching you play!" Mary Eva glowed.

"So looking at my timepiece and the hour, why the visit at this time of the night?" Mr. Parsell asked.

"Well," Leggett seemed to stumble for words to explain his appearance. "I actually came by to ensure that Mary Eva had been successful in getting all the things she had brought out to help with the luncheon back home. I felt badly that we had all just left her and her friends there to clean up and I just wanted to verify that everything went okay."

"It did," Mary Eva replied. "We had no problems."

Then Leggett added a more truthful line. "I also wanted to say thank you to her for all that she did before the day came to an end."

"It was my honor and a true privilege to have been a part of it. Thank you, Mr. William Leggett, for requesting our help." Mary Eva smiled broadly and gave a slight bow of her head as she finished speaking.

There was an awkward silence for a moment. Mr. Parsell looked at the two young people there and cleared his throat to speak.

"Well, it is getting late and church service will come early tomorrow no matter what one does the night before," he said.

"Yes, well, sorry for the late intrusion," Leggett replied.

"Not at all, son," Mr. Parsell answered. "I look forward to the day when we can sit, at a reasonable hour, and talk about all that took place today. In the meantime, I do hope you have a nice night."

Mr. Parsell reached out and shook hands with William.

"Thank you sir," William said.

Leggett now stepped back toward the street and away from the door. "And, again, thank you Mary Eva for all that you did."

She smiled and gave a wave before her father closed the door.

He waved back and headed up the street. He thought about how wonderful it would be to have someone with him throughout his life who would always want to share memories of this special day.

Leggett realized that he was aching all over his body each time his foot hit the ground. Each muscle seemed to groan and joint creaked when he moved. But a positive inner feeling from the day helped guide his steps forward on his walk back toward his room where he was boarding.

Great day! Those two words played over in his head. All glory to God! He did not need to remind himself of this truth as it was the very fiber of his being and he raised a prayer of praise heavenward.

Leggett's thoughts then drifted off to Gummere's last comments and his boast about winning the game the next week down in Princeton.

Another game.

With so much energy expended with this first contest, what would a second contest even mean to them now? He knew they would have to get ready for the game. But it would be really hard to not have an emotional letdown which could so easily happen with all the drama spent on the game today.

The next game. What would they improve on? How could they get better? When would they practice?

He chuckled as he thought about how odd he must be as his preparations crossed over in his mind. Here I am already thinking ahead after the momentous events of this day. I am as bad as some general, now more consumed by the whole endless war instead of reflecting on the joys of the battle victory just won.

Enjoy tonight this victory the Lord has given you, he told himself.

As he moved up George Street and crossed over to continue up Somerset, he glanced up at the Old Queens building that marked off Rutgers College situated atop the small hill.

The weather vane was fully engaged catching the strong breeze trying to blow past it. The entire structure looked majestic against the moonlit glow of the night.

Leggett stopped.

"Here's to you, my lady," he said out loud as if the stone walls of this structure could hear.

"Who knows, besides God, what our futures may hold. But after today no man alive may ever take away this one simple and irrefutable fact. That Rutgers College, today, won the first football game ever played between two colleges. Yes, you are the victor. And tonight, Old Queens, you are the champion of all colleges in this great country. Thanks first to God for making this day. And God bless the United States of America and Rutgers College forever!"

43
"The Aftermath"
November 16, 1869
Rutgers Campus

President Campbell held up the letter that had arrived earlier in the day from Princeton.

"So, gentlemen. Do you all you agree with President McCosh at the College of New Jersey? There should be no third contest and this football competition now officially comes to an end?"

"I think his logic is clear. We have seen it too. The students have become distracted from their studies and are losing their focus on the critical elements of their academic learning. That is no surprise with the amount of time they have allowed themselves to expend playing these games."

"The first game truly served a purpose. A great outlet with the events around us that were transpiring. But it is time to get our scholarly structure back on track."

"I agree. It is not like these games will ever be something someone will be able to earn a living doing."

"Or that the college will ever see as a viable means for securing any type of funding with boys out there each week playing a game. Face it. We need to get them back on track before they forget that their future needs to start aligning with classwork and our college needs to get back to our true work with research and publishing."

"And your thoughts?" President Campbell was now looking directly at the men he had assigned to get the students in better physical condition as more of a form of punishment. He also was aware from what he had been told that these three men in front of him might have the strongest objections to cancelling future contests.

"Do you also agree we stop the contests between the two colleges?" President Campbell asked the three of them.

Atherton and Kellogg looked at each other and shook their heads in agreement. True, they had been the faculty members who were the most responsible for the training that had helped prepare the students. But they also believed firmly in the academic mission of the college and while physical fitness of their youth was important, academics was being sacrificed with all the time being spent on game preparations.

Hasbrouck, who had assisted the Rutgers players, nodded in agreement too. "I support a reprieve from the football contests with the College of New Jersey."

"Very well. Then we must let the students know. As of today, there will be no more contests to distract them from their studies. We return to normal and the expectation is that no challenges by any student is to be made with another college with any sport or academic competition until further notice."

Campbell had stood up as he made the declaration. "That is our position that we will enforce." Then, turning to face the group he added, "For now. Understood?"

"Yes sir."

"Very good gentlemen. Have a good day."

After the rest of the staff filtered out of his office, Campbell looked to Cook and Murray who he had requested to remain behind with him for a moment.

"So the lads really lost that second game six to zero?" Campbell asked.

"That is what was shared," Cook replied.

"Crushed," Murray interjected.

"Well, never the matter with that."

Campbell spoke as he moved about his desk as he prepared to get back to other affairs of the campus besides this new football competition talk.

"What I liked hearing is what was told to me when last I was speaking with a member of the state legislature who resides here in New Brunswick. He said the word is all across the state that Rutgers College won that first challenge. That first game ever played is all people will always recall. Who cares about what took place later. Rutgers won the game that mattered."

"True, true," Cook and Murray echoed each other.

"Very well. Back to a focus on scholastic studies," Campbell announced.

Campbell smiled at the two professors. "It seems like only yesterday I shared with you my concerns about our college's standing. How fast things can change. Who would have thought that a boy's game could be so uplifting? I truly feel that event put us on the right track now. It did more to further our reputation and bring a positive report about our college from the Board beyond anything we had thought about on our own."

Murray turned to Cook as they walked out of the President's office and back out on to the campus grounds.

"Do you really think no student cares if Rutgers never wins another football game against Princeton?" Murray asked.

"Student?" Cook shot back. "Heck I care that our lads at Rutgers win again in the future and I bet the same is true with almost every part of the faculty. Imagine hearing that from someone among the alumni or if that is the thought of that member from the state legislature Dr. Campbell was referring too? No, Dr. Murray, I believe every loyal son of Rutgers cares when we will win – again!"

"So how does Rutgers win again if our boys do not play again?"

"The stop is temporary," Cook predicted. "Oh, old men can make our formal edicts. But this game caught too much of our people's spirit and their desire to compete to simply go away. They will play again. You heard President Campbell say it best. Just not now."

"I am as amazed as Dr. Campbell that the results of that victory seemed to carry over so strongly among all groups associated with the college."

"Competition and winning are strange things. Compete to win and not just to play. It stirs the blood. You and I know that well from our work with the land grant victory. The lads now know it with their exploits in the athletics domain."

"I suppose," Murray replied. "But when I think about the future do you really see this sports thing being that big or that important in the end? I mean, it was just a game."

"Just a game?" Cook repeated. "Victory is what builds pride in any group or institution. Small or large? Time will tell about whether it is this game or another that matters in the future. But they will compete again Dr. Murray. It is in our blood. And if this game does end up catching on as the true test of might between two colleges, then one thing will always be there in our honor. That the boys from Rutgers won the first contest ever."

"Dr. Campbell is right, though. Lose game two after winning game one; who cares?"

Cook laughed.

"Oh we care, Dr. Murray. Do not fool yourself. I can see us lobbying for a game three if we had won game two just to keep proving our ability to beat them each time. The loss makes it easier to dismiss a future contest. But mark my words, we will play again in the future. There will also be many people demanding that we exert whatever is necessary at our college's disposal to secure a win."

"Imagine taking the limited funding we have from our educational resources to support a game. That would not seem possible."

"It is not only possible, Dr. Murray. I believe it is probable."

"And why do you believe this so strongly?"

Pulling a copy of a paper with newsprint from his bag, Cook pointed to an article within the several page publication.

"Do you know what this is?" Cook asked.

"No, I cannot say that I am aware of what this is without reading it."

"This is a copy of the brand new student newspaper that is being published here at Rutgers. Our young men have lobbied to have a paper of their own so that they can chronicle their points of view as well as what they deem to be the most important events happening in their lives."

"Interesting, but what does that have to do with your prediction that we will steal the funds out of the educational piggy bank to pay for sports contests here on our campus?"

"The paper is called *The Targum*."

Murray glanced at the paper and back again at his colleague with a quizzical expression on his face.

"Dr. Murray, I cannot believe you do not see the significance at first blush but let me further explain," Cook stated folding the student newsprint paper so the article of the game remained on top.

"As you may not be aware, the founding of the college paper at Rutgers was a major struggle and engaged numerous parties in the process. Both staff and students, as well as the local Fredonian press, all had a vested interest in how it would appear. Initially billed as a literary periodical, the students recently rose up to demand that they be allowed to print what they felt were the most relevant and critical topics to them. This has all transpired in the past two years so the passion among the students is very high."

"A side story, even the naming of the paper was controversial. As the story goes, the name of the paper was hatched in the room of Tunis G. Bergen, Class of 1867. The word used in the title of the newspaper came from the classroom of our own college president, Dr. Campbell. Students discovered it through their intensive studies of Hebrew literature. The students insist to us the title was picked due to its link with the academic depth it evoked. There are others who talk about a secondary meaning to the students. It is supposed to be an insiders joke about the cheat sheets that students supposedly created to assist with getting ahead in their classes and on their exams."

"Seems an inappropriate title for our college then and maybe something we should change," Dr. Murray quipped. "But again, what does that side story have to do with your prediction."

Dr. Cook continued without acknowledging the comment.

"The point is, the students are running the show in this free press setting. Students like Pruyn, Griffis and Knapp, who is now their senior editor, forged together a plan to turn the annual into a monthly publication. They have provided energy with both gathering resources through subscriptions along with the basics of actually publishing a paper."

"The students, not the staff, determine what they print. The students, not the professional press, determine what is newsworthy. The students are the ones invested in what becomes the permanent record of our college or what is an event to be forgotten."

"It is the combination of these things that leads to my prediction. First we have the critical influence of the press retelling the story of the football game. Next you have the cost and energy which makes the paper important to the students. Add the recent events with winning and this is where I know that my future prediction of the importance of that sports contest has future traction."

"You see, Dr. Murray, in that limited space that the students have and where they can say anything about any topic in the world that is available to them, they elected to use a whole segment to replay the events of that contest with the team from Princeton. Take a moment to read that article and their version and their school mates who actually participated are elevated to heroic status much like the Roman gladiators were in an earlier time."

"Okay. I think I see your point," Dr. Murray replied.

"But it gets bigger, Dr. Murray. Next take the exploits of those students and move forward several years to when they have graduated and are now successful businessmen themselves and earning enough that they want to donate back to the college as alumni. The positive memories that will be evoked are the ones where they are most likely going to want to contribute to sustain these memories. Hence, the glory of that first contest victory becomes immortalized in a way that no one ever wants it to be forgotten. To do that means supporting it into the future through whatever funding is necessary."

"In the end, my friend, they may easily forget what you and I taught on a random day in a lecture hall but they will not lose that cherished memory of vanquishing the evil that had haunted them from across the state. This football game they played becomes the stuff of legends. Monuments get built or, more importantly to us, money gets spent to find the power to victory again."

"Incredible."

"Yes, winning always is."

44
November 17, 1869
Campus in Princeton

President McCosh looked out across the street at the town of Princeton from his home.

The dirt from the leaves which had been whipped up off the ground in the wind from the prior night had left their mark and he made a mental note that he needed to bring this to the help's attention. It was a sure sign that the weather had changed and winter was firmly on its way.

"So is there anything else, sir?"

He turned back to look again at the student guest seated in the high-back, black leather chair. He had to work hard to maintain his administrative look and not smile. Truth be told, this was not easy to do.

In this young man was what he hoped all in his charge would aspire to be.

The passion. The desire to succeed. The love of God, family, country and school. And a relentless will to win no matter what the challenge.

He had articulated his point and that of his teammates as well as any of the courtroom lawyers or evangelical preachers he had ever heard before. And, in so many ways, he really wished he had the latitude to reward this student for his efforts.

But that option, for now, was simply not in the works. There was no pathway where he could allow them to play again.

"No, son, there is not."

He watched as the student took a deep breath, disappointment clear in the manner in which his shoulders now pulled down at his sides.

Yet, as he stood to leave, this student reached out his hand. He politely thanked President McCosh for making the time for him and for hearing his request in full before rendering his final decision.

The student leaned back toward the chair and collected his overcoat. He then turned once again and thanked President McCosh for all he had done and exited the room.

And, in that step, McCosh saw that this young man still had hope. It was clear to him that this son of Old Nassau believed like him, that, if not today then maybe tomorrow. As the student disappeared from sight, McCosh wondered to himself if his faculty had that same sense of hope and resiliency.

They certainly had a passion to argue against any change. They definitely had a desire to not see the students engaged in anything beyond their pre-determined avenue of study.

And in that firmness of direction and tradition that they preached, McCosh wondered if they were right about what was best for everyone's future or if they were simply mimicking a past and the way they had once been taught because it was the only thing they knew?

McCosh moved over to his desk and thumbed through the never ending stack of papers which appeared thrice each day for his purview. One, on top, was the response from Campbell up at Rutgers agreeing that they, too, would cease the football competition right away.

Oh, how he wished he could clear his boys from Princeton to play one more time.

When he had heard they had lost that first contest at Rutgers he was in shock. Instantly, he started hatching ways that the school could help the students in the next game so that they could attain a level of revenge.

Revenge. Who was he kidding about the students getting revenge? He wanted to beat them as badly as any of the players.

Then when he learned they had completely blanked the lads from Rutgers in that second contest, he practically danced across his office floor. Princeton was back in its rightful place as the winning school. McCosh clearly saw a third victory in the cards and with it a cleansing of the rotten taste he had once felt after that first contest.

It would have provided true redemption for that initial loss. A win would have made them the clear champions when folks counted total wins at two victories to one upset victory by Rutgers. That would set the record straight.

But time was not on his side or on the side of the players for a third contest. The faculty had virtually threatened to revolt and walk out if a directive did not appear banning any further distractions from study hours or lectures.

As much as he enjoyed the spirit this game injected into this rivalry with Rutgers College and as much as he wanted to see all in Princeton emerge victorious; he knew this was not the time or even the cause right now to fall on one's sword. A faculty revolution was the last thing the Board would want to see. He reminded himself he was relatively new in his role in Princeton and winning this fight was not likely.

He fully understood that there would be a better day for a battle over bringing the College of New Jersey into the modern era over the objections of the classic traditionalists who cried foul at any change. There was also a better day to fight on the football field with Rutgers again and teach them a lesson about who was the best. He smiled again as he thought about how the report came in from that second game. "We totally dominated them," was the one line explanation given to him by an aide.

But oh, how he wished they could just play and win one more game with bragging rights at stake.

"President McCosh?"
It was a young tutor standing nervously at his door.
"Yes?"

"I was supposed to come by and hear if there is any message for the faculty advisors to deliver to the student body this evening?" the tutor anxiously asked of the College President.

"Yes. Please pass on to them that I will be there shortly myself. You can offer them that I plan to tell them what I believe will make them happy about not allowing worldly distractions among the students while they complete their coursework this year."

"Very good sir," the tutor answered. "I will let them know you will be with them shortly."

McCosh stood and put on his overcoat and scarf. While he reached for his gloves and hat he paused for just one more second.

"Yes," he said out loud to himself while no one else was present. "I will have our young academicians return their full attention to their studies."

Pulling on his gloves he opened the door and stared at the cold wintery environs in front of him. Then he spoke out loud with the same clear voice to no one in particular. Or maybe his comment was meant for everyone in Princeton to hear.

"One day, we will settle that score with Rutgers College. We will eventually win that third contest. And then we will win many more. Again we will prove we are the academic and athletic superiors of that other college in New Jersey!"

Then, for emphasis he added.

"And with victory, it will make us the best college in this whole grand country. And that, my dear people of Princeton, is something for you to be proud about with your students here at Old Nassau!"

With that, he headed to the faculty gathering where they were awaiting his announcement about eliminating the next contest from the schedule.

As McCosh walked out to the meeting there was no way he could have known he was also heading forward toward a nation awaiting the growth of college football and all the pride, unity and glory it can bring to all members of a college community.

45
"After the Graduation Ceremony"
Spring 1870
Princeton Campus

They walked across the grounds and away from the East College building structure that had housed him over the past year. Classmates waved hello and good-bye at the same time as they moved past each other one final time.

His brother had already headed out on an earlier train leaving with his mother and a large collection of the family-owned items that had adorned their rooms. There had been a few crates even as Spartan as their existence had been while living in the campus proper.

"There appears to have been a great deal of construction here on campus even since you first started," his father noted as they looked at the new structures around them. "With the remarks from President McCosh and other graduates, there does not seem to be an end to expansion in sight either."

"That will be a benefit for future students," young Will Gummere replied.

Stopping then at a point near the commons area and looking back toward Nassau Hall, which was still the central focus of the college, his father stood next to his son and placed his arm around his son's shoulders.

Unsure of the meaning behind this sudden physical gesture, Gummere froze in place.

"From the look of things and your time here, I would say that those who follow behind you will owe you a great deal of gratitude too."

"Sir?"

"Come now. I have read not only of your academic accomplishments and the letters from your professors acknowledging your excellence with personal scholarly efforts. From every student planning to still attend here next year to the father of every other student who has now graduated too, all I hear is how their sons are impressed by you and awed by your leadership among their ranks."

"That is kind of them to say," Will replied cautiously to his father.

"Kind has nothing to do with it William. Parents rarely praise someone else's child in this type of setting unless they feel compelled to do it because of the basic truth and evidence behind the compliment."

Will was unsure what to say next, so he just listened as his father continued.

"People typically do what they are told to do by leaders, William, regardless of how they have been assigned. On the other hand, people respect and actually follow leaders when they have selected them from within their own ranks. Inherit a post and that man will be in an operational position to do no more than manage. To be placed in a post at the bequest of those around you and that man is a leader in the truest sense of the word."

Turning now to look directly at his son, the elder Gummere continued.

"I have heard about how when challenges arose, you stepped up as your classmates' choice to be their voice. I have heard about your role as captain of this new sport that has emerged to test the strength and will of the college body and soul."

"That is impressive William. That is proving yourself among your peers. That is being successful among your fellow students and rising above the crowd to set yourself apart in a positive and powerful way that will not be forgotten."

His father smiled.

"You have attained more than I could have predicted. You have established a legacy here that those around you and those who will follow you will never forget. You have created a foundation that will be a part of this college for generations to come. From what I have heard, the impression and difference you have made may be as lasting as these new stone structures that have risen around you and that we have just marveled at."

His father paused for just a second before he finished his thoughts.

"I am proud of you William. I am proud of what you have accomplished. I am also excited about the great man I believe you now will become."

"Thank you, sir."

"I love you son."

"I love you too Dad."

His father gave William a hug before separating,

The emotional exchange was a first that Will could remember with his father. It was so far removed from their normal formal interactions. All Will had ever known of he and his father were the required public actions of the strict, male parent and the obedient, compliant child.

Will wiped a tear from his eye.

With that, the two men walked off toward the future, both returning back to their roles expected of the business class in society. Will vowed to himself, as he walked off the campus pathway and back on to the public streets, that he would work to fulfill his father's prediction about him.

Still on the Princeton campus, in a back room of a dorm hall, two other students spoke about what they planned to do at their college where they were enrolled to attend in the next academic year.

"Who do you think they will select as the captain?"

"I have several ideas but we will have to wait and see."

"And do you think they will let us play again?"

"Not only will they let us play, I believe before we know it they will be asking for try-outs among the students here to guarantee they have the best team representing the college versus just a team selected among the students who sign up."

"And what makes you think that will happen?"

The other student stared directly into his classmate's eyes. There was no hesitation as he responded to the rationale behind his prediction.

"Because they want to continue to prove that the first football game loss was a fluke. They want to beat Rutgers just as badly as the students all do. You will see. One day, in the not too distant future, they will be banging on doors seeking out those who can carry the banner of the school in a way that all know that we are the best. And to be the best, we must be the champions at the sport that matters most. And that for us, my friend, is football!"

AFTERWARD
November 5, 1938
Seventy Years Later
The New Rutgers Stadium

It did not feel as cold as the last time they had taken her out, she thought to herself.
The car ride here had been smooth compared with her memory of the last one she had been on. They did not take her out as often as they used to do.
But what should she expect they do?
She knew it was difficult moving a 94 year old lady around.

Now seated, after being assisted to her seat, she pulled her blanket tighter around her to fight off the crisp cold air of that November afternoon.
She looked around at those who had climbed into the stands and had assembled around her.
There must have been thousands there in that crowd she guessed. It was loud. There was so much yelling and calling out all at one time. It almost made any other normal volume talk impossible for her to detect.

Yes, it had been a long time since she had been to a college football game.

She still read the newspapers, when she did not fall asleep with them in her lap.
She still listened to the radio, when she did not fall asleep with it droning on.
She had not forgotten about many of the big events that had passed. The World War where the doughboys had etched their legacy by helping free Europe from the threat of Kaiser Wilhelm. The wonderful jazz music she loved from the social settings that soothed people through the failure of Prohibition. The awful day that word of the great stock market crash was broadcast and then the times as the President explained that the country was fighting off economic loss in what was now being called the Great Depression.
She was also keenly aware of new tales coming out of Europe where a dictator had risen to power in Germany and talk was common about

another collision course with a second possible war that could impact countries across the world.

But behind all that massive major news that engulfed everyone each day, she felt like she had that secret so many forgot that made life so worthwhile. Regardless of world and national headlines, she still had her memories of all the people and love that had been shared.

And those thoughts were what dominated her remaining minutes on this planet now.

She thought of the warmth of family that never ends and is rekindled through magical times like Christmas and birthdays.

And then there is the glory of the hope for tomorrow that one can revel in through the eyes of one's own grandchildren. A renewal in life that takes place through their little smiles and dreams that life never really ends. And she now watched this reality appear again most recently with the growth of her great grandchildren.

That sight was a comfort to one as they grew older.

Her fingers rubbed together unconsciously and her lips smacked as she smelled a familiar fragrance in the air about her. Fresh popped and buttered popcorn!

Oh, how she loved that smell. And there was a time when she would savor every bite of a deep container of that wonderful buttery food. There was a day when you could not have stopped her from racing into line and buying a bag.

But now as she reminded herself about the uncooked kernels that always were in every batch, for a person without permanent solid teeth, that was not the best choice for her today.

"Grandma," she heard an exasperated voice as a hand repeatedly tapped her on the shoulder. "Are you off day-dreaming again? Mom, I think she has fallen asleep!"

She looked at the woman seated next to her on her right. It was her granddaughter, Kate, and she smiled at her to reassure her that she was awake and not dead.

"I'm fine dear," she said, unsure with all the noise around her if her own voice had been loud enough to be heard by someone else.

"Look, Grandma. Down there! That is our Allison."

She tried to follow the direction of her granddaughter's finger as it pointed to a group down on the field in front of her in that part of the giant bowl below.

"Where?" she asked, still unable to make out what was being shown.

"There," came back the same voice, a little more frustrated in sound this time. "Can't you see her? Can't you see Allison?"

She nodded just to get her granddaughter to relax. She knew she could barely make out the liver spots on the back of her own hand anymore let alone a figure so far away. But no need to aggravate her granddaughter today.

"Mom!" She heard a second voice call to her. "Can you see what Kate is showing you?"

"Yes dear," she replied to the woman seated on the other side of her granddaughter.

"I don't think she can see her," her granddaughter stated to that woman.

If you believe that my dear, she thought to herself, *then why are you asking me if I can see?*

The other two women then switched seats.

Her own daughter was now seated next to her. She was no youngster any more either. Her hair was white and her face showed the signs of 74 years well spent in the sun.

"Mom," this woman now seated next to her tapped her hand gently. "Kate wants you to know that your great granddaughter is down there on the sideline with the other students from Douglas College cheering on the Rutgers team. See, she is in the color guard with the band!"

Every time Anna spoke, she always thought the same thing and her heart felt lighter. Oh, how her daughter still sounded like that sweet little girl she knew she would always love. 70 years swept away in an instant and she saw that five year old at her side instead. She patted her daughter's hand back.

"Mom, do you remember when you and Dad said that one day that might be me down there on the field? Can you remember that time?"

Oh, how she could remember that time. That day. That moment.

The memories always flowed through so fast. Just like the pace of real time movies at a theatre, the visions never slowed down.

She thought about Christopher and what a wonderful husband he had been to her. He had been a marvelous father to two young children, her Anna and Jonathan. He had adopted them completely, not just in name but also with his heart, after they had married.

She thought back to the years that had taken them from one spot to the next but always, regardless of where they landed, back to the New Jersey college campuses where they had first met.

She thought back to the weddings and new births that had grown their family so large.

And yes, as she looked back at Anna her daughter, she remembered that day so long ago. She could never forget when they had watched that first football game together. It was the day she knew that as a family they would forever be together.

"Mom, they are going to have the only remaining player down on the field from that original team. He is about to be introduced now."

"Aren't they all dead?" she smiled as she asked since she knew this would get a rise out of her daughter if she could hear what she had just said.

In the background that last original Rutgers football player, George Large, had made it to the field. The address system noted that he was now the last surviving member from the original game. It was then announced, in a more somber tone, that the last Princeton player, William Preston Lane, had passed away that morning.

There was a moment of silence held to remember the deceased Princeton player.

All on both sides of the crowd were respectful.

When the next announcement was made, she immediately recognized the voice.

It was the voice of that young fellow from that radio sports show which she so much enjoyed listening to each day. He was the radio announcer who had visited her in her room not that long ago when she had shared her story of the first game. Funny, she thought. He is also the public address announcer at the stadium.

"Yes, let's have another round of applause for the final player from the first college football game in history!" His voice belted out through the public address system. It rang across the ears of thousands seated in that stadium around her.

She smiled.

Well, nice to know the sportscaster had kept his word after losing their bet!

After the applause for George Large started to slow, Mr. Large was escorted from the field so the game could resume.

With a wave of his hat to the crowd, there was one more roar from the Rutgers faithful and even from the spectators who hailed from Princeton for the last founder of the first game. One could clearly define George Large that day as a man who had served a major purpose in the life of his college and for the history of the sport.

Young people started jumping up and down again and were yelling loudly as the players from both teams started to re-take the field for the second half.

Elizabeth's daughter leaned in to speak to her again. She felt her daughter's gentle hand lovingly rub her arm through that scarlet and black blanket she had with her all the time now.

"Mom, whenever you feel ready to go, let us know and we can get you out of the cold here. We want to take you out with us later to eat at the restaurant with Allison when her band finishes up and the game ends. I know she would love to see you."

Elizabeth smiled but said nothing back to her daughter this time.

Her mind did not want to leave the wonderful film it was playing of days spent with her daughter, Anna, and her son, Jonathan, during their youth.

She watched again as the pictures etched in her mind flipped through the memories of so many of those long-ago special days.

The one when she and Christopher were married.

The one when Jonathan enrolled at Rutgers and how proud Christopher had been.

The one where Anna was married to Troy and how Christopher had walked her down the aisle. Oh how those tears of a proud father had fallen from his face as he sat next to her in the front row of the church and watched the ceremony with her that day.

The one when they announced the birth of their first grandchild. The one when they announced each of the grandchildren.

The one when she was there when they brought her great granddaughter home from the hospital. That same great granddaughter was the one now carrying on a family tradition of a love of college football on the field below her today.

Her mind only knew how to run the happy memories. She had been blessed.

Now she heard the glee club chorus sing the Rutgers fight song, "*RU, Rah, Rah, RU, RU, Rah, Rah!*"

It cut into her thoughts and she smiled again to think about the joy of the full college experience and what it had meant for her and for her family as well as for so many others.

Without it, she would never have met Christopher and taken his last name.

Without it, she may never have broken out of a small provincial town.

Without it, the joy she had shared with her children, grandchildren and now a great grandchild, would never have been as deeply fun and rewarding.

"*On the banks of the Old Raritan,*" was now being sung by voices across the stadium.

She looked over at Anna, forever that little girl in her eyes.

She looked over at Kate, forever that sweet little grandchild to her.

She looked down toward the field where she knew her first great grandchild was now enrolled in college and loving the experience.

It all felt so good. It all felt so right.

She swayed with the crowd as they sang on with their song to honor Rutgers.

It was a song that even a girl from Princeton had grown to love after her family saw it as their alma mater now.

It was a song in so many ways about their home and hers.

Yes, without question, it was a song that spoke to the story of her life.

And she smiled heavenward.

Yes Christopher. Our lives have been blessed.

I will never forget that moment that I realized I had fallen in love with you and how that led to the beginning of all the wonders our life would bring.

She saw the loving community spirit on display as the fans continued to sing and cheer.

She reflected again on how grateful she was that this game was invented that allowed one's true passion in life to be seen by others beyond the formal façade people too often feel we must create for ourselves.

And then she glanced in the direction of the announcer's booth.

She knew sitting inside was another historian who now would always ensure the story around her cherished memory remained straight for future generations. It felt good to know that would not change even after she was gone.

And it mattered to her not simply because of her personal family story of love.

No, it mattered to us all. Because on that same day she had fallen in love with her future husband, Rutgers and Princeton took a chance and played in the first college football game in history. It was the day that a whole nation was destined to fall in love with a sport!

And she knew, as old as she now was, that the foundation of one's love was something that should never be misrepresented or forgotten by anyone.

POSTSCRIPT
Present Day

Joey and Gianna thumbed through their mother's old things.

They should have done this a long time ago. But every time someone had suggested they help their mother downsize the clutter, there had always been something better to do.

They both had families and homes and Gianna even had a grandchild of her own to care for now. So like the lyrics in Harry Chapin's *Cats in the Cradle* song, they all stayed perpetually too busy to spend a day climbing up into the cramped, unfinished space in the rafters above the second floor of the house filled with so many old things that needed purging.

But today became the day they had been putting off for so long.

Rusty, torn, rotted or worn out, they worked their way through whatever had been stored in the corners of the attic far away from anyone's eyes or personal use.

Slowly they filtered through the dust and cobwebs and separated each item into one of three piles.

Toss away. Donate. Keep.

Gianna paused as she glanced at the three designated areas and noted that almost everything had landed in the going to the dump grouping. Three things graced the donated pile while nothing had found its way to the save area.

Outdated gifts and old plates with random chips on them. Stained clothing held for years for the predicted use with some next child. Toys with missing parts and faded surfaces. Odds and ends that could not be defined. Each piece was placed on top of the last that had been deposited in the disposal pile. Together it created a small mountain of what was about to be expunged from their lives.

While she and her brother believed each item belonged in the disposal category, it did not stop both of them from holding each object one last time in an effort to try and pull out one last happy prior memory of when it held so much more meaning in their or someone's life.

A smile or a happy tear would come to their face as they saw an old toy they or one of their children had once cherished, purchased, and played with. However, even when there was some specific recollection from the past, the emotional desire to put it in the keep pile evaporated quickly as the reality of their own homes with no additional storage space came back into view.

"Check this one out."

Her brother's words cut into her depressing observation that most of what had been saved up here for so many years was heading to a junk heap.

"That's one of our Grandmother Allison's old scrapbooks," Gianna somehow recognized the object in front of her as her brother pried apart the pages.

Dried out and very poorly aged, the paper that carried various notes once penned by hand on to it, fell like confetti to the ground.

"Looks like mice found some nesting material and used up the majority of what this once held," Joey exclaimed.

Several other items, long separated from the glue corners that once held them to the scrapbook pages, now slid out from the binder and littered the floor.

A playbill cover to some off Broadway show. A series of tickets to a night club. A birthday card that moisture had devoured the signature and message it once contained. Several clippings from old newspapers with national and world news headlines or local stories that must have included some neighborhood figure someone must have known.

With each, the browning of the paper had made the writing basically impossible to read. Still it was obvious with the way this binder had once been put together, that each piece of memorabilia was so important at one time even if those clues to their significance were too distant in the past for anyone to now know why.

"Look at this," Joey announced as he moved to the final pages of the binder. "Some type of fancy letterhead with a radio station logo it looks like and a second letter stapled to it that is still intact."

"What's it say?"

Joey pulled the paper closer to his eyes to read as the light was fading from the already dark attic area.

"It appears to be some type of radio letterhead on this paper. It looks like this note was written on December 1, 1939. It starts out with someone expressing sorrow about something and then the note is announcing a winner of some kind."

"Just read it to me if the note is that short," Gianna said.

Joey nodded and read the note out loud.

"First, let me say that I was sorry to hear the news and I send my condolences to you and your family. She won our little bet, as you know. I thought you might like to have this letter that she wrote me just before she passed. Please know that she opened a seasoned announcer's eyes and taught him about the heart that is supposed to be there within the true intended purpose of the game. That will never be forgotten. Nor will I ever let anyone ever forget the date of that first game."

"Does it say who wrote it?" Gianna asked.

"I cannot make out the signature," Joey replied.

"What does the letter stapled to that note say?"

They both shifted their attention to the second document.

Cleanly typed on a standard sheet of paper, Joey could clearly make out each word. Again, he read out loud for his sister.

I am dictating this message to a lovely nurse who has agreed to type for me as my hands just do not seem able to do the writing they used to do any longer. To begin, I did want to let you know that I appreciated that you honored our little wager. I genuinely hope that I did not hurt your feelings or damage your pride when I won. At the same time, while this was sad for you, the reality is that most of us older ladies never forget what was always basically true.

I also know that the names used in the story I told you may have been scrambled slightly with what each person actually did or did not do. I apologize for that as I know you wanted your facts. But know there was no malice in any error made as the personal details simply get fuzzy for everyone when matching any exactness of an old tale with the true events and the timing in which it took place. But while the details and names of who actually accomplished or said certain things may have grown fuzzy over the years, the outcomes I told you about have never changed.

And you see, those outcomes are what actually matter and not the particulars of which person did or said what. Historians too often lose this direction and then they try to debate new outcomes. They lose sight of the basic truths. The story I told you never deviated from those core truths.

I hope you remember that with this lesson.

Never forget it all started with a love of a school and a love of a game combining that day in New Brunswick. From that day in 1869 and on, nothing on college campuses would ever again be the same. The lads from Princeton and those at Rutgers set the football world in motion.

And that, my good fellow, is pure history.

All the best to those who come after me as it is my time to pass this memory on. Whether they also cheer for the scarlet or some other team, I hope those who watch the game and those athletes who play never forget what the true meaning of the game was supposed to be about. I hope its ability to bring people together lasts forever with its power to generate joy through the pure love of a game. Really it is a simple game that can forge collegial bonds while fostering loyalty and devotion to a school. It also proves to be a perfect recipe for uniting family through a common cause.

And as you now must agree: This all began in 1869 at Rutgers College.

One lucky lady.

"I cannot make out the signature after that final line at the end of this typed letter," Joey said as he finished reading. "You want to try to make it out?"
"I know who it was from," Gianna responded. "I don't need to see the signature. That was Elizabeth, our great, great, great grandmother."

"Interesting. Toss or save?" Joey asked, gesturing with the paper toward the disposal pile.
"We save this one. Some things simply cannot be replaced," Gianna stated as she reached forward and carefully took the paper from her brother's hand.
As she shifted back up to her feet, she looked down at her younger sibling. When was the last time she had told him that she loved him?
She leaned over and ran her fingers through his hair. She then gave him a gentle kiss on the crown of his head.

Looking up, Joey asked, "What was that for?"
"Thanks for going through all mom's old stuff with me. I really loved sharing some old memories together."
"Love you too, sis."
Then she held the letter up for emphasis.
"And remember that some things in life, like love little brother, should never be lost or forgotten."

Ω

The Real Players and Historical Figures

November 6, 2019 was the 150th birthday of the first college football game ever played. It took place between Rutgers and Princeton. This is a fact.

However, in completing any work of historical fiction, the reader is hopefully inspired by what they have read to explore beyond the novel to research the time period to find what can be documented through firsthand accounts and primary materials. To that end, there is a sample list of resources at the end of this work to help provide some guidance on where to start.

While real figures and events help outline this work, the plot that is to make the events easier to read about today requires fictionalization of certain areas, especially any dialogue. This is done to allow the reader to feel more connected with that moment in time and to advance the plot.

To this end Christopher Adkins and Elizabeth Warren are fictional characters created to draw upon the actual social issues within this time period while advancing the storyline.

On the other hand, many of the other names used are those of individuals who actually existed and played roles in both the real first football game in New Brunswick as well as in roles that impacted the world around them at this story's timeframe in history. Hopefully, this has been done in what is interpreted by the reader as a respectful manner to honor those who played such a crucial role in our past. Again, while the dialogue used by these real people in these settings was simply created to serve the plot of the story; many of these men and women who are named did help shape the Rutgers and Princeton University communities we know today.

It is important to continue to highlight that the figures used in the story include many of the names, if not the thoughts and words, of the actual first college football players in American history. This was done to respect those who actually played in that first game within the context of the story. At the same time, any comparisons of actual language or characterization with the people within this tale are purely the creation of the author.

<u>Historical Places and Events: A Short Summary</u>

Princeton College was chartered by the Crown in 1746.

The *New Light Presbyterian Church* played a critical role in the formation of this institution. It was originally given the name of the *College of New Jersey* and was not officially named Princeton until 1896. The reference to *Nassau Hall* as one of the longest standing college facilities is also correct. Other places in Princeton, like Judge Olden's home (*Drumthwacket*), Professor Aycock's home, as well as the President's house all existed at that time in 1869.

Rutgers College was originally known as *Old Queens College* and was associated with the Dutch Reformed Church. Rutgers had separated its official ties to the *Dutch Reformed Church* in 1864 while the Seminary still remained in New Brunswick.

Rutgers was chartered by the Crown in 1766. This date has been debated as a second charter was issued in 1770. For a while, 1770 was also considered the official year of the College's founding at one time before the 1766 date was restored as the official charter date at this time.

The *Old Queens building* was the main structure on the Rutgers campus in 1869 and still has a prominent place in the layout of the current campus grounds. The bell in the cupola was donated by namesake Henry Rutgers. Buildings like *Van Nest Hall, Schanck Observatory, and Riverstede* (George Cook's home) have structures that were all present at that time in 1869 and can still be seen today. Riverstede was actually converted into a Rutgers University building after being donated to the College by George Cook. It has recently served as the Social Work Annex administrative site.

Student John Wyckoff did board while enrolled in school in a home along Bayard Street. <u>*Northrop's*</u> was an establishment, some called a resort, in New Brunswick. One of the original players alluded to the teams dining there after the first game in an article that appeared years later about that time period.

The street names used in this work existed in Trenton, Princeton and New Brunswick. The overview of the landscape and the changing face of each community based upon industrial and manufacturing growth is also a portrayal of what was taking place during that time period.

A local justice, James S. Nevius, was paid to conduct an investigation of Rutgers students to determine which one of them had been involved with the destruction of the campus latrine.

The actual playing site used for the first football game was located between Sicard and College Avenue. The area at that time was an open field that was used for a variety of purposes. Eventually other structures were built in this location including the school gymnasium (affectionately known as the "Barn"). A plaque remains on the spot commemorating where the first game was played and dirt from this area has been sent to the College Football Hall of Fame in Atlanta, Georgia to memorialize its role in the first game.

Trains played a critical role in commerce and travel throughout the country in 1869. This was also true for transport between the cities of Philadelphia, Trenton, New Brunswick, and New York. Princeton had two stops for passengers who rode on the Central NJ Railroad.

The Morrill Act created land grant colleges across the country. This promoted new college growth and altered the pathway for existing colleges through this financing. Rutgers did win the bid through the efforts of Dr. Cook and Dr. Murray which was fiercely contested between the two colleges within New Jersey. Princeton had also bid but it was not awarded the Morrill Act funding.

Women's Rights speaker *Lucy Stone* visited Princeton. There are reports that she had a rude welcome from the audience when she spoke there. *Elizabeth Cady Stanton* was the first woman (January 20, 1869) reported to have spoken to the assembled Congress on the topic of women's rights.

Halloween traditions have existed for a long time. The people of New Brunswick, like many across the country with varied immigrant populations, most likely followed practices that were similar in fashion to what was described within the story.

Ghost stories about the grounds on and near Rutgers have been shared over the years. One story talks about the ghost of Catherine Livingston waiting for Alexander Hamilton's return to Old Queens. Another links the history of the mortuary that existed on College Avenue (near the tunnel location) in a location that became a Rutgers College facility, Miller Hall. Miller Hall (it became a student residence hall) sits at the site of the old McDede Burial Company property that operated in the late 1800s. Ghostly sounds have been reported to be heard throughout the structure ranging from creaking boards to unexplained footsteps in the hallways.

The tunnel under New Brunswick is a part of its early working history as well as a setting of local lore. The character's trail that is followed in this story is derived from an actual map from that time period that outlines the underground pathway of what had once been a copper mining operation. In the map, it runs underneath the streets listed in the story. The tunnel's use as a portal with the Underground Railroad is one of the local tales reported in New Brunswick. The actions referenced with the story of the Underground Railroad are accurate. The name *Cornelius Cornell* was reported to be known as a local watch. There is no verification that exists of who this person with this name actually was. The reality that New Jersey, even though it was a northern state in the Civil War, had many residents with pro-slave sympathies is one of the sad truths of that time period related to New Jersey state history.

The stories about New Jersey and the American Revolution are accurate. Washington and many other famous leaders in that time period did fight through these locations. The debates about the cannon and incidents that took place on the campuses of the two colleges go back to these events. This episode in New Jersey history became known as the "cannon wars" between Princeton and Rutgers. Supposedly the rivalry finally ended when Princeton buried the cannon (which had the contested ownership) in concrete. There was a task force in 1875 which actually studied and tried to resolve this debate between colleges and communities about who owned what cannon. Rutgers College has a cannon now on its grounds but that cannon is not the original cannon from the "cannon wars."

Billiards was a popular game with interest rapidly growing in the 1800s. Variations of this table top game were evolving in this time period. The version of the billiards game referenced in this story was becoming more common in the late 1860s.

Black Friday (on September 24, 1869) was an event in US history engineered between robber barons (although this term did not exist at that time) Jay Gould and James Fiske. In an attempt to capture the gold market, they had manipulated investors. Their actions even involved staff close to the newly elected President, U.S. Grant, in the scandal. Individual wealth was impacted and the aftershock also raised fears about the stability of the United States economy.

The musical titles of songs referenced in this story all existed at this story's time period. These song titles include:
-Brahms Lullabye
-The Man on the Flying Trapeze
-8th Regiment of NY March
-Johnny I Hardly Knew You
-When Johnny Comes Marching Home Again
-What a Friend in Jesus
-God Save Ireland
-Champagne Charlie

-Tramp, Tramp, Tramp
-Princeton Alma Mater
-Battle Cry of Freedom

The story of the origination of the London Football Association and the federation football league rules also has a historical foundation. Ebeneezer Cobb Morley and the meeting at the tavern is part of its history. The fact that the games of soccer and rugby were not cleanly defined actually lends credence to the likelihood of the version of football played at Rutgers that first time was some combination of these two sports. The evolution of the games over time produced the style of play we see today in all three sports.

Princeton did expel students for misbehavior as a part of its discipline consequence with their students. The expulsion depicted in this story on the eve of the football game though is not factual (and the character Lawrence Joueur is entirely fictional).

Princeton's *baseball team* did defeat the Rutgers team by the embarrassing score of 40 to 2 in May of 1866.

There was a Japanese student named *Kusakabe Taro* who was enrolled at Rutgers. He was one of a group who did come to the United States and to Rutgers College to study. His personal family history is linked to the Samuri in Japan. Staff members, like Dr. Murray, would maintain a relationship with the country of Japan and several staff actually went to Japan to work there. There is a cemetery marker for some of the Japanese students who died while they were enrolled at Rutgers. The markers for these students can still be located by visitors to the Willow Grove Cemetery.

The *grave site for William Van Arsdale* also exists in the Willow Grove Cemetery. He was a police officer in New Brunswick who fell through the ice while on duty in December 1856 by the docks and drowned. He left behind a family of a wife and six children. As the story goes, all they found was his cap on the frozen ice where he had supposedly fallen in.

The *admissions process* for the Rutgers College Scientific School did make accommodations for students to be admitted when compared with the traditional entrance expectations during this time period. The coursework within this program of studies also emphasized a different track from the traditional course of studies (Classical) common at Princeton at that time.

Dinosaur fragments were found in New Jersey marl pits. A full hadrosaurus was excavated in New Jersey in 1858.

The <u>Cook Campus</u> is named for the work at Rutgers, and across the state of New Jersey, by Dr. George Cook. It is symbolic of the advances that were accomplished on the campus with agricultural practices and a course of studies that would become known as agricultural engineering. Whether the Malthusian theory that food would run in short supply with exponential population growth was a driving basis for his work is not known; but Cook's experimental lab station revolutionized the farming industry in the state of New Jersey and it became known as the "Garden State."

<u>Douglass College</u> opened in 1918. It was the female college counterpart to the campus with an all-male enrollment at Rutgers College on the other side of New Brunswick.

The Rutgers song, *On the Banks of the Old Raritan*, was written in 1873 by Howard Newton Fuller (Class of 1874).

The Rutgers fight song, *The Bells Must Ring* (with the lyric "Rutgers Rah"), was not written until 1931.

The phrase, "*Keep Chopping Wood*," to explain not to quit and to just continue to do one's job is attributed to many individuals. For Rutgers University and college football, it was first used as the mantra of the Rutgers football team under Coach Greg Schiano in 2005 and not reported as having been used by anyone to motivate a team back in 1869.

The Names and the People

Rutgers President Reverend <u>William Henry Campbell</u> and Princeton President <u>James McCosh</u> were both in charge of their respective colleges at the time of the first football game. President McCosh did write for the *Nassau Literary Magazine* an article which advocated for a change in the name for the college in Princeton away from its 1869 *College of New Jersey* title.

<u>Professor George Cook</u> was Rutgers most famous staff member at that time and maybe of all time. His wife was named *Mary*. He was the state geologist and his work on the Rutgers campus with agriculture led to the naming of Cook Campus after his work.

<u>Professor David Murray</u> was recruited to Rutgers College by Dr. Cook. His wife's name was *Martha*. He was well known for his work in mathematics and he did go abroad to work in Japan.

Other Rutgers staff names (*Meyer, Kellogg, Atherton, Doolittle, Reilly, Cooper*) were active Rutgers faculty in this time period.

In 1865 Rutgers alumnus *John Voorhees married Hannah Mary* (who was the sister of an 1869 Rutgers student and member of the first football team as a player, George Large).

Isaac Hasbrouck and Edward Bowser were staff members who worked with Dr. Murray in the math department. Hasbrouck had a wife who was named Lucy. He also was a tutor for Japanese students while at Rutgers. Bowser would eventually become acknowledged for his writing in the field of mathematics.

John Mclean was the president at the College of New Jersey right before President McCosh. Arnold Guyot was a professor at Princeton. A famous 1867 photo of the Princeton staff was taken in front of Guyot's home located on Nassau Street and included the entire faculty for the 1867-1868 school year.

Judge Charles Smith Olden was the 19th Governor of the state of New Jersey from 1860 to 1863. In 1869 he was serving on the highest court in New Jersey. His home, *Drumthwacket*, is located in Princeton and the story of the property and Judge Olden are linked together in many ways with the history of Princeton as well as the history of New Jersey.

The Players

Princeton Original Football Team Roster*:
William Gummere (Class of 1870 was the Captain)
Jacob Edwin Michael (Class of 1871 known as "Big Mike")
Homer Dutch Boughner (lived until age 90)
George Billmeyer (never graduated and became president of a railcar manufacturer)
Charles Seth "Pipe Stems" Lane (oldest of three brothers at Princeton, youngest was also on the team)
Chauncey "Chaunce" Field (became a medical doctor)
"Frank" Burt (poet)
William Frazier Henley "Billy" Buck (Class of 1870 was also the first Princeton baseball team captain)
William Bynum "Tar Heel" Glen (Class of 1870 went to VMI first and served in the Confederate army)
William Wetmore "Flag" Flagler (born in Morristown, NJ and also a gymnast)
James Winthrop "Calf" Hageman (became a Presbyterian minister)
William "Preston" Lane (last surviving member of the original Princeton team, died in November 1938)

George "G" Mann (at age 16 he was the youngest member of the Princeton team)
"Dave" Mixsell (lawyer and roommate of teammate Charlie Darst in 1869)
"Charlie" Barrett (became a Presbyterian minister)
William "Grandfather" Chambers (died 8 years after graduation)
Charles "Charlie" Darst (also a baseball player at Princeton in 1867 and 1868)
Lee Hampton "Honeymoon" Nissley (shortstop on the Princeton baseball team)
Hughes "Olly" Oliphant (also a gymnast)
Charles Joel "Charlie" Parker (Class of 1870 was son of NJ Governor Joel Parker)
Jerome "Jerry" Sharp (catcher on Princeton baseball team)
Alexander "Van" Van Rensselaer (Captain of 1870 Princeton football team that defeated Rutgers)
John Green "Colonel" Wier (became a lawyer in Kentucky)
Thomas "Tom" Young (became a broker on the New York Stock Exchange)
Note that 25th Princeton player's name is not confirmed
*Information from David Nathan's research

Princeton Players Extended Notes:

William Gummere was the captain of the Princeton first football team. His hometown was Trenton, New Jersey where he was born on June 24, 1852. His father had a law office in Trenton. He graduated from Princeton in 1870. He went on to study law and he eventually served as the Chief Justice of the New Jersey State Supreme Court. As the story goes in one of his most famous rulings on the court he determined that a child's life, in a lawsuit, was only worth one dollar to the parents after the child was killed in a railroad accident. This position resulted in building his permanent reputation.

Jacob Edwin "Big Mike" Michael was born in 1848. He was Gummere's roommate in 1869-1870. He graduated from Princeton in 1871. He went into medicine where he became the chairman of anatomy and clinical surgery and then the chairman of obstetrics.

Homer Davenport "Dutch" Boughner (Class of 1871) and **George Billmeyer** (Class of 1871) were the "captains of the enemy's goal" for Princeton in that first football game.

Rutgers Original Football Team Roster:
William James Leggett (Class of 1872 was the Captain)
D.D. Williamson
E.D. Delamater
S.G. Gano
G.R. Dixon
G.H. Stevens
J.A. Van Neste
M.M. Ball
F.E. Allen
W.H. McKee
J.O. Van Fleet
G.S. Willits
G.H. Large
T.W. Clemens
J.W. Herbert
P.V. Huyssoon
D.T. Hawsxhurst
C.L. Pruyn
E.D. Gilmore
C. Rockefeller
W.J. Hill
W.S. Lasher
J.H. Wyckoff
A.I. Martine
G.E. Pace

Rutgers Players Extended Notes*:

William James Leggett was the captain of the first Rutgers football team. He was born in 1848. He was a member of the Rutgers Class of 1872. He became a Pastor in the Dutch Reformed Church. He was married in New Brunswick, in May 1876, to **Mary Eva Parsell** and together they had seven children.

Mary Eva Parsell lived in New Brunswick and was the daughter of **Major John V. A. Parsell** and Fannie Price. Her brother was John Henry Parsell (born in 1853).

George Hall Large was born in 1850 and he graduated from Rutgers in 1872. He was originally from Whitehouse Station where his father was a dealer in lumber, coal and iron ores. Large became a lawyer after graduation and served as a State Senator.

John Wayne Herbert, Jr. was a member of the first football team at Rutgers. He was in the Scientific Section of the college and he was born in 1853. His father had been a civil engineer and John won a prize for his work with minerology while he was a student at Rutgers. He became an attorney after graduation.

Robert Adrain (born 1853) was a student at Rutgers who did not play in the first football game. His grandfather (**Robert Adrain**) was a Rutgers mathematician and professor from 1825-1827 and had previously served at Queens College from 1809-1813.

Joen Alfred Van Neste was a member of the first football team and after graduation became a pastor in the Reformed Church. His father was killed as a soldier in the Civil War.

William Henry McKee was admitted to Rutgers without a required math curriculum and went on to become a clergyman in the Protestant Episcopal Church. His whereabouts later in life was unknown to his classmates.

Thomas Clemens was a member of the first team. He was born in 1849. He was raised by an uncle and aunt in New York City. At the age of 12 to 14 he became a member of the fife and drums corps with his brother's military unit during the Civil War. While working on a farm one summer local taxpayers heard him speak at a meeting and supported his entry to college. After graduation he became an attorney and practiced law.

Madison Monroe Ball was a member of the first football team. He was born in 1841. He also served for three years in the military during the Civil War. He was a part of the 91st NY Infantry and suffered a wartime leg injury in battle at Donaldson, Louisiana.

Douwe Ditmars Williamson was a member of the first team. After graduation he became an architect.

John Henry Wyckoff lived at 84 Bayard Street.

George Dixon and Stephen Gano were the designated "captains of the enemy's goal." According to one source, Gano is credited with scoring the first point in college football history.

*Biographical information mainly from the Rutgers Class archives

The Game

Records for the description of the first game at Rutgers in this story came from a variety of sources however no source of the events exist that were printed that day (November 6, 1869) referencing the contest itself. While the Rutgers school publication, *The Targum,* carried the story as an overview of the contest, it was written by a student writer for the November publication that came out later that month in 1869. Still, many consider it the best source of information about what transpired in the timeframe closest to the actual event. Other reports that filtered through newspapers were typically provided by original team members many years afterward.
What tends to be accepted as factual includes:

Pre-game:

-A letter was exchanged between students at both colleges for the game challenge
-The rules outlined in the story for how the game was to be played are accurate according to the earliest sources that explained the contest
-Princeton players did take the 10:00 am train to go to New Brunswick the day of the game
-Princeton students were treated by Rutgers students to a pre-game meal after checking on billiards rooms and walking about the town of New Brunswick
-Princeton did adopt the 7th Regiment cheer (known as the sky rocket cheer) as a major college cheer for their school although the players (not fans) did the cheering at the first game and no record exists of if this is what they actually cheered that first day
-Wooden fence rail was around the field and people sat on it to watch the game (which could be considered the first football stands in use from which to watch a football game)

-Some claim the first tailgate party happened this day when fans waiting for the game sat on the back gate of their horse drawn wagons (behind their horse's tail) and had refreshments they had prepared for a midday meal
-There were fans present to watch the game although estimates on crowd size varies from under a hundred in attendance to several hundred present

The Contest Itself:

-The order of the scoring in the story is what the earliest sources reported
-Rutgers scored the first college football point ever
-The style of play was violent and physical as players crashed into each other without protection
-Several Rutgers players wore scarlet head covers and this became the first use of a "school color" to identify team members in a football game
-The football offensive formation which became known as the "flying wedge" was used by both teams
-Rutgers had a player accidently help Princeton score a goal by sending the ball the wrong way
-George Large and Michael Jacobs crashed into the fans on the fence breaking the fence
-A Rutgers professor who came by was angered at the style of play and announced the players would come to "No Christian End."
-Leggett gave an inspirational and tactical speech that led the Rutgers players to their last two scores
-The final score was Rutgers 6 and Princeton 4

Post Game:

-Players from both teams gathered after the game at a popular tavern in New Brunswick known as Northrop's (according to the Daily Fredonian article about the time)
-There is one source (written years later from a Princeton player, Preston Lane) which indicated that the Princeton players were chased out of town after the game but the Northrop's function was recorded closer to the actual date

-One week later after the first contest, the second game was played between the two colleges and Princeton shut out Rutgers in this contest
-The third game was scheduled but it was not played as faculty at both schools indicated the game was becoming a distraction to the academic studying the students were supposed to be engaged in
-Princeton would win all football games with Rutgers until Rutgers won again in November 1938. The victory by Rutgers that day was by a score of 20-18. The game that day was held in their new stadium in front of 22,500 people. At this time, the last game played in the rivalry series took place on September 27, 1980 with Rutgers beating Princeton 44 to 13 (with the author present). Overall Princeton leads the series 53-17-1.
-In 1938 the game had the last living player from the original 1869 game in attendance
-The last living player for each team were Robert Preston Lane for Princeton (passed away on November 5, 1938 before the 1938 game) and George Large for Rutgers (who passed away in 1939)

A plaque designating the names of the Rutgers players was placed in the College Avenue gym. Pictures of the Rutgers players can be seen in the composite of the first college football game ever played.

The College Football Hall of Fame (Atlanta, Georgia) has soil from the original field at Rutgers on display

Conclusion

Historical fiction places an interesting spin on what may have taken place within the construct of an actual historical time period. For an author, writing in this manner allows one to use their imagination while still participating as a researcher to help provide a realistic lens into what life was like in a time period and during an event.

For the reader, it hopefully leads to an interest in that time period or event and results in a desire for the reader to research that material further. It should be noted that this is also the desired outcome for writers of non-fiction work. The reality is that any written work is often driven by a single question of what is truly factual complicated by the limited documents and other materials left behind to provide clues into the past.

So what is real and what is imagined?

Maybe the concept of a Princeton gal falling in love and marrying a Rutgers man and then years later becoming a Rutgers University fan is too farfetched?

It is true that Elizabeth and Christopher Adkins are fictional characters in this story. But do various alliances ever change in deep-set real life college rivalries? Has a Michigan or Oklahoma family ever found that a new alliance finds them rooting for Ohio State or Nebraska?

I look at the pathways that both my daughters took in attending Virginia Tech shadowed against my past where I had gone to Rutgers and rooted against Virginia Tech as a Rutgers rival in the old Big East Conference.

Both my daughters each loved their college experience. The fall weekly football games were an integral part of that social memory for each of them and helped define their identity with the college. It became ingrained to where they now continue to passionately root for the Hokies each Saturday years later with spouses and children in tow.

When my wife and I attended our first Virginia Tech football game as proud parents, we watched from the nosebleed seats as our older daughter came onto the field as a part of the VT color guard. Instantly we were captivated. As the notes hit to "Enter Sandman" and the players raced onto the field, the exuberance of what would eventually one day be both my girls "bouncing along" with the crowd was always fun to see.

Now years later, as my granddaughter gets decked out in orange and maroon for a game even when it is only on television, it makes watching a bowl game a family event that goes well beyond the food and other fanfare of any other activity we are a part of during the year.

Oh the magic that college football can have over you when it involves those you love.

Yes, I was and still am a loyal son of Rutgers having attended there as an undergrad and graduate student. If you asked me when I graduated if this would ever change I would emphatically have said no. This singular rooting for the Scarlet Knights was all I knew on the college scene and all I ever thought I could be loyal to when it came to college sports.

But from where I now stand, while I do still cheer for RU whenever they take the field, I unabashedly also cheer for those Hokies too!

So maybe anything is possible even when it is shared within the realm of a fictionalized story line.

However, there is one specific item in this work that is not imagined. There are basic facts that cannot be changed no matter who is telling this tale.

Rutgers beat Princeton 6 to 4 on a field in New Brunswick, New Jersey that day on November 6, 1869.

November 6, 2019 marks the 150th birthdate of that game.

It was the first college football game ever played.

And Rutgers won!

And the rest, as they say, is history…

$$\Omega$$

General Selected List of Sources Used

Aero View of New Brunswick, NJ, 1910, https://www.loc.gov/resource/g3814n.pm005240/

Beat Visitor, *The 1869 Targum Article: America's First College Football Game.*

Beers, F.W., *Map of the City of Trenton*, New Jersey, 1870.

C., "Reflections from Senior Year," *Nassau Literary Magazine*, Volume 26, Number 4, April 1, 1870, Papers of Princeton, Princeton University Library, The Trustees of Princeton University, 2009-2019.

C.H.H., "The Value of a College Reputation," *Nassau Literary Magazine*, Volume 26, Number 1, June 1, 1869, Papers of Princeton, Princeton University Library, The Trustees of Princeton University, 2009-2019.

Class of 1872 Rutgers History to 1917, https://archive.org/stream/classof1872rutge00rutg/classof1872rutge00rutg_djvu.txt

Class of 1873 Rutgers College, Library of Congress, Internet Archive, https://babel.hathitrust.org/cgi/pt?id=loc.ark:/13960/t3gx57f1c;view=1up;seq=5

Cunningham, John T., *New Jersey: America's Main Road*, 1976.

Davis, Parke, H., *Twenty-four Stalwart Men and a Goliath*.

Demarest, William H.S., *A History of Rutgers College 1766-1924*, https://archive.org/stream/historyofrutgers00dema/historyofrutgers00dema_djvu.txt

"The First Game: November 6, 1869," Official Site of Rutgers Athletics, http://www.scareletknights.com/sports/2017/6/11/sports-m-football-archive-first-game-html.aspx

Frusciano, Tom, *Rutgers University Vault*, Whitman Publishing, 2008.

"Group on Nassau Street" (photo), The Princeton Historical Society, https://princeton.pastperfectonline.com/photo/49C5A99A-2AE4-4BC7-8F62-003448266565

Gummere Family of Princeton, N.J., http://politicalgraveyard.com/families/15123.html

Guide to Historic Sites in Central New Jersey, 4th Ed., Editor George Dawson, The Raritan-Millstone Heritage Alliance, Inc.

Herbert, John W., "Rutgers v. Princeton: Beginning of 100 Years of College Football," (Original article written for AP in 1933), *The Daily Utah Chronicle*, Thursday, November 6, 1969, Newspapers.com 2017.

"Howe Insurance 1870's," (photo) https://princetonol.com/history/

"Late William Preston Lane was Member of First Team to Play for Princeton: The Oldsters used the "T" Formation, *The Morning Herald*, Hagerstown. Md., Tuesday, November 7, 1944, Newspapers.com 2017.

Map of City of New Brunswick, N.J.,
https://www.loc.gov/resource/g3814n.wd000574/
Map of Princeton and College of New Jersey,
https://www.loc.gov/resource/g3813mm.gla00126/?sp=45&q=Princeton+nj+maps
M'cosh, President, "Need of Upper Schools in the United States," *Nassau Literary Magazine*, Volume 26, Number 1, June 1, 1869, Papers of Princeton, Princeton University Library, The Trustees of Princeton University, 2009-2019.
Myers, William Starr, ed., *The Story of New Jersey*, Volume I, 1945.

N., "What is in a Name," *Nassau Literary Magazine*, Volume 26, Number 4, April 1, 1870, Papers of Princeton, Princeton University Library, The Trustees of Princeton University, 2009-2019.
Nathan, David (Guest columnist), *Biographies of Princeton Players, 1869 Football Team*.
"No Christian End! The Beginnings of College Football in America," Originally Published in *The Journey to Camp: The Origins of American Football to 1889*, The Professional Football Researchers Association Books.

"Olla-podrida," *Nassau Literary Magazine*, Volume 26, Number 4, April 1, 1870, Papers of Princeton,

Princeton University Library, The Trustees of Princeton University, 2009-2019.
Pictures of Princeton 1870s, Princeton Historical Society,
https://princeton.pastperfectonline.com/photo
Plan of the City of New Brunswick, Actual Survey, Published by Marcelus & Ternune & Letson, 1829,
https://www.loc.gov/resource/g3814n.Ja002032/
Plump, Wendy, *First Smackdown: The Football Game That Started It All*,
http://www.princetonmagazine.com
Princeton Original Football Players,
https://paw.princeton.edu/article/biographies-princetons-first-football-players

Rutgers Past Presidents, https://www.rutgers.edu/about/history/past-presidents/

Rutgers through the Years,

https://web.archive.org/web/20070120202924/http://ruweb.rutgers.edu/timeline/1800.htm
Rutgers University Campus Information Services Historical Tour Guide Manual, 2004 revision, compiled by Chuck Del Camp.

Schmidt, George, *Princeton and Rutgers: Two Colonial Colleges of New Jersey*, 1964.

VaPasule, C.C., *Map Showing Location of Tunnel Constructed for Copper Mining about 1780 near Rutgers College*, New Brunswick, N.J.

Weinreb, Michael, *Season of Saturdays A History of College Football in 14 Games*, Scribner, Simon & Schuster, Inc., 2015.

Princeton Information, www.Princeton.edu
Rutgers Information, www.Rutgers.edu

Printed in Great Britain
by Amazon